BENEATH THE SICILIAN STARS

LINDSAY MARIE MORRIS

Storm
PUBLISHING

ALSO BY LINDSAY MARIE MORRIS

The Last Letter from Sicily

*To the 600,000 Italians branded as "enemy aliens"
on December 8, 1941*

ONE

DECEMBER 7, 1941

Pittsburg, California

Static crackled through the aging speaker as Annalisa Aiello's father, Vincenzo, turned the radio dial in search of the right station. The soft orange glow of the vacuum tubes was almost too faint to be seen in the late Sunday morning light.

The sun poured through the window, reflecting off the glass covering their family portrait. Annalisa and Papà gazed out with deep-set eyes above chiseled cheekbones, while her older brother Mario's features favored those of her mother, Maria, with a more pointed chin. His face was distinguished by a pencil-eraser-sized mole on his left cheek. Together they smiled broadly in that bittersweet moment just before they said their goodbyes.

The photograph was taken with Mario's box camera on the day the Aiellos sent him off with the Navy to Honolulu—so far from the only home he'd really known. It was a world apart from what was sometimes a challenging life in the East Bay city of Pittsburg, California, where Annalisa had grown up. Her parents had arrived two decades earlier, fresh from Italy with baby Mario in tow.

The dial landed on the right frequency, and Annalisa heard the familiar singsong jingle of *The Jell-O Program Starring Jack Benny*. The entertainer launched into a humorous intro, while the sixteen-year-old hunched over math homework on the coffee table. Pots and pans banged in the kitchen as her mother prepared their afternoon supper. The faint scent of garlic permeated the air.

Annalisa scribbled answers to the various equations, some more challenging than the rest. But half of her attention remained on Benny and the program she hated to miss.

About fifteen minutes in, she set down her pencil, and leaned in beside Papà, who laughed heartily as Benny acted out the parts of Dr. Jekyll and Mr. Hyde. It was a spoof on a film she and her father had seen downtown at the California Theatre.

She remembered how Spencer Tracy had acted out the different sides of the composite figure. Hyde was unpredictable and critical while Dr. Jekyll was gentlemanly and charming. In a funny way, the duality reminded her of her mother.

There were rare moments when Mamma smiled in wistful reflection, channeling her memories of growing up in Isola delle Femmine, Sicily. It was in these instances Annalisa would learn things, like how her mother grew up surrounded by the aroma of her own father's fresh baked bread and helped fill *cannoli* for his bakery.

"We used fresh sheep's milk *ricotta*, so we could only really make them in the winter months," Mamma had once recalled with a softness in her voice. "That was back when we didn't have refrigeration."

Then Annalisa had smiled, eager to learn more. But the moment had passed, and she had seen her mother's face harden.

"You're slouching again," she'd snapped. "Who's going to want to marry a girl who can't sit upright in church?"

The teenager often wondered when she might meet a man who would want to be her husband. Several boys had interested her over the years, but those were crushes, really. While she chatted some with classmates who sat to her sides, she never spent time with them outside school. She didn't dare bring anyone home for fear of what they'd think, how they might judge her immigrant parents.

She glanced at her father, who was absorbed in the program. At least he spoke English, unlike her mother. Still, his thick Sicilian accent sometimes clouded his words, leaving store clerks and church parishioners staring without comprehension. Worse still were the laughs and name calling of neighbor children that still haunted her dreams.

She thought about it as the laughter rang out in Benny's studio audience. But then something peculiar happened.

Benny was cut off midsentence as another man's clipped voice suddenly took command over the air waves.

"We interrupt this program to bring you this special announcement live from Honolulu, Hawaii. We have witnessed this morning the severe bombing of Pearl Harbor and the attack on the city of Honolulu by the Empire of Japan. There has been serious fighting in the air and sea. More than three hundred and fifty men have been reported killed by a direct bomb on Hickam Field. Witnesses report that at least three ships were attacked and the USS *Oklahoma* was set afire. This is a developing story."

Benny's monologue resumed along with the laughter. It was as if the whole event hadn't happened. But at that same moment, Annalisa's pale brown eyes met those of her father. Something terrible had happened in Honolulu.

They rose from the couch and left Benny's nasal voice and

the sickening laughs behind. Fear and confusion must have washed over their faces, because the moment they entered the kitchen and her mother turned, her eyes were wide with her own concern.

"What happened?" She inhaled sharply as if bracing herself for what was to come.

Annalisa took a deep breath of her own and relayed what they had heard. "There was a bombing in Honolulu." She spoke in a flat voice, scarcely believing the words herself. "Three battleships were hit. They say it was Japan."

Mamma clutched the halter of her sauce-stained yellow apron. "Mario... Oh my God, my son is there!"

She sank into a stiff-backed wooden chair and buried her face against the well-worn table.

"We don't know that anything happened to Mario." Papà slid into a chair to her right. Annalisa saw him reach for Mamma's hand as she pulled away.

"They didn't say anything about his ship." Her father clasped his own hands.

Annalisa thought about the latest postcard from Hawaii that sat back in the living room on the coffee table. She remembered straining to read Mario's messy handwriting. In just a few lines, he'd shared how lucky he felt to have been stationed at Pearl Harbor aboard the USS *Arizona*.

Why had he decided to leave them? She still couldn't understand. Sure, Mamma was strict, and Papà had probably pushed him too hard to follow in his footsteps and become a fisherman. But did he have to travel so far away, to some place that was now so clearly dangerous?

He'd written about the swaying coconut palms and stunning blue warm water—so different from the chill of the murky brownish Sacramento–San Joaquin River Delta watershed. Never satisfied with life in Pittsburg, where he'd been bullied and teased for being Italian, he'd finally found a place where he was welcome.

But none of that mattered if he were in danger—or worse.

She tugged at the horn amulet around her neck, the one he'd given her to ensure her own luck and safety. Imagine that.

With her eyes closed to hold back the tears, she mouthed a silent prayer. "Please, God. Let Mario be OK."

TWO

MAY 1919

Isola delle Femmine, Sicily

For thousands of years fishermen had stood as Vincenzo Aiello did now, at the side of a large wooden *gozzo* boat, net clasped in his calloused hands while he and twenty-nine other men worked together to lift their portion of a two-ton net called the *tonnara* from the shimmering azure sea. Their bronzed arms strained with effort, muscles bulging as they rhythmically tugged at the woven linen. The aged boat, its paint faded and chipped, creaked beneath their feet from the heavy load.

May's warm, dry sirocco winds had brought them—the fishermen but also hundreds of bluefin tuna, each weighing in at several hundred pounds, caught by surprise in netted corridors. Screeching seagulls circled as the men chanted the rhythmic *cialoma*. They raised their voices as they came to the chorus, "*E amòla, e amòla!*" and they dragged in the net until it formed the *camera della morte*, the chamber of death. There, enormous fish desperately flopped from side to side, partially caught between the threads. It was time for what the men called the *mattanza*, the massacre.

Vincenzo held the net with one hand as he leaned over with a spear, jabbing at the flopping fish alongside his comrades. The blue topaz-toned waters soon took on an equally vibrant ruby hue as blood splattered and soaked white shirts so they turned pink, matching the men's sunburned faces.

"Praise his name! Praise Jesus," the so-called *rais*, leader of this hunt, shouted.

"Amen!" responded the men, adrenaline coursing through their veins while they shoved the enormous fish into the hold, where fins skidded across the rough wooden surface.

It lasted no more than twenty minutes, and then they were done, the fruits of the season in tow. But it was hardly worth the effort, for there were fewer and smaller fish than in years past. People were desperate, traditions were fading. And since he'd returned from the Great War, Vincenzo counted fewer fishermen. He was used to celebrating the *mattanza* with up to two dozen more men. Gone were those days, he thought as he helped unload the day's catch.

"I can't take it anymore." His friend Velio wrung pink, frothy liquid from his shirt onto the dusty ground. "I'm going. We've saved enough money, and Gemma and I are on the next boat out of here."

Vincenzo didn't have to ask where. About half of Isola delle Femmine had fled its sun-kissed-but-cursed shore for a new life across the globe. California. He liked how the name sounded. It had become synonymous with the word *promise*. The promise of a better life, free from the rural poverty that rocked Sicily.

"You don't think it's ever going to change?" Vincenzo asked, his eyes wide.

Velio shook his head. "It's time. Time for you, too, my friend. Think about it."

· · ·

And so, Vincenzo thought about it as he wended his way down the cactus-lined lane to a little white-washed apartment building and sighed heavily as he pushed through the wooden door.

"You're home early." His wife, Maria, brushed a chestnut curl from her heart-shaped face. "What's wrong?"

"Oh, you know." Vincenzo slipped off his soiled sleeveless shirt. "There were only forty men today and half the catch of last year."

"But it's money, right?" She handed him a clean collared shirt from the laundry basket on the kitchen table.

"Some money, yes..." He slid his arms into the sleeves and began to button up. "But enough about me. You said this morning you had news?"

"Good news, I hope." She averted her eyes.

He took her hand. "I could use some good news."

"I didn't want to tell you earlier because I know how you are on *mattanza* day. You need to focus..."

"Tell me." He took her other hand.

She looked down. "Well, it's just that... Well... we're going to have a baby."

For a moment, the little apartment seemed to shrink, its walls pressing inward as if the air had been sucked from the dimly lit room where they stood. Then he exhaled, and everything expanded again. The news was wonderful—so why did it leave a flicker of panic?

"A baby." He wrapped her in a hug, wanting to root himself in the moment and safeguard her.

"Yes," she breathed into his chest. "A baby."

He brushed a tear from his eye. It had been five months since their wedding night. Both of them wanted children—more than anything. And now?

"What are we going to do?" she whispered.

"What do you mean?"

She looked up, and he saw she, too, had tears in her eyes. "We can barely feed ourselves. Another mouth? Can you imagine?"

He couldn't imagine. The paltry catch, the smaller crew, and now a baby? He shook his head. There had to be a solution. He thought of his sister, Costanza, and her husband, Giuseppe Cardinale. His brother-in-law had chosen the sea rather than taking over his grandmother's store and had sold the building for a new boat. The couple had yet to bear children of their own.

He'd never asked Giuseppe for assistance. He'd always been too proud, even now, after the war, when everyone seemed to be struggling. But the time had come. He knew it as well as he could sense the best spot to drop his net and when the wind was just right.

They needed a plan before it was too late. It was time to go.

"Maybe Costanza can help."

MAY 1920

Isola delle Femmine

Vincenzo grasped a medium-sized flat rock and twisted to the right before tossing it discus-style into the sapphire sea.

"Ah!" said Giuseppe. "It bounced three times with that throw."

He patted Vincenzo on the back. "Good one!"

The two watched as a wave crashed onto the rocky shore just a few feet from where they stood.

"I can't believe you're leaving." Giuseppe's voice was soft, his hazel eyes fixed on the sea-foam before them.

"It's too bad you can't join us." Vincenzo plucked another smooth rock, weighing it in his palm.

Giuseppe sighed. "We both know it's for the best. Besides,

with the new baby coming, your sister will have her hands full. More mouths to feed."

Vincenzo nodded. Little Mario was enough for his wife, Maria, especially after the complications. She'd given birth two months early. The midwife said early delivery was common in cases like hers. Then there was Maria's depression. Her dark eyes were like caverns, swallowing all light. He'd never be able to repay his sister for what she did to save her during that period.

They would never have guessed that five months later Costanza would get pregnant, too. After that, her promise to help them was so much more than she and Giuseppe had bargained for, and Vincenzo was beyond grateful.

Giuseppe tossed his own smooth stone and Vincenzo watched it skip. "We've lived through how many *mattanze?* And still, you never know what the spring will bring."

He turned and faced Vincenzo with a slight tightness to his jaw. "But I have no regrets. We're happy to have our family—however God intended."

Again, Vincenzo nodded, slower this time, as he bent down and lifted a large, flat rock. He held it in a moment of silence, for some things were better left unsaid. Shifting the weight from hand to hand, he pondered their pact—and the burden that would haunt them across an ocean.

He wound up and released the stone into the receding waves, watching it plunk through the surface. All that remained were ripples. Their decision was necessary, vital for their futures.

It had taken longer than Vincenzo hoped, but he was finally following his destiny—even if it meant carrying the weight of their choice to California.

He was following the path hundreds of other village men had carved before him, beginning with his distant relatives, Pietro and Rosario Aiello.

The brothers had set off in the nineteenth century, during Italy's Great Unification, the *Risorgimento*, which despite all its promises left people in Sicily so hungry they were eating plaster off the wall for wheat. The men landed in New Orleans where they found work in oyster beds—until a yellow fever outbreak.

They fled for Oregon in pursuit of Columbia River salmon before heading south to San Francisco. There may have been gold in California's hills, but they were more interested in fish. And they soon set their sights on the Sacramento–San Joaquin River Delta's fertile fishing grounds and a burgeoning fishing village at New York Landing.

The Aiellos had hopped on a train and jumped off at the new village, which locals then called Black Diamond for its coal. Pietro returned to Isola delle Femmine to prepare his family to join him and let fellow villagers know about the opportunities across the ocean. And so, the migrations began, drawing Sicilians to what soon grew to become a town that locals renamed Pittsburg after the city to the east, reflecting its new steel mill.

Soon, Vincenzo would join them.

There was a time when all Vincenzo knew and aspired to be was an Isola delle Femmine tuna hunter. Everything changed in the spring of 1915. For the first time in his life, he would miss the annual *mattanza*. Instead, he boarded a boat for the mainland. From there, he rode north and marched with strangers to the Austrian border. He'd left everyone and everything he'd known back home, including Maria, who'd stained his new uniform with her tears.

The baker's daughter and a nun's niece, Maria was wholesome and devout, never without her Madonna delle Grazie pendant, patterned after the statue who, wearing a crown surrounded by a halo of golden stars, held her crowned baby Jesus on her right side. Legend had it that a fisherman discovered the Blessed Virgin's simulacrum in Scalo della Madonna, a cove not far from where the community would build a church and call it Maria Santissima delle Grazie, Maria's namesake and Isola delle Femmine's patron.

It was there in the Holy Mother's church that Vincenzo first locked eyes with her as she sang among the assembled choir of young women clad in white gowns with ivory mantillas. He had seen her before, handing out loaves of bread in her father's shop, but on that particular Sunday, golden light cascaded down through the windows above the vaulted ceilings and played upon her warm olive complexion while adding a hint of mystery to her deep brown eyes. He wondered just who this angel was before him.

Had he not gotten up the courage to ask her father for permission to court her, he might have lost her to the cloth, for she had long thought she might follow in her aunt's footsteps to the convent. As they strolled the stone streets hand in hand, always saving some room for the Holy Spirit between them (as directed by that aunt who accompanied as chaperone), he strengthened his resolve to become the man worthy of this sweet and pious girl's affections.

In late June, he placed an order at her father's bakery for the village's customary St. Peter's key-shaped cake, a treat to symbolize his desire to fully open his heart. By July's Maria Santissima delle Grazie Feast Day, their families had begun to talk about a wedding. She was set on springtime, and he was in no rush. Little did he know that was when he'd be called to serve.

Marriage would have to wait until he returned more than three years later. He'd left as barely more than a boy and returned as a battle-tested man. And there she was, his dark-eyed angel, ready and willing to continue where they'd left off, still holding the key to his heart. But they both knew it would not unlock paradise in a country devastated by war. He wanted a better life like those other Aiellos had promised existed on the other side. He wasn't going to wait until he had to eat the plaster off his walls. And he certainly couldn't ask Giuseppe for anything more.

Vincenzo shook his head and squeezed the stone in his palm, bringing himself back to the present and the uncertainty that lay ahead. He stared out at the silhouette of the Spanish-era watchtower that stood on the islet across the way. It had stood there for at least three centuries and bore witness to the ebbs and flows of the tuna hunt. His father, his grandfather, his great-grandfather... they all heeded the call of the sea, all genuflected to the God that delivered them fish. Year after year after year.

The sun was setting now, leaving the tower to be swallowed by shadows. He launched his rock through the air and watched as it skipped twice, once for the present and again for the future. He stared at the ripples it left behind, dissipating in the orange glow that reflected off the gentle blue surface. He felt a chill as water trickled over his bare toes. It was time to go. But first he had a gift.

He reached into his pocket and grasped his trusty well-worn wooden net shuttle, the same elongated tool he'd used since he was a boy when he first started repairing fishing nets. It had been a present, carved by hand by his favorite uncle.

He placed it in Giuseppe's hand. "For the little one."

"Are you sure?" Giuseppe offered it back. "What if he doesn't use it? Who knows what will come of the next generation?"

Vincenzo shook his head, his gaze fixed on the tower as it faded into the darkness. "Seawater runs in our blood. He may not use it now, but one day he'll see its worth. It's part of who we are. Keep it safe for him, so that he'll understand where we come from. The future is uncertain, but one day he'll lead the way."

THREE
OCTOBER 1930

Pittsburg, California

Vincenzo struggled to keep his eyes open as Father Christopher rambled about the meaning of the upcoming All Souls' Day. He took a deep breath. The air was thick with the scent of frankincense and candle wax. To his right sat a woman in a black shawl with a matching lace mantilla, holding a blood-red rosary in her withered hands, while to his left a younger man with a dark suit and fedora nodded his head. In the pew in front of him, two small children—a boy and girl—shifted restlessly in their seats before their mother turned to hand them a stuffed bear to play with between them.

He fixed his gaze on the center aisle, where stained glass windows cast colorful patterns on the stone floor. Then he glanced at his wristwatch. In just ten minutes, he would have a chance to slip out after Communion and set up his weekly collection table in front of the church.

As a member of the Ex-Combattenti, the Italian veterans' group, he was tasked with collecting funds that would eventually be distributed to war widows and orphans back in Italy.

Even after all these years, the nation struggled. The government had printed extra money to fund arms during the war, which led to severe inflation. By 1920's end, the lira had plummeted to just one-sixth of its 1913 value. The recent Depression only made matters worse. It was an uphill battle, compounded by the loss of those the war left behind. During that time, a veteran named Benito Mussolini had risen to power with pockets full of promises to restore order and enact reform. But it had been eight years, and Vincenzo wondered whether the man they called il Duce could ever truly deliver. In the meantime, he saw his charitable work with the Ex-Combattenti as critical, and each week, he put out a collection box and solicited donations from church parishioners.

On those Sundays, he'd often sit apart from his family toward the back, where he could easily scoot out the door and set up a card table outside.

"Have a moment for our war orphans?" he'd ask as the parishioners walked past.

Many of them wanted to see pictures. Boy, did Vincenzo have pictures! He would fan the faded photographs out on the rickety table, its surface scratched but otherwise smooth with age. He'd point to wide-eyed children left behind in the war, and the parishioners, particularly the older women, would stop and sigh before reaching into their handbags to deposit a bit of change in the tin canister Vincenzo had set on the table's edge.

It was time for Communion now. He watched his son, Mario, rise, followed by Maria, holding the hand of little Annalisa, who was still too young to accept the Eucharist. Mario would soon be eleven. In just a few years, he'd be old enough to bring aboard the fishing boat. It would give Vincenzo more time to bond with his boy. He might even bring him with him when he fished in Alaska.

There was money to be made following the fish up to Bristol Bay. It was hard, competitive work, but by summer's end, it was worthwhile. The kids could count on a new pair of shoes each year and meat on the table at least once a week. Plus, he'd have enough left over to send his sister's family in Sicily. She'd never asked for it, but it was the least he could do considering what she'd sacrificed for him.

Still, he knew the time apart wasn't easy on Maria. She, who had waited more than three years for him to return during the war, was now left back at home with the children for three months of the year. And when he was home, he spent more time on his boat than helping change the diapers or witness little milestones. It was no wonder "Mamma" was Mario's first word. He even missed Annalisa's August birth. As a result, his marital relationship with Maria often seemed strained. She'd exhale a heavy sigh when he arrived late to supper, and when they crawled in bed, she often turned her back to him. And he'd awake to a cold spot next to him where she'd once stayed to snuggle in the morning light. He wondered if she regretted the choice they made.

He watched as she settled back in their pew, pulling out that darn rosary of hers. Perhaps she would have been more content as a nun after all. Then again, he knew she'd not trade anything for her children. He was the problem, but this was the life of a fisherman. He sighed, for he had no solution.

He felt a hand on his shoulder. It was his friend, Giovanni Scotto, another fisherman. And he realized the rest of his pew was waiting on him. He stood and entered the line.

As he inched forward, his gaze drifted to the rose-shaped stained glass window behind the altar. The sun was shining through, promising a beautiful day and bathing the congregation in streams of purple and blue light. He would play Maria's favorite record when he got home and maybe ask her to dance. Tonight, he would be hers.

* * *

Annalisa held her mother's hand as they crossed the street, following Mario, who raced ahead.

"Careful!" Mamma shouted. "That boy. Someday he's going to get hit."

Annalisa hoped not. Mario wasn't just her big brother; he was her best friend. He let her play with his Erector Set and taught her how to build a fort with couch cushions.

Mario was sitting on the front porch when they arrived at their apartment. They lived in a side-by-side duplex next to the DeRosa family, who had three older children. Mr. DeRosa fished with Annalisa's father but spoke better English. It helped that Mrs. DeRosa was born and raised in California. And unlike Annalisa's parents, Mr. DeRosa had applied for citizenship.

"I'm King of the Hill." Mario stood and stretched out his arms. "Welcome to my kingdom."

"Very funny, little man," their mother said.

"Mamma, can we play outside?" Mario rubbed at his mole.

"Only if you promise to watch your sister."

"I promise, I promise." Mario made the sign of the cross.

"I'll just be in the kitchen preparing pasta for our lunch. Don't stay out too long."

Mario smiled at Annalisa after their mother had entered the apartment. "How about we go to the park?"

"Mamma said not too long."

"So, we won't stay long. How about it?"

"OK!" Annalisa followed her brother as he scampered up the street.

When they got to the park, three big boys were sitting on the swings. They turned toward the Aiello children.

"Annalisa, we should leave," Mario said in Sicilian.

"What's that?" asked one of the boys, who had reddish hair. "Did I hear a dumb dago?"

"That's right." Another boy with light brown hair laughed. "A couple of spaghetti benders."

"Leave us alone." Mario stepped forward.

"Or what? You'll tell your fisherman father? My Pops could beat him up, no problem."

"I said, leave us alone!" Mario clenched his fists as he raised his voice.

The third boy, whose face was covered in freckles, jumped out of his swing and shoved Mario. Mario pushed him back, and then the two boys wrestled on the ground. The other two boys jumped in and soon had Mario pinned.

"Stop it, stop it! You're hurting him!" Annalisa shouted.

"Let him go," someone called out.

Annalisa turned to see the youngest DeRosa boy.

"You can't pick on someone your own size?" He placed his hands on his hips.

"Come on. Let's get out of here," the freckle-faced boy said. The two other boys followed him away, but not before turning to spit in the DeRosa boy's direction.

"Go back to Italy, you dumb dagos!"

"Are you OK?" The DeRosa boy frowned.

Mario nodded, and Annalisa could almost feel his shame. Tears streamed down his dirty cheeks, and his lip was split. Her body rippled with rage. How could those boys do that to her big brother?

"Come on." The DeRosa boy waved them forward. "I'll walk you back home. You can come to my apartment to wash up. You don't want your Mamma to see you looking like that."

* * *

Mario's split lip gave it away.

Vincenzo noticed during dinner. But he waited until Maria was doing the dishes to ask about it.

"Are you in some kind of trouble?" His voice was low and hushed.

Mario shook his head.

"Papà, what's a dago?" Annalisa asked.

"Shh," Mario said.

"Is that what happened? Someone called you a dago, and you hit him?"

"It was nothing." Mario looked down.

Vincenzo leaned forward, projecting a sharp whisper. "Listen, both of you. I don't want any fighting, you hear me? This ends now."

"They started it!" Mario frowned.

"Remember Jesus's words." Vincenzo raised his hand to his face. "You turn the other cheek."

"But, Papà, they told us their father was going to beat you up," Mario said.

"Don't worry about me, son. You just take care of that sister of yours and stay out of trouble, you hear?"

"Yes, Papà," he mumbled, again looking down.

Vincenzo patted his son's hand. He knew what it was like to be the target of prejudice. He experienced it first while serving with the Alpini. The northern Italian soldiers often made jokes about Sicilians being genetically inferior and uncivilized. Here in the United States, he'd read about lynchings of Italians. He'd also seen editorials about how immigrants, including Italians, were taking away jobs. These boys must have heard such rhetoric at home from their parents. This was a heavy cross to bear, and he wished his children didn't have to carry it, too.

"Listen to me." He took their hands as he carefully chose his words. It wasn't right but neither was violence. "There will always be people in this world who want nothing more than to make you feel small. But that's because they feel small themselves. You come from a long line of strong, hardworking fishermen. And your Papà fought in the Great War. You can be proud of where you came from and even prouder to be an American, just like them. So, I don't want to hear about any more fights. You are better than that. Do you understand?"

Both children nodded their heads.

"Good. Now, go clean up that lip, Mario. You don't want to scare your mother."

The children left the table, Mario with his head down and shoulders slumped. Vincenzo worried about his sensitive boy. Would things have been better had they stayed in Sicily?

He shook his head. In many ways, it would have made it harder. With distance they could avoid the discomfort about the difficult decision he and Maria had made.

His thoughts turned to his Sicilian family. What kind of life was their son leading? What trials and joys did he face? He couldn't help wondering how things might have turned out had they chosen differently.

FOUR

OCTOBER 1930

Isola delle Femmine, Sicily

Alberto Cardinale stood as still as possible while his father, Giuseppe, straightened a blue kerchief he'd wrapped around his neck and secured with a round silver pin.

"*Credere, obbedire, combattere,*" Papà read from the pin's inscription. "I suppose you are prepared to believe, obey, and fight?"

"Yes, Papà." Alberto's nearly eleven-year-old voice wavered between childhood and the tone he aimed to master.

"Good boy." His father patted the shoulder of Alberto's black button-down shirt. "I'm proud of you."

"You'll be even prouder if we get there on time." His nine-year-old sister Cristina rolled her light brown eyes.

Alberto gave her a grin, pulled his black beanie over his curly dark brown hair, and raced out the door ahead of her to Piazza Umberto I.

"Wait!" she called after him, scuffing her black dress shoes as she ran along the unpaved road to catch up.

. . .

It was the morning of the eighth anniversary of the March on Rome, a mass demonstration that resulted in Benito Mussolini's ascension to power. To celebrate, the town was invited—in truth, obligated—to attend a state-sponsored parade followed by a grand *festa*.

Nearly everyone was present when they arrived in front of the Church of Maria Santissima delle Grazie. Alberto's school principal, Signor Caruso, handed each youngster a black banner bearing the Fascist symbol: a gold eagle clutching a bundle of sticks in its talons.

Alberto and Cristina carried their banners to the end of a line of dozens of other children who stood on a platform. The Balilla, like Alberto, dressed in black shirts and gray knee-length pants, whereas boys fifteen to eighteen, the Avanguardisti, wore green blazers and matching long pants. Meanwhile, the Piccole Italiane, like Cristina, wore dark skirts and white blouses, and their older counterparts, Giovani Italiane, ages fourteen through eighteen, wore longer skirts with black ties over their blouses.

A crowd had already begun to gather around them. Alberto recognized many of the villagers, some of whom held posters of Mussolini, while nearly everyone chanted, "Duce, Duce, Duce!"

Suddenly, he heard the crash of cymbals and the blare of trumpets as the local marching band began a rendition of "Giovinezza," the Fascist Party's official hymn, which the children sang.

Alberto belted out the lyrics about heroic people and the immortality of the Fatherland in which men of faith and ideals could be born again. He scanned the audience. Many stood with their right arms raised stiffly in the Saluto Romano, the Fascist salute, as they sang along.

His eyes settled on an older woman his mother knew from church. Her mouth was closed, and she crossed her arms over her chest rather than extending the Saluto Romano. Perhaps she was cold or uncomfortable standing in the crowd. Or was it something else? He shook his head and continued to sing.

The children sang about how Mussolini's regime was remaking Italians. The lyrics praised il Duce's preparation for war, Italian labor, and national glory while emphasizing youth as the driving force. Alberto heard sniffling and saw many tears.

The anthem ended with a final crash, and Alberto sat down at the platform's edge while his sister chatted with a friend. His neckerchief was too tight, but he resisted the urge to tug at it.

"If only il Duce could have seen that." Papà approached and patted Alberto on the head.

Alberto's cheeks flushed as he quickly looked around and was thankful no one was watching. He would be eleven soon, after all. Almost old enough to join the fishermen in their swordfish and tuna hunts. He ran his finger across the silver medal below his chin. He wanted more.

Since his toddler years, he'd dreamed of being a professional soccer player. While his mother and sister waved to Papà as he and his crewmen rowed from the shore near Piano Ponente, Alberto had his head turned in the opposite direction. He focused on the soccer field, next to where the men would spread their nets to dry.

It wasn't long before Alberto and his neighbor boys, other fishermen's sons, were out on that field themselves. They played nearly every Sunday, dribbling and sometimes elbowing one another in pursuit of the much-coveted goal.

They'd play from after Mass to late afternoon—until his mother, Costanza, would open the window and shout, "Al-ber-tino Card-in-ale!"

Their apartment was one street away from the field, but he could hear her loud and clear. It was dinnertime at the Cardinales—at least for Mamma and the children. Papà was frequently out on expeditions to the waters around the island of Lampedusa near Tunisia in search of more fish.

He was never around to watch Alberto dribble the ball down the field or when he scored a goal from twenty feet away. With the exception of state-sponsored parades, it seemed nothing came between the man and his fishing.

Each night they ate without his father, the boy silently affirmed that he would not follow in his footsteps. Alberto was part of Italy's future. And it certainly wasn't going to be on a fishing boat.

He often thought instead about men like Signor Caruso, respected as a Fascist elder and school principal. Men like him lived on the other side of town with the merchants, teachers, and the village doctor. Why couldn't his father be more like them?

And then there were men like his uncle Vincenzo, who somehow escaped Isola delle Femmine completely and today sent Alberto gifts from America, like that pair of knee-length woolen pants he never wore and the oblong-shaped leather ball that he didn't know what to do with.

The lively buzz of revelers brought Alberto back to the present. He loosened his neckerchief and took a deep breath. His father looked so happy, happier than he'd seen him in a long time. And he was glad to bask in that glow, even if it meant having to sing publicly in an uncomfortable uniform.

But at that moment this year's festival awaited his arrival. An accordion player began a popular tune accompanied by the rhythm of a woman with a tambourine. He saw Cristina and her friends race toward a series of vibrantly colored *carretti* unhitched from the backs of horses and donkeys. Each hand-painted wooden side panel told a story, illustrating scenes from the Bible or popular fairy tales. Inside, vendors had loaded large quantities of roasted nuts and sugary fruit candies. Savory and sweet scents clung to the crisp afternoon air, enticing *festa*-goers of all ages to come and partake as they made their way to hastily erected carnival game stalls.

"Come on, let's win some prizes," Cristina called over her shoulder with a big smile and wide eyes.

Alberto nodded and trailed his younger sister to a booth where a red-and-white-striped awning shaded a man with a handlebar mustache. Several rows of dusty bottles stood before a wall of prizes ranging from plush teddy bears to blue-eyed dolls. Alberto watched as Cristina took an armful of brightly colored rubber rings, which she tossed and managed to land around the neck of three bottles.

"What aim this one has," the man remarked as he fetched a large red ball. "Now it's your turn, little man."

Alberto took his rings and concentrated, trying not to get distracted by the persistent calls of hawkers, the buzz of disparate conversations, and the laughter of other children from nearby stalls as he tossed his first ring toward the bottles. He missed. He tried until he was out of rings.

"Better luck next time," the man said.

"You can have my ball." Cristina extended it in Alberto's direction.

"Are you sure?" he asked.

She nodded. "You're the ball player."

He held the prize under his arm as he trotted over to the next game. This time, it was a beanbag toss. He mouthed a little prayer before clenching his first beanbag in his fist, winding up his pitch, and releasing. He hit one target, a painted red-faced wooden clown.

"Lucky shot!" Cristina taunted from the side.

He wound up again and released another beanbag. He missed.

"So close!" Cristina giggled.

Alberto smiled as he shook his head. The siblings' closeness in age naturally put them in healthy competition. But it was always in good fun.

After drawing in a deep breath, he singled out his next

clown target. It was blue, but like him, it had a little dark spot on its right cheek. He tightened his grip on the beanbag. How many times had his classmates remarked that he had something on his face, some even swatting at it? He stared angrily at the clown with the mole and inhaled sharply before he slammed his beanbag right into its red, open mouth before knocking it down.

The man in the stall gave him a handful of hard candy, which Alberto shared with his sister.

They played there all afternoon, stopping only for supper with their parents: *arancini* and *cannoli*, washed down with a sparkling *aranciata*. They returned to the games until the sun had set, and they heard their father call, "Come along, *ragazzi!*"

Alberto dribbled the ball in front of him as he joined his family. They followed the other villagers toward the beach overlooking the islet, where the centuries-old Spanish tower stood bathed in moonlight.

He sat on a smooth rock to his sister's left and waited. Then they saw a spark shoot up into the sky and, with a loud boom, it exploded into a burst of shimmering red light, further illuminating the aging tower. Moments later, another burst, this time green. Then yellow, then orange, and soon they'd witnessed a rainbow's worth of hues as the pyrotechnics fizzed, popped, boomed, and sparkled before leaving a puff of smoke and the smell of rotting eggs.

Villagers oohed and aahed and, when it was done, erupted in applause and more shouts of "Duce! Duce! Duce!"

Alberto leaned back on the rock and stared up at the sliver of a moon that looked like a sideways grin, and he smiled back. The day had marked another year of fascism, another chance to honor the advancements of Mussolini and the greatness of Mother Italy.

Look to the future, the fascist elders had urged, but never forget the greatness of Rome and all that the people had achieved. Forget the Greeks, the Muslims, the Normans, and the Spanish who came after—for once, all of Italy belonged to the same empire. Regional rivalries could no longer endure as a New Rome was dawning.

For a ten-year-old boy, it was thrilling. One day, he would be a part of the nation's grandeur.

Maybe then his father would really be happy.

FIVE

FEBRUARY 1933

Annalisa sprawled out on the worn hooked rug decorated with rows of diamond shapes, each filled with pink-and-blue floral designs, covering the living room's dark hardwood floor. But her eyes were not on the intricate floral motif nor the walnut-framed chair with the cane back and seat nor the pale blue tufted sofa above her. Instead, she ran her index finger along the smooth mahogany planking of Mario's latest model boat she had placed before her. Her brother had spent a week piecing it all together, constructing the cabin and affixing the cast metal deck fittings. It had a radio-controlled motor, and she couldn't wait to see her brother maneuver it in the river water not far from where fishermen would cast off. Maybe she'd even have a chance to wave to her father on his full-sized weather-worn but sturdy boat he'd named *The Maria* after her mother and Isola delle Femmine's patron saint she'd always heard about.

She tugged at the little cotton American flag extending from a tiny post on the boat's stern. It was a miniature version of the one that flapped outside her apartment, the one her mother had mended after part of it tore in the wind. When she ran out of white thread, she used yellow. Now, there was a little yellow line in one of the white stripes. You couldn't really see it, because the flag usually just draped down from the metal pole Mr. DeRosa let her father attach to the side of their front window. But Annalisa knew it was there, and it reminded her how her family was different.

It wasn't just the neighborhood bullies. She'd seen the way people looked at her father when he set up his table outside the church and spoke with his thick accent. And she was tired of having to correct people when they mispronounced her name as "Anna" instead of "Ahn-nah." Why couldn't she have a name like Sarah or Margaret?

Papà always told her she should be proud to be American. So why did they always speak Sicilian at home? And why was it that her mother still didn't speak English?

"Whatcha doing with my boat?" Mario's voice cracked in surprise as he padded into the room in white socks.

Annalisa quickly sat up. "I was pretending it was in the ocean."

Mario shook his head and squatted next to her with a smile. "All that green in the rug must be the algae, right?"

Annalisa wrinkled her brow. "What's algae?"

"It's a plant that floats in the waves." He traced his finger across the leaves that surrounded the roses. "Listen, I don't mind you playing with it; just be careful, OK?"

Annalisa nodded and made the sign of the cross like she'd seen her mother so often do.

"Say, did you hear about the bridge?" Mario settled onto the floor.

"What bridge? Over the river?"

"No." Mario shook his head. "It's a great big one they're building down in San Francisco. I read about it in the newspaper. It's going to be part of a gigantic highway that runs all the way from Alaska to South America."

Annalisa's eyes widened as she thought about the southern continent she'd seen on Mario's globe. "That's really far!"

"What's really far, *mia cara?*" Papà settled onto the couch with a glass of water.

Mario rose to pick up a newspaper from the boxy coffee table.

"I was telling her about the highway they're going to build after they finish the new bridge." He pointed to a headline. "See, it says it here."

Mario absently ran his finger over the mole on his left cheek while their father scanned the page, the man's lips curling into a smile.

"It says here there will be a groundbreaking next Sunday! How would you kids like to go see it?"

Mario raised his eyebrows and smiled. "To San Francisco?"

Annalisa had never been to San Francisco. All she knew was that it was a big city by the ocean. Maybe they could take Mario's model boat there. With that many people, they might not feel so out of place.

"That's right, and perhaps Mr. Scotto would like to go; then we'd have a ride," Her father leaned forward with a grin.

"Where is Giovanni taking you?" Mamma entered the room, wearing a yellow-checked apron and holding a white dish towel.

Annalisa looked at her father, who slid back a bit on the sofa. "We were talking about this new bridge they're building in San Francisco, and, well, I thought we could take the kids to the groundbreaking ceremony next Sunday. There will be a parade and airplanes and..."

"Vincenzo." Mamma raised her brows along with her voice. "It's a Sunday."

Annalisa gazed back at her father who sighed and looked at

the floor. "Maria, it's at two o'clock, well after Mass. I just thought it would be special for the kids."

Annalisa nodded as she looked at her mother, praying that she would say "yes." Sundays offered a special opportunity to spend time with her father after Mass. He was always so tired on other days when he'd return home after long hours on the water, stinking of fish and sweat. And he was gone come summer. She dreaded it this year, because this time he was going to bring Mario. She'd be all alone with her mother, who was always telling her to brush her hair, stand up straight, and say prayers before meals and at bedtime.

She heard Mamma sigh. "All right. But I'm staying here. Someone has to cook your dinner."

Annalisa saw her father's shoulders tense. "But, Maria, this would be fun for the whole family."

Her mother shook her head. "You can have fun going to that big city, squeezed into Giovanni's little car. I am perfectly happy here."

Papà released a sharp exhale. "Maria... you never get out. Maybe we can have dinner in the city?"

Her mother slid a loose curly brown tendril behind her ear. "It will be good for you to spend some time with the children for once."

Her father's pale eyes got big beneath his bushy black brows, and he clenched the couch cushion. "Fine. The three of us will go, and we'll tell you all about it."

"Good." Mamma frowned, and she flicked the towel over her shoulder as she left the room.

Annalisa looked at Mario and then followed his eyes to her father who sighed heavily. "It's not every day that you can witness history. We never saw this kind of thing back in Sicily, I'll tell you that much. Your cousins are missing out. But we'll have fun, won't we?"

"Yes, Papà!" Annalisa shared a smile with Mario.

They were going far away from little Pittsburg to the big city with new people, practically a new world. She wasn't going to be like her mother, stuck in the past and tied to her Old-World ways. Her father was inviting them to see just what fun the future had in store. More than anything, she wanted to be a part of that.

FEBRUARY 26, 1933

California

Annalisa carried her sauce-stained plate to the kitchen. She didn't want her mother to have any reason not to let her go to San Francisco. She smiled at Mario, realizing that he, holding his dish, must be thinking the same.

Her mother looked at her and shook her head before running to Annalisa's side and tugging on her pale pink skirt.

"Look at what you've done to that dress!" Mamma raised her voice. "Go to your room and change into something else. You're lucky you have such nice clothes considering how often you soil them."

Annalisa stomped through the kitchen down the hall to her room where she opened her closet. Toward the front hung a mint-green dress with a white rounded collar tied at the front with a pink satin bow. She yanked it from the hanger and slid it over her head before skipping back to the kitchen to show her mother.

She saw Mamma's eyes harden as she exchanged a look with Papà who was leaning on the windowsill across from her. "You're going to let her out of the apartment looking like that?"

Her father frowned. "What's wrong? I think she looks beautiful—like a pretty flower. Come here, *mia cara!*"

Annalisa avoided her mother's eyes as she slid under her

father's arm. Mamma threw her hands up and left the room in a huff.

"Let me look at you." Papà smoothed Annalisa's waistless skirt.

"Now, let's make you a pretty bow." He retied the pink ribbon and patted down her staticky chin-length hair. "There. All better."

He helped her slide into her navy-blue wool peacoat that he had bought her last winter. She'd grown an inch since then and the sleeves were a little short, but she felt as pretty as a princess in her father's smiling eyes.

After calling goodbye to her mother, the two headed out front where Mario sat on the stoop, dressed in his own navy peacoat over a brown double-breasted flannel suit with knicker pants above red and blue argyle socks. He'd smoothed his curly brown hair into a right-side part.

"So, Mamma made you change your dress?" he asked as they waited for Mr. Scotto.

She nodded, looking down at her scuffed Mary Janes.

"Well, I think you look swell." Mario flashed her a grin.

She smiled as she plopped down on the stoop beside him and leaned her head on his shoulder. "Thank you."

The birds were chirping in the big sweetgum tree growing out of the patch of grass closer to the street. Its rough, grayish-brown branches were bare except for the spiky seed pods Mario called "gumballs." Several had fallen on the ground. Either her father or Mr. DeRosa would have to sweep the sidewalk soon.

Then she heard a honk and the sputtering of an engine as Mr. Scotto's familiar boxy, black Model T slowed to a stop. The man, who was older than her father with silver-streaked curls above a wiry frame, leaned toward the passenger seat.

"Who's ready for San Francisco?" he called out with a wide grin.

"Me! Me! Me!" Annalisa squealed, jumping to her feet.

Papà opened the dusty door and waited for Mario to slide onto the back bench before lifting Annalisa and placing her beside her brother. The leather seat was cracked with white patches showing through and the car reeked of fish, but Annalisa was thrilled to be going on this big adventure.

The two men talked in hushed voices in the front, occasionally erupting in chuckles. Annalisa clung to the seat edge as the car bounced and rattled.

"Are you scared?" Mario offered her a soft smile.

She shook her head, but she had never been so frightened. It wasn't the first time she'd been in Mr. Scotto's car, but the last time her father was driving. She wasn't sure she trusted the older man behind the wheel.

"Why don't we play the alphabet game?" Mario suggested.

"The alphabet game?" She loosened her grip from the seat.

"Yeah, you just have to look outside for all the letters in the order of the alphabet. So, for example, see the license plate on the car ahead of us? It has an 'A.' So, there's your first letter."

Annalisa scanned their surroundings. "There's a sign for Brookside Drive!"

"There's your 'B.'" Mario pressed his face into the window. "And that over there is for the city of Concord, our 'C.'"

Annalisa liked this game. She was soon craning her neck and calling out more finds. "J" was harder, but she spotted the word "junction." It wasn't until they landed on the letter "Q" when she found herself truly stuck. But as they crossed into the forest hills, she was soon distracted by the tall, graceful trees lining the road's edge. Their bark was reddish and looked fuzzy as if they were covered with a shaggy coat.

"They call them redwoods." Her father turned around in his seat. "They say they are the tallest trees on the planet and they're right here in California. And some of them are thousands of years old."

Annalisa's mouth dropped open as she pressed her face to

the window and peered up toward the treetops. She had never seen anything as big or old—maybe Mount Diablo where her father had taken them to see snow. But that was a mountain. And these trees were so different from the ones that she'd seen in her own neighborhood.

They descended from the forest to a small town, where they passed a gas station and a little market. The sign for the latter read QUALITY GROCERY. She nudged Mario and pointed.

He nodded at her discovery of the elusive letter "Q." "We're almost finished with the game. And we'll be there before you know it."

It took a while for Mr. Scotto to find a parking spot as he slowed and stopped for hordes of people crossing the street. Many more congregated on sidewalks. Annalisa had never seen such a crowd.

They stepped out of the car and were greeted by a cool gust of wind. Annalisa balled her fists and shoved them in her pockets. Her father placed a warm hand on her left shoulder and drew her close to his side.

"They call this the Marina District," Papà said. "Believe it or not, they say this place used to be covered in sand dunes."

Annalisa tilted her head. "What's a sand dune?"

Her father smiled. "It's little mountains of sand that you can climb on."

It sounded fun to her. "Where did they go?"

Mr. Scotto turned toward her from her father's right. "The people leveled the area for industrial plants." He waved his hand in a horizontal line. "Then, of course, there was the earthquake that destroyed it all. But they built it back up for a world's fair, and now, as you can see, it's been redeveloped for housing."

Annalisa looked past the crowd of chattering people to

boxy-shaped houses with flat roofs and barrel-shaped fronts. They almost looked like big boats.

She tugged on Mario's sleeve as he strolled to her left. "They're like your model ship!"

He nodded and a smile spread across his face. "It's like the whole neighborhood is a harbor."

Annalisa was so immersed in thoughts about all things nautical that she hadn't realized how long they'd been marching with what seemed to be many thousands of people streaming like a giant ribbon along the streets. A chilling wind blew a briny, fishy scent, and she could now see the glistening ocean. It was so much bluer and more expansive than the water back home.

Seagulls screeched from above as the four followed the other people onto a large sandy field near the water's edge. There, the wind whipped through Annalisa's hair. And she wished she would have worn her hat like the pretty ladies in their woolen berets and cloches to her left and right.

Then she heard a man's tentative voice. "Testing. One, two, three. Testing."

The cacophony around them dulled to whispers. And Annalisa saw several people making the sign of the cross as a man dressed in a purple cassock with a matching tall shield-shaped hat stepped to a microphone on a wooden platform far ahead of them. Behind him stood a piano and several chairs on which other men sat.

The man cleared his throat and began to speak in a booming voice that seemed to silence everyone around her.

"Paul once said, 'Not that I have already obtained all this, or have already been made perfect, but I press on to take hold of that for which Christ Jesus took hold of me.'" He clasped his hands in front of him. "'Brothers, I do not consider myself yet to have taken hold of it. But one thing I do: Forgetting what is behind and straining toward what is ahead, I press on toward the goal to win the prize for which God has called me heaven-ward in Christ Jesus.'"

He paused and Annalisa only heard the sound of crashing waves.

Again, the man cleared his throat before speaking. "The nature of the Christian journey is ongoing in our pursuit of spiritual maturity. We are meant to focus on the future rather than remain rooted in the past. It is the time to embrace the progress this bridge will represent as we collectively press on toward our goals and build on the success of this city, this state, and this nation. We are building not only a bridge of concrete and steel but a path forward to the prize for which God has called us."

"Amen!" Someone shouted, soon followed by a chorus of other amens.

The holy man raised his hands and the crowd again grew silent. "May the Lord above bless you on this banner day and for all the days of your life. And may His light shine upon the builders of this bridge, which will stand as a beacon of hope for a brighter future."

When he bowed his head, it seemed that everyone—even her father, Mr. Scotto, and Mario—erupted in applause. Looking up once more, he tapped the microphone, and the clapping stopped. A man with slicked back hair and a thin mustache rose from his chair in a gray double-breasted suit and stepped to the holy man's right side. The two men shook hands before the suited man spoke.

"Thank you, Archbishop Gilroy." He turned his head from left to right. "Ladies and gentlemen, I am pleased to present to you a special treat. We have in our presence the incomparable Lee Roberts, composer of 'Smiles,' who has put together a special tune he calls 'Ode to California.' Let's give the gentleman a warm welcome!"

A slender man with brown hair combed in a sleek right-side part stepped to his right and bowed before crossing to the piano on the far left of the platform. He settled onto the bench, adjusted his sheet music, and began pounding on the keys with both hands.

It was a lively and dramatic melody; faster than the songs they played on the organ at church. A lady to Annalisa's right started to tap her foot and the man she was with took her hand. He drew the woman in so they were close together before they moved apart, holding hands and extending their arms outward in a swinging motion, accompanied by some fancy footwork. They laughed as they danced and people began circling them, turning their attention away from Lee Roberts on stage.

Annalisa watched as other couples began swinging and stepping in time with the music.

Then her father turned to her. "May I have this dance, *mia cara?*"

She nodded without hesitation as a smile tugged at the corner of her lips. Papà slipped his arm through hers before the two of them began hopping forward and then backward, while snapping their fingers, before turning and taking each other's hands and swaying to the music.

"Hey, hey, hey!" chanted Mr. Scotto as he and Mario clapped their hands and tapped their feet.

Annalisa giggled as she and Papà continued their dance, a *contradanza* her father had learned in Sicily. Her father smiled down at her as they swung back and forth, and he held her tight as they hopped.

Soon other people had joined Mario and Mr. Scotto in calling out, "Hey, hey, hey!" and clapping their hands. And Lee Roberts continued to pound out his passionate tune written for California.

As Annalisa hopped and swayed, she felt love all around her—for her brother and father and even Mr. Scotto, but also for this dance that reminded her of where her family came from. Her father rarely talked about the old country, but she'd heard her parents arguing about it recently. Mamma cried and said something about what they'd left behind. Perhaps it was all too painful. Annalisa didn't want to ask questions and make her mother sad. The woman was grumpy enough as it was.

The song ended and Annalisa collapsed in her father's arms with which he gave her a sweaty hug. Then she turned back to the stage where people in black robes had begun lining up, and men wearing dark suits with white hats, carrying brass instruments and drums, shuffled in behind them.

The mustachioed announcer explained that this was the San Francisco Municipal Band and Chorus. They launched into a "Hallelujah," and men began spreading out coats so ladies could sit on the sandy ground. Annalisa plopped down next to Mario who was already seated.

"Sure is a lot of religious stuff in this program, don't you think?" He rolled his eyes.

Annalisa tilted her head. "What do you mean?"

Mario scooted closer. "I mean, I know it's Sunday and all, but we had the archbishop here to start the program, and now they're rejoicing about God."

"What's wrong with that?" Annalisa asked.

"I don't know." Mario shifted his eyes to the stage. "It just makes me think about Mamma and how she's always praying her novenas and kissing her Maria delle Grazie pendant. With all this talk about leaving the past behind for the future, they're still holding on to ancient religious stuff. You know what I'm saying?"

Annalisa turned toward the chorus and listened to their joyful refrain. She nodded.

"I'll tell you one thing," Mario said. "This bridge is going to change things. And one day, it's going to get us out of here."

Annalisa frowned. "You want to leave?"

Mario inhaled as he lifted his chin. "Why not? I mean, look around you, the world's so much bigger than Pittsburg and all the wannabe big shots and bullies. With this bridge we'll have a chance to see it all—go to South America if we want to!"

"And see monkeys and jaguars and sloths?" Her eyes widened.

Mario nodded. "And big rivers and jungles and mountains and volcanoes."

Annalisa smiled as she thought of the possibility—a chance to break free from the bullies and stares, boring church and prayers, grouchy mothers, and everything that always stood in the way.

"And you'd take me with you?"

Mario grinned back. "Of course I will."

The song ended and the announcer turned the microphone over to an older gentleman with glasses and a bowler hat, who said he had a message from President Herbert Hoover.

The president's proclamation sounded a lot like the archbishop's except he didn't quote scripture. He spoke of how progress, prosperity, and peace were connected with that of humanity and how this bridge was a path forward, building on what the nation had gained over the past four years in its economic recovery.

It didn't mean much to Annalisa, who knew a new president, Franklin Delano Roosevelt, would soon be in office, someone who excited her father. Papà said the man would rescue the country from the Depression. She wasn't sure what it was, but Mario told her "depressed" meant "sad." As she looked around her now, she saw nothing but happy faces. And she smiled along with them.

Then the man on the stage finished reading President Hoover's proclamation and the mustachioed announcer returned and shook his hand.

"And now, let us turn our attention behind me to where members of the United States Navy have gathered for a rendition of 'To the Colors,' which will be followed by a twenty-one-gun salute." Annalisa stood on her tiptoes and saw movement just beyond the stage, closer to the water's edge, but she couldn't really see what was going on.

Papà tapped her on the shoulder just as her right foot was starting to cramp from standing on her toes. "Need a lift?"

She nodded, and he helped her onto his back. She pushed her head past the side of his smoothly shaved right cheek as she draped her arms over his firm shoulders.

She could now see a row of seven cannons, which resembled tin toys Mario had on his bedroom shelf.

Alongside the cannons, seven men stiffly held their hands at their sides. They wore white hats with shiny black brims over dark blue, gold-buttoned double-breasted suits with stripes on the ends of their sleeves.

An eighth man, dressed in the same uniform, lifted a brass horn, raised it to his lips, and began to play a tune that seemed to make everyone around her stand a little straighter and for some reason place their hands on their hearts.

Then it was quiet except for the screech of a nearby seagull and the sound of the waves lapping the shore.

Annalisa heard a man shout something and then the men behind the cannons began lifting shiny canisters, which they shoved into the back of the weapons. Suddenly, she heard a loud boom, closely followed by another and another and another. The blasts continued. It almost sounded like fireworks, but there were no pretty colors or shapes, just clouds of smoke enveloping the men, whom she could now barely see.

Her heart leapt with anticipation—for what, she did not know. No one around her spoke; all had their eyes fixed on the spectacle beyond the stage. And then, for a moment, it was quiet. The men emerged from the smoke and marched forward with their hands raised to their hat brims in a salute to the crowd, who rewarded them with wild applause.

But the excitement did not stop there. Annalisa heard a

deep humming sound coming from the sky and suddenly she saw a cluster of light gray propeller-driven planes with yellow wings approaching. They formed a V-shape as they soared above the ocean, tipping their wings to the right in a synchronized fashion. Audience members whistled, shouted, and clapped above their heads.

The V-shape circled high above the ocean's surface and then swooped above the awe-struck crowd. Ladies and gentlemen grasped their hats as the planes passed overhead. And Annalisa buried her face in her father's wavy black hair until the humming grew fainter. Then she looked back up to see the planes head toward a tree-lined island across from them. She saw Mario tent his dark eyes in their direction even after another man stepped up to the microphone and began speaking. What did her brother see? She didn't want to miss any of it.

"Papà," she whispered in her father's ear. "I want to go down now."

Her father nodded his head and lowered himself so she could slide down to the sandy ground. She approached Mario who seemed lost in thought as he rubbed at his mole. "What are you looking at?" she asked.

"It's called Angel Island," he said. "Papà told me about it. Immigrants go there before they enter America."

"Did Mamma and Papà go there?"

Mario shook his head. "Don't you know? They came in through New York and traveled all the way to California by train. Mostly Chinese people come in through Angel Island."

Annalisa had seen Chinese people, but she didn't know any of them. They seemed so different from her and her family. But if Mario was right, and she was sure he was, it meant they had come to the United States on big boats just like her parents had, only across a different ocean.

"Mario and Annalisa!" Papà broke her from her spell.

She turned to see a shiny black truck pull up in front of the stage, dragging a large steel framed grate-covered box. It was followed by another long low cart upon which a large orange wooden structure jostled. Her eyes traced its outline—two triangle shapes connected by an upside-down arch on two large orange feet—as several people in the audience oohed and aahed.

"What's that supposed to be?" Annalisa asked Mario.

He smiled and squatted next to her. "The Golden Gate Bridge, of course."

She nodded and shifted her gaze back toward the water, trying to imagine it stretching across.

"But it's so small," she said. "I thought cars were going to drive across it on their way to Alaska and South America."

Mario chuckled and shook his head. "It's a model, like my ships and boats. The real bridge is going to be bigger than anyone's ever seen around here. It's going to knock your socks off!"

She tried to imagine it, but again she heard oohs coupled with laughter. She turned to see a cloud of hundreds of birds pouring out from the metal box. A man held open the grate door of what she realized had been their cage. They were pigeons, wildly flapping their wings until they'd congregated in a large dark cluster that swirled up and out into a whirlwind pattern that grew increasingly closer to them.

Several audience members held their hands over their heads as the birds circled above. And the mustachioed announcer explained that these weren't just any pigeons.

"Ladies and gentlemen, these are carrier pigeons, and they are going to carry the message about today's event across California." He smiled broadly. "Maybe even to other states. And you were here to see it."

The pigeons flapped their wings and soared above and beyond the field, seeming to make their way back toward the Marina District. And Annalisa wondered if the pigeons could possibly speak. She'd heard that people could teach parrots to do so.

Her thoughts were fixed on those pigeons and the message of hope they'd share as the four made their way back to Mr. Scotto's car. She found herself nearly skipping between her two favorite people, Mario and her father. If only they didn't have to return to little Pittsburg and her grumpy old mother.

She didn't want the day to end, but she was certain there would be brighter and more exciting years ahead.

SIX

APRIL 1939

Alberto pulled the flyer from his pocket and read it once more.

"Work the Palermo shipyards! Good pay!"

What it lacked in detail, it delivered in intrigue. The twenty-year-old had been looking for a sign, some direction in his life after returning from his eighteen months of compulsory military service at the naval base in Taranto.

Between gunnery practice and navigation drills, he'd cleaned and repaired enough ship parts that he was certain he would fit right in at the shipyard. It was a chance to make a living in the big city yet near enough to home that he could still see his family. A bright spot compared to the village's fading fishing tradition.

"What are you reading, son?" Papà settled to his right on the worn mauve sofa.

"Just something I found on the church's bulletin board," Alberto said. "Here, look."

He handed the flyer to his father.

"Palermo, eh?" Papà lifted his hazel eyes. "You'd want to work the shipyards?"

"It's something, Papà." Alberto grasped the armrest. "Besides, it's not that far away. I could come back for Sunday suppers."

His father nodded and sighed as he rubbed his thumb absently at the corner of the flyer. He didn't hand it back. "You've really given it some thought."

"Yes, Papà."

His father was quiet for a moment. Then he began drumming his fingers of his free hand, a habit Alberto recognized as something he did while working through a problem. Like the times he'd seen him hunched over the kitchen table, poring over bills.

Then, he frowned. "It's hard work, you know."

"What else is there to do?" Alberto raised his shoulders. "I've no education, and you know as well as I do there's no future in fishing."

Papà stopped tapping, and his gaze dropped into his lap as if he was inspecting some invisible stain. For the first time he looked old. It was more than just the lines in his face, etched by years of exposure to sun and sea. He seemed burdened by a heavy weight.

"You sound so much like your Uncle Vincenzo." His father shook his head, his voice softer now, tinged with something that wasn't quite regret. But it wasn't approval either. "At least you're not going to America."

Alberto took a deep breath. "Papà, this will be good for us all. I'll send money back to you and Mamma."

He saw his father's jaw tighten. Then, he nodded, placing the flyer on the worn wooden coffee table. "That's very kind of you, but living in the city won't be cheap. See how things are before you make any of those types of promises."

Alberto nodded. "Thank you, Papà."

"For what?" His father smiled.

"For understanding."

Papà released a short breath—nearly a laugh but minus the joy. He leaned back and stared out as if beyond the thin apartment walls and Alberto wondered if he saw the sea. "Half of this village left twenty years ago, and we may never see any of them again."

His soft, low voice wavered slightly before he turned to Alberto again. "At least I know you'll be back for some pasta now and then."

Their eyes met, Papà's so much lighter than his, as if they reflected the distance Alberto had always felt between them. But when his father pulled him into a hug, his grip was firm, hanging onto him longer than usual. He felt emotion emanate from the man's stolid exterior. And Alberto knew it was grief—not just for his son's departure but also for the fisherman he would never become.

Alberto heard the whistle blow, and he turned to see the black locomotive approaching. Behind him stood his parents, next to his sister Cristina, who held her baby, Teodoro, with her husband, Franco, at her side. There was no one else on the platform—just a few pigeons pecking at crumbs.

Had he alone answered the call of that flyer someone had tacked to the church bulletin board? His chest tightened with the thought. Perhaps other men had seen something he'd missed between the lines or knew something he didn't.

He adjusted his grip on his two suitcases, the weight shifting between his feet, as he reflected on the warmth of his father's embrace and his mother's parting prayer. Neither had asked him to stay.

Just thinking of it made his heart beat a bit faster. Here he was, neither a fisherman nor a scholar. He had no land or shop

—nothing to his name. There was no clear path before him—just a vague invitation to opportunity coupled with hope. A desire for something greater, rising from the fear of remaining rooted to a destiny that never felt like his.

As the locomotive drew closer, he swallowed hard. Just what would await him in the big city?

Then he felt a hand on his shoulder. Alberto turned to see his father. The older man said nothing at first, just slipped an oblong wooden ring into his son's hand. "I've been meaning to give this to you."

Alberto looked down to see a net shuttle. It was smooth in his palm, as if worn down by generations and experiences.

"It was your uncle's. He wanted you to have it. It's something to remember where you came from."

"Thank you, Papà." Alberto grasped his father in a hug as his mother squeezed him from behind.

The train slowed to a stop, and he turned to say goodbye.

"See you Sunday?" His mother's eyes were hopeful.

"Sunday." He stepped onto the train.

He slid his suitcases onto a rack above a hardwood bench next to a window. Once seated, he waved to his family, who remained on the platform. He saw Papà's sad eyes and thought about the shuttle in his pocket, wondering whether he'd made the right choice. Whether he should have stayed and fulfilled his father's vision of a fisherman's destiny. But the time had come, and he was going to be a part of Italy's future.

The train blew another whistle and rumbled slightly as it started up again. Running his finger over the smooth wooden shuttle, he thought about all the times he'd watched his father and the other fishermen repairing their nets just steps from his soccer field. Their rough, calloused fingers tugged at the linen threads that tied them to their past. He had never once held such a tool, as it wasn't his place, not his dream. Now he was surprised by how well it fit in his hand. He slipped it back into his pocket.

Alberto watched as the train passed buildings and then sped past the deep blue sea and through green fields punctuated with patches of yellow wood sorrel and the random red poppy. Then, after several stops, he was no longer alone on his journey. Families said their goodbyes before mostly men entered.

Gradually, fields turned into rows of buildings, and after about forty minutes had passed, he had arrived at Palermo Centrale. He stood and pulled down his luggage, following a line out to the station. Noise met him from all directions as people pushed and shoved their way through the crush. He counted at least nine other platforms, many with trains waiting on the tracks. Above him was a large glass canopy with iron framing held up by sickle trusses.

His stomach growled as he smelled the deep-fried scent of *arancini* emanating from a vendor's cart. And he weaved his way over to purchase one of the rice balls. It was warm and dense and delicious to its meaty center, and he washed it down with water from a bottle his mother had packed.

Then he reentered the wave of people undulating toward the arched doors of the station exit to a queue of *carretti*, horse-drawn carriages. He waited his turn until a *carretta* driver waved and then descended from his perch to help Alberto load his luggage. The brown horse snorted and tossed his red-and-green-tasseled head as Alberto boarded the wooden cart. He got a good look at its richly decorated side. The panels featured a carved battle scene in vibrant shades of red, yellow, blue, green, and brown. At the center, a cavaliere led the charge of five other knights against a golden castle's gatekeepers. It appeared the horsemen were winning just as the showy horse-led *carretti* seemed to dominate the road over the shiny honking cars and buses.

He asked the driver to take him to a neighborhood near the

port. As the horse clip-clopped along the streets that alternated between unpaved and cobblestone, Alberto saw and heard vendors hawking their wares from colorful market stalls, children playing soccer in the street, and women hanging faded laundry from their balconies. The aroma of fresh-baked bread mingled with the stench of vehicle fumes. The sunlight filtered through the narrow alleyways and cast shadows on graffiti-covered aging walls.

"Borgo Vecchio!" shouted the driver as he pulled the horse's reins to bring the journey to a stop.

He hopped off the edge of the *carretta* and helped Alberto descend along with his luggage. Alberto paid him and then watched the driver whip the horse to set the *carretta* back in motion.

He stood there in the middle of the street, staring up at rows of dangling T-shirts, underwear, and slacks. A horn beeped, and he awoke to his senses, waddling with his heavy luggage to the street's side to let a car pass.

"Hey, *paesano*!" someone shouted from above.

Alberto waved at the elderly gentleman, who leaned out his window.

"Looking for a place to stay?"

Alberto nodded.

"Come on up." The man beckoned him.

Alberto couldn't believe his luck as he took a deep breath and carried both suitcases toward the building.

"This door?" He pointed to a street-level red door beneath the man's window.

"That door." The man nodded. "Come upstairs."

Alberto set the suitcases down to turn the knob and entered a dimly lit first floor. There, he saw another door to what he assumed was an apartment. He placed the suitcases at the base of a marble staircase and climbed up, passing a peeling copy of the *Last Supper*.

The older man emerged from one of the two doors on the second floor.

"I see you left your luggage downstairs, which is good. That's where we have an open apartment. Come, let me show you."

So, Alberto went back downstairs, closely followed by the gentleman who introduced himself as Signor Ambrosino. The latter pulled a set of keys from his pocket and opened the door. "And here it is," Signor Ambrosino said. The men entered a slightly musty room with peeling yellow walls rimmed with what Alberto recognized as black mold.

"It needs a bit of cleaning," Signor Ambrosino ran his finger along the dusty living room windowsill. "But you can't beat the rent."

The two discussed the details as they walked through the three compact rooms. There was a bare bed left behind in the bedroom, an ice box, a sink, and a wood-burning stove in the kitchen, and a tiny bathroom where the water ran cold. It was cramped, damp, and smelled of decay.

Still, Alberto said, "I'll take it."

He handed Signor Ambrosino much of what was left in his wallet. Then the man bid him good luck and left him to settle into his new home.

Home. He felt a sudden wave of panic. It was really happening. He was on his own to fend for himself—no one to manage finances or cook for him. With that thought his stomach growled. He had no food. And how was he going to eat or sleep surrounded by that mold?

"Wait," Alberto called up the stairs. "Where can I buy groceries?"

"A block to your left." Signor Ambrosino gestured, and soon Alberto was on his way.

The store was small, with most items on display behind the counter. In addition to a loaf of bread, a bottle of wine, a bucket, and a dish towel, Alberto pointed to a bottle of vinegar. Then the shopkeeper carefully bagged Alberto's purchases.

As soon as he arrived back at his new apartment, he poured the vinegar into the bucket, added water, and then used the dish towel to wash the walls with the solution. Tending to the inevitable mold was a weekend ritual in his family apartment. The spores often grew in homes by the sea, particularly when it was more humid, and his mother swore vinegar could kill them. Wiping down the walls and taking out the trash had been his task, while Cristina helped in the kitchen and cleaned up after supper.

Within an hour, the apartment smelled strongly of vinegar but was free of mold. He opened the window to air the place out before washing up and pulling out the wine and bread.

It was hardly a meal, but then again, he barely cooked and knew he needed to conserve his savings—at least until his first paycheck. With that thought, he finished eating the loaf, swallowed some wine, and shuffled into the dim bedroom.

He'd need some linens, but for his first night he would have to make do. He sat on the thin mattress, trying not to think of who had slept there last. Instead, he focused on what had to be done: getting some decent sleep and rising early enough to make it to the shipyard, so he could get a job and pay his new bills. Was it really so simple? He lay down and stared at the ceiling where he saw a patch of mold.

He sighed, inhaling the still-acidic air, as he considered his father's words: It's hard work, you know. It wasn't just the new job; all of it would be taxing—at least for a while.

That was his last thought before he sank into a deep sleep, so fatigued by his eventful day, in need of rest for what was to come.

· · ·

The next morning, he awoke to the sound of a ship's horn blowing. He yawned, breathed in the vinegary air, and sat up.

It was Monday.

Still wearing the same clothing as the day prior, he pulled a black brimmed cap over his messy hair, and raced out the door, wending his way down the cobblestone streets to an open gate between the corner of two buildings where an overhead sign marked the shipyard entrance.

A buzz of voices greeted him. There appeared to be hundreds of men, congregated at various stations, welding metal, tinkering at wooden scaffolding, carrying materials, and crossing his path as he stepped forth in search of who might be in charge.

Drawing closer to the water, he saw more than two dozen hulking steel ships docked. Seagulls glided and called to him as he made his way past an area of enormous steel sheets laid out in the reflected sun. Ahead of him, he spotted a small wood-paneled building where he assumed he would find an office.

As he crossed the threshold, he was assaulted with the stench of tobacco that had yellowed the otherwise bare walls. A paunchy middle-aged man jolted up in his seat. His wooden desk was stacked with weathered ledgers and loosely rolled drafting paper, their fingerprint-stained edges curling from use. Pencils, paperclips, and rubber bands lay scattered in disarray. At the center, a sooty glass tray brimmed with half-smoked cigars and an inch of gray ash.

"Can I help you?" The man gave Alberto a cold stare.

"I'm here for the shipyard job." He wrung his cap in his suddenly sweaty hands.

"Skills?" The man's nut-brown eyes seemed to size him up.

"I was in the Regia Marina."

The man tilted his head. "Where did you say you're from?"

"Isola delle Femmine."

A knowing grin spread across the man's face; his eyes now

lit with amusement. "Strong, sturdy men from the village." He tapped a fat, callused finger on one of the few bare spots of his desk. "We'll put you on general labor. How does that sound?"

"Good." Alberto's grip on his cap loosened as he exhaled with relief. "When can I start?"

"Eager, aren't you?" The man let out a low, throaty chuckle.

He plucked a half-smoked cigar from the ashtray, rolling it between his fingers before slipping it between his thin lips. Striking a match from a green-and-yellow book, he cupped his hand around the flame, letting it catch at the cigar's tip. After a deep inhale, he paused, then exhaled a slow ribbon of smoke before settling his gaze on Alberto once more.

"Let's see what you can do," he said before raising his voice. "Ascanio!"

Alberto turned to see a wide-eyed man with an athletic build freeze in the doorway.

"Yes, Francesco?" He glanced at Alberto.

Francesco puffed at his cigar. "Get this young man out there, will you?"

"Come." Ascanio led Alberto through the clamor of the shipyard. The air was thick with the briny scent of seawater mixed with the sharpness of sawdust. Alberto strained to hear Ascanio's small talk between the sounds of striking hammers, scraping metal, and a persistent hum, punctuated with laughter and curses.

"See these wood beams?" Ascanio stopped and pointed.

Alberto nodded.

"We're going to carry those from here to there." Ascanio gestured toward carpenters hammering together a scaffolding.

Alberto bent down and reached for a beam.

"Wait!" Ascanio held up his hand. "You need gloves. You don't want any slivers."

He left briefly to retrieve a pair of cotton gloves, which he handed to Alberto.

"Now, watch what I am doing and follow along."

Alberto grasped the corner of the beam just as Ascanio was doing. It was heavier than it looked.

"Now we're going to carry it to where there's an open space on the ground. See that?"

Alberto saw, and the two men walked about fifty feet carrying the beam before they squatted to lower it to the ground.

"Now what?" Alberto wiped his brow.

Ascanio rolled his eyes. "We do it again."

And so, they did, about fifty more times, until they had laid out enough beams for the carpenters to work with.

There was a rhythm to it, with a goal-oriented discipline that reminded Alberto of his military training. Still, his coworkers were jocular—in some cases crude with their stories of escapades with women—and Alberto found himself absorbed in laughter as he made fast friends with the men.

By the day's end, Alberto's shirt was soaked through, his back hurt, and he was certain he had developed a sunburn on his forehead and the back of his neck. But for the first time in a while, he'd done something productive. And he slept well that night.

SEVEN

JUNE 1940

Palermo, Sicily

Too tired for dinner, Alberto had just laid down after a long day at the shipyard when he heard a rapping at his door.

"Just a moment." He threw on a shirt and smoothed his curly brown hair into its center part before opening the door a crack.

Signor Ambrosino stood with his age-spotted hand resting on the wall. For a moment, Alberto wondered if something had happened to the rent he'd shoved under the door earlier in the week.

"Did you hear the news?" The landlord leaned forward.

Alberto shook his head. "I don't have a radio."

"There's going to be a speech. Il Duce. Monday evening."

"Il Duce is coming here for a speech?" Alberto raised his eyebrows.

Signor Ambrosino shook his balding head. "No. They've set up loudspeakers in all public places. They've been repeating it every fifteen minutes. I assume it's a big deal."

Alberto nodded slowly. "Do you think it has anything to do with the war?"

"Smart boy," Signor Ambrosino chuckled. "Of course, I think it has something to do with the war. What else do you think he'd be talking about? A new train line? Just make sure you're somewhere where you can hear the speech."

Alberto closed the door and padded back into his bedroom, where he threw himself onto his rumpled sheets.

War. It was only a matter of time. Everyone talked about it at the work site. No doubt Italy would join Germany, its Pact of Steel partner. The question had just been when. And now all signs pointed to Monday. Alberto had questioned Germany's motives in their latest invasions, but he decided Mussolini knew what was best for Italy. In the meantime, he needed to get some sleep. He'd promised his mother he'd come to Isola delle Femmine tomorrow, as he had every two weeks since moving to Palermo.

It surprised him how much he looked forward to the trips. Sure, he enjoyed the camaraderie of his coworkers and the energy of the gritty city, but he often found himself reflecting on simpler times, dribbling the soccer ball down the field or suiting up for Sabato Fascista. Plus, there was the promise of his mother's meals—so much better than his attempts at ragù over what was often overcooked pasta.

The next morning, he was awakened by the distant crow of a rooster. He thought he was already back in his old village. Then he saw the peeling yellow paint of his moldy room, and it all came flooding back to him.

He rubbed his eyes and inhaled the vinegary air before rising and stepping into the cold shower. Then he slipped into some clean clothes and headed out the door for Mass.

When he arrived, the church buzzed as if it were an auditorium rather than a holy place with voices rising to the vaulted ceilings. There, blond angels peered down with wide blue eyes. Behind him, a woman expressed her reservations, as she had two sons of military age. Another next to him whipped her head around.

"Mussolini is always right," she hissed, parroting a frequently stated slogan.

The pipe organ played the opening hymn, further silencing the congregants. Then the tall, lithe priest, dressed in a green vestment, seemed to glide to the gilded altar.

During the homily, he pounded his fist on the lectern with passion as he spoke about how God had delivered a leader, Mussolini, who would move mountains to achieve greatness for his people. The past conquests of Albania and Abyssinia and even involvement in the Spanish Civil War proved that this man knew what was best for the nation. It was time to open hearts and minds to whatever came from the next day's announcement.

After Mass, Alberto made his way to the Palermo Centrale train station, passing a building upon which someone had scrawled DUCE DUCE DUCE! He chuckled at the irony of their vandalism in the name of law and order.

Aboard the train, he heard more people speculating about the announcement. Several commented that it would no doubt be a quick war. And Alberto smiled to think about how France would soon bow to the likes of Italy.

When the train finally rolled into Isola delle Femmine, he was happy to see his family lined up on the platform waiting for him. There was also a new poster advertising that Monday evening's speech would be broadcast from Piazza Umberto I.

"Will you stay for the speech?" his father asked as they embraced.

Alberto shook his head. "You know I can't, Papà. I have work tomorrow."

"Well, at least you'll have time for the afternoon supper. Your mother made *casarecce al pesce spada e melanzane*."

"Swordfish with eggplant? My favorite!"

"Your Mamma knows." Papà patted his son on the back.

As they headed toward his parents' apartment, Alberto turned to Cristina. His sister seemed quieter than usual; her light eyes clouded with worry.

"You're wondering what this will mean for Franco."

She sighed. "Of course, I am. I don't know what the kids and I would do without him around."

"Well, we don't know anything for certain just yet. Besides, people are saying it won't last long."

When they arrived, Franco was seated in the living room with his two young children, baby Remo and two-year-old Teodoro. The son of the village cobbler had married Cristina when she was just sixteen, and they started their family not long after. Franco's father had earned an elevated status after he set aside his wooden lasts, rasps, and files to brave the battlefield. Franco didn't just wear good shoes; he had some big ones to fill. So, despite Cristina's reservations, Alberto knew Franco, who had in the past year returned from his own stint of compulsory service, would be eager to join a fight.

Alberto nodded to his brother-in-law before he stepped into the steamy kitchen and kissed his mother.

Then he returned to the living room, where he settled onto the mauve couch to his brother-in-law's left and his father's right. Teodoro waddled up and saluted him with a tiny hand.

"You're preparing him for the Balilla already?" Alberto asked, staring down into his nephew's hazel eyes.

"He picked it up from one of the parades." Franco brushed a dark curl from his forehead. "You know how it goes. So, how is big-city life treating you?"

"We're building a new ship, about one hundred and seven

meters long, for more than two hundred men." He held out his arms to demonstrate just how big. "It's a real beauty."

Franco smiled, revealing the dimple in his left cheek. "I'd heard about some of those ships. Can you imagine taking one of those out for fishing? You could catch a whale or two with one of those."

"So, how are things here?" Alberto asked.

Franco's eyes shifted to Papà.

"What is it?" Alberto asked, turning toward his father.

"It's just my heart." Papà shook his head. And Alberto sensed embarrassment in the man's long, thin gray-stubbled face, so unlike his own with his pointed chin and full cheeks. "The doctor says the fishing is too much for me."

"You've been having heart problems?" Alberto frowned.

"I just get worn out." Giuseppe tapped his chest. "Getting old, I suppose."

Alberto shook his head. "Fifty's not that old, Papà. Did something happen? Why did you see a doctor?"

Again, he saw Franco look at his father. There was an awkward silence.

"Come on, Papà." Cristina emerged from the kitchen with a frown. "Why don't you tell Alberto what really happened?"

"It was nothing," his father said quickly.

"He fell out of the boat." Cristina threw up her arms. "It was definitely something. Papà, you passed out, and we had to get the doctor. You're lucky it happened here and not when you were rowing near Tunisia."

"Papà, why didn't you tell me?" Alberto grasped the edge of his seat. It was something to cling to with this floor-dropping news. His solid, stolid father needed help. And when it happened, his son wasn't there for him.

"Enough." His father waved his hand. "It's all taken care of now."

"So, you're not fishing anymore?"

Papà shook his head. "Not since last month."

"What are you doing for money?" Alberto raised his eyebrows. Fishing wasn't just a passion; it was how he supported his family, a family the man so rarely saw all those years, following the fish to regular earnings.

Alberto had long resented that drive, but as an adult, he finally understood the sacrifice. In a way, the man was truly the hero he'd long sought. But all those years of enduring the elements and changing tides had caught up with him. Now he needed to take better care of himself.

"We still have those checks from your uncle in America." His father's eyes shifted. "Anyway, at least I had a chance to participate in one last *mattanza*. My last and maybe the last for the village if we start this war."

Alberto frowned. "We don't know Mussolini's going to declare war."

"Sure, we do." Franco tilted his head. "What do you think they're planning to do with all those ships you've been building?"

Alberto nodded slowly and stared across the room to where little Teodoro was pounding together two wooden blocks. Clop clop. The dull thud seemed to echo through the silence, like the beat of a drum. Clop clop, like the march of soldiers advancing on a battlefield.

He was part of the machine preparing for a war, one he, with his job, would likely never fight. But the conflict would still affect everyone in the room. Franco would be called to serve, while Alberto would tinker with his own blocks of wood. These boys would go months—maybe years—without seeing their father's return, while he swept up bolts and debris. His sister would have to keep the little family going, while he fetched tools. His parents were clearly going to be financially strained—

perhaps even more with a war. And ships would sail from the shipyard into battle, targeted by enemies from other nations, inevitably leading to untold casualties on both sides.

It was a war he hadn't chosen but one his hands had helped build. The older men, including his father, told stories of valor and heroism set against the backdrop of hunger and fear on the Austro-Hungarian border. Alberto knew there were many others who never came home. It was a war that changed Europe, leaving unhealed wounds and shattered lives. Somehow history was repeating itself.

The men sat in silence, absorbed in their own thoughts, the June heat suddenly stifling the little room. And just when Alberto thought he could take it no more, his mother appeared in her green apron calling, "Food is ready!"

The family made their way to the rectangular dining room table as Mamma and Cristina ladled the swordfish and eggplant pasta onto everyone's plates. Then once they were seated, Papà began grace.

"Thank you, Lord, for bringing us all together." He closed his eyes. "We are so proud of our only son. May you continue to bless him, our daughter, and her lovely family. And may il Duce's speech tomorrow mean good things for our future and the future of Italy. Amen."

"Amen," everyone answered in unison.

Alberto looked around the table and thought about how this day might be the family's last together in a long time. He wondered what good would truly come for their future and that of Italy with war afoot.

The brief visit left him pondering all that would no longer be so mundane for the rest of his family as he kept pressing on. There was a new, urgent need to help his father in the shadow of a looming threat he'd for too long overlooked, always taking Sicily's safety for granted.

Later, he could not help but notice tears in his sister's eyes as they said their goodbyes. At just fourteen months apart, they'd shared a bond tighter than many of the siblings he knew. Growing up, she'd been more than a sister; she was his best friend, someone who shared a longing for a father tied to the sea. It was no wonder she married early after he went away. He drew her in for an extra hard hug.

"Everything is going to be all right," he whispered in her ear, and she nodded into his chest.

They separated, and he turned to his mother, who seemed to feel the need to re-part his curly hair. "Keep making us proud."

"I will, Mamma." He returned her sad smile, and then it was time to board the train.

As he slid onto the bench, he noticed someone had carved the words "*Credere, obbedire, combattere*" into the grains of wood. Soon he'd learn the extent to which all of Italy would be asked to rise and believe, obey, and fight.

War was all the talk of Alberto's fellow laborers the next morning at the shipyards.

Ascanio and another man named Fausto chatted with him while the three pushed wheelbarrows full of piping to a welding site.

"It's a chance to restore Italy to what it was in the Roman Empire," Fausto said over his shoulder.

"What do you know about the Roman Empire?" Ascanio chuckled.

"I know we were respected." Fausto slowed his wheelbarrow to a stop. "Think about it. All those promises they fed us during the Great War. Austria-Hungary and Dalmatia would be ours for the taking. And then what? We walked away with nothing after all those lives lost. This war's going to be different."

Ascanio clicked his tongue. "You're certainly not going to fight it."

Fausto shook his head. "We're fighting it. We're building the ships."

"What do you have to say for yourself, Albertino?" Ascanio asked suddenly.

Alberto wasn't listening. He was thinking about his father and his heart condition, something furthest from the day's big event but monumental to him. After all, while his father hadn't said it, it was clear that his uncle's checks weren't enough to pay for his parents' apartment. And he knew Cristina and Franco couldn't do it with their family expenses.

"How long have you worked here?" Alberto asked.

Ascanio turned his eyes upward as if counting. "A year and a half."

Fausto raised his index finger. "About a year for me."

"Why do you ask?" Ascanio tilted his head.

"Don't you ever want to do more around here?" Alberto spread his arms. "I mean, really working on the ships."

"Sometimes, sure." Ascanio nodded. "But then I wouldn't get to chew the fat with this goofball." He messed up Fausto's shaggy salt-and-pepper hair.

Fausto shoved him away and turned toward Alberto. "Sounds like you have some aspirations there, young man."

"Just thinking." Alberto regretted that he'd even mentioned it.

"You know what I'm thinking?" Ascanio winked. "I'm thinking they might let us out early."

"Better slow down so we don't have to move too much more before then." Fausto smiled.

"I don't know about you two, but I don't want to get fired so early on the job." Alberto pushed his wheelbarrow ahead. "Some of us need the money, you know."

"Listen to that one," Fausto chuckled. "It was a joke."

Just then, a whistle blew, the whistle that typically marked the end of their shift.

"See?" Ascanio grinned. "What did I tell you? They're letting us out early."

The streets were pulsating with frenetic energy as Alberto wended through the throngs of Palermitani gathered at the entrance of Mercato Borgo Vecchio. Brilliantly hued awnings stretched over stalls nearly overflowing with fresh produce. Women in colorful headscarves haggled over prices of plump red tomatoes, long green squashes, and deep purple eggplants, desperate for a last-minute deal. The heavy aroma of ripe fruit mingled with the pungent scent of cured meats and cheeses.

The crowds grew denser as Alberto inched closer to the market's heart, which beat along with the cacophony of shoppers' chatter and the rumbling of passing carts across the uneven street. He felt the heat of their bodies and saw their eyes wide in anticipation as they turned toward the loudspeaker perched above a rickety wooden platform.

Meanwhile, the vendors, who typically extolled the virtues of everything from oranges ("Sweet as a lover's kiss!") to melons ("Like sunshine in a rind!") and lingered to entice the after-work crowd, couldn't pack up their colorful offerings fast enough.

Around him, Alberto saw and heard a large group of people begin chanting, "Duce! Duce! Duce!" louder and louder between party slogans. It was as if the entire neighborhood was preparing for a grand Fascist parade.

He slid through the crush and found a spot near some

particularly stinky salted fish. The space was quickly filling up, and it was getting harder to breathe.

Suddenly, there was a crackling sound, and everyone quieted down. Then a sharp voice pierced through the silence over the loudspeaker, introducing "the founder of the empire."

The mass of people erupted in applause, joining the roaring sound from the speakers of audience members in Rome. Again, there was silence as everyone leaned forward, waiting for Mussolini to speak.

And finally, there it was, the gravelly voice of il Duce himself.

"Soldiers, sailors, and aviators! Blackshirts of the revolution and of the legions! Men and women of Italy, of the Empire, and of the kingdom of Albania! Pay heed! An hour appointed by destiny has struck in the heavens of our Fatherland."

It seemed everyone in the market and on the other side of the loudspeaker cheered.

"The declaration of war has already been delivered..."

More cheers broke out, and people began shouting, "War! War! War!"

"Shh!" an older woman said.

Mussolini continued through the cheering in Rome. "We go to battle against the plutocratic and reactionary democracies of the west, who at every moment have hindered our advance and have often endangered the very existence of the Italian people."

"Yes, yes, yes!" someone shouted.

"Recent historical events can be summarized in the following phrases: promises, threats, blackmail, and finally to crown the edifice, the ignoble siege by the fifty-two states of the League of Nations. Our conscience is absolutely tranquil."

Cheers seemed to drown Mussolini out, but he raised his voice to continue. He spoke of how—despite Fascist Italy's efforts to avoid conflict—Europe plunged into turmoil and how rigid adherence to old treaties without considering necessary revisions contributed to the conflict.

The nation, he said, must enter the war out of a sense of honor, duty, and future interests. He spoke about how it was a chance to resolve issues related to maritime boundaries and ensure free access to the ocean for Italy's people. This was but a phase in the logical development of the nation's revolution, a struggle of industrious nations against the exploitative. He made it clear that he did not wish to involve neighboring countries such as Switzerland, Yugoslavia, Greece, Turkey, and Egypt unless provoked. And finally, he affirmed his loyalty to Germany and expressed his confidence in Italy's unity and strength.

"The single order of the day is categorical and obligatory for all. It already spreads and fires hearts from the Alps to the Indian Ocean: victory!"

The people erupted into more cheers.

"And we will win." Mussolini's voice was forceful. "In order to finally give a long period of peace with justice to Italy, to Europe, and to the world. People of Italy! Rush to arms and show your tenacity, your courage, your valor!"

Alberto looked all around him. People were crying and hugging strangers, and then he realized the speaker had turned off. The speech was over. Yes, Mussolini had declared war, and yes, that meant great changes were to come, but there was something in the stinky air, an electricity that seemed to charge everything and everyone around him.

He was back to the parades of his youth, the energy that sustained his people through the years following the war and after the Depression, the force that elevated Sicily with grand promises and pronouncements. Mussolini sounded so confident, so certain of victory, and Alberto wanted it to be true. Perhaps this war could be something good for the nation, something to reflect on with pride, knowing that he had worked on the battleships. Like the revolutions of republics past and Italy's ultimate unification, surely there was a greater reason to fight.

At that moment, moved by Mussolini's words and warmed by the heat of bodies spread throughout the market, he felt stronger and more certain of his place than he'd ever felt in his past. Now was a moment to celebrate. He joined the sweaty group in a hoarse rendition of "Giovinezza" as they filtered out into the promising light that still shone over that fateful June evening.

The next morning was certainly less joyous. Francesco had tasked him to sweep up the carpenters' dropped screws and nails. At the very least, he could count on Ascanio's acerbic wit.

"They say we have to close the shutters and turn off lights tonight." Alberto pushed his broom. It had been all the talk among the men that morning. Having to essentially hide wasn't something he hadn't anticipated would come after Mussolini's rousing call to action. "Do you think the French and English are going to strike?"

"If they do, it's their funeral." Ascanio knelt with the dust-pan. "Have you seen what they brought in last night?"

Alberto had noticed. Two enormous zeppelin-like balloons were hovering over the harbor, anchored to the ground by a series of chains woven into what looked like a net, presumably intended to catch enemy aircraft. Additionally, clusters of men in military uniforms were sitting around a cannon-like contraption pointed at the sky.

This was the air defense, and while it was supposed to serve as a comfort, it reminded Alberto that the harbor area, including the shipyard, was a military target.

The same thought registered when he was awakened later that night by the wail of sirens. He didn't just work at a military target site; he lived just a short walk from the waterfront.

Anything that happened to the shipyard would happen in his backyard.

He went to his living room, opened his shutters, and stared out at the empty street. Not a soul was out at this time of night —especially not with the siren blaring. But then he saw something—a woman's pale face in another open window across the street. Just as he saw her, she turned in his direction, and they made eye contact.

Embarrassed, he stepped back from the window, as he wasn't wearing a shirt. He quickly pulled one on, and when he looked out the window again, she was gone. So, too, was the siren. All was quiet.

He returned to bed and lay there for a long time in the stillness, wondering if he was safe to even be there. But then his mind wandered to more pleasant thoughts, those of the woman he'd seen.

Alberto had always been shy around girls growing up, too self-conscious about the silly mole on his cheek. And then he went to Taranto for his compulsory service, away from members of the opposite sex. He'd seen plenty of attractive women pass him on the streets and sit across from him on the train. But they were sophisticated city ladies and certainly wouldn't pay attention to a laborer like him. He wondered what this neighbor woman's story was, if she was lying in her own bed thinking about him in an effort to ward off fear. It made him chuckle.

Then the sirens started up again, this time pulsing three times rather than the prolonged whining. He knew he probably shouldn't, that it could put him in harm's way, but returned to the window and was rewarded with another glimpse of the woman. This time, she wasn't looking in his direction. But he could see her soft features, a small nose and gently rounded cheeks. Her hair was fair and fell just past her shoulders.

She turned suddenly and nodded. He tipped his chin up and raised his hand in a wave. She waved back and nodded again before leaving the window. He waited for a moment more before returning to bed, where, when he finally fell asleep, he dreamed of a fair-haired angel, who could guide him to a world without fear and serve instead as a beacon of light.

Each night thereafter, from the moment he turned out the lights, he paced in front of his window, waiting for a glimpse of the woman across the way. But there were no more sirens, no reason for her to be looking out.

He thought of her as he tackled his grunt work, everything from moving materials and equipment to bringing more rivets to the riveter. He thought of her in church when he knelt before a nineteenth-century wooden statue of St. Anne with a young Virgin Mary. Perhaps, if he ever had the chance to meet her, she could offer such comfort and grounding. It was something he sought amid the uncertainty and confusion that clouded his support for Mussolini's fascist ideals and desire to assert the nation's rightful position as one of Europe's greatest powers.

And he was thinking of her again as he was just leaving Mass on the morning of June 23, when he heard the rattling wail of a siren. He stood in the center of the piazza and froze in place.

He looked around at the other congregants who had emptied into the square, their eyes just as wide as his. The siren stopped, leaving them in tense silence. Then he heard a loud squawk. He saw a single seagull in the bright blue, empty sky.

The people around him erupted in nervous laughter.

A false alarm, Alberto thought, as he and the crowd resumed their movement.

He walked for half an hour and heard nothing more. He reached Palermo Centrale and waited on a crowded platform for the reliable *chug-a-chug-a* sound of the train for Isola delle Femmine.

. . .

His father stood at the station alone this time to greet him, and he was glad for that. He wanted some time to talk to him. He had spent so much of his childhood yearning for such precious moments, always watching his father disappear into the horizon on his boat. Finally, with his fishing livelihood gone, they had time to talk. It was a mixed blessing.

"How is the heart, Papà?" He glanced at him from the side as they walked.

"Don't you worry." His father gazed straight ahead.

Alberto saw a frown on his father's weathered face. His calloused hands were balled in fists as he moved forward at a slower pace than Alberto remembered.

"Are you sure you're all right, Papà?"

His father let out a deep breath, heavy on the sea breeze. "It's just hard, you know. Not being able to fish."

He paused, his voice quieter now. "If I didn't have the two grandsons, I don't know what I'd have to live for."

Alberto nodded, feeling a tightness in his chest. His father had so rarely expressed his emotions. He'd seen him shed a tear just once in his life—when Alberto's *nonna* died of heart failure. "How is the money, Papà?"

His father stopped mid-stride and looked down, as if examining his scuffed shoe. And Alberto knew his father was too proud to admit defeat.

"You know I can help you," Alberto said softly.

"That's very kind of you, son, but you need the money for your own living expenses. It's not cheap in the city."

"I'm serious, Papà. I can help."

His father's hands, which had not been there to support Alberto's baby steps or clap in support of his soccer matches, took those of his son and gave them a squeeze. "Thank you. As soon as I can, I'll repay you."

"Don't worry about it, Papà. Besides, I'm working my way up at the shipyard. Before you know it, I'll be one of those welders or carpenters."

His father pressed his lips together into something resembling a smile, but his eyes seemed far away, as if he were replaying a filmstrip of the few precious moments they'd shared together. Alberto wondered if his father felt any sense of regret.

"Good boy." Papà pulled him in for a hug. "I'm proud of you."

Alberto shut his eyes, absorbing his father's warmth and a feeling he had chased for years. Now that he had it, he wasn't sure it was enough, if a single hug could erase the distance between them.

They arrived at the apartment around noon, just in time for Mamma to serve *riso con zafferano e cozze*, saffron-infused rice with mussels.

Cristina, Franco, and the boys were there, but Franco was quieter than usual.

"Did you hear the news about Trapani?" Papà asked, breaking through a moment of silence after grace.

"I did." Alberto nodded. "They say it was the French. Thirty people were killed."

"But you're safe in Palermo?" Cristina held her fork above her plate.

"I think so." Alberto dug in. "We've had a couple of false alarms, that's all. How about here?"

"No alarms." Cristina shook her head and put down her fork. "Not in Isola. But we do have some news."

She looked at Franco, her fingers tensing at the edge of the table.

"I've been assigned to Libya," he said in a flat voice. His green eyes met Cristina's.

His sister's plump lips parted slightly but released no words. Instead, she straightened her back with stiff shoulders and reached for her wine glass. As she raised it to her mouth, he saw a slight tremor in her hand.

"Libya?" Alberto asked. "When?"

"In two weeks."

Alberto grabbed the edge of his seat, desiring its firmness in this state of the unknown. His sister shifted her gaze to her plate where she poked her fork at a mussel. She'd not yet eaten a bite. He knew, for her sake, he had to reflect strength even if it amounted to false hope. "Well, from everything I'm hearing, this war won't last too long. After all, Germany already occupied Paris."

Cristina raised her head to offer a small smile. Gone was the confident girl who often upstaged her older brother in games and studies. In that unconvincing expression, he saw resignation and unspoken fear.

He was aware of the sudden silence that swept across the little table punctuated only by the scraping of silverware and the creak of his father's chair as he reached for the bread basket. Even the little ones were uncharacteristically quiet with Remo in his wooden high chair, pushing a fistful of rice in his mouth, and Teodoro inspecting a mussel shell.

Alberto lifted a forkful of the saffron-scented rice, so vibrant in its yellow hue, a sharp contrast to the looming shadow of war, the uninvited guest that sat at their table. He chewed slowly, processing the food almost mechanically, for he'd lost his appetite. But he knew his mother had worked hard to prepare it. It was important to keep rituals going—even in the face of the unknown. People still needed food, there were still tasks and obligations, and despite the war, life had to go on.

At some point conversation resumed. It was small talk, but healthy dialogue nonetheless, punctuated by the occasional outburst from little Remo. Alberto watched Cristina scoop up the baby and make cooing noises to soothe him. And he thought of how hard it would be for his sister to manage tending to her little boys alone.

"Let me know if you need anything," he said to her later, before he boarded his train.

"Thank you, big brother." Her eyes were moist, as he pulled her in for a tight hug. "We're going to be just fine."

The weather was still pleasant when he exited the train to Palermo Centrale and merged with others returning from their respective villages to the city.

He reflected on his day. He'd promised his father he'd help him, and he implied the same to Cristina. Now he just needed to make some more money. He thought about the scaffolding carpenters, the welders, and the painters. Any one of those jobs would be ideal. He just needed training. And in order to get that training, he'd need to assert himself and ask.

He was just turning onto his little cobblestoned street when he heard a loud buzz from above. Three silver planes flew overhead. And at the same moment he saw them, there was a burst of what at first sounded like fireworks, but was in fact, machine gunfire.

He ran down the street with his hands over his ears until he reached his door and entered his apartment. The earth began to rumble, and he heard what sounded like the loudest, closest firework. His ears began to ring as the floor continued to shake with the window rattling where he stood in the living room. He didn't know where else to go, so he slid under his bed like he'd done as a boy when playing hide-and-go seek. Then, there was a sense of safety in the spot beneath the place he'd dream. Now he was aware of how dangerous it could actually be as the wooden frame creaked while shifting from side to side. Still, he didn't dare move—except involuntarily, for his chest was heaving in hyperventilation.

Whereas in the past he could rely on a laughing Cristina eventually spotting him, he shook at the thought of being pulled out by a British soldier. Or getting blown to smithereens. Pressed to the shivering yet warm floor, his body frozen in terror despite the June heat, he reflected on what he'd heard about Trapani, of Franco's service, of the unseen enemies who could one day roam Palermo's streets, and how his work had helped prepare Italy for this fight. He wondered if his landlord, Signor Ambrosino, had found refuge. Then he considered the safety of the angel-faced woman across the street. Such were the thoughts that consumed him for about half an hour amid nearly nonstop shaking and banging of furniture. All the while, the phantom planes continued to emit their sawing sounds.

Then, at some point, he was aware it had passed, for he heard nothing but the tweeting of nearby birds. He marveled at the resilience of nature, that song could arise from violence and terror. Then came a siren, which he optimistically deduced meant "All clear."

Waiting for a moment, he slid back out from under his bed and crawled to the living room window. He opened the shutters to an empty street; there appeared to be no damage. He looked across and found himself overjoyed to see his neighbor, peering out the window just as she had on the night of the first siren. She raised her thin eyebrows and nodded. He smiled, perhaps a bit too broadly, for they still hadn't met. But he felt a rush of relief. She waved and disappeared from the window.

He stood there for a few minutes more, staring at the woman's window, until a thought occurred to him. The sounds he heard were no doubt coming from the waterfront. Against his better judgment, he decided to take a walk to survey the damage.

He could hear the crackling flames before he saw them and felt the heat. One of the destroyers the crew had been tirelessly finishing had been hit and was now a smoldering hunk of steel, sinking in the sea. Beyond the shipyard, there was a long stretch of ruined homes. He was aware of the wail of sirens, but this time those of ambulances racing to rescue the people trapped in the piles of rubble. He considered the news from Trapani and wondered just how many people in Palermo had now been wounded, how many had perished, and considered how he could sleep the night without knowing when and where the next bombs would fall. Within those thoughts he was painfully aware: This was only the beginning.

EIGHT

MAY 1941

Vincenzo slid on his cotton gloves and, leaning over the stern of his wood-hulled *gozzo* boat, began to draw in the drifting net, passing it back to his twenty-one-year-old son, Mario, who stood behind him.

"Look at that!" He picked apart the linen webbing to extract a plump male shad.

The eight-pound fish wriggled as he passed it to Mario, who tossed it into the boat's rear hold.

Vincenzo tugged again at the net, pulling it toward him and revealing two more fish. He carefully picked each out of the webbing before handing it to Mario to stash away.

"One day, this will be your boat." He drew in more netting, proud of how far he'd come. Life would have been different had they stayed in Sicily, had they not made that choice. Still, as he stared into the murky water, he couldn't help but think back to the deceptively gentle turquoise waves that splashed into rocky coves and the rhythms of nature that drew in migratory herons and cormorants, who sometimes fished alongside the men in their boats. He thought about his village's twin stone towers, one on land, the other built atop Isola delle Femmine's homonymous islet. Both once served to protect against pirates and stood the testament of time. For centuries, they'd stood, but not nearly as long as the village's fishing tradition. Now he wondered who might provide it protection. It was fading, even among his family. Costanza had written that Alberto had left for the city. Whether he'd realized it or not, he'd cut himself from the long line of fishermen. But Vincenzo knew you could never truly break free from the pull of the sea.

He turned to his son. "You've been awfully quiet. Is something wrong?"

Mario shifted his gaze and cleared his throat. "I've been thinking, Papà. I met with a recruiter the other day..."

"A recruiter? What do you mean, a recruiter?" Vincenzo paused.

"The Navy, Papà. I want to join the Navy. Think about it: I can sail the world."

Vincenzo stared into his son's dark eyes, and thought about a photograph Costanza had sent him. They reminded him of Alberto's—he, too, wanted to see more.

"But you do see the world." He yanked the net. "Every summer when we fish Bristol Bay."

He thought of the way Mario had marveled at the sight of a moose sipping from the edge of the vast watershed, the host of the world's largest sockeye salmon run. They'd also spotted their fair share of bald eagles soaring above or perched in shoreline trees.

The bird was a symbol of freedom and strength, representing philosophies that differed greatly depending on where on Earth you stood. The fascist eagle clutched an axe tied to a bundle of sticks, a symbol of unity with a hint of violence. Meanwhile, the American eagle extended its legs, revealing one talon holding an olive branch opposite another full of arrows—signifying a desire for peace but a readiness for war.

He'd left behind the first before it took flight, trading enforced unity for freedom's uneasy promise. Now his son was asserting his own freedom to fly. This sensitive boy wanted to soar like the eagle along with an organization known for both peacekeeping and violence. Vincenzo knew he had to release him from his talons. Still, he wanted to hold on.

"Papà, it's just that... I want to do something on my own for once. Sail the seas. Meet new people."

Vincenzo took a deep breath. He hadn't expected this. He steadied himself in the gently rocking boat, aware of a sense of instability. Their world was changing.

His hands shook as he gripped the damp mesh of the net and pulled it up, hand over hand to reveal the thrashing fish, its silver scales caught between the fine threads. He'd performed the action countless times, as if he was born knowing how. Yet here he was, struggling. For Mario, as with Alberto, tradition was fading away.

"So, you don't want to fish anymore? Is that it?"

He handed Mario a smaller shad.

"I didn't say that." Mario nearly dropped the wriggling fish as he tossed it into the wooden hold. He wiped his wet hands on his denim work trousers. "Besides, I already signed up."

"Signed up?" Vincenzo's hands froze just above an undersized fish that desperately twisted in the net. It deserved a chance to grow and find its way to the ocean. He released it from the fine threads and tossed it back into the water where it darted away. "Why didn't you tell me?"

"Because..." Mario sighed as he absently tapped at the hold. "This is why. You don't understand."

Vincenzo released a deep breath as he squeezed the netting, its mesh digging into his calloused fingers leaving red marks. "So, where are they sending you?"

"Camp Stoneman first for basic training and then to Hawaii."

Vincenzo frowned. He turned and looked at his son. Mario had his mother's eyes. And now those eyes wanted to see more. "The islands? But that's so far away."

Water lapped the side of the boat, and Vincenzo slackened his grip.

"It's time, Papà. You were my age when you entered the service, right?"

Vincenzo turned back toward the stern and looked out at the grassy shore. There was a wide world beyond the Sacramento-San Joaquin River Delta.

He reflected on his own youth, the thrill tinged with trepidation as he embarked on his journey, leaving Sicily his first time. "But that was different. It was compulsory. And there was a war."

Mario flicked at the water with his fingertips, sending ripples across the surface. Vincenzo wondered how soon his son would lose the calluses on his hands. "I'll come back and help you, of course. But..." He chuckled. "Fishing was never really my thing, you know?"

Vincenzo did know. Mario was the same boy who dropped his first fish back into the water.

"He's still alive, Papà!" he'd cried out in horror at what they'd done.

Back then, Mario couldn't make the connection between the fish in the net and the filets on the dinner plates. It took a couple of years before Vincenzo could trust him with stashing their catch in the hold. Later, the boy would complain about the long stretches of silence, which Vincenzo prized for its reflective space. And Mario would wriggle his nose at the stench, something Vincenzo considered akin to cologne. It was the scent of hard work, a reminder of his own first fishing experiences with his father, a man who was light-hearted yet disciplined, whose legacy he sought to share. Now who would pass it on?

"We'll miss you." Vincenzo stared out into the murky water.

"I said I'll be back," Mario sighed. "Besides, I'd miss Mamma's cooking too much."

Vincenzo turned to his son. He was no longer the little boy he'd dragged with him on their first fishing excursion. He was a man, someone who wanted more in life—just as he had when he set sail for America. He couldn't blame Mario, but it didn't make it any easier.

He nodded sadly and cleared his throat. "Speaking of supper... we'd better wrap this up. Help me with the rest of the net."

The two men fell back into their old rhythm, with Vincenzo passing the net back to Mario between picking out the fish until they'd lifted the entire net, which lay pooled at their feet.

Then it was time to head to the cannery to unload their precious cargo. There they'd have to work quickly to preserve the fish's freshness. But Vincenzo sensed his boy couldn't leave the fish or this place soon enough.

* * *

Annalisa and her mother were nearly finished preparing dinner when Papà and Mario arrived home.

"I made *spaghetti ai ricci di mare*," Mamma called out. "There was a special on sea urchins at the market."

"Papà!" Annalisa ran to her father for a hug. She inhaled his familiar stinky fish scent.

"How is my little girl?" He patted her head.

"Papà, I'm going to be fifteen!" She rolled her eyes and pulled away. "Did you catch a lot of fish?"

"It was a good day for the season." Her father shifted his gaze, and she wondered why he suddenly seemed sad. She looked to Mario who flashed her a small smile. Maybe it was only her imagination.

"Dinner's ready," Mamma called, and Annalisa raced to help her mother bring plates to the table.

As she was setting silverware, she saw her father exchange a look with Mario. "Are you going to tell them, or should I?"

"Tell us what, Papà?" Annalisa clutched a fork.

"Did something happen?" Mamma gasped.

"Why don't we all sit down first?" Mario pulled out his chair.

Annalisa eyed her brother as she settled into her seat. Something was definitely wrong.

Mario cleared his throat. "I'm going to Hawaii."

"Hawaii? The islands?" Annalisa suddenly felt as if the floor had dropped beneath her.

"The islands. I've joined the Navy."

"The Navy?" Mamma's eyes widened, and her voice rose. "Why would you do that?"

"The boy has always liked boats." Papà sighed. "And he says he wants to see the world."

"But you do see the world." Annalisa tilted her head. "What about all those times you went with Papà to Alaska?"

"That's what I said." Her father nodded.

Mario was silent as he looked down at his plate.

Annalisa felt a lump in her throat. "So, you're what... just leaving?"

"I start basic training in a couple of weeks." Mario spoke slowly, still looking at his plate.

"I don't understand why you have to leave." Annalisa dropped her silverware as she stood and then ran from the table.

She raced to her room and slammed the door, sliding to the floor in tears. How could Mario do this—leave her?

She heard a knock.

"Can I come in?"

She took a deep breath, wiped her eyes, and stood up to open the door to Mario.

"What's wrong? It's not like I'm going away forever, you know."

"Promise?" she said as he enveloped her in a warm hug.

"Promise."

"And you won't let anyone mess with you?" she whispered into his chest.

"No one's going to mess with me. It's the Navy. These are professionals."

"You know what I mean." She released herself from his embrace. She was thinking of all the times she, his little sister, had stood up for him against neighborhood bullies.

He stepped over to her bed and sat down.

"Maybe you can come out and visit. See for yourself how things are."

"I'd like that." She slid beside him.

"If nothing else, it'd be a tropical vacation. I hear Hawaiians grow coconuts on their palm trees. Just think about all the coconuts I'll be eating."

She shoved him playfully. "While I'm here babysitting Mamma and Papà."

"They can take care of themselves."

"Oh yeah? When was the last time Mamma went anywhere without her interpreter? You'd think after—what—twenty, twenty-one years they'd have learned at least enough English to know the difference between tooth powder and talcum."

Mario laughed. "They're not that bad. Papà knows plenty of English. You should hear him at the cannery. He doesn't let them shortchange him for what he brings in."

"All I'm saying is that it isn't easy. And now I'll be alone, and... I'll miss you."

Again, she felt her eyes water.

"It's going to be OK." Mario wiped away one of her tears. "Just pretend it's another summer in Alaska."

She nodded and rubbed her eyes.

"I have an idea." Mario traced his mole with a fingertip. "How about we spend a whole day together tomorrow—just the two of us?"

She swallowed. "But I have school."

"Consider it a field trip." He smiled. "I'll come by during lunch and pick you up. You'll only miss a few classes."

She smiled back. "Latin, history, and home ec."

"I know a great historic place where you can speak Latin and even sew if you'd like."

She tilted her head. "Where's that?"

"The old Black Diamond Mines." He gestured as if they were right behind him. "There's a beautiful graveyard there where my buddies and I like to hang out. But you have to hike to it."

"A graveyard?" She raised her eyebrows. "Why would you hang out in a graveyard?"

"It's just a place I go with some of my friends," he said quietly. "I mean, there's not really any other place you can go in town to just have some peace from your parents."

"But how will we get there?"

"One of the guys can lend me his car." Mario stood up, offering her his hand. "Are you up for it?"

She took his hand and rose to her feet. "You bet I am."

After lunch the next day, Annalisa slipped out of the school's front door and waited in the shade of a sycamore tree. The light filtered through the big fuzzy leaves, dappling the gravel ground with specks of gold.

A group of teachers passed to enter the building, and she tugged at her shoulder-length brown hair and checked her leather wristwatch. She watched happy-go-lucky students walking side by side. While she was friendly with her classmates, there was no one with whom she felt so close. She'd never felt like she truly belonged in this little town.

A girl nodded as she passed her and she cracked a shy smile. She was anxious not to be seen by too many more people before she skipped her next three classes. This would be her first time being truant. Perhaps the principal's secretary would think it was a mistake and not call her parents. Then she thought about it some more. Even if they called, her mother would probably answer, and, as she didn't speak English, the conversation would be cut short. A wave of relief settled over her. And then she heard the honk of a horn.

She turned to see her brother waving from a shiny black two-door car.

"How do you like your carriage, Cinderella? It's a Chevrolet Standard Mercury, the cheapest six-cylinder on the market."

Annalisa laughed and got in.

"It has a radio." He fiddled with the dial, landing on "Three Little Fishies" by Kay Kyser.

The two sang about three fish from a pool in a meadow who defy their mother by swimming over a dam and out to sea only to encounter a shark. Mario tapped on the steering wheel as they shouted the "Boop boop dit-tem dat-tem what-tem Chu!" chorus along with the singer.

They made their way onto Sommerville Road. There, Mario slowed the car to a crawl as they zigzagged their way up a gravel route past showy wildflowers, pines, and blooming buckeyes to a flat parking lot.

Just as they stepped out of the car, Annalisa screamed.

"Look!" She pointed to a yellow-striped black snake.

"That?" Mario laughed. "He's harmless. There are all sorts of his kind around here. Lizards, too."

She shook her head. "Great. A bunch of reptiles."

"Bluebirds and meadowlarks, too."

"That's better." Annalisa smiled.

"Come on, scaredy cat." He slugged her shoulder. "Let's go on a little hike to the cemetery."

"Speaking of scary..." She raised her eyebrows.

"What? You believe in ghosts?"

"Naw, I'm kidding." She grinned. "Show me the cemetery!"

The sun was high, and Annalisa wished she had brought a hat. She was certain she would burn. And then how would she explain herself? *Oh yeah,* she thought with a smile. *I'll blame Mario.*

"How much longer?" She panted as the path looped once more.

He pointed. "See that tall juniper tree over there?"

A tall, thin juniper tree top stuck up from a hillside.

"Yeah?"

"Well, that marks the cemetery's spot. Just keep your eyes on that tree, and we'll be there in no time."

As they got closer, Annalisa suddenly saw a twin to the juniper she was focused on, along with a few pepper trees and a couple of pines. Between them, laid out in a square fenced-off area, were worn-down gravestones. She read one: "Georg Adam. Died November 7, 1873. 1873! These are old."

"But he wasn't," Mario said quietly. "Look what it says."

"Aged three months?" She frowned. "How sad."

Little Georg wasn't the only infant represented among the buried in the yard. Many of the young children's tombstones featured lambs or rosebuds. There were many women, too. And Annalisa wondered if they'd died in childbirth.

"What a sad place." She swept her eyes across the field of stones.

"But it's peaceful, too, don't you think?" Mario asked.

She examined a few more worn and cracked tombstones.

"You're right. It's peaceful. And you wouldn't even know this cemetery is here. It's like a discovery."

"Yeah, well, now you've discovered it." Mario chuckled. "You want to take a couple of pictures?"

"You brought your camera?" she asked excitedly.

"Sure did." He pulled his Brownie box camera out of his knapsack. "Smile!"

Annalisa shook her head. "And you'll show these to Mamma and Papà and tell them I went to the cemetery on a school day? Hmph. No, sir."

"Come on." He lifted his camera. "I want to bring some photos of my little sister to Hawaii."

"OK." She sat on a curved lower branch of a pepper tree and smiled. "Now's your turn."

Mario handed her the camera and knelt on the ground where he threw up his hands in a victorious pose. She held the camera and stared down into the viewfinder before snapping the photo.

"These are going to be great." She smiled.

Annalisa and Mario plopped down together on the tree branch where they could cool off. The siblings sat in silence, listening to the chirping of birds and the breeze sweeping through the tall grasses on the surrounding hills.

"So, you're really leaving?" She fixed her lips in a pout.

Mario nodded, looking down at the lawn below them. Then he reached up and unhooked a gold chain that was around his neck.

"Here, I want you to have this." He placed the necklace in her hand.

She looked down and ran her thumb and forefinger over the twisted gold horn amulet that hung from the chain. She recognized it as something her father had given Mario when he'd turned thirteen, a traditional Italian good luck charm for their first Bristol Bay fishing excursion.

"Your *cornicello*?" She shook her head. "I couldn't!"

"It's a symbol of strength, something you've always represented in my life." His cheeks reddened as he shifted his gaze. "Plus, they say it wards off the evil eye."

"Like my Latin teacher is going to give me for skipping class today?"

He laughed and slugged her shoulder.

"I'm serious. Wear it for me, OK? It will keep you safe while I'm gone."

She took the clasp in her fingers and secured the chain around her neck.

"I'll wear it every day and everywhere I go." She tugged at it. "But you have to promise me you'll come back for it."

"I promise." He held up his pinky, and she locked her little finger in his.

He looked at his wristwatch and then stood up. "It's getting late. We'd better turn around or else Mamma will have a stroke."

They walked back in silence, Annalisa feeling the weight of her brother's departure becoming more real with each step. She walked slower, yearning to hold on to the moment. She was sad when they finally reached the car, but somehow tugging on the horn charm already made her feel better.

"By the way, thanks." She stepped into the car. "For everything."

"No need to get mushy," he said. "I'll be back before you know it."

NINE
DECEMBER 8, 1941

Pittsburg, California

The sun streamed in through the shutters, painting golden lines across the ceiling. It was the first thing Annalisa saw when she awoke.

She heard a radio announcer's voice, and suddenly she remembered what happened at Honolulu's Pearl Harbor. Mario was there. Was Mario OK?

She ran down the hall to the living room, where her parents paced.

"Why did you let him go? Why would you let our boy go?" Mamma sobbed.

"Just listen, will you?" Papà turned up the volume.

"Early reports indicate that multiple battleships, including the USS *Oklahoma*, the USS *West Virginia*, and the USS *Arizona*, have been severely damaged or sunk. More than two thousand and four hundred Americans are presumed dead with many more injured."

"USS *Arizona*!" Annalisa brought her hand to her mouth. "That's Mario's ship!"

"Our boy!" Mamma shouted. "What has happened to our boy?"

"I'm not going to school today," Annalisa said. "I can't until we know something."

"Vincenzo!" Mamma huffed. "Call the school and tell them she won't be coming."

Papà rose quickly and left the room to make the call.

The family stayed glued to the radio set for the next hour until they heard the voice of the President of the United States say, "Yesterday, December 7, 1941—a date which will live in infamy—the United States of America was suddenly and deliberately attacked by naval and air forces of the Empire of Japan..."

"What is he saying?" her mother hissed. "Is he going to declare war?"

"Shh, Mamma, I'm listening." Annalisa closed her eyes to focus on the speech. "He says the attack was unprovoked and occurred while America was in peace talks with Japan... He says it's obvious that Japan planned it... and that very many American lives have been lost..."

"Did he say anything about your brother's ship?" Mamma's eyes widened.

"No, but now he says the American people are ready to defend themselves and that he is requesting Congress to declare war. So, yes, he's asking for war."

"Meanwhile, we know nothing about Mario." Papà shook his head. "Turn that off. I can't take it anymore."

Annalisa turned the knob to shut off the radio.

"We would have heard something by now." Mamma's eyes were clouded with tears. "If Mario was alive, he would have sent us a telegram. He wouldn't have wanted us to worry."

Annalisa tugged at the horn amulet. She knew her mother was right. And she was certain something had happened to her brother.

* * *

After a quiet and simple supper of fava bean soup with crusty bread, Vincenzo slid out of his chair and carried his dishes to the kitchen. He heard Maria shuffle in as he ran water over his bowl.

He looked in the window above the sink and saw their reflections. She had her head down as if studying her dirty dish. His eyes shifted to the juniper tree in their backyard.

He remembered when he'd help Mr. DeRosa plant it, how he'd stood Mario beside it to show him it was the same height and how his son marveled at its dusty blue berries. Now, it towered above the tiny fenced-off yard, having nearly outgrown its space. So many years passed. So many memories between.

He shut off the water. "First thing in the morning, I will telephone the Navy. The number is with all that paperwork he gave us to hold on to."

Maria released a sob, and he turned to her. He took her dishes from her hands, placed them in the sink behind him, and drew her in for a hug. As he clutched her head of curls to his chest, he realized it had been a long time since they'd embraced. She sobbed harder, her tears soaking through his shirt.

He said nothing for a while, just stood there and held her in the kitchen. His own eyes grew misty as he remembered holding her when she announced she was first pregnant. He thought about the sacrifice they made, how he'd decided to ensure they could live a better life. And now, here they were on the other side, and he was powerless.

He heard a soft creak in the floor and shifted his eyes to the doorway where Annalisa had entered. As soon as he made eye contact, he saw her tears.

"What are we going to do?" Her voice was soft as if she spoke from far away.

Vincenzo motioned for her, and she placed her plates in the

sink before slipping under his extended arm. He pulled her in next to Maria and felt her collapse in tears.

What could he say? What solace could he offer? So much was unknown. This was bigger than them—an attack on the nation, now made deeply personal. He thought of his family in Sicily. Would they have heard, too?

"Don't you worry," he said finally and squeezed them. "We'll know more in the morning. For now, we just need to be strong for Mario."

"And pray." Maria turned her pointed chin upward.

"And pray." He nodded.

Vincenzo sat up in bed, dripping in sweat from a nightmare. He'd dreamed about Mario, trapped in his ship and pounding on a door to get out.

He checked his wristwatch. It was 11 o'clock. And someone was indeed pounding on the door. Was he still dreaming?

More banging.

"Vincenzo, what is happening?" Maria's frightened voice sounded small as she pulled the heavy oxblood red covers over her head of chestnut curls.

"Open up!" someone shouted from the other side of the door.

"Papà?" Annalisa called out from her room.

Vincenzo cleared his throat. "One moment!" He pulled on a robe and slid into his slippers.

More banging.

Vincenzo approached the door cautiously. He unlocked it and opened it a crack to see three men standing on the porch. Two were wearing suits, and one wore a navy-blue police uniform.

"Vincenzo Aiello?" the fat and balding cop, who stood between the suited men, asked.

"Yes." Vincenzo rubbed his eyes. He scanned the men. The cop stood between a tall, slim man with red hair and a matching thin red mustache, and another man with sandy brown hair and an athletic build. He could see their breath in the chilly air.

"You're gonna need to come with us," the cop said.

"What do you mean, officer?" He tried to stay calm.

The red-mustachioed man stepped forward and revealed an ID. He was an FBI agent. And Vincenzo gathered that so too was the other man in the suit.

"By order of the President of the United States, you are under arrest," the red-mustachioed agent said.

"Under a-arrest? For wha-what?" Vincenzo stammered.

"We're not at liberty to say." The sandy brown-haired agent shifted his eyes. "We need you to come with us now."

"I don't understand." Vincenzo stepped back.

"We don't want any trouble." The cop fingered his pistol.

"Now. Come with us now." The red-mustachioed agent enunciated each word, and the cop held up a set of handcuffs. The two agents grabbed Vincenzo by each arm, and then he felt the scratch of cold metal on his wrists. *Click.*

"No!" Maria screamed. She was suddenly behind him, standing there barefoot in her lacy white nightgown and sobbing.

"Ma'am. This is a federal matter. We need everyone's cooperation, OK?" one agent said.

And before he could comprehend what was happening, the men stuffed Vincenzo into the back of a dark car. He looked back toward the house. Maria was on her knees on the cold front porch, screaming, "No! No! No!"

"Where are you taking me?" he asked the cop, who slid in beside him. The officer ignored him.

Meanwhile, the agents whispered in the front seats. Vincenzo caught a glimpse of the mustachioed agent's steely blue eyes in the rearview mirror. He was younger than he'd initially appeared, likely about the same age as Mario. Perhaps they'd gone to school together.

Mario. What had happened to Mario?

Surely this was all a misunderstanding, a case of mistaken identity, perhaps. Vincenzo wondered whether he had done something wrong.

* * *

Annalisa tiptoed down the hallway to the living room. It was suddenly quiet. Eerily so. Where was Mamma?

The door opened, and her mother entered. She was shivering, and her face was covered in tears.

"Mamma! What happened?"

Her mother dropped to her knees, sobbing and pulling at her hair.

"Mamma, why don't you sit down?" Annalisa tugged her mother's right arm.

Her mother slowly stood up and shuffled to Papà's favorite chair, where she collapsed. Annalisa stroked her head.

"They took him," Mamma said.

"Why?" Annalisa frowned. "Where? Who?"

"I don't know. They said something about the president. Imagine. They can just come in here and take your father like that."

Annalisa knelt next to her mother and hugged her.

"It's going to be OK, Mamma." She was still absorbing the shock of it all. "I'm sure it was just a misunderstanding. Papà's probably on his way back here now."

"This is what they do in Italy... to the Communists. Not here. Not to my husband. The man works hard for a living. He's a good man. There's no reason..."

It made no sense. Annalisa felt her mother's fearful tremors and realized that she too was shaking.

"Mamma, what can we do?" A tear traveled down her cheek.

"Wait. They have to tell us something."

Annalisa trusted she was right. As grumpy and difficult as she was, Mamma had always been honest. She'd always drilled into her daughter that lying was a sin. But she saw her tug at her Madonna delle Grazie pendant, and it made her wonder if her mother was truly certain.

DECEMBER 8, 1941

801 Silver Avenue, San Francisco, California

Vincenzo and the men were on the road for about four hours, winding their way through small towns to Fremont and near San Jose all the way to the San Francisco Bay before they pulled through a gated entrance and into a parking lot. The stark two-story brick Silver Avenue Detention center loomed before them, and he felt a sudden chill.

"Here we are." The red-mustachioed cop exited the front seat and opened the door for Vincenzo.

The men led him up a set of stairs between two columns past which stood a wooden door. The brown-haired cop knocked, and a darker-haired man in a matching police uniform answered.

The brown-haired cop chuckled. "We brought you an Italian delicacy."

"Yeah, one of those spaghetti benders," said the red-mustachioed cop.

The dark-haired cop grasped Vincenzo's shoulder. "Come with me."

Vincenzo shuffled forward, nearly tripping on his right slipper.

The cop brought him to a dim windowless room, where he patted him down and proceeded to ask questions.

"Name?" the cop barked.

"Vincenzo Aiello." His voice shook. "I think there has been a mistake..."

"Just answer the questions. Date of birth?"

"1896. The thirteenth of September."

"Where did they pick you up?"

"P-P-Pittsburg."

"Are you an American citizen?"

"I've lived here twenty-one years..."

The cop wrote something on the notepad he was holding. "So, no? You are not a citizen?"

"No."

"Thank you for your cooperation." The cop closed his notebook. "Follow me."

Muffled voices echoed down the hallway, as Vincenzo followed the cop past yellowed walls to a large, brightly lit room with high ceilings and wooden floors, resembling a school gymnasium. But instead of sports equipment, he saw rows of occupied triple bunk beds. His eyes settled first on the men at the center of the room, who appeared to be of some Asian descent. He turned his head and saw rows of Caucasian men on the periphery.

"Find yourself a bunk and make yourself comfortable." The cop turned to leave.

"Wait! How long am I here?"

"About five days before they send you to Montana," the cop said over his shoulder.

"Montana? Wait!" shouted Vincenzo. It was not just another state; it had to be about a thousand miles away. This wasn't going to be a short stay in a holding cell like when a fellow fisherman was picked up after a fistfight. That man spent the night before his wife brought him home. It was all the talk during unloading at the cannery.

In Vincenzo's case, who knew if and when he could even see his family? And what about Mario? Would either of them be able to come home?

December 9, 1941

Pittsburg, CA

Light poured through the window, illuminating the bed where Annalisa lay in a tearful embrace with her mother. Perhaps there would be some information today, Annalisa thought as she wriggled out of her mother's arms and sat up.

She stepped into the kitchen to start the coffee and fix breakfast. With grounds and water, she filled the Moka pot and set it on the stove. She pulled three cups out of the cupboard and then began to cry.

Where had they taken Papà? And what about Mario? She fingered the horn amulet around her neck. Why hadn't they heard anything?

Soon, it would be Christmas. But it couldn't be. She sank into a seat at the wooden kitchen table, and she looked at their respective chairs. It didn't feel real.

Suddenly, Annalisa heard a sizzling sound, and she turned to the stove, where water had dripped from the coffee pot and onto the burner. She turned off the stove and then sat back down.

She would not go to school again today. It didn't matter that she had a geometry test yesterday and a term paper due Thursday. She wasn't going anywhere until there were answers.

Mamma appeared in the doorway.

"I overslept." Her voice was flat as she sank into the adjacent chair.

Annalisa rose and poured her mother a cup of coffee. The two sipped in silence.

Then someone knocked at the door.

Mamma looked at her, and Annalisa nodded and rose.

She opened the door to a man in a blue uniform holding a yellow envelope.

"You received a telegram," the man said.

"Thank you." Annalisa felt a mixed sense of dread and anticipation as she took the envelope before bidding the man farewell.

"What is it?" Mamma asked as Annalisa reappeared in the kitchen.

"Western Union." Annalisa tore open the envelope. "It says it's from Washington, D.C.," she added as she began to read the telegram, translating for her mother.

"Dear Mrs. Maria Aiello of Pittsburg, California,

The Secretary of War decreed me to express his deep regret that your son, Private Mario R. Aiello, was..."

"What?" Mamma shouted. "Keep reading."

"...k-k-killed in action in defense of his country in Hawaii on December 7, 1941."

"No!" her mother screamed, sinking to the floor in tears.

Annalisa's hands shook as she continued reading, *"No remains can be transferred to the United States..."*

She paused and wiped away a tear.

"...until after terminations of hostilities when the Quartermaster General will, if possible, and upon request of the next of kin, bring the remains to the United States for final interment."

Mamma pounded the floor and kicked her feet, and Annalisa sank to the floor beside her. Together they collapsed in a fit of tears.

"So that's it?" Her mother's voice was ragged. "My boy has been... killed, and they can't give us his remains?"

Annalisa wiped her eyes and swallowed. "That's what it says."

"And only if it's possible after the war?" Mamma leaned her head against the cabinet.

"I think that's right." Annalisa scanned the letter once more.

The two sat for a moment in silence. Annalisa thought about her brother's promise. He'd even pinky-sworn on it. And he'd given her his good luck charm! She shouldn't have let him. She grasped the amulet in her fist as she closed her tearing eyes.

"I hope it was quick." Mamma wiped away her tears. "I pray to God that my boy didn't suffer."

Annalisa nodded. "I'm sure it was, Mamma."

The phone rang, and Annalisa looked at her mother before rising to answer the call.

"Yes?" she breathed into the receiver.

"Annalisa..." She heard a distant voice over the line.

"Papà, is that you?"

"Is it your father?" Mamma shouted. "Where is he?"

"Tell your mother I'm in San Francisco at a place called Silver Avenue Detention Center," Papà said. "But they say it's only five days. Then, for some reason, they're sending me to Montana."

"Montana?" Annalisa was confused. "Did they even say why they arrested you?"

"I've heard nothing yet."

"I don't understand. Who were these people? Why did they do this?"

"It was the FBI... and I know. None of this makes much sense. Did you hear from Mario?"

"About that... Papà... he's gone." Her voice shook. "We... got... a letter."

Her words were met with silence.

"Are you still there, Papà?"

"I'm here." He inhaled sharply. "Are they sending him back?"

"No, Papà." Annalisa sobbed. "They said they can't until hostilities are over."

She heard her father clear his throat. "What does that mean now that there's a war?"

"I'm not sure, Papà." She swallowed. "I'm so sorry."

"Why are you sorry?" he asked in a soft voice.

"It's just that... you are dealing with enough over there."

The line was quiet for a moment.

"Papà? Are you there?"

Again, her father cleared his throat, and she could tell he, too, had been crying by the shakiness of his voice. "I'm glad you told me. Listen, we'll talk more when we can. Maybe this arrest was just a huge misunderstanding, and they'll send me back home at the end of this week instead of Montana."

"I hope so, Papà." Annalisa cradled the receiver. "I love you."

"You didn't let me talk to my husband?" Mamma slammed her fist on the table, after Annalisa hung up.

"He said he didn't have much time to talk, Mamma." Annalisa leaned her head back into the wall. "He's at a place called the Silver Avenue Detention Center in San Francisco. They said he'll be there for at least five days, and then he'll be sent to Montana."

"Montana?!" Mamma's voice rose. "Why would they send him to another state so far away? What is going on here? First, our son is killed, and then they take his father. It makes no sense."

"I know, Mamma," Annalisa said quietly. "I don't understand any of it either. It's like some big nightmare that we're both having. And I just want to wake up."

"Annalisa, you have to do something." Her mother leaned

forward. "Call this Silver Avenue Detention Center and tell them this is a big mistake."

"Mamma, they're not going to listen to me."

"Do it now," her mother shouted.

"All right, Mamma, all right."

Annalisa called the operator and asked to be connected to the Silver Avenue Detention Center in San Francisco.

"Yes?" a man answered.

Annalisa cleared her throat. "Hi, uh, my father is at your detention center. I'm afraid there's been some kind of mistake."

"Is your father an enemy alien?"

She frowned. "Excuse me?"

"Enemy alien," the man repeated in a flat voice. "Is he German, Italian, or Japanese?"

"Italian."

"They're sending the Italians to Montana in five days."

"But why?" Annalisa squeezed the receiver.

The man sighed. "I am not at liberty to say, Miss."

"But why?" she asked again, this time louder.

"By order of the President of the United States, Miss." The man raised his voice in response. "Now, if you excuse me, it's been a very busy day. I wish you the very best. Goodbye."

"Wait..."

The phone disconnected, and Annalisa stared at the receiver a few moments before she hung up.

"So, what did they say?" Mamma asked, her eyes red from tears.

"Nothing," Annalisa sighed and sank into her seat before her cold coffee.

TEN

DECEMBER 11, 1941

Palermo, Sicily

Once again, there was talk of another Mussolini speech. All work was to stop at noon on Thursday, December 11, so that citizens could gather around strategically placed loudspeakers for the big event.

"I bet he's going to weigh in on this war between Japan and America." Fausto held up his broom.

Ascanio tapped his head. "*Stupido*, he's going to declare war on America. Why else would he stop work for a speech?"

Fausto nodded. "That's what I said: He's going to weigh in with war."

"That's not at all what you said." Ascanio rolled his eyes. "Anyway, if nothing else, there will be more pronouncements like 'Italy will make the Mediterranean an Italian lake.'" He imitated Mussolini's gravelly voice and puffed out his chin as he spoke.

Fausto responded with a Fascist salute, and the two began to laugh uncontrollably.

Alberto ignored them as he focused on the task at hand,

touching up a stainless-steel plate with a bright shade of red. He enjoyed the break from the monotony of fetching and cleaning up after the carpenters, riveters, welders, and pipefitters. The red would stand out, a regal entrance for Italy's Navy as they battled for their place in the sea.

He worked to the rhythm of hammers clanging against metal, accompanied by the fizz and hiss as sparks flew from welders nearby. The air was thick with the stench of oil and the briny scent of the sea, a smell he'd become accustomed to while working the docks. But there was something more: a palpable tension hanging on every breath and echoing through each spoken word in the lead-up to the day's eagerly anticipated broadcast.

The whistle blew, and the men gathered around a loudspeaker management had set up specially for the occasion. Everyone stopped talking and seemed to lean in, waiting for il Duce's distinct voice. Someone had turned on the speaker and they could hear a crowd in Rome cheering for Mussolini, but soon the clamor died down, and Mussolini began to speak.

"Fighters of land, sea, and air! Blackshirts of the revolution and of the legions; men and women of Italy, of the Empire, and of the Kingdom of Albania: listen!

"This is another day of solemn decisions in the history of Italy, and of memorable events destined to imprint a new course in the history of the continents."

He heard the people cheering in Rome, and the men on his side clapped and shook their fists.

"The powers of the Pact of Steel, Fascist Italy, and national-socialist Germany, ever more closely united, stand beside heroic Japan against the United States of America. The Tripartite has grown into a military alliance that amasses around its flags two hundred and fifty million men resolute for victory in everything.

"Neither the Axis nor Japan desired the expansion of this

conflict. One man, a single man, an authentic democratic despot, through an infinite series of provocations, deceiving with a supreme fraud the very populations of his own county, has desired this war and has prepared it day by day with diabolical pertinacity."

"He means Roosevelt," Ascanio whispered. Alberto put his finger to his lips.

"The formidable blows which have already been inflicted over the immense expanse of the Pacific against the American forces demonstrate the resoluteness of the soldiers of the Rising Sun. I say, and you all feel, that it is a privilege to fight with them.

"Today, the Tripartite Alliance, in the fullness of its moral and material means, is a powerful instrument for war and the secure guarantee of victory; tomorrow it will be the creator and organizer of a just peace between the peoples.

"Italian men and women, standing once again, be worthy of this great hour. We will be victorious!" Mussolini concluded, and the speakers were shut off.

"*Viva Italia!*" shouted the men. "Duce! Duce! Duce!"

Several men began singing "Giovinezza," and Alberto reflected on how much had changed since the days he'd taken part in the March on Rome parades as a boy. He thought about the chorus that spoke to the optimism and resilience of youth, even in the face of challenges.

"*Youth, Youth, Spring of beauty, In the hardship of life, your song rings and goes!*"

Such hardships were now omnipresent. The city had endured at least a dozen bombings scattered between the months of January, July, and September. While most involved small numbers of medium bombers and caused minor damage and few deaths, September was particularly deadly, resulting in seventy casualties. He remembered the dark photograph from one of the month's newspapers, the blurry shape of a child, lifeless as a stuffed doll, lying in a pile of building rubble. But the past couple of months had been quiet. Was there cause for optimism?

The men linked arms and swayed as they continued to sing.

"*For tomorrow's war. For labor's glory, for peace and for the laurel, for the shame of those who have disowned our Fatherland.*"

He remembered how Mussolini had once said, "We must become a warlike nation." Prior to Italy's involvement in the current conflict, he'd seen the evidence in the colonization of Libya, the occupation of Somalia, the conquest of the Horn of Africa, the war with Abyssinia, the nation's involvement with the Spanish Civil War, and the war with Albania. As a boy, he'd marched proudly with his wooden gun, training "for tomorrow's war." Then he served his peacetime stint with the Regia Marina before serving his country "for labor's glory" among the builders of their battleships.

But this war was different, closer to home and more taxing on Italy's people. Alberto thought about the sawing sounds of the planes, the whining sirens, the crumbled buildings, and the lives shattered. He wondered what might change now that Italy was at war with America, too. Would things—could things—get worse? What about the rations? Sugar, soap, oils, flour, and pasta were all in short supply. Just how much more could they take?

The men continued to sing, their voices growing hoarse with the effort.

"*The poets and the artisans, the lords and the countrymen, with an Italian's pride swear loyalty to Mussolini. There is no poor neighborhood, which does not send its ranks, which does not unfurl the flags of redeeming Fascism.*"

Alberto thought about the slogan "Mussolini is always right," emblazoned on walls across the city. Mussolini had explained the rations were a consequence of the bad behavior of those farmers who did not bring grain to the national warehouses. If he was right, which Alberto was beginning to doubt, that was also the cost of war.

Still, it hurt to see his mother reduced to serving up bone broth soup with a side of bread that he was sure was now being made with sawdust or some other disgusting filler. Somehow, black market merchants had access to all these goods and more, and they were selling them to desperate people like his family at exorbitant prices.

But there was little time to dwell on what the future would bring, for the whistle blew, signaling it was back to work.

"Alberto, what do we have here?" Francesco startled him.

He turned around to see the superintendent smiling.

"Very good work on that panel. No streaks. How about we try you out for a few days with the painters?"

Alberto nodded his head. "I'd like that."

"Good." Francesco placed his hands in his pockets. "In the meantime, I need you to help sweep under the scaffolding over there. How about it?"

"Of course." Alberto ran to get a broom.

ELEVEN
DECEMBER 14–15, 1941

Fort Missoula, Missoula, Montana

Vincenzo's teeth chattered as he hugged his knees above his cold, slippered feet. He'd disembarked from what had been a pleasantly warm, if frustrating, train ride and now rode in the back of a tarp-covered military truck alongside eight Japanese men and one other Italian. He tried to keep his distance from the strangers, but each time the truck ran over a bump, they'd fall atop one another like dominos.

Finally, after at least an hour, they arrived at Fort Missoula, Montana, and the truck rolled to a stop.

"Here we are. Home, sweet home, gentlemen," a man called out in a deep, jovial voice, as he untied the closed flap and let a gust of frigid air into the back of the truck.

Vincenzo turned toward the opening, slid forward after the men in front of him, climbed out, and sank his slippered feet into ankle-deep snow. He blinked as his eyes adjusted to his spotlight-lit surroundings. They were standing in between a row of one-story, white-paneled buildings. Beyond those stretched a fence topped with barbed wire, and he could see shadowy guard towers looming at least forty feet above the ground and casting long shadows at four corners.

It was midnight California time, and he wasn't sure how many hours ahead Missoula was. But after a long night and groggy day on the train and his bumpy ride, he needed some rest. He looked down at his pajama pants and slippers, realizing he was in desperate need of some real clothes.

"Follow me," said the man, who wore the khaki wool suit of a soldier.

Vincenzo and the other nine men trailed the soldier through the door of one of the white buildings, where they entered a large dormitory of sorts. It smelled musty, like sweaty socks, but it was warm. Several men craned their necks from their spots on metal bunk beds that stood in rows and filled the place from wall to wall.

"There should be enough room for all of you." The soldier brushed a hand through his light, close-cropped hair. "Wake-up is at six a.m. You'll be served breakfast and then appear for roll call at eight. Don't be late. Lunch is at noon, dinner is at six, and the second roll call is at eight p.m. Got it?"

"Yes," mumbled Vincenzo and several other exhausted men in unison.

He spotted an empty top bunk in the middle of the room and quickly claimed it by pulling off his robe and draping it over the bed. There, illuminated in the faint glow from the spotlight out the window, he saw a folded pair of dark pants, a matching button-down shirt, and rolled-up woolen socks.

He pushed these under his pillow and climbed up into the bed, taking care not to wake the man snoring on the bunk below.

He lay on his back and watched the spotlight sweep across the ceiling through the windows. And the next thing he knew, a bell was ringing. He looked at his watch, which read 5 o'clock, and realized Missoula was an hour ahead of California since the soldier from the prior evening had mentioned a 6 a.m. wake-up. He rewound his watch and climbed down the ladder, where he came face to face with his bunkmate.

"Aldo." The man sat up and extended his hand. "Aldo Rosso."

He was younger, with wavy brown hair and matching stubble on his olive-toned face.

"Vincenzo. Vincenzo Aiello."

"What brings you to Bella Vista, Vincenzo Aiello?"

He spoke in Italian in what sounded like a northern dialect.

Vincenzo tilted his head. "Is that what they call this place?"

"That's what we call it. You came in the night. Just wait until you see the lovely view." He motioned toward the windows.

"I honestly don't know why I'm here. They came and took me."

Aldo nodded. "So, you're an American?"

"Well, I live near San Francisco, but I came here about twenty-one years ago from outside of Palermo."

"Ah, Sicily." Aldo swung his legs to the bed's side. "I come from Rome. I was a cook on the Conte Biancamano, a luxury ship like you've never seen. They stopped and arrested us in the Panama Canal back in April."

"April?" Vincenzo asked. "But that was before Pearl Harbor. On what grounds?"

Aldo leaned forward. "They accused us of espionage, and it didn't help that our ship was inoperable. They claimed it was on the grounds of sabotage, too."

"How many of you are here?"

Aldo looked up as if counting. "Between the Conte Bianca-mano, a merchant marine ship, and employees of the World's Fair... I'd say about a thousand."

"A thousand? That's a village worth!"

A whistle blew, and the men stopped talking and turned.

"Breakfast time," a pale young soldier with mousy brown hair called out.

"It's like being back in the military," Vincenzo said to Aldo.

"You served?"

Vincenzo nodded. "Sure did—as part of the Alpini."

"I was too young. The war was ending by the time I reached eighteen."

"I fought all the Isonzo battles," Vincenzo reflected with pride. "Caporetto, too. And then a few years later, we set sail for America."

The two men stepped into a line that snaked out the door and ended in a large, wood-paneled mess hall.

"So, what's for breakfast, anyway?" Vincenzo was famished.

"Bacon, eggs, and buttered toast."

"Seriously?"

Aldo nodded excitedly. "Seriously. And they let me cook some nights. You're from Sicily... you'll love my *spiedini*."

The thought of the rolled-up breaded tenderloin skewers made his stomach growl. He liked the way Maria filled them with onions and bay leaf, the perfect aromatics to flavor the tenderized cuts of meat.

"Well... we'll see how long I end up staying. I think there was a huge misunderstanding."

He heard a snicker and caught the eye of another man, who seemed to know otherwise.

TWELVE
DECEMBER 28, 1941

Pittsburg, California

Annalisa awoke to the pitter-patter of rain. She rose from her bed and slid into her fuzzy slippers and terry-cloth robe. She could hear and smell breakfast being prepared down the hall.

However, food was far from her mind. She'd had a dream about Mario. He was calling her name, and when she finally saw him, he was treading water as his boat sank. He'd survived, and no one knew he was still alive.

But now, in the pale light of morning, she remembered. She ran her finger and thumb over the twist of the horn charm around her neck. The pain was there all over again.

She slipped into the kitchen, trying to avoid her mother's gaze, for she knew she would start crying.

"Good morning." Her mother spoke quietly as she set down a plate of eggs.

Annalisa nodded and dug into her food.

"We say prayers, don't we?" Her mother's dark eyes seemed to bore holes in Annalisa's skull.

"To who? What? God?" Annalisa pounded her fists on the table. "What kind of God would take Mario away? And now Papà, too."

Mamma glared at her. "I don't understand you. Now you don't believe in God? What's the matter with you?"

Annalisa stared back at her mother. Had things been different, Mario might have stayed. Maybe he'd have gone to school. But her mother had driven him away. She was just an old, superstitious, and unhappy woman. And that was her fault, not her father's. He'd worked too hard to deserve what had happened to him.

"Fine." Annalisa made the sign of the cross before digging back into the eggs.

Her mother sighed and sat down, burying her face in her hands.

They heard a knock at the door.

"Coming," Annalisa called.

"You can't go to the door like that!" Mamma hissed. "You don't want people to see you in your pajamas!"

Annalisa ignored her and stomped to the door where she found not one but three policemen.

"Good morning, Miss." A tall and skinny cop looked her up and down.

Annalisa's face grew warm as she tugged at her robe. "Can I help you?"

"We're here for a routine check..." The man leaned forward into the doorway, and she backed up. "We just need a few minutes of your time... We're here to check for any contraband."

"What's contraband?" Annalisa glanced at her mother who stood awkwardly behind her.

Another cop with a receding hairline put his hand on the doorframe. "We're specifically looking for weapons, cameras, and shortwave radios. Do you have anything like that?"

"Annalisa, what do these men want?" Mamma asked in an exasperated tone.

Annalisa translated.

"Why would they want that?" Mamma's eyes darted to the men.

"We don't have anything here." Annalisa ignored her mother.

"So, then you wouldn't mind if we had a quick look then, would you?" a third officer with curly dark hair said.

Annalisa thought about her brother's camera sitting on her nightstand. He'd left it with her when they sent him off, but not before posing with them for a final family photo. She didn't want to part with it, but she knew the police officers would find it right away.

"Wait... I have a camera." And the police officers followed her to her room, where she pointed to it.

The curly-haired cop picked up the box camera and looked at it from each angle before handing it to the tall officer.

Annalisa felt panic rise within. "It was my brother's camera, and he's..."

"I'm sorry, Miss, but we do have to take it." The tall officer tossed the camera into a paper bag he was carrying.

"Annalisa, what's happening?" Mamma cried from behind them.

Annalisa swallowed to hold back tears. "My mother and I want to know why you need our camera."

"Government orders, Miss," the tall cop said.

Annalisa tried to translate, but she was unclear and scared.

Meanwhile, the other two cops had begun searching the apartment.

"Hey, Jarvis!" a shorter, balding cop called from the kitchen. "Look what I found!"

He was holding up a flashlight.

"Contraband. Hand it over here." The tall cop named Jarvis held out his hands.

"Check it out." The balding cop held up an Italian newspaper.

"Fascist propaganda!" Jarvis snatched the paper and began tearing it up into shreds on the floor. "All right. I think we're finished here, aren't we, boys?"

The other two men nodded.

"Thanks for your time, ladies." Jarvis motioned for the others to join him in leaving.

Annalisa stood frozen in front of the door for a few moments after they left.

"What was that all about?" Mamma sounded just as frightened as angry. "First, they took your father, now they took a flashlight and your brother's camera. Why?"

"They said something about the government," Annalisa mumbled, still staring at the door.

"I thought we left that kind of government behind in Italy!" Mamma sobbed as she began sweeping up the shredded newspaper.

All Annalisa could think about was Mario's camera, another piece of him, taken away.

DECEMBER 31, 1941

Pittsburg, California

Annalisa checked her watch. It was half past eleven. Soon, the neighbors would bang their pots and pans to celebrate the birth of 1942. But Annalisa had her mind on more pressing matters. She'd heard on the news earlier that there was a new travel restriction for Italians, Germans, and Japanese people the announcer called "enemy aliens." Being one of those restricted, her mother could not travel more than five miles away from her home.

"I don't understand it." Mamma wrung her hands as she paced. "Your father will be in Montana for who knows how long. They searched our home, and now we're practically homebound."

"At least I can still travel." Annalisa glanced again at her watch. She wasn't sure what she was waiting for; so much uncertainty lay ahead.

"I should have listened to your father and learned English." Mamma sighed. "Then we would have been able to apply for citizenship and avoid this enemy alien business."

Annalisa nodded. "Yes, you should have."

Mamma stopped pacing and looked at her daughter.

"You know your father wrote again."

"I saw. The censors crossed out most of his letter. He must not be too happy."

Mamma held up two fingers. "They only let the man write twice a week and about a paragraph per letter at that."

Annalisa wondered what lay between the lines of her father's letters. Were they feeding him... torturing him? She shook her head. There had to be something they could do.

"Maybe I can visit him?"

"Are you serious?" Mamma tilted her head with a frown. "I can't travel over five miles, and I'm not having my sixteen-year-old daughter travel alone."

"But, Mamma, he's all alone out there."

Her mother sighed. "Unfortunately, for now, letters will have to do. Maybe my New Year's wish will come true, and he'll come home soon."

"That was my wish, too," Annalisa said quietly.

Just then, they heard the clatter of pots and pans. 1942 had arrived.

FEBRUARY 1942

Pittsburg, California

It was a dreary, gray day when Annalisa and her mother marched downtown with a letter and package for Papà.

As usual, they received their fair share of dirty looks from people who seemed to know Mamma was an enemy alien.

"Wop!" hissed an older woman, and Annalisa blushed. She tugged at the horn amulet. *Please let them leave us alone.*

As she waited in line, Annalisa spotted a sign. It was written partially in Italian.

"Mamma. It says enemy aliens are supposed to register by the end of this week."

Her mother frowned. "But they know I'm an alien. They searched our home, didn't they? They took my husband, didn't they?"

When they reached the front of the line, Annalisa asked about the registration. The cashier nodded and pointed to a booth that had been set up just to the right of the register. There sat a fair-haired lady, tapping her fingernails.

"Who is the alien?" she asked.

"My mother." Annalisa cringed at the word. "She doesn't speak English."

"All right." The woman handed her a sheet of paper. "I'm going to need you or your mother to fill out this identification form. It's only a few questions. And then I need to get her fingerprint."

"We can do that." Annalisa translated to her mother.

"My fingerprint?" Mamma asked. "What is this? Am I being arrested?"

"Is there a problem?" The woman raised an eyebrow.

"No problem." Annalisa held up the paper. "Say, it says

here that my mother needs two photographs? We don't have those."

"She has thirty days to produce two photographs," the woman said. "Just bring them here when you get them."

Annalisa helped her mother finish filling out the form, and then Mamma stuck her right index finger into an ink pad and onto the paper.

"Just get us those two photographs," the woman reminded them. "Then you'll have your little alien booklet ready in about a week."

Annalisa stared at the typewritten letter her mother had handed her.

"It says we have to leave." She frowned.

"What do you mean?" Mamma wrinkled her brow.

"They say it's because of the steel mill and military base." Annalisa lowered the paper and shook her head. "I'm not sure how you're a threat to either of those."

"This is nonsense!" Mamma's voice rose. "When do they expect us to leave?"

Annalisa swallowed. "They've only given us three days."

"Three days?" her mother shouted. "But where would we go? Everything is here—your school, our friends..."

"Calm down, Mamma. The letter lists a few places where we can go. I could check the newspaper for rental listings."

"I don't understand," her mother sighed as Annalisa fetched the morning's paper.

She flipped to the real estate section and ran her finger down the page. "Mamma, don't worry. I'll take care of it."

Annalisa got to work, pen in hand, circling every listing that fell within the cities the government letter specified.

When she was done, she presented the paper to her mother.

"There are several apartments available in Concord." Annalisa pointed to the newsprint. "It's only ten miles away, and I found some job listings there."

"What kinds of jobs?" Mamma asked.

"There are plenty of listings for house cleaning. You could easily get one of those jobs. You don't need to know English to scrub a floor or wash some dishes. And look, I even found some job options for me."

"You?" Her mother pointed at her with a laugh. "Work? I can barely get you to set the table."

Annalisa frowned and shook her head. "That's not true, Mamma. Besides, I'm sixteen years old. Old enough to start pulling my weight around here."

"So, tell me about Concord." Her mother's tone softened. "Isn't that the name of a grape?"

"Yes, the really sweet purple ones."

Mamma gazed out the window. "Maybe our life there will be sweeter."

Annalisa nodded. She certainly hoped so.

FEBRUARY 24, 1942

Concord, California

The Greyhound bus came to a stop, and Annalisa and Mamma set foot for the first time in Concord. They stood on a street corner in front of a row of houses with manicured lawns as several cars whizzed past, and Annalisa fished a piece of paper out of her shirt pocket.

"Unbelievable." Her mother huffed. "You don't know where we're going?"

Annalisa ignored her mother's tone. She was tired—from all the preparation and all of the criticism from her mother.

"We're not far." She looked both ways as they crossed. "It's at the corner of Pacheco and Grant streets."

They walked for about fifteen minutes, stopping now and then to adjust their suitcases in the shade of sycamore and eucalyptus trees before they spotted a large square sheltered by an enormous pergola around which grew thick, woody vines.

"Wisteria," her mother said. "We had it in Sicily. It blossoms purple or white in the spring."

"It's a good omen, Mamma." Annalisa set down a suitcase and reached up to touch one of the spiral vines. Then she adjusted her necklace, considering another omen.

After they both set down their luggage, they each sat down on a suitcase beneath the pergola. Then Annalisa rose, leading her mother where her little map indicated.

The apartment was only a block away from the pretty square, which the map labeled as Pacheco. The building was large and white with stucco walls, arched doorways and windows, a rounded turret, and a red-tiled roof. Several of the units had balconies with wrought-iron railings.

They walked up Spanish-tiled brown steps to the black wrought-iron front door framed with a subtle seashell pattern and rang the bell. After a few moments, they could see an older woman in a black-and-gold dress descend a flight of stairs.

"You must be the Aiellos." She wrapped her bright red nails around the side of the door to let them in. "You can leave your luggage downstairs for now."

The woman, whose name was Mrs. Ruffrano, led them up a reddish-brown staircase beneath a white door at the end of a white stucco hallway.

"Are you sure one bedroom is big enough for the two of you?" Mrs. Ruffrano asked.

Annalisa nodded as the landlady opened the door. In addition to the one bedroom, there was a small living room, a smaller kitchen, and a tiny bathroom. At least there was a shower. The walls were the same gleaming shade of white as the hallway above a shiny hardwood floor.

"Rent is due on the first of the month." Mrs. Ruffrano crossed her arms. "No exceptions."

Again, Annalisa nodded. She opened a door to join her mother on the balcony, which looked out into a broad-leafed sycamore tree and beyond that, the quiet street.

"We're going to need some curtains," Mamma said to Annalisa.

"I can bring some up," Mrs. Ruffrano responded in Sicilian.

"You speak Sicilian?" Annalisa's eyes widened.

"Sure. My family came here after the last war. We're from Catania."

"Beautiful city." Mamma's eyes lifted in reflection. "We come from just outside Palermo."

"I'll tell you what." Mrs. Ruffrano tapped on the balcony rail. "You'll get the Sicilian discount—half off your first month's rent. Just make sure you pay on time."

"Thank you, thank you," Mamma breathed. "God bless you!"

Mrs. Ruffrano smiled. "All right then. Let's get your things so you can settle in."

The women followed the landlady back down the stairs to the entrance, where Annalisa noticed a wooden mallard duck positioned on a small table.

"This is Giacomo." Mrs. Ruffrano patted the painted figure's head. "He watches the door for me."

Then she shouted down the hall, "Tony! Tony! Get over here. Two ladies need your help."

A balding man wearing a sleeveless undershirt that hugged his round belly appeared in the hallway.

"I was listening to the radio program," he said gruffly.

"You can listen later." Mrs. Ruffrano pointed to the suitcases.

"All right, all right." Tony took the two suitcases up the stairs. Mamma and Annalisa followed him up with the two other suitcases.

"Thank you, sir." Annalisa bowed her head.

"Don't mention it," Tony mumbled. "Welcome to the neighborhood."

THIRTEEN
FEBRUARY 1942

Fort Missoula, Missoula, Montana

Vincenzo stood in knee-deep snow, staring up and out at the snow-covered trees on the mountains beyond the rows and rows of white stucco buildings. A gust of bitter cold blew, chilling him to his bones as he trudged forth, the crunching of his boots echoing into the blanket of silence.

His thoughts drifted back to late 1917 and the Battle of Caporetto, when he'd braved a similar chill. It was the twelfth battle along the Isonzo River against Austria-Hungary, and Italy had seen limited success, experiencing heavy casualties. Along with his comrades, Vincenzo was exhausted. He was tired of enduring the mud and cold, his uniform caked with filth despite his efforts to stay clean. Supplies were scarce, and he felt the persistent gnaw of hunger that kept him up at night. It was no surprise the overall troop morale was low. More than 600,000 battle-scarred men either deserted or surrendered. But not Vincenzo, for he'd made a promise to himself that he would hold on, fight to the finish—if not for himself but for the pride of his future wife. She didn't deserve to marry a coward.

Now, as his knees knocked from nerves and the frigid air, he thought back to how he'd somehow managed to survive both the cold and Austria's relentless offensive. He remembered huddling in the trenches, absorbing the warmth and fear of his comrades amid relentless artillery shell explosions and poisonous gasses. He couldn't forget the smell of burning flesh and acrid smoke that clung to his uniform and weather-worn skin. Yet through it all, he held onto the hope that he'd see Maria on the other side. They could build a future there, and he'd leave behind the horrors of war.

He closed his eyes as flakes pelted his face. He'd survived Caporetto. Surely, he could endure this chapter, too.

It had been two months since he'd arrived at so-called Bella Vista, and thus far, the views were nothing but foreboding, especially with the four boxy, elevated guard towers. Someone was always watching, his movements were regulated, shaped by a rigid schedule and the concrete presence of barbed wire.

He was frustrated. There was little information, no matter whom he asked. What he did know was that he had a so-called loyalty hearing today. He'd finally hear what he did wrong and why he was here.

"What kind of hearing is this if I can't bring in a lawyer?" he'd asked, but the guard told him it was not possible.

He checked his watch. It was a quarter to twelve. He trekked through the drift to the courtroom in building T-1. If only he had access to one of his suits. All he had was a camp-issued gray sweater, slate-colored pants, and boots that were a size too large.

He entered the building to a blast of warmth, a sharp contrast from the outdoors. A guard greeted him and led him up narrow stairs to a wood-paneled room where three men in suits stood chatting near the entrance. They stopped talking when he stepped into the room, his boots leaving a trail of watery prints behind him.

"Please be seated." A slim man with wire-rim glasses pointed to a wooden chair behind a rectangular wooden table.

Vincenzo felt the men watch him as he settled into a seat positioned across from an elevated table, flanked by two American flags. A portrait of President Franklin Roosevelt hung on the wall.

Just then, three more men walked through the door and slid into chairs behind the table in front of him. The others piled onto a bench to Vincenzo's right.

Everyone was quiet for a moment as they settled into their respective seats. Then a gray-haired gentleman with a long face stood from behind the elevated table.

"All rise." And everyone did.

"My name is Bradley Jones of San Francisco and to my left and right are Emmett Gould and Douglas Kerry, also from the Bay Area. We have gathered here today in the presence of U.S. Attorney Scott Fitzgibbon, William Pratt representing the Immigration and Naturalization Service, and Donald Martin from the Federal Bureau of Investigation for the loyalty hearing of Vincenzo Aiello, age forty-five, of Pittsburg, California. Mr. Aiello, do you attest that these facts are correct?"

"Yes, sir." Vincenzo was calm. He'd done nothing wrong. This was all a mistake. Surely, they'd send him home today.

"All right, everyone, please be seated." Jones tapped the table. "Now we may begin the hearing. Mr. Martin, will you provide me with the evidence?"

The FBI representative wore a dark suit with a dark blue tie that matched his beady eyes. He gave Vincenzo a quick, cold glance as he pulled out a folder.

"Let the record show Mr. Aiello was witnessed on several occasions soliciting funds for Italian nationals." Martin raised his finger.

"What do you mean, soliciting funds?" Vincenzo heard his voice rising.

"Silence," Jones met his eyes. "Please let Mr. Martin continue."

Vincenzo felt his face grow warm and his palms begin to sweat.

"Yes, Mr. Aiello was seen soliciting funds with a Fascist organization."

"Mr. Martin," Jones interrupted the FBI representative. "Are we certain this organization was Fascist?"

"Allegedly Fascist," Martin said.

"But that's not true," Vincenzo mumbled.

"Silence, please, Mr. Aiello." Jones turned his penetrating brown eyes in his direction and paused for a moment. "Gentlemen, is there any further evidence?"

They shook their heads in silence.

Jones cleared his throat. "Mr. Aiello, you've heard the evidence against you. What have you to say for yourself? You may now speak."

"I'm innocent." Vincenzo's throat tightened with each word. "I'm a veteran of the Great War. Italy fought on the same side as America. We've lived in America for more than twenty years. I'm no Fascist. We left before the March on Rome. My son gave his life for America!"

"Mr. Aiello." Jones's voice was as sharp as his eyes. "Despite the fact you say you're no Fascist, you've maintained contact with Italian nationals who may be Fascists. Let's say your contacts through Italian channels made requests for you to do something. Would you do it?"

"That depends, sir." Of course, he'd do anything for Costanza and her family. Why wouldn't a brother help? Especially after what they'd done for him.

"Let me restate the question: Would you do anything to harm the United States if requested to do so through Italian channels?"

What was he talking about?

"Of course not!" Vincenzo nearly shouted.

Jones paused and scowled before returning his attention to his papers. "Thank you. Let's take a five-minute recess."

Vincenzo watched as the six other men walked out of the courtroom, leaving him shaking in his seat. Above the hissing of the radiator, he could hear muffled voices outside the room. He stared across at the portrait of President Roosevelt. Was this president who had spoken so warmly to the American people responsible for the nighttime arrests of innocent men who were sent away to prison camps? If so, Vincenzo decided he was worse than what he'd heard of the Fascists. At least with the Fascists, they simply raided your house and fed you cod liver oil until you soiled yourself.

Vincenzo tapped his fingers on the wooden tabletop. What were the men going to decide? Would he receive a harsher punishment? And for what? Sending money to poor housewives and orphans? It didn't make any sense.

To his left, out of the corner of his eye, he saw a crow fly past the window. He turned and saw one of the camp's framing mountains, its snowy summit shimmering in the midday afternoon sun above patches of deep green pines. The other Italians had called this view Bella Vista, and at that moment, he thought he might understand why. It wasn't just the arresting view; it was a glimpse of freedom, beyond the barbed wire. But from where he sat, the snow-covered peak was insurmountable, for it seemed to him the men had already decided his fate.

The six men entered the room with the same three sitting on the bench to his right and the other three sitting at the table in the front.

"Please rise," Jones said.

Everyone stood. Vincenzo felt himself begin to shake.

"On behalf of the United States, we have determined that

the defendant is potentially dangerous and a threat to national security and therefore will continue to be interned."

"No!" Vincenzo cried out, tears streaming.

What did it all mean? For how long would he be punished for an unknown crime? It was as if he was stuck in a dream. If only he could wake up. But no, this was real. And his fate was out of his hands. Where had he gone wrong?

A guard appeared at his side and put his hand on his shoulder. Vincenzo wiped his eyes and rose. The guard took him by the hand and led him out the door.

"Where are you taking me?" he asked.

"It's time for lunch." The guard's smile made Vincenzo's stomach churn.

FOURTEEN
MARCH 1942

Palermo, Sicily

Alberto dipped his brush into a can of navy-blue paint and reflected on how the color was a symbol of naval pride, something he once felt as he worked on the ships for the Regia Marina so long ago. Now he worked behind the scenes, making ships battle-ready with coats of paint to protect them from the elements as well as to distinguish them from the enemy.

He looked down as some of the blue paint splattered on his coveralls. He was just as proud of his uniform today as he was of his sailor suit. Each drop of paint was another stripe on his shoulder, for he'd graduated beyond the work of general laborer to a job he felt had meaning. And it didn't hurt that it paid well —especially now that mail had been cut off from the U.S. and his parents wouldn't see money from Uncle Vincenzo.

He wondered if his family knew anyone attacked at Pearl Harbor. There was no way to know while America was the enemy. He reached into his pocket and traced the grooves of the wooden net shuttle passed down from his uncle. It was his good luck charm, but more than that, it was a tie to his mother's brother, a man he didn't remember. He felt sorry for him being ruled by a hypocritical president, who, il Duce said, was responsible for the moral decline of its people.

"Make sure you get the corners, too." He heard Francesco's voice from behind him. "They're the most vulnerable spots."

Alberto nodded and adjusted his position so he could reach the bottom edges of the panel he was working on. The painting foreman had already drilled into him the importance of doing so. A missed spot could lead to corrosion of the metal, and Alberto didn't want to be responsible for anything that could put a battleship at risk. Not with the future of Italy at stake.

The whistle blew, and he hammered the lid of his paint can back in place before carrying it to the locker alongside his fellow painters. After they'd locked up, he headed back to his apartment.

As he made his way through the streets, he passed an empty lot where a dozen kids played soccer between two sets of orange cones. He stopped and watched as the tallest of the boys dribbled the ball past two other boys before kicking it hard so that it bounced through the cones and landed in front of Alberto.

He rolled his foot over the top of the ball, bringing it to a stop, and kicked it back to the boy. The boy smiled before another player cut in and stole the ball, bringing it in the opposite direction.

Alberto stayed for a few minutes, watching the game, and thinking back to when he, too, thought the world revolved around soccer. That was before civic duty in the form of naval service kicked in. He'd set aside his dreams for another day. And now he didn't see when that day would come. It had been years since he'd touched a soccer ball. It wouldn't be long before these boys, too, would heed the call to serve the Fatherland.

"Excuse me," he heard a female voice say.

He turned to see the fair-haired woman from the building across the street from him. The woman from his dreams, here in the flesh and not just a face in a window. His pulse quickened and he realized he was standing mouth agape. He closed his lips and swallowed.

"And so, we finally meet," he said.

She flashed a pretty smile. "I was just coming to pick up my brother, Lorenzo."

"Which one's your brother?" Alberto asked.

"The tall one." She pointed to the boy who'd scored the first goal.

"So, you live with Lorenzo?" Alberto asked.

"And my Mamma." She brushed a loose lock from her face. "I'm Vittoria."

"Alberto." He shook her extended hand.

Lorenzo ran toward them. "Lorenzo, this is Alberto." Vittoria tilted her head in his direction. "He lives across the street."

"You play soccer?" Lorenzo's light brown eyes widened.

Alberto nodded. "I did once. But that was a long time ago."

The three began walking back toward their street, Lorenzo regaling them with highlights from the day's game. Alberto walked in silence, listening but also watching Vittoria smiling at her brother through the corner of his eye.

"Well, here we are." Vittoria rose to her toes and clasped her hands. "It was a pleasure to finally meet you, Alberto."

He liked the way his name sounded in her mouth. "A pleasure." He nodded.

And they went their respective ways.

He was tired that night and fell into a deep sleep in which he dreamed he was back in Isola delle Femmine, swimming from the shore to the islet on which the old Spanish watchtower, mirroring that of another in the village, stood and not much else. He reached his destination from which he could see the twin tower. But he wasn't alone. He looked to his right and saw Vittoria there, smiling at him. She was wearing a violet-colored bathing suit, and she dived into the waves, beckoning him to join. Just as he did, he heard a siren.

The siren continued blaring, and he opened his eyes in the darkness. Another air raid?

He checked his watch and saw he'd been asleep for three hours. Tiptoeing to the living room window, he peeked through his shutters. There were no signs of life on the street.

He returned to his bed, praying it was a false alarm. But then he heard the low hum of an overhead plane followed by the *rat-tat-tat* of machine gunfire. He pulled the cover over his head and lay very still, waiting and listening to the shooting until, at some point, he must have fallen back asleep. For he awoke with a start to the sound of an explosion. The room rattled as if hit with an earthquake as he heard a series of loud booms reminiscent of a fireworks finale, only louder. He clung to his bed's wooden frame, and when the shaking subsided, he made his way to the window.

It was daylight and while he didn't see anyone, it wasn't long before he heard the sirens of emergency vehicles. He looked at his watch. It was already 7:25, and he had to be at work at 8. He began to see people passing his window in the street, their eyes blank and steps slow and deliberate, as they faced another day in the aftermath of an air raid.

When he emerged from his apartment, greeted with an acrid, burning smell, he heard a loud crackling sound. Turning toward the north pier, he saw it.

Fire was pouring out of three nearly sunken steamships and an enormous tanker. Around them, about two dozen other ships were singed, many with damaged or missing masts. But what really stood out were the floating bodies. He felt sick and promptly vomited, his breakfast mingling with the diesel fuel and other dark substances that floated on the water's greasy surface.

He was so caught up in what he saw that he almost didn't hear the shipyard whistle blow. Everyone at his work site seemed to be gathered for an impromptu meeting. Ascanio nodded as he slid in behind him.

"Gentlemen, as you have no doubt seen, last night's air raid resulted in significant damage to many of our ships," said Francesco to the group. "The emergency crews are in the process of fishing out the bodies, but I'm going to need all of your hands today to clean up. There's a lot of debris that will need to be cleared and it needs to be removed today for health and safety reasons. Once that's done, we'll assess what can be salvaged from the ships that didn't sink, and I'm afraid some of these are a lost cause. Are there any questions?"

No one raised a hand.

"All right then." Francesco slid his hands in his pockets. "Let's get to work."

FIFTEEN

MARCH 1942

Fort Missoula, Missoula, Montana

Dear Maria and Annalisa,

I think of you every day. I am well. The food is good. There are some famous musicians here, and they like to perform concerts. They are taking care of me. I cannot complain.

How is the new apartment?

Love,
Your husband and father

Vincenzo couldn't complain because if he did, the censors might block his letter from even going out. This was one of just two short letters and one postcard a week he was allowed to send.

He folded the light blue pre-folded paper, which was 6 inches wide by 14.75 inches long. About twenty-four widely spaced black lines were printed for his use, a reminder that his word allowance was limited. He could only write on one side. Once the letter was folded, the other side became the envelope.

"Vincenzo!" Aldo called up to him from below the bunk. "There's a performance tonight. They're doing *La Traviata*. Are you coming?"

He set the letter to his side and hopped down from his bed. "I wouldn't miss it!"

Several famous musicians and singers were among the thousand internees from Italy. The current show was one for which they'd been practicing for the better part of a month.

Vincenzo followed Aldo out the door into the frigid evening air, and the two walked to the white stucco recreation building, where a large wood-paneled, high-ceilinged room had been set aside for entertainment.

The performers had built their own stage, and several dozen mismatched wooden chairs in the audience were already filling up when the two men arrived. They settled in mid-row seats.

Vincenzo watched as the musicians set up their instruments in the flickering light onstage. There were men with flutes and other woodwinds, several brass instruments, a large golden harp, drums, a piano, and string instruments. The orchestra sat up straight and waited along with the audience. Then the violinist and violist raised their instruments as the pianist began pounding away in a lively tune. The actors entered, some men wearing pastel-colored gowns, with wine glasses in their hands. The song began with the male character wearing a dark suit and singing about drinking with joyous abandon and everyone else dancing around him onstage. Men in the audience whistled as one actor wearing a lacy red dress sang his part as the female lead in the duet.

Vincenzo had never seen an opera but was certainly familiar with the opening's drinking song. He laughed, sang along with the audience, and raised his hand with an imaginary beverage. He gathered that the female character, Violetta, was supposed to be a courtesan. By Act 2, she'd left behind her profession for her love for the young nobleman Alfredo, who sang with her in the beginning. There was a particularly moving scene between the man playing Alfredo's father and the man playing Violetta. The audience clapped as Violetta hit impressive high notes in a song about leaving Alfredo. In the next scene, the characters appeared at a ball, each wearing brightly colored papier mâché masks, as acting couples swayed and danced to the music from the side of the stage. There, Alfredo confronted Violetta and her new lover, who challenged Alfredo to a duel.

Vincenzo looked around and saw all the men leaning in, captivated by the performance. Then Act 3 began.

The audience learned Violetta was dying. Alfredo had survived the duel, and his father had told him the truth about why Violetta had left him. Then the man playing Alfredo appeared at the man playing Violetta's side. Violetta wore a long white nightgown as he and Alfredo performed a final duet before crumpling in Alfredo's arms.

The audience erupted in applause, and Vincenzo rose with the others in a standing ovation as several men whistled and called out, "*Bravi!*" to the cast assembled onstage.

"They were incredible!" Vincenzo shouted over the buzz of the other men leaving the theater.

"See, Bella Vista isn't all bad." Aldo raised his voice in response.

"They deserve a real audience," Vincenzo said.

Aldo grinned. "Aren't we enough of an audience?"

"I'm serious. The camp could raise money by charging locals for tickets to these shows."

Aldo stopped and put his hands on his wide hips. "Who's going to propose this plan to the camp administration?"

"I will."

Vincenzo stood in front of the mirror at the communal bathroom's sink, razor in hand.

"Think I should grow a beard?" he asked Aldo.

"It's definitely a goal worth pursuing," Aldo nodded.

He ran his hands over his head. "I could grow my hair out, too."

"You'd fit in with the mountain men around here."

Vincenzo stared in the mirror and noticed fine wrinkles around his pale eyes. He looked older and the gray hairs on his face didn't help. He shook his head and lathered up before raising the razor to his stubble.

Aldo chuckled. "I thought you wanted a beard. You'll never get there at this rate!"

"I've changed my mind." Vincenzo stretched and carefully shaved his neck.

Aldo watched him. "You never know if they'll need a couple of extra actors to play ladies in upcoming operas."

"Speaking of which..." Vincenzo stretched his upper lip to attack his mustache. "I shared my plan with one of the guards. That guy Jenson."

"What's he going to do with that information?" Aldo spoke into the mirror. "You have to talk to someone in charge."

"I'm working on it. I figure if I tell enough people, word will get to the people in charge. And then they'll think it's their idea."

Aldo smiled. "That's brilliant."

Vincenzo felt his face for remaining stubble. "So, what are you cooking for supper tonight?"

"You'll never believe it, but they got us eggplant. Just think of all the recipes I can make using eggplant!"

"*Pasta alla Norma*, of course." Vincenzo set down the razor.

"Or I could pound out strips and roll it up with bread crumbs as *involtini di melanzane*."

"Sounds delicious!" Vincenzo turned on the faucet and splashed his freshly shaven face.

"*Che bella!*" Aldo puckered up his lips.

"You're not so bad yourself." Vincenzo winked.

Roll call ended, and the men began to disperse, many returning to their bunks to read or play cards. Vincenzo stayed behind and waited to get the INS officer in charge's attention.

"Excuse me, sir."

"Yes?" The brunet man whose name tag read Thomas turned to him.

"Sir, I was thinking… This camp could use some extra money… you know, for supplies and food. And we have these world-class opera singers and a fabulous orchestra…"

"And you think we oughta charge admission from the public?" The officer nodded. "I know, I know. Nichols told me about your idea."

"And do you think we can do it?"

Thomas ran a hand through his hair. "That's above my pay grade. But I'll tell you what. I can tell Campbell when he's back in town on Friday. He's the guy who needs to send it up the flagpole for INS approval."

"You'd do that?"

"Sure, why not?" The officer winked. "We could use some extra interaction with the public. Us guys get kind of stir-crazy. And some extra funds might mean better food. And we all want that, right?"

SIXTEEN

APRIL 1942

Annalisa pulled a snug crimson sweater over her crisp, white blouse and smoothed out her pleated, plaid knee-length skirt. She slipped her white bobby-socked feet into a pair of black-and-white saddle shoes, checked herself in the mirror, adjusted her horn necklace, and raced off before her mother could remind her to eat breakfast.

It was Saturday morning and promised to be a busy day at Reede's variety store, where she'd been working for the past month. With a slogan of "If Reede's doesn't have it, then you don't need it," the store had just about everything—from craft, cleaning, and party supplies to candy, cosmetics, and basic apparel. And it was just two blocks from her apartment, at a busy intersection on the other side of Pacheco Square.

Mr. Reede, an older gentleman with round, rimless glasses, had hired her on the spot when she dropped by one day after school. And since then, she had been working the 4 p.m. to 7 p.m. shift on weekdays and from 10 a.m. to 1:30 p.m. on Saturdays.

In addition to working the cash register, she would take turns walking the store aisles, watching for shoplifters, and answering questions. During that time, Mr. Reede would oversee the register. It was just temporary, he'd told her, until he could find someone to share her shift. The store had recently seen two employees turn in their work aprons. One had left for the Navy, and the other had gone off to college.

When she arrived, she was surprised to see Mr. Reede walking with his arm around a tall young man with copper-red hair and pale blue eyes, surrounded by a smattering of freckles.

"Good morning, Annalisa!" Mr. Reede called to her. "I was just giving Sam here the grand tour. Sam, Annalisa. Annalisa, Sam."

She nodded and found herself blushing as Sam turned in her direction. She wasn't sure why.

"Annalisa, weren't you saying you lived on the northwest side of Pacheco Square?" Mr. Reede asked.

"I do." She still felt her cheeks burn. Sam was looking directly at her now.

"So do I." Sam's eyes widened. "On Pacheco, near Grant Street."

"Really?" she asked. "That's where I live. I'm right at the corner."

"The Rosal Apartments?"

She nodded. "That's right."

"Then I'm your next-door neighbor." He smiled. "My Ma and I are in the house just to the left if you're standing with your back to your building."

She knew the house. She passed it every day and wondered why she'd never seen him.

"Well, I'll let you kids get acquainted while I stroll the aisles," said Mr. Reede.

Sam slid in next to her, behind the register. He was standing close enough that she could smell cigarette smoke.

Her pulse quickened. "Have you used one of these machines before?"

Sam leaned against the counter. "Sure. I used to work at Rexall's down the street."

"The drugstore with the soda fountain!"

"That's the one." He nodded. "I never saw you there, though."

Annalisa twisted her amulet on its chain. "I'm new in town."

A boy approached the cash register with a handful of candies. Annalisa rang him up and handed him back some change while Sam watched.

"Seems like a piece of cake." He tapped the counter. "So, where are you from, anyway?"

Annalisa closed the register. "Pittsburg."

Sam raised his bushy red eyebrows. "Up by the steel mill and Camp Stoneman?"

She nodded. "That's right."

"Your old man works at either of them?"

She took a deep breath. "No, he is... was a fisherman."

"Oh, I'm sorry." Sam's freckled face reddened, nearly matching his hair.

"He's not dead," Annalisa said quickly and tugged at the ends of her hair. "He... had to go to Montana."

"So, he's a cowboy now?"

Another customer approached the register, this time with a board game and a dozen socks.

"Your turn." Annalisa stepped back, and Sam slowly rang the customer up.

"How are we doing here?" Mr. Reede said, returning from his stroll.

"Good." Sam looked at Annalisa. "Right?"

"Right."

"That's what I like to hear," Mr. Reede said. "Now, Annalisa, it's your turn to stop the shoplifters."

Annalisa nodded. "Well, I'll see you in a bit." She met Sam's blue eyes.

"See you." He flashed her a toothy grin.

Sam waited for her when their shift ended.

"I thought you could use some company on the long walk home," he joked.

Annalisa rolled her eyes. "Yes, two blocks are so long."

The two cut through Pacheco Square, Sam reaching up to touch the tassels of wisteria as they passed beneath the pergola up toward Grant Street.

"So what year are you in school?" He pulled down a blossom and sniffed it.

"I'm finishing my second year." She caught his blue eyes. "You?"

"Same." He tossed the blossom on the gravel path.

"I'm surprised I haven't seen you before."

His lips curled into a sly smile. "Mount Diablo's a big school. Besides, I'm not exactly what you'd call a model student."

She raised her eyebrows. "You mean you skip classes?"

He nodded. "Sure. Every now and then, I like to drive up to Black Diamond Mines."

"You ever go to the cemetery?"

"Sure do." He nodded again. "You know it?"

"Yeah, I've been there before." She smiled. "During a school day, too."

"Really?" Sam stopped walking and turned to her. "I wouldn't have pegged you for the truant type."

"There's a lot you don't know about me."

They were standing between her apartment and his house now.

"Well, Annalisa." He tapped her shoe with his toe. "I look forward to learning more."

Monday came and Annalisa pulled on a pale blue fitted sweater over a brown pleated skirt before sliding into a pair of matching brown loafers. She ran her hands through her wavy brown hair before pinning up both sides.

"Breakfast is ready." Mamma stuck her head in the doorway. She was already dressed in her cleaning lady uniform.

"I'm not hungry, Mamma."

"That's the third day in a row you're not eating breakfast. What? You think you're too fat?"

"No, Mamma. I'm just not hungry."

"Well, at least take the lunch I made you."

Annalisa sighed and took the brown bag her mother handed her before racing out the door.

Once she reached the front of the apartment complex, she stopped and looked to her left. There was no sign of activity from Sam's house, so she walked to Grant Street and turned left.

Annalisa was two blocks up when she heard a horn beep. Sam was there, leaning out the window of a boxy blue Ford.

"Want a ride?"

"I'm almost there."

"Are you sure? Come on, hop in!"

She opened the door and climbed in. The front bench seat was smooth leather and smelled of cigarettes.

But instead of stopping at the school, Sam took a turn and sped up.

"Where are we going?" Annalisa asked nervously.

"To the cemetery."

"But I have a history test."

"You can make it up tomorrow." He turned to her. "Come on, it's a beautiful day. Live a little."

She held on tight to the door handle as they hit a curve. He was driving fast, but her mind was racing even faster. *What if we have an accident? What if the principal calls Mamma? Does Sam like me?*

Soon, she could see yellow hills in the distance, the same hills she remembered from her excursion with Mario. She smiled and then felt a wave of sadness as she always did. Poor Mario.

The car slowed as they hit the curved road at the entrance to the park.

"We're almost there now," Sam said, and Annalisa remembered.

They made their way up the gravelly road until they rolled into the parking lot.

"It's about a ten-or-so-minute walk from here. Think you can do that in those shoes?"

Annalisa looked down at her loafers. "Sure."

She wasn't so sure about halfway to the graveyard when she felt her shoe rub against a blister. But she looked ahead at the top of the juniper bush, her sign that there wasn't that much farther to go.

"So, why'd you come to Concord of all places if your old man's in Montana?" Sam asked suddenly.

She paused, crouching down to rub her blister. "My family's Italian."

"What does that have to do with anything?" He tilted his head. "I'm Irish."

"It has to do with everything," she sighed. "My mother's not a citizen, and the steel mill and Camp Stoneman are in Pittsburg, so they told us we had to leave."

"They thought your mother was going to do something to the steel mill?" He laughed.

"It's actually not that funny." Annalisa was getting warm and was certain she'd have a sunburn.

"Sorry." Sam pressed his lips together. "I guess with us being at war with Italy, the government is being cautious. But I didn't know. So, it's just you and your Ma?"

"Yeah." She stared at the golden-grass-lined road ahead.

"While your Pops is playing cowboy and avoiding all this Italian stuff?"

"It's not like that." She waved her hand. "They took him away."

"What do you mean? Arrested him?"

"Yeah." She kicked at a pebble. "Something like that. How about you?"

"Me?" He reached into his pocket and pulled out a pack of cigarettes.

"Yeah, what about your father? I've only seen your mom."

"He may as well be in jail for all I care." He lit a cigarette. "Want one?"

She eyed the pack. "Why not?" He lit another cigarette and handed it to her. She placed it between her thumb and forefinger, raised it to her lips, and took a deep drag. Then she launched into a fit of coughing.

"You've never smoked before, have you?" He laughed. "Try taking a smaller sip of it, like this."

He brought the cigarette to his lips and lightly inhaled. Then he exhaled, releasing the smoke slowly in a thin, wispy trail.

She tried again, this time taking a lighter drag. Again, she coughed, but less violently.

"Not bad for your first time," he said. "It takes a bit of practice."

She inhaled once more, slowly and lightly, and exhaled without coughing. She smiled.

"There you go." He patted her on the back, and she felt warmth flood her body. "You're a natural."

The grassy fenced-in graveyard appeared before them, cracked tombstones rising from the uneven ground. Sam dropped his cigarette and stubbed it out with his toe, and Annalisa followed suit.

"There it is." He pointed to a pepper tree. "My favorite place to sit."

He slid onto a low branch, the same branch she'd sat on with Mario. When Mario was still alive.

Tears filled her eyes, and soon she was crying.

"Hey." Sam took her hand. "What's going on? Is this about your Pops?"

"No." She took a deep breath. "My brother. He brought me here last time, and he..."

"What happened?"

She ran her thumb and forefinger over the twist of her horn charm. "His ship sank at Pearl Harbor."

"Oh my God," Sam said. "That's awful. You sure have been through a lot."

He drew her in for a hug.

She cried harder into his shoulder. Then he kissed her on the top of the head. Instinctively, she raised her face toward him. He kissed her again, this time on the lips—a long, deep kiss.

"Feel better?"

She nodded, and he pulled her in again.

She broke away.

"What is it?" he asked.

"It's just..." She wrung her hands. "We're in a cemetery."

He winked. "I'm sure the ghosts have seen their fair share."

She shifted her gaze. "Anyway, it's getting late, and we have work today."

"Relax." He took her right hand and massaged her palm. "We have time."

"No, we really should go." She withdrew her hand.

"Why?" He grinned. "Your boyfriend will get mad?"

She shook her head. "I don't have a boyfriend."

"I'd like to change that." He leaned in for another kiss.

SEVENTEEN
APRIL 1942

Fort Missoula, Missoula, Montana

Hon. Edward Ennis
Alien Enemy Control Unit
Department of Justice
Washington, D.C.

Dear Sir:
I wish to petition for a rehearing of my case. At the time of my hearing, it was apparent that I did not have all the facts. There was not even an attorney to represent me. Instead, I was limited to answering questions I was not prepared for and not able to defend myself against all the accusations. My wife and I have been in this country for twenty-two years, and I have never once broken the law or disobeyed any regulations. It is my hope that you will provide me with a new hearing, as there is nothing on my record to show any doubt about my loyalty to this country.

Sincerely yours,
Vincenzo Aiello

The scent of clover perfumed the air. Spring delivered deep shades of green to the lawn and surrounding hillsides, and the vibrant purple irises planted just outside the barracks were in full bloom. Vincenzo finally understood why they called this place Bella Vista.

The mild weather beckoned the men from the buildings, many engaging in a game of soccer or bocce ball on the fields and courts they maintained themselves. Meanwhile, Vincenzo could see the Japanese men had convinced the guards to give them golf clubs, which they were using to putt balls on a makeshift course.

Warmer days also meant that Vincenzo's musician and singer friends could expect larger crowds to come in from the surrounding towns to see what the camp had touted as "world-class entertainment." Even the guards seemed to enjoy the shows.

Working as he did on Saturday nights at the ticket counter gave Vincenzo a chance to interact with people from outside the barbed wire fence. People leaned forward in hushed silence as the violinist sawed at his rich red-brown instrument or roared in laughter as the men wearing dresses warbled their high notes. It was clear these attendees weren't afraid of the Italians onstage.

As he sat behind the ticket window, he remembered when he had saved up to take the family to see a vaudeville act at Pittsburg's California Theatre. They'd lined up beneath the marquee, which was flanked by a stone woman with a dagger on one side and a flute-playing nymph on the other. And they'd followed the stream of fancy people, those for whom such a ticket was not a luxury, into the airy golden theater and sat in velvet seats beneath an ornate ceiling lamp surrounded by decorative radiating lines in shades of soft blues and pinks accentuated by gold highlights.

That was while Mario was just a boy and Annalisa was a toddler. At some point during the show, Maria nudged him.

"Where is Mario?" she whispered.

"I let him go to the bathroom by himself," Vincenzo said.

"Why would you do that?" Maria hissed, and people shushed her.

The actors on stage stopped their bit, and one pointed to the left.

Vincenzo panned across the stage to see his son climbing up to join the actors. The audience laughed, and Vincenzo got up and had to excuse himself while pushing his way across his row to the aisle. He then ran up the side of the theater and scooped up his little boy.

"But, Papà!" Mario whined. "I wanted to sing."

Vincenzo brushed a tear from his eye with the memory of a little boy, whose exuberance once could not be contained. They'd been so embarrassed that night that they left the theater immediately. And, Vincenzo thought, they were afterward likely too hard on the boy. It was no wonder he chose to break out on his own, to join the Navy, to perhaps escape the confines of the world his parents had created.

"Is everything all right?" an older woman asked from the other side of the ticket window.

"Everything is all right." He smiled. "Enjoy the show."

He waited until the last person in line stepped up to the window and then closed up the makeshift box office to sneak into the theater.

They were putting on a production of *La Bohème*, some songs from which Vincenzo was familiar, particularly "Musetta's Waltz."

The opera started with a scene from Christmas Eve with three Bohemian friends, painters Rodolfo and Marcello and philosopher Colline, who were cold and hungry. Their musician friend, Schaunard, appeared bearing gifts of food, fuel, and money. The friends went off to celebrate, leaving behind Rodolfo, who promised to join them later.

Vincenzo was happy to see that some of the money earned from the performances had gone to providing better-quality costumes.

Then a man named Eduardo, wearing a blonde wig and pink dress, came on the stage as Mimì, with whom Rodolfo fell in love at first sight.

They shared a duet, "O soave fanciulla," about the love that had blossomed between them.

The two lovers joined the others at a café where Musetta, Marcello's former lover (played by a man named Gino), arrived on the arm of a wealthy, older admirer.

The fact that "Musetta" was much taller than Guido, who was playing the older gentleman, made the audience laugh. But Gino stayed in character.

Vincenzo leaned in and watched as Musetta and Marcello got back together, and Musetta managed to shed herself of the older gentleman.

But by Act 3, it was clear that romance was not easy for either couple. Mimì was in poor health, and she and Rodolfo decided to break up because of her illness and their poverty. Meanwhile, Musetta and Marcello had a fight that led to a breakup.

Act 4 began with Rodolfo and Marcello collectively lamenting their now lonely lives. Their friends came to bring them food for a meal, which Musetta interrupted to inform the men that Mimì was very ill and yearned to reunite with Rodolfo. The friends rallied around Mimì with Musetta selling her earrings and Colline his coat so they could buy medicine. But despite their efforts, Mimì died in the end.

Vincenzo had seen the rehearsals, and yet he found himself overcome with emotion. Yes, the opera was depressing, but it was more than that. He was thinking about the camaraderie of the internees, how they looked forward to the simple things like pasta dinners and time on the bocce court. These comprised their Bella Vista, their beautiful view despite the fact each was suffering some sort of loss: displacement from their home and family or, in his case, additionally, the loss of a loved one.

Vincenzo walked alone through the cool grass back toward the bunkhouse. He could hear laughter and chatter of audience members leaving the compound for life beyond the barbed wire. For two hours he'd been among the free, sharing laughter and tears, and now the spell was broken. He was back in his state of limbo.

JUNE 1, 1942

Fort Missoula, Missoula, Montana

A bolt of lightning zigzagged across the sky. Moments later thunder rumbled, causing the glass panes to shake and startling Vincenzo and Aldo, who were peering out the window.

The rain had cooled down what had been a hot day, but what really burned Vincenzo was a letter.

"Have you ever been to Texas?" Aldo asked.

The Department of Justice was transferring Vincenzo to a new camp, Dodd Field, in San Antonio. He wasn't sure why, but from what he gathered it was part of the drill: prisoner rotation to other camps throughout the country.

He shook his head. "Are you kidding me? Aside from when I entered New York and took the train to California, I've done no traveling before coming here. I'm not sure why they're keeping me, let alone sending me so far south."

It didn't make sense. According to his hearing, Vincenzo's big crime was membership in an organization, a club to which he no longer belonged because of his circumstances. What threat could he pose at this point?

They stood before the window in silence, listening to the pitter-patter of the rain blessing the hills. The dim light of a hanging bulb cast long shadows over them, further darkening Vincenzo's thoughts.

"So, what are you going to do?" Aldo asked.

"What else can I do?" Vincenzo replied to his friend's reflection. "Maybe things will be different there."

"I heard it's even hotter down there. And humid, too."

Again, thunder rumbled outside. "I mean, maybe I'll get a rehearing."

"Perhaps." His friend smiled with his sandy-brown eyes. "Or they'll keep you for another nine months."

Vincenzo nodded and swallowed. Maybe Aldo was right.

"Hey, don't look so sad, *paesano!*" Aldo patted him on the back. "This is your chance to visit someplace new. Although I'll tell you one thing; you won't find as good of a cook down there in Texas."

He winked and flashed a toothy grin. "Or internees as handsome."

JUNE 9, 1942

Dodd Field, San Antonio, Texas

Vincenzo stepped across the white-hot gravel alongside a guard whose name tag read Wilkinson to a long row of pyramidal khaki tents mounted on wooden foundations.

"This one." Wilkinson lifted a canvas flap. "We call them Victory Huts."

Inside was a triangular layout of three thin metal cots, two of which sagged under the weight of their sleeping occupants, one of whom appeared to be Japanese, his upright chest rising and falling with shallow breaths. The other lay on his side, his fair skin flushed and glistening with sweat beneath a head full of ash-blond hair. German, Vincenzo guessed. A crumpled pack of cigarettes and a worn box of cards sat on a single wooden table surrounded by three chairs sat at the center of the hut. The thin walls were stained in dust and mildew and seemed to trap the stifling heat that made the air thick and heavy, difficult to breathe.

"Enjoy your new home." Wilkinson turned to leave.

Exhausted from his trip, Vincenzo settled onto the empty cot. There were no sheets, but it was so hot, it didn't matter. It didn't take long for him to fall asleep.

He awoke in a pool of perspiration to the sound of whispers.

"You woke him!" the fair-haired man said, and Vincenzo heard his distinctly German accent.

Vincenzo sat up and wiped his forehead. "What time is it?"

"A quarter after eleven." The German watched him with piercing blue eyes from his seat at the table.

"We were just playing a game." The Japanese man held up a card. His shiny black hair was flecked with silver. "Care to join us?"

Vincenzo sat down, and the German, whose name was Ernst, explained that the point of the game was matching a card in hand with any of the same number or figurehead in the center, which they called the board.

"It's based on a Japanese game, but we don't have the right cards," added the other man, named Satow.

Vincenzo sat down as Satow carefully reshuffled the cards and then passed each man a hand of seven. He placed six new cards face up on the board and set the rest of the deck to the side.

Vincenzo looked at his cards. He had a two and four of spades, a nine of hearts, a six and ten of diamonds, and a two and five of clubs. On the table were a ten and queen of clubs, an eight of spades, an ace and seven of diamonds, and a four of hearts.

He grabbed the ten of clubs and the four of hearts.

"It's similar to a game we played in Italy," Vincenzo said.

"Matching-card games are universal." Ernst passed his turn. "But they require no skill like soccer."

"Ten people, ten colors," Satow scooped up the seven of diamonds, the eight of spades, and the queen of clubs. Then he replenished the board with five new cards.

"He speaks in riddles." Ernst shook his head.

"No, I just mean everyone has their own tastes." Satow tapped his cards.

Ernst shifted his blue eyes in Vincenzo's direction. "What about you, Vincenzo? Are you a soccer player?"

"I played when I was young." Vincenzo grabbed a card from the board. "Now I am more of a bocce player."

"You're not that old," Ernst grabbed two cards from the board.

"I'll be forty-six in September."

"My birthday is next month." Satow pocketed three more cards. "I'm two years older than you. Ah, look, I have just one card left."

Satow replenished the board.

"We'll see how long that lasts." Vincenzo snatched up three more cards. "Now I also have just one left."

Ernst grabbed three as well.

"There goes my chance." Satow replenished the board.

"So, where did you come from, Vincenzo?" Ernst grabbed a card after Vincenzo passed his turn.

"Missoula, Montana, but before that I..."

"I win!" Satow interrupted him.

"I believe this is a game well-suited for the tricky Japanese." Ernst grinned.

"Said by the man whose nation used lightning war in Poland and France." Satow shook his head.

Ernst rolled his eyes. "Anyway, Vincenzo, you were saying?"

"I live in California. How about you?"

"Multnomah County, Oregon," said Ernst.

"Alaska." Satow replied.

"Alaska?" Vincenzo's eyes widened. "Really? What part?"

"Southeastern."

"We fished across the water in Bristol Bay most summers." Vincenzo ran a card between his fingers. A young Mario's face flashed before him. It all seemed so long ago.

"I used to fish where I come from, but Japanese aren't allowed to do so in Alaska." Satow's dark eyes shifted. "Not since 1937 when my countrymen showed up with diesel-powered boats."

Vincenzo nodded. "Heard about that. Unfair competition."

"Since then, I worked at a cannery," Satow sighed.

"It seems we all touched the water in some way," said Ernst. "I'm a shipbuilder."

"Doesn't America need shipbuilders with the war?" Vincenzo tilted his head.

"Not potentially dangerous ones like me." Ernst pointed to his chest.

The men were quiet for a moment. Vincenzo reflected on his hearing and how he, too, had been labeled as "potentially dangerous." He looked at Ernst and Satow and shook his head. They had all been branded by a government that called itself a democracy and subjected to a state of limbo between prison camps. For what? Simply belonging to the wrong organization? Or as in the case of Satow, perhaps because of the shape of his eyes.

"I'll tell you what's dangerous." Satow gathered the cards to put them away. "The heat here."

"It's already too hot to be outside." Ernst tugged at his

sweaty collar. "By noon, you'll be too hot to sit up. We lie around on our cots most of the day to keep cool."

"And we take lots of cold showers." Satow chuckled.

Vincenzo took a deep breath. The humidity was oppressive, and he was sweating from parts of his body he didn't even know perspired.

"It's only June, and it's already this hot?" He wiped his brow.

"You'll get used to it," Ernst sighed.

Vincenzo nodded. He was already feeling a strange camaraderie with these men with whom he'd not have previously interacted. Not that there weren't Japanese and Germans in Missoula; they just kept their distance. Now there wasn't a choice, and he was glad to see they weren't too different from himself.

"Well, thanks for the game. It was a nice distraction."

"Of course." Satow nodded.

Vincenzo followed the men as they left the table and sprawled out on their respective cots. As he lay there, staring up at the canvas roof, he thought about how, despite their differences, these men had found a way to connect. And in a world torn apart by xenophobia and prejudices, that was something.

The dwarf nodded. "An ancient guardian. The Masters created it, as they did me. Though I must say, Yig is far more dangerous, so it was logical they sealed him in the city when they left. Others … other guardians were not sealed. The dragon, for one."

Liv nodded and looked at Wincott. "We need to seal the valley. If what he says is true … if Yig or others like it were to get out … nothing could stop them."

"Myrrhmyth," Wincott breathed, nodding slowly.

Ruddlefunt nodded. "Yes, the dragon. You know it?"

"No, no one has seen it in generations. It's said to haunt the mountains east of here, blocking the old trade routes. The Company and the Guild have been trying to expand their territories to the east far longer than I've been alive, but a long time ago, they gave up—most these days say it's because the paths are nonexistent or too rough to make trade profitable. But it's the dragon."

Ruddlefunt looked at him quizzically. "This Company and Guild you mention. I have not heard of them. Do they work for the King?"

"The Erdor and Expanse Trading Company—the *Company*—is owned by the Queen. The Guild is independent—a merchant network formed by former Company men some two hundred years ago before it was taken over by Mordren's royal family," Wincott explained. "How long have you been down here?"

"As I told the candidate, a very long time."

"Candidate?" Liv inquired.

"Yes, the young fellow, tall, a bit gangly, no shoes. What did you call him?"

"Sish," said Wincott. *My son.*

Liv eyed the old thief inquisitively and then turned to the dwarf.

"Why do you call him the candidate?" she asked.

"He successfully traversed the first two trials to gain entry to the Grand Valley of the Lords of Roan. He is now the candidate. If he can traverse the valley safely to the Storeroom, he may access the Wealth."

"And he's the only one?" Wincott pressed.

Ruddlefunt nodded. "Yes, but no candidate has ever survived, and I daresay he likely hasn't either. Yig doesn't crawl out of his cave for nothing. Which reminds me, that girl you brought with you: I've never seen anyone quite able to do what she can do."

Wincott lifted his eyebrows. "Well, yes, it is. An amazing coincidence, I'll admit. Now can we get back to the problem at hand? My boy is in the bottom of that valley, and that snake-thing might be hunting him as we speak."

"Yig," said Ruddlefunt.

"Pffft," snorted Liv. "You don't care one wit about him. Never have. You want that treasure."

Wincott's face grew red. He pointed a finger at her and said, "You're wrong."

The thief turned away from the pointless conversation and searched the room for another doorway or passageway out, anything, really, that might make it easier to get to the valley bottom.

Liv stood still and watched him quietly, her arms crossed.

"They're probably all dead; that *thing* wasn't taking prisoners. We need to seal the cavern off and get out of here," she said.

"Yig," Ruddlefunt said again.

"Flee? Are you kidding?" Wincott questioned her, an incredulous look on his face. He took on a mocking tone. "But I thought you were a *Dungeoneer*—sworn to protect the weak, fight evil, and uphold justice! *Flee*. Are you kidding me?"

"It's the only rational thing to do," she said evenly.

"A wizard would say that," Wincott shot back. "What is it you want to keep hidden down there anyway? Want to keep it just for yourself?"

Liv scoffed, "No, you old fool. The Grand Valley was sealed for a reason. The Wealth isn't some trunk of jewels you can carry out of here and cash in at the market. It's dangerous, and the people who built this city knew it. That's why they protected it and it's been locked away all these centuries. If it gets out … well, that snake-thing will be the least of our worries."

"Yig."

Wincott and Liv turned toward the dwarf and yelled in unison, "Stop saying that!"

The dwarf's eyes widened in surprise. "Its name … its name is Yig not *snake-thing*. I see the people of the world have grown more crude with time. Perhaps the Masters were wise to seal me in here."

"What's a Yig?" Wincott asked.

Liv stepped toward the dwarf and crouched in front of him, her hands on his shoulders. "Are you … did I hear you say *Yig*?"

EIGHTEEN
JUNE 1942

Palermo, Sicily

A low rumbling noise disturbed the calm, and the boys on the soccer field turned to Alberto.

Everyone froze for a moment, their eyes wide and mouths open. Just then, a bolt of lightning slashed through the sky.

"It's only a storm," Alberto called to the boys.

In the four months that Alberto had been volunteering as soccer coach, there had been no bombings. Things were peaceful despite the annoying rations and blackout hours, grim reminders of the fact the nation was still at war.

After a week hunched over and inhaling paint, he looked forward to Sundays when he alternated between visiting his family in Isola delle Femmine and sharing techniques with the twelve- and thirteen-year-old boys who showed up to sharpen their skills and take part in scrimmages.

One of those boys was Lorenzo, and so Alberto could also look forward to face time with Vittoria.

He learned that she was a primary school teacher and had taught several of the boys in their younger years. So having their teacher and coach cheer them on from the sidelines boosted their confidence, which they needed at a time of so much uncertainty.

"Just think of what these children have seen." Vittoria shook her head as they walked back, while Lorenzo ran ahead.

"It's not at all like when we were kids," Alberto agreed.

"I never understood why il Duce decided to enter this war. He bragged about millions of bayonets, and what good does that do when bombs are raining down on you?"

Alberto sighed as the weight of her words pressed on him. Part of him agreed. But he'd grown up trusting in the gospel of Mussolini. He often wondered what it would have been like to live somewhere else, for example, in the United States. Would he be a different person just because of the leadership? Fascism had given him discipline and strengthened his character.

"I guess there are just some things we'll never understand because we're not close enough to the issues," he said slowly.

"I suppose you're right." She wiped a raindrop from her eye.

It was drizzling now, with the pitter-patter of rain forming puddles in their path as they ran between colorful storefront awnings. Lorenzo was well on his way home.

"Why don't we stop for a coffee until it lets up?" Alberto pulled Vittoria with him into the doorway of a café.

"Sure, why not?" She fixed her dripping hair.

They settled into wobbly chairs and Alberto asked the waiter for two coffees.

Vittoria smiled at him from across the little round table when the waiter left.

"What?"

"Nothing." Her eyes seemed to sparkle. "It's just that... Well, I've been wondering when you were finally going to ask me out."

He smiled. "Are we out?"

"I'll count this as a date." She nodded. "Even if the coffee's made of barley."

He felt warmth spread over him.

"Then I'm glad I finally got up the courage."

They sat in silence for a moment, just smiling at one another.

The waiter served each a *caffè d'orzo* before tiptoeing away.

"So, what's next?" Vittoria asked.

"What do you mean?"

She leaned forward. "I mean, what do you see next in your life?"

He sighed and looked up at the wood-paneled ceiling.

"I used to think about the future, but all that changed with the war."

She tilted her head. "What would you have done differently?"

He shifted his gaze to the rain pelting the window and watched a drop slide down to the sill. "A long time ago, I wanted to be a soccer player. But that was impractical for a village kid like me. After I served with the Regia Marina, I figured I could use my skills here in Palermo. And well, I'll see what happens. Maybe one day I'll be the foreman. Or at least have a role in building one of the great ships that lead us to victory."

He met her pale brown eyes. "So, what about you? What made you decide to become a teacher?"

She shifted her gaze and smiled. "Oh, the usual. I wanted to make a difference for our future generations."

He sipped his bitter ersatz coffee and inhaled its earthy scent. "Did you always want to teach?"

She nodded. "I had a lower secondary history teacher who took me aside after I did well on a test. He liked the way I broke down the concepts and connected the dots."

"In what way?" Alberto leaned forward.

"Well." She twirled a stray strand of her light brown hair. "I wrote one paper about how Italy has been torn between unity and individualism, starting as far back as the Roman Empire. It was arguably the greatest empire the world has ever known, but its collapse led to fragmentation and competing kingdoms, which persisted throughout medieval times and even after the Risorgimento. You and I both know that even today regional divides remain strong. The South will never have the resources or industry of the North. It's part of our identity as Sicilians to hunger for the love of our Fatherland."

He nodded and clutched his cup. "But that's changing, isn't it? I mean, look at what il Duce has done for us to make things more efficient. He's restored our pride in national identity."

She shifted her eyes. "I suppose we'll see what happens."

They sipped their coffees and waited for the rain to stop. Then they walked, hand in hand, to their street and stopped. He didn't want the moment to end.

"I'll see you soon?"

She squeezed his hand. "I'll have my Mamma make you some dinner. How about you come over tomorrow night?"

"I'd like that."

NINETEEN
JULY 1942

Annalisa glanced to her left as she and her mother descended the Spanish tiled stairs to the sycamore-shaded sidewalk. Sam's Model A sat in his driveway, and she knew he must be sleeping in. She would definitely not find him at Queen of All Saints Catholic Church, where they were headed.

A large cream-colored crucifix sculpture separated four sets of windows above the church's wooden front door that opened to face her high school. It was as if Jesus was always there to remind her of her sins, ones she couldn't bear to bring up when her mother dragged her along for confession.

She'd lied to her mother more times than she could count on both hands. And she was certain the Lord would look down on her for the number of times she'd ditched class. That was, of course, if there really was a Jesus... or God for that matter.

Ever since she placed Mario's *cornicello* around her neck, she hadn't felt like wearing her cross. For one thing, there would be too much gold. She knew the old Italian ladies liked to load up on their crucifix and saint pendants, but she didn't care to pretend anymore. She blamed God for everything that had happened to her family.

Her mother was quite the opposite. She'd come home from her cleaning-lady job, and pull out her rosary before even changing out of her uniform in seemingly endless rounds of novenas. She clung to her precious beads as if that was going to change something. It was as if she were suspended in animation, so fixed in her old ways and focused on the past.

Someone had to face the future. And Annalisa knew that had become her role, something she increasingly resented.

At least she had Sam. He offered a chance to escape from her problems, the nightmares that haunted her, and the dreams that could never come true. That, and the fact she found herself mesmerized by his pale blue eyes, which seemed to twinkle when he smiled at her. And in those moments, nothing else mattered.

As she and her mother settled into the wooden pews and Mass started, she found herself drifting far beyond the vaulted ceilings as she reflected on her and Sam's most recent trip up to the cemetery.

"I brought you something," he said, as he parked the Model A in the gravel lot.

He reached into the backseat and pulled up a bulging, dark brown rucksack. After unlacing the top, he slid his hand in and extracted a glass bottle, dripping with condensation.

"Beer?" Her mouth dropped open. "Where and how did you get it?"

He flashed a grin under his freckled cheeks. "I have my ways."

He pulled out a metal bottle opener and slid off the cap before extending the beer in her direction.

"What if someone sees us with it?" She quickly grabbed the bottle and placed it at her feet.

He shook his head as he pulled out his own bottle and opened it. "Relax."

He took a long sip and exited the car with the bottle in his right hand and his rucksack over his shoulder. Annalisa grabbed her bottle and scrambled out the door.

"This way we have something to drink along the way." Sam took another sip. "Go ahead, have some. It will cool you off."

Annalisa had tried wine and even tasted her father's grappa, but she'd never come across a bottle of beer at her parents' apartment. She raised the bottle and sniffed. It reminded her of the scent of baking bread.

She took a tentative sip and spat it out. "Yuck. It's bitter. How can you drink that stuff?"

Sam laughed and downed the rest of his bottle, which he tossed on the ground.

"Don't do that." Annalisa reached down and picked up the bottle. "We don't need to leave more evidence that we've been drinking."

He took it from her hand, lowered his rucksack, and stuffed it inside. She heard a clang as he did so.

She gasped. "Just how much beer did you bring?"

"Enough for the two of us." He slipped his arms through the straps so it rested on his back. "Relax. It's just beer. My old man used to drink the hard stuff."

He tugged at the ends of the pack's straps, and Annalisa sensed tension in the air. She raised her bottle again to fill the silence.

She took a long sip and gulped the beer down. "I guess it's not so bad." The sun was beating down on them, and after she finished her bottle, Sam handed her another. She was glad to have something to quench her thirst, and the more she drank, the less bitter it tasted.

By the time they reached the graveyard, she was asking for a third beer. It made her head feel light, like she could drift away on the summer breeze.

Sam motioned for her to join him on the pepper tree branch. She giggled as she slid next to him and slumped against his shoulder.

"You're drunk as a skunk," he laughed.

"Am not!" She tried to sit up straight. "So, anyhow, where did you get the beer?"

"At the store." He slid his arm around her. "I just told them I was buying it for my old man, and they didn't care."

"Did your father drink a lot?" She held back a hiccup.

Sam dropped his arm, and he readjusted himself on the branch. "I don't want to talk about it."

She nodded and straightened. Sam never wanted to discuss his father. She thought about her own father and how much she missed him. She couldn't imagine being separated from him as long as it seemed Sam had been. The thought brought tears to her eyes.

"Annalisa, what's wrong?" Sam slid down from the branch and stepped in front of her. He took her hands. "I didn't mean anything by what I said. It's just, well..."

She shook her head and swallowed a sob. "No, it's not that. I was just thinking about my Papà and..."

"You really want to see him again." Sam squeezed her hands.

She nodded, suppressing a hiccup.

"Maybe we can go see him some time." He ran his thumbs over her knuckles.

"But how?" she asked. "He's all the way down in Texas."

Sam smiled and tapped her knees. "I've got a car, don't I?"

She shook her head. "It's awfully far. And besides, my mom would never allow it."

"Well, I, for one, would love to take a trip along old Route

66. Imagine all there is to see. Sure beats Contra Costa County!"

She smiled. "Isn't that the truth? Well, it's a nice thought. There's only so much that can be said in his short letters. It'd be nice to just sit down and talk to him again."

"You're lucky, you know," Sam said softly.

She nodded and slid down from the branch. He pulled her toward him and began to kiss her, gently first, and then with hunger. She reached up to run her hands through his carrot-red hair, and as she did, he slid his hands up her blouse and began stroking her chest.

She dropped her arms, and he drew back. "Sorry, I got a little carried away."

"It's OK." She placed her hand on his chest. "You just surprised me, that's all."

She leaned in for a kiss, and he pressed her against the tree trunk as he ran his lips down her neck and began unbuttoning her blouse.

She hiccupped loudly, and he stopped. "What a way to kill the mood," he chuckled, breaking away.

The church organ pulled her back to the present, and her mother nudged her. "Why aren't you singing?"

She looked over her mother's shoulder and flipped her hymnal to the right page. But she didn't feel like following along. She was tired of doing what her mother told her. She was sick of having to manage their affairs. More than anything, she wanted to be with Sam. She closed the hymnal and slid out of the pew.

"Annalisa!" her mother hissed, but she didn't stop.

She walked down the side of the church to the back and slipped outside. It was a beautiful, sunny day. She wandered back to her street, pausing on the sidewalk in front of Sam's house. She didn't want to bother his mother, so she went to his window and tapped three times.

Sam pulled back his yellowed curtain and met her eyes with a wide grin. He lifted his window.

"What are you doing here?" he asked. "I thought you were at church."

She smiled. "I was, but I got bored."

He grinned back. "Want to take a ride?"

She nodded.

"Great. Meet me at the car."

Annalisa clutched the wrought-iron railing as she slowly climbed the tiled steps to her apartment. She fished in her pocket for her key and realized she must have dropped it along the way. She giggled as she sat down in front of her door and leaned her head against it.

"Drunk as a skunk!" she laughed and then hiccupped.

So, this is what it felt like to be Sam, to not care, to just be. For too long she had tried to do the right thing. In the past seven months, she had to grow up fast as if she was the parent to her enemy alien mother with her Old-World ways. She was tired of trying to make sense of a mixed-up world that stole her brother and imprisoned her father. Didn't she deserve a break? Wasn't she, a teenager, allowed to have some fun?

She heard footsteps on the other side of the door.

"Annalisa, is that you?" her mother called out.

She sighed and rose to her feet. "Yes, Mamma."

Her mother opened the door and leaned into the hallway.

"Where have you been?" She sniffed the air. "You've been drinking alcohol!"

"So what?" Annalisa said a bit too loudly.

Annalisa heard Mrs. Ruffrano's door open below them. "Is everything all right?" the landlady called up.

"Get inside!" Mamma grabbed Annalisa by the shoulder and pulled her into the apartment.

"Yes, everything is fine," she called down to Mrs. Ruffrano before closing the door.

Annalisa rubbed her shoulder as she faced her glaring mother. "That hurt," she whined.

"Good." Mamma put her hands on her hips. "It will give you something to think about next time you decide to run off to God knows where with God knows who and get drunk. Did it even occur to you that I would be worried about you?"

Annalisa stared back at her mother. "I'm tired of caring. I'm done."

Mamma scowled at her. "After all we've been through. What would your father say?"

Annalisa clenched her fists. "He'd understand. You never did. You talk about how much you miss him, but you barely spoke to him while he was around. It's like you were jealous of what Mario and I had with him. You're just a bitter old woman stuck in the past. Not like Papà. Papà got out and did something with his life."

"A lot of good that did him," Mamma snapped. "Now go to the room. I'll sleep on the couch. I don't want to see any more of your drunk face tonight."

"Fine." Annalisa stomped down the hall. She slammed the door behind her before collapsing on her bed in tears. No wonder Mario had left. Living with her overbearing mother was miserable—especially without having her father there as a buffer. She drove Mario away. Her father joined that stupid club to get away from her, too. She knew it had to be true. And now both of them were gone, leaving her behind. She screamed into her pillow before releasing a hiccup. Then she laughed. At least she had Sam on her side.

TWENTY
AUGUST 1942

Sicily

Dinner at Vittoria's apartment quickly became an evening routine. He'd pack up his paint supplies and bring them to the paint locker before heading home to change for supper across the street.

He sat in the dimly lit dining room across from Lorenzo and next to Vittoria while petite Signora Ferrante flitted between the kitchen and the long oval table, her silvery hair pulled up in a messy bun, making sure he had enough food. She then loaded him up with a sack to bring home.

"Mamma, he's not going to starve between now and tomorrow's dinner." Vittoria laughed.

One evening, Signora Ferrante asked him to help her with the dishes.

"You go spend some time with your brother," she told Vittoria.

And Alberto suddenly felt nervous.

He brought a stack of plates to the kitchen and found

Signora Ferrante standing there with her hands on her small hips.

"Young man," she said with a stern and steady voice. "I would like to know your intentions."

He swallowed and looked down at her. "I have the best intentions."

"Good." She nodded. "So, what are your plans with my daughter?"

He'd thought of it often. "I would like to marry her someday."

She stared at him with a frown, her hands still positioned on her hips.

"Someday? And you would take care of my daughter?"

"Yes, Signora Ferrante."

He felt his mouth dry.

She continued to stare, and suddenly her lips curled into a smile. "Then you have my permission to ask my daughter to marry you."

"Thank you, Signora Ferrante." He exhaled in relief.

"So, when will you ask my daughter?"

He took a deep breath. "With your permission, Signora Ferrante, I'd like to bring her to meet my family first."

"And you are visiting your family on Sunday, is that correct?"

"That's correct." He nodded.

"Yes." She patted him on the cheek. "You have my blessing."

Vittoria held Alberto's hand as they stood on the platform in Palermo Centrale, waiting for their train.

She wore a white peplum blouse with a navy-blue pleated A-line skirt, and he knew she'd dressed up for the occasion.

"Tell me what your family's like." She released her hand to fix her hair.

"They're just your typical family. Why? Are you nervous?"

"Of course, I'm nervous." She laughed. "I've never met a man's family before."

"Then I should be nervous. I've never brought a woman home before."

"Not ever?" She gave a little smile.

"Never."

He drew her in for a kiss.

The train arrived, and they boarded, Vittoria carrying a sack of black-market-purchased food that Signora Ferrante had sent with them.

They watched as people got on and off as the big city buildings gave way to the fields and, finally, views of the sea.

"So, tell me about this place, Isola delle Femmine." Vittoria leaned on Alberto's shoulder. "Is it true the island had a women's prison?"

Alberto laughed and lowered his head onto hers. "The truth is we're not entirely sure. The prison story is probably just a legend. My father says the name more likely comes from the area's links to Byzantine General Euphemius or the Arabic word *fim* or 'entrance,' which described the *tonnara*."

Vittoria squeezed his hand. "Now you're the one teaching the history lesson."

When they rolled to the stop, Alberto pointed to his father and Cristina, the only people on the platform.

They exited and met Papà's warm and proud embrace. "Welcome to Isola delle Femmine. I've heard so much about you."

"Thank you." Vittoria smiled at Alberto. "I'm happy to meet all of you."

"Here, let me take that." Cristina reached for the bag. "Is this what I think it is?"

"Olive oil and flour," Vittoria said.

"My mother will love you!"

Alberto smiled. He was glad his sister was already hitting it off with Vittoria. They passed the Church of Maria Santissima delle Grazie, and Papà told Vittoria about how Alberto had served there as an altar boy and about the time that Alberto had fallen asleep during Mass while kneeling at the priest's side.

Vittoria laughed. "I can't wait to hear all of your Alberto stories."

They arrived at the apartment to the smell of garlic and anchovies.

"Mamma is cooking *pasta chi vruoccoli arriminati*." Cristina grinned.

"Sit down, sit down." Mamma emerged from the kitchen in a red apron.

Once everyone was seated, she served pasta with sautéed cauliflower topped with anchovies, raisins, pine nuts, capers, and toasted bread crumbs.

"Mamma, you shopped the black market for us?" Alberto knew the answer.

"It's a special occasion." She smiled.

"It looks delicious," said Vittoria.

Everyone turned to Papà, who led the table in grace.

"And I'd like to make a toast. To Vittoria for being a source of light in these dark times for our son."

Everyone raised their glasses and sipped wine before digging into supper. Everyone except for Alberto. He cleared his throat, and the table turned to him as he stood.

"Everyone, I've brought Vittoria here because she is—as you say, Papà—the light in my life."

He paused and looked down at Vittoria, whose pale brown eyes shone.

"Vittoria? Will you marry me?"

Vittoria burst into tears. And for a moment, the rest of the table looked uncomfortable.

But then she spoke. "Yes, Alberto. I will marry you."

And his family cheered.

"Praise Jesus, our son is going to get married." Papà clapped his hands.

After dinner, Mamma stopped Alberto before he joined the others in the living room.

"Son, I have something for you."

She brought him to her bedroom, where she opened a dark wooden box and pulled out a gold ring with a single round ruby.

"This was your Aunt Maria's ring. She gave it to me before they left for America. In some ways you remind me of her... Anyway, I want you to give it to Vittoria."

Alberto picked up the ring and held it in the light. "It's beautiful. Thank you, Mamma."

She hugged him. "I am so proud of you."

Later, after they'd boarded the train and waved goodbye to his family from the window, Alberto reached into his pocket and, when Vittoria wasn't looking, put the ring into the palm of her hand.

"It was my aunt's."

She slipped it on her ring finger with tears in her eyes.

"This is all really happening, isn't it?"

He nodded. "You asked me what I planned for my life. While it's hard to plan in war, I am happy to know you will be my wife."

He took her newly ringed hand and kissed it. Just as he had inherited his uncle's netting shuttle, now Vittoria had his aunt's ring. Now they were both connected in a way to two people who had broken free to embrace their own future.

"You truly are the light in my life."

She was, after all, his beacon of hope, something he needed to get through the bleaker, more frightening days. It was fitting she was a teacher for she'd taught him how to love. But it was more than that. Vittoria had a sense of purpose, a conviction he admired and wished to share in his own life. It was as if she'd been placed in that window to guide him.

He ran his finger across her smooth palm, so delicate for someone with such grit. She'd shared some of her lesson plans, and one stood out: a question of whether one could truly escape the weight of the past. She'd reflected on the valor of Giuseppe Garibaldi, who led the charge of Italian unification, guided by the philosophy that confronting outmoded divisions would lead to a more stable future. Could they possibly escape past mistakes and embrace their own destiny?

TWENTY-ONE
AUGUST 1942

Dodd Field, San Antonio, Texas

Two months passed since Vincenzo said goodbye to his tent-mate Satow. Theirs had been a brief friendship, forged by necessity. It was too hot and cramped a space to share with someone he disliked. And the two had bonded over their Alaska adventures with stories of whale sightings and fish tales. But after just a couple of weeks, the so-called Issei, the first-generation Japanese, received orders to ship out to a camp in New Mexico.

Another four men, all German, were added to the tent, crowding the already stifling setting. For the first few weeks, Ernst did his best to translate the other men's German. Vincenzo even learned a few German phrases, so he could thank his tent-mates and greet them. But as the summer grew hotter, he lost his patience. They weren't trying to learn Italian; why should he struggle to be understood?

He found himself withdrawing and even ignoring their invitations to play cards. Soon, it was clear Ernst had given up. The man began speaking solely in German. But in a way, Vincenzo was relieved. It was simply easier to avoid speech when every hot breath added to the steamy interior. And after days of lying around, waiting for the meal bell to ring, there was only so much to discuss.

It reminded him of his efforts to squeeze his messages back home to the regulated twenty-four lines. He chose not to complain to his family about the unpleasant air and his lack of sleep. And unlike Bella Vista, food certainly wasn't worth writing home about. It was all about the "economy of words," as Mario had once so simply put it. His son had made the statement in reference to a poem he'd shared with Vincenzo—something by a gentleman named Auden.

"Listen to how he packs so much meaning into just four stanzas." Mario explained that stanzas were sections of the whole poem.

Then he read something about stopping all the clocks and sounds of the telephone and barking dog—essentially so the right mood could be set for mourning. In fact, the whole poem seemed pretty somber. But there was a passage about planes writing in the sky along with people releasing birds with black bows around their necks.

It made Vincenzo think back to the air show and the hundreds of carrier pigeons that were released in San Francisco during the Golden Gate Bridge groundbreaking ceremony nearly a decade ago. Those birds had nothing to weigh them down; they were released into a bright afternoon so full of hope and promise for the future. He'd wanted that more than anything for his children—for them to soar unencumbered by the hardships so many Sicilians faced post-war.

He remembered the way the birds had formed a ring above before finding their way together. Was his family still circling without him there to lead the way? Or were they now too weighed down by the black bow of mourning to truly take flight?

He searched his overheated head for the last line, something Mario had underlined on the page. And then he remembered: "For nothing now can come to any good."

At the time, he'd urged his son to read happier prose. Instead, he'd seen the boy grow more frustrated with his homework, more restless as they sat in the boat, waiting for the fish to come. But they never came fast enough, and now he knew his son yearned for something more—just as he had so long ago when he left Sicily for California.

He'd raised his concern with Maria, who took it upon herself to introduce Mario to Bible passages. She'd given him a rosary for his eighteenth birthday. The Lord only knew where that ended up.

Maria had fastened a black bow around her neck a long time ago—before Mario's death. She'd made the decision not to learn English or leave the apartment much, tethering her to her circumstances.

He remembered the Saint Peter's key cake he'd given her. If only it had unlocked paradise rather than the limbo she'd endured, waiting all those years for his battle-weary return. Did she resent him as she cooked and cleaned and disciplined while he spent his days drifting away? Did she regret the choice they'd made?

He'd more than made up for all the time he lost with the kids, but it came at the cost of neglecting their mother and her needs. He never asked her what she wanted from life. She'd made one of the greatest sacrifices, and over time, he'd taken her for granted. Now she was back in that limbo state—all because he joined a club and put his extra energy into giving back to those less fortunate back in Sicily. Perhaps charity should have started at home—his Pittsburg apartment.

He let himself fall backwards onto the stiff cot so it creaked beneath his diminished weight. Above him the tent roof sagged in the thick, heavy air. All he wanted to do was sleep, anything to escape the oppressive heat and lack of conversation.

Maybe after a nap, he could write down a few coherent thoughts, practicing the economy of words, while saving his family from the less pleasant details that would only add to the weight of those black bows they now wore around their necks. Better yet, perhaps he'd awake to news of a rehearing. It could happen. After all, even an internee could dream. They couldn't take that away. Could they?

TWENTY-TWO
SEPTEMBER 1942

California

Annalisa giggled. Sam was making faces at her from where he stood at the end of aisle two

"If I didn't know any better, I'd say he was flirting." Mr. Reede set down a box on the register counter.

Annalisa laughed harder.

"Well, you're certainly Miss Giggles," the store owner said. "Just make sure you aren't laughing in front of the customers."

"I won't, Mr. Reede."

"Good girl." He smiled over his shoulder as he carried the box to the storeroom.

"So." Sam placed his hands on the counter. "Did you tell your Ma about studying?"

Annalisa nodded. She had, in fact, fibbed to her mother that she would be studying at a classmate's house that night. Sam hadn't yet told her why she had to tell the lie. All she knew was that he had brought the car today.

"Good girl." Sam imitated Mr. Reede's higher voice.

She was not at all a good girl lately. She'd skipped geometry so many times she was sure she was going to flunk. Pretty soon, it'd be the same with history, which was the period after. But when it came to riding with Sam, she just couldn't say no.

"So, when are you going to tell me?" She twisted her horn charm.

"How about we just drive and find out? It's part of the adventure, right?"

She loved his spontaneity and appreciated that while he couldn't care less about school, he was diligent with work.

Mr. Reede returned from the storeroom. "Th-th-that's all, folks!" he stuttered like Porky Pig.

Annalisa took off her apron and handed it to her boss. And Sam followed.

"Thanks, Mr. Reede," she said as the two of them exited the store.

As soon as they were out the door, Sam pulled out his box of cigarettes and lit one for her. She puffed dramatically, imagining she was Greta Garbo, as they walked to his dusty blue Model A. Then she dropped the cigarette and stubbed it out with her toe before slipping into the passenger seat.

Sam revved up the engine, and they took off, speeding down the streets. She thought about their relationship. She often counted on her fingers just how long they'd been a couple: about six months now. There was something about Sam. He made everything seem easier if not more thrilling. She'd cried a lot less, and when she did break down, he'd listen while offering a shoulder. She'd never had a friend like him, someone who didn't seem to judge her or eye her as different. He didn't care who her parents were. With him, she belonged.

"Hey, we're in Pittsburg." She looked out the window, suddenly aware of her surroundings.

"That's right." He slowed to a stop in a quiet neighborhood near the harbor. "Here we are." He opened her door. "My lady?"

She took his hand and climbed out.

"But why Pittsburg? What's here?"

He led her up a walkway to the door of an apartment. And she was surprised when he swung open the door.

"How'd you do that?"

"I picked the lock earlier this week." He winked.

"But whose apartment is this?" Her voice raised in alarm.

"Some Italian." Sam waved his hand. "They sure aren't here anymore."

She peered into the dark entrance. "How'd you know they were gone?"

"The newspaper had their picture and address."

Annalisa remembered those papers. For two straight weeks, the county paper had featured photographs and the names and addresses of all the Italians who were kicked out of Pittsburg. Her mother's picture was among them.

"But it was someone's home." She shook her head. "That's breaking and entering."

"Sure, it is." Sam grinned. "But no one's going to catch us. Come on, what are you afraid of?"

She followed Sam into the apartment past Palm Sunday fronds woven into a cross above a painting of Jesus into a dark living room lit by the glow of the moon out the window. She could make out a blue velvet couch and a matching blue-and-white rug.

Sam plopped down on the couch and motioned for her to join him. She hesitated, then sat down beside him.

"Think about it: No one's going to show up." He patted her thigh. "Just pretend it's our house."

She couldn't see but imagined his blue eyes sparkling.

"I'll be right back," he said. And he left the room.

She wasn't so sure about this place. It just felt wrong. But she knew she couldn't tell Sam that and ruin his fun.

"Look what I found." He held up two bottles and handed one to her.

"Go on, drink it. Don't be so worried."

She pulled the cork out and tilted her head to take a deep sip.

"Yuck!" She spat the rancid wine all over the rug.

"Oops, I guess that one must have gone bad." He took a sip from the other bottle before passing it her way. "We can share this one. It's pretty good."

She took a swig. "It's grappa. My Papà loves grappa."

"Hey." Sam laughed. "That sorta rhymes."

She took another sip. "It does. Doesn't it?" She passed him back the bottle.

The two laughed heartily and suddenly fell silent. She could tell he was looking at her.

"You're so pretty." He stroked her cheek.

She giggled. "It's nearly pitch-black in here. You can't see me."

"That's not true. I see you, and you're beautiful."

He handed her the bottle again, and she took a big gulp.

She was feeling lightheaded. She liked the way she felt.

He began to kiss her. She closed her eyes and let him kiss her deeper.

She ran her hands through his hair, and he started to unbutton her blouse.

"Hey." Her body tensed.

"Don't worry. We'll go slow."

He kissed her again, and she felt him fumbling with her bra. She stopped him and then took it off herself.

He kissed her breasts and pulled her closer, his hands slipping down the waistband of her skirt. Suddenly, he was on top of her, running his hands all over her. She kissed him back, hungrily.

"Do you want this?" he asked.

She said nothing, instead reaching down his trousers.

Before she knew it, he had entered her. She didn't push him away. She watched him in the shadows, thrusting into her. And she knew only that she wanted more.

In that same moment, he stopped and rolled over on the couch next to her, breathing heavily.

"You stopped?" she asked timidly. She wondered if she'd done something wrong.

"I finished." He took her hand.

"Was I... all right?" she stammered.

"You are incredible."

They lay there for several minutes in a sweaty embrace, their bodies still warm from their shared heat. The air was thick with a salty scent intermingled with the underlying smoke she'd come to appreciate. His firm chest rose and fell in a peaceful rhythm. She traced her finger along his outstretched arm, running it along the hairs and rougher patches, so different from her smooth skin. She checked her necklace. The horn amulet was still there. She certainly felt lucky, but it was more than that, wasn't it? There was a feeling of safeness; she was grounded.

"What time is it?" She curled into his firm chest, reluctant to leave.

He held up his wrist in the moonlight. "It's after eight."

"Jeepers!" she said. "I need to get back home now."

"Come on, relax." He ran his hand through her hair.

"Do you want to explain to my mother?" She pulled her clothes back on.

"All right." He zipped up his pants and straightened his shirt.

They rode back in silence, and when she entered her apartment, she briefly wondered if she looked any different now.

"So, do you feel prepared for your history test?" her mother asked.

"I do, Mamma. Very much prepared."

TWENTY-THREE
SEPTEMBER 1942

Camp Forrest, Tullahoma, Tennessee

The train's closed shutters glowed, indicating that it was morning. Vincenzo had been aboard for more than thirty hours, anxiously awaiting arrival at a new camp.

He could feel the train start to slow until it jolted him forward at its stop. The guards aboard rounded up the prisoners, pushing him out onto a platform. There, he and the other dozens of men were met by troops, who herded them like animals into the backs of trucks mounted with machine guns.

Squeezed between four Japanese men, he could feel each bump in the road as the vehicles sped off.

The trucks entered the barbed wire gates and rumbled through a dense forest before they stopped in front of a row of ten green wooden huts that faced a second, identical row of ten huts. The two men in the front of the truck walked to the back and let the internees out.

"Single file," barked a young man with heavily pomaded hair, and when at first the men did not line up, he and several other men began shoving them into place so there were five single-file lines of men standing in what formed rows. One by one, each row of five men was rounded up and delivered to one of the huts.

When it came time for Vincenzo to be delivered, he looked to his right and left and saw two Italians and two Germans he'd not yet met. A soldier with wavy brown hair motioned for them to follow across sharp gravel to the hut's entrance.

The interior of the hut was just as spartan as that he'd lived in at Dodd Field. The beds were bare save for a folded blanket and a green uniform at the foot; there were no sheets or pillowcases.

"You are to put those uniforms on," said the man who'd led them into the hut. "Breakfast is after reveille."

The five men sat on their claimed cots in silence, staring at the concrete floor. Then Vincenzo rose, turned toward the wall, and began changing into the green button-down shirt and matching pants. The other men stood and followed quietly in suit.

There was soon the sound of a bugle. Vincenzo followed the other men as they trudged outside, across the gravel, following other men who knew where the mess hall was.

He waited in line between his Italian roommates and tried to make conversation.

"We were at Dodd Field together. Ernesto and Fino, right?"

The men nodded.

"Vincenzo Aiello."

"Well, at least the food looks good." Ernesto shifted his chocolate-brown eyes to the serving counter. "I don't know about you, but I'm famished."

A mess hall server slopped a scoop of scrambled eggs on each of their metal trays alongside a slim piece of bacon.

Vincenzo spotted the German roommates and signaled for them to join them.

One of the men shook his head, and the two sat elsewhere.

"What's wrong with them?" Vincenzo asked, gesturing in their direction.

Fino shrugged his muscular shoulders as he settled in his seat across from him. "They sat near me on the train. Talked in German the whole way. So, how long have you been behind barbed wire, Vincenzo?"

He counted on his hand. "About nine months now. You?"

"I was taken from San Francisco in February." Ernesto pushed a black curl from his forehead.

"They got me around the same time in Los Angeles." Fino dug into his eggs.

"That's about when they made my family leave our home." Vincenzo nibbled at the bacon. "They evacuated a third of our city. Can you imagine?"

"They didn't make my family move." Ernesto swished his fork through the yellow clumps. "They just had to get some silly passports, with their photographs and fingerprints. This government. I'll tell you; I should have stayed in Pisa."

"The way they rounded us up." Fino pounded on the table. "For no crime. What kind of government does that?"

"And they accuse us of Fascism," Vincenzo said. "So, what did they get you for?"

"I am... was the editor of an Italian-language newspaper." Ernesto took a bite. "Sure, we had editorials about Mussolini. He was doing good things, making the trains run on time and whatnot. Even Roosevelt praised his efficiency. But then Americani changed their minds."

"They accused me of writing a letter praising Mussolini." Fino shook his head. "I didn't write any letter like that. And then they had to go and bring up the Balilla and the Avanguardisti. As if we had any choice but to join the Fascist youth!"

"I was a member of the Ex-Combattenti." Vincenzo took a sip of water.

"Thank you for your service." Ernesto raised his glass. "I was too young to join the war."

"Thank you, but apparently being a war veteran makes you a Fascist." Vincenzo shook his head. "I left the country two years before the March on Rome. I didn't know anything about Fascism except what I read here in the papers."

"Well, if nothing else, being an internee is a ticket to seeing the United States." Fino waved his hand dismissively.

The three finished their breakfast and headed back to their hut. The air in the tent was thick with the musty stench of damp canvas coupled with the pungent musk of unwashed clothes. A single bulb hung from the center, casting shadows on the wooden beams and illuminating the two Germans crouched in the corner, fixated on something on the floor. The taller of the two, with closely cropped dark hair, held an upside-down glass in a tensed hand. The other fair-haired, slightly stocky man peered down at his side.

"It's a black widow," the fair-haired man muttered in English, presumably for his audience. His voice held a mix of wonder and unease.

"Got her." The dark-haired man slammed the glass hard onto the wooden floor.

"She could have bitten us in our sleep," the first man said over his shoulder to the others.

"So, we Italians have met." Vincenzo's eyes shifted to the trapped spider beneath the glass. "Who do we have to thank for catching the spider?"

"Karsten." The darker-haired man slipped a piece of paper beneath the glass and carried the trap out the door.

"Alrich." The man with the lighter hair stood, smoothing out his stiff green pants.

Vincenzo and the other Italians introduced themselves.

Karsten returned to the group and plopped down on the

edge of his cot. "Those spiders were all over the bathroom, too. They're bound to bite someone one of these days."

"So, what's there to do here?" Vincenzo scanned the tight quarters. "Aside from getting bitten, of course."

Karsten ran his hand through his hair, which looked redder as he sat in the dim light. "The guards said that we will start what they call Americanization classes tomorrow."

"What does that mean?" Ernesto asked as he and the other Italian men silently claimed bunks and sat down.

"We are supposed to work on improving our English and learning the Constitution," Alrich explained.

Ernesto chuckled and slapped his thigh. "The Constitution that allows the government to round people up in the middle of the night without fair trials?"

Karsten nodded his head as he reached for a cigarette. "*Ja*, that one."

Just then, they heard the pitter-patter of rain on the wooden A-frame roof, filling the silence of their shared contemplation. Vincenzo leaned back against the hut's frame and a cold drop of water landed on his head before dripping in his right eye. He wiped it with his cotton sleeve before turning to see its source: a leak through a gap in the corner.

"Look at that." He scooted away. "Water's coming right in."

He pushed his cot out of the way. Water was beginning to pool into a puddle on the floor. The other men stood and moved to the other side of the hut, away from the leak.

The rain came down harder.

"We need to do something." Vincenzo watched the water spurt through the gap. "I'm going out there to find someone to help."

"I'm coming with you," said Karsten.

The two men marched out the door into the downpour and ran through puddles to the nearest guard station.

"Yes?" The guard glanced up from a magazine.

"Our hut is flooding," Vincenzo panted. "We need to patch up the wall or something."

"It will stop raining soon." The guard looked at his watch as if he knew the time the rain would cease.

"You don't understand." Vincenzo raised his voice. He was losing his patience. "Water is bursting through our wall into our hut."

"Just wait it out and try to stay out of the water." The guard turned back to his magazine.

The two prisoners returned to the hut, defeated.

"What did they say?" Fino asked.

"They won't help us," said Vincenzo. "Come on, let's gather our blankets. We don't need them, anyway."

"You want to mop up the water?" Alrich raised his eyebrows. "But it's still coming out of the wall."

"I'm a fisherman." Vincenzo smiled. "I'm used to cleaning up standing water. Help me stuff these in the gap."

The men got to work, shoving blankets into the space between the wall and setting aside a couple to mop up the floor. When they were done, Vincenzo and Karsten went out to replenish their blanket supply.

They returned to find the other men sound asleep. The air was thick with the scent of wet canvas mingled with damp earth and body odor. Vincenzo curled up on his own bare, soaked cot and listened as the rain slowed to a drip and birds began chirping again in the trees. Then he drifted off to sleep.

TWENTY-FOUR
SEPTEMBER 1942

Palermo, Sicily

Alberto took Vittoria's hand as they strolled along the path of Foro Italico, overlooking the deep azure waves of the Tyrrhenian Sea and the crenellated rooflines of Castello Utveggio atop Mount Pellegrino.

"My Mamma used to take us here in our strollers." Vittoria smoothed the skirt of her sky-blue shirtwaist dress as it caught in the light breeze.

"What was it like growing up in the big city?" Alberto asked.

"I never really thought much about it... I guess I'm just used to seeing more people."

"And cars."

"Yes, we do have lots of cars." She pointed toward the street. "But we have places like this, too."

Alberto paused and slid onto a bench, and she joined him. His eyes settled on an oleander shrub with vibrant red blossoms poking out from dull greenish gray leaves. Beyond it, closer to the sea, two identical boys stood, one holding tight to the string of a bright yellow kite, while his twin pointed at its blue streamers.

Alberto watched as the boys' mother nodded at two passing men in dark uniforms, aptly called Blackshirts, the paramilitary wing of the Fascist Party. Their presence patrolling the park added to his sense of security, making him feel nothing could penetrate the bubble of calm that surrounded them.

"It's pleasant here," he said. "The city's so spread out; this brings everyone together."

Vittoria nodded. "It's been here since the sixteenth century. The viceroy wanted the people to have their own walking path."

"Just like how il Duce..."

"Let's not talk about him." Vittoria's eyes shifted.

"Why?" Alberto raised his brows. "He's done a lot of good for this country. That's someone who's really brought us together as a people."

"But he also brought us into this war, one we weren't prepared for." Vittoria tapped his thigh. "Think about it. How many people have died? All those ships that have blown up. All of that could have been avoided."

Alberto had thought about it—a lot. After all, he had been tasked with cleaning up after several of those ship explosions. And while there hadn't been any bombings since March, he still had nightmares about the sights and sounds with which he'd grown uncomfortably familiar. He reached into his pocket and squeezed his wooden net shuttle. Perhaps it had kept him safe.

"You're right." He stood. "Let's not talk about it."

She rose with him, and they continued their stroll in silence, absorbing the colorful sights and sounds of people who had survived terror and continued to endure rations but were, at that moment, happy to embrace a beautiful autumn day.

A seagull shrieked as it soared above and then dive-bombed into the sea to catch a fish. The sun was setting, its orange light seeming to dissolve in the contrasting water, while streaks of pastel pink splashed across the sky.

Alberto wanted to hold on to the moment, like a pearl in a shell, for here he was with the woman he loved in one of the prettiest places in Palermo.

"There's so much history here," Vittoria said as they passed statues along the path.

Alberto nodded.

"Do you think this war will end soon?" She turned to him.

Alberto thought about it for a moment. "The Pact of Steel is dominating the Allies. It can't be much longer."

"I hope you're right." She clasped her hands as if in prayer. "I worry about children like Lorenzo... my students... our children. What will become of them? What world are we leaving them?"

Alberto nodded. He'd grown up listening to stories about how his father and uncle had clashed with the Austro-Hungarian army on snowy mountainous terrain. There was hand-to-hand combat and poisonous gases. For a young boy, it was the stuff of nightmares. And yet, there were times when—with toy soldiers in his hands—he'd reenact the Battle of Vittorio Veneto, which led to the surrender of 300,000 Austro-Hungarian soldiers and ultimately, the collapse of the Habsburg Empire. In his years marching with the Fascist youth, he'd spun wooden guns in preparation for future war victories. There was always the question of when, not whether, one would be called to fight. Up ahead, a man stood at the center of a small crowd, speaking about the need for unity in Italy. His voice carried despite his slight stature.

"*Viva Italia!*" someone shouted.

"It is also a time for us to find peace and end this war." The speaker raised his fist. "Our people have died. Our families are suffering."

His audience stopped cheering and exchanged nervous looks. Just then, a group of Blackshirts swooped in to listen.

The crowd began to rapidly disperse.

"We should go," Alberto whispered. But before they could leave, one of the Blackshirts spoke.

"What's all this?"

"I am just a citizen voicing my concerns," the man said loudly.

"We'll show you what to be concerned about." Another Blackshirt shoved the man to the ground.

Alberto stood frozen, watching the Blackshirts pile onto the man. Together, they pummeled his face. Then they stood, leaving the man bleeding on the ground.

"Does anyone else have something to say?" A Blackshirt dusted off his pants. "Any concerns?"

The other Blackshirts laughed and patted each other on the back as they left the scene.

"Are you all right?" Alberto crouched down beside the protester.

"How can they do that?" The man spat out blood. "What kind of country is this where we must suffer in silence?"

"You have to be careful," Alberto said. "You don't know who's watching."

He and Vittoria left the park, shaken by the sudden realization of just how oppressive the regime had become. He had seen the poster where a man dressed in full military regalia held his index finger to his lips beside the message, "Beware! The enemy is listening!" He wondered how many other people, like the man in the park, had been brutally silenced for simply stating the obvious, the facts that the government wished to sweep under the rug. And he wondered if there could ever be peace in a place rife with such violence.

As they walked back toward Borgo Vecchio, Alberto thought about his family back in Isola delle Femmine, particularly his father. Amid the Isonzo battles, his family's patriarch had fought for God and country. He forged a legacy of honor and bravery, which he'd instilled in his children's hearts. And yet, when the moment came, Alberto found himself paralyzed, unable to stand up in the face of injustice and oppression.

"You've been quiet." Vittoria frowned as they neared their street. "I can tell that really affected you."

He nodded and sighed. "I should have said something. I could have done something. It wasn't right what happened."

"But who knows what those men would have done to you." Vittoria took his hand.

"I feel like I've been drifting." He waved his hand. "Like I'm powerless with all this uncertainty, but I know I can do more. It reminds me of the nets my father would drop. They really got beaten up in the waves and with the fish swimming through. But there was this strength woven in them. I want that to be a part of me, too."

Vittoria squeezed his hand and nodded. "It is. And when the time is right, you'll find a way to stand up. I know you will."

He swallowed, reached his other hand into his pocket, and squeezed the wooden shuttle, and silently vowed to make the right decision next time.

TWENTY-FIVE

DECEMBER 1942

"Hail Mary, full of grace," Annalisa prayed alongside her mother on the kneeler. "The Lord is with thee. Blessed art thou amongst women and blessed is the fruit of thy womb, Jesus."

It was the Feast of the Immaculate Conception, and although it was a Tuesday, her mother insisted that she take the morning off to pay tribute to the Madonna at Queen of All Saints Catholic Church.

The sun poured through red, yellow, and blue stained glass windows in the vaulted ceiling, illuminating what was an otherwise dark day for Annalisa: the day after the anniversary of the date that would live in infamy, Mario's death, and a year since her father's arrest. She was supposed to be strong for her mother. That meant no skipping out to hightail it to the cemetery with Sam when it was all she wanted to do. But how could she be strong when she had to leave church twice to run to the bathroom to throw up?

It must have been something she ate, she thought, although

she'd not eaten since the night before. Maybe food poisoning just took that long to affect your system.

After Mass, she waved goodbye to her mother and ran across the street to school. But instead of going to class, she slipped into the ladies' room. She was sick again.

She flushed the toilet, and when she emerged from the stall, she made eye contact in the mirror with her chemistry teacher, Miss Chambers.

The older woman nodded at her. "Are you OK?"

"It's nothing... just food poisoning." She adjusted her horn necklace.

"You look pale," Miss Chambers said. "I think you should see Mrs. Thompson."

In her year at Mount Diablo High School, Annalisa had never set foot in the school nurse's office.

"I don't know..."

"Come on, let's go." Miss Chambers took Annalisa by the arm.

They walked down the hall and descended the stairs to a room just to the left of the gymnasium. And Miss Chambers knocked on the door.

Mrs. Thompson, an older woman with silver hair and thick glasses, wearing a white cap and matching jumper, answered and led them into her tiny white walled room. There was a single metal cot with a thin mattress on one side and wooden desk and chair on the other.

Miss Chambers introduced Annalisa, and the nurse nodded. "How can I help you?"

"Well, I don't want to speak for Annalisa." Miss Chambers flashed a smile. "But she seems ill."

"What kind of illness?" Mrs. Thompson frowned.

"Annalisa, why don't you describe what you feel?" Miss Chambers placed her warm hand on Annalisa's shoulder.

"It's nothing; I just threw up." Annalisa stared down at the gray-and-white tiles.

"And just this once?" Mrs. Thompson raised her gray eyebrows.

Annalisa shook her head. "Well, no, actually. Earlier at the church and a few times last week."

"I see." Mrs. Thompson nodded. "And how would you say you've been feeling lately? Any fatigue?"

Annalisa thought about it. "Well, yes. But it's probably just because I work after school."

"But you've been feeling more tired than usual?" the nurse asked.

Annalisa tugged at her horn charm. "I guess so. Maybe I ought to cut back on my hours?"

"Miss Chambers." The nurse turned toward the teacher. "I'd like to examine Annalisa."

"Oh yes." Miss Chambers's eyes were on Annalisa. "Of course. I'll leave you to it."

She turned and stepped to the door before stopping and turning her blonde head. "Take care."

"Thank you." Annalisa was suddenly frightened by the prospect of being alone with the nurse.

Mrs. Thompson closed the door. "So, tell me, Annalisa. When was the last time you experienced your monthly cycle?"

Annalisa blushed. "I'm not sure. It's been a while."

"Think about it. Did you have your cycle last month?"

She bit her lip. "No, I guess not."

"I see." The nurse nodded with a frown. "Young lady, it seems to me that you may be pregnant."

Annalisa was stunned. "What?"

"Pregnant," Mrs. Thompson repeated. "I'm going to have to telephone your mother."

"No." Annalisa shook her head rapidly. "Please don't do that. I'm sure there's some other explanation. I've just been going through a hard time. It's the anniversary of my brother's death and my father... Well, he's away in Tennessee..."

The nurse sat in a wooden chair. "My dear, I'm afraid all signs point in the direction of pregnancy. That is, of course, unless you can tell me you haven't engaged in sexual activity."

Annalisa's cheeks were hot. "I better go. I have class."

She ran out of the nurse's office and raced to her English class. She was fifteen minutes late, but she'd at least done her reading assignment. Still, she found herself unable to concentrate. Was she actually pregnant? She looked down at her belly. If she was pregnant, just how long could she hide it?

"Annalisa?" Miss Miller asked. "How would you characterize Elizabeth Bennet's interactions with Mr. Darcy?"

Annalisa's mind went blank. She stared at the teacher in silence.

Miss Miller shook her head. "Perhaps she showed prejudice?"

"Yes." Annalisa nodded.

"And can you tell me why she might have shown prejudice toward Mr. Darcy?"

Again, Annalisa stared at her teacher.

Miss Miller sighed. "Mary? Can you help Annalisa out?"

"Well, it all started when Mr. Darcy refused to dance with her."

"Good, Mary. Annalisa, does that help?"

Annalisa nodded, feeling her cheeks burn. The bell rang.

"Annalisa, may I have a word with you?" Miss Miller asked.

Annalisa went to the teacher's desk as students filed out of the room.

"It seems to me that you have not completed your reading assignment." Miss Miller tapped a pencil.

"I did read it. It's just..." She felt herself tear up.

"It's OK." Miss Miller patted Annalisa's arm. "I know Jane Austen isn't for everyone. But between not reading and not showing up to class, I might not be able to pass you this semester."

"But I did read it," she said. "And I promise I'll come to class more often. I've just been sick a few times. That's all."

"All right." Miss Miller sighed. "I'm counting on you."

Annalisa felt her stomach flip. "Well, I should go. I don't want to be late for my next class."

She scurried out of the room and headed down the hall to the bathroom, where she again vomited. Now she was certain. The nurse was right; she was pregnant.

Annalisa had just stepped out the door when she saw Sam standing in his driveway.

"You weren't at work last night." He furrowed his brow. "Are you mad at me?"

"No, I... was sick." She twisted her horn amulet. "It was nothing really."

"Are you sure?" He tilted his head.

"Yeah, it was nothing." She scraped the toe of her saddle shoe against a crack in the sidewalk.

"Swell! Well, I thought we might want to sneak out this afternoon. Hit the cemetery with me?"

She shook her head. "I'm not sure that's such a good idea. I have a chemistry test."

She didn't, but she definitely needed to be seen by her chemistry teacher. After all, the woman had been genuinely concerned for her health. She owed her something, that was for sure.

"Darn. Well, maybe tomorrow then?"

She swallowed. "Maybe tomorrow."

That evening, she told Mr. Reede she was sick again. She needed to tell Sam what was going on, but they had to be alone. She couldn't keep this from him any longer.

. . .

The next morning, as she walked to school, she heard a horn beep, and she stopped. It was Sam, leaning his head full of messy red hair out the window of his Model A.

"I guess you were sick?" he asked, and for the first time she noticed rust on the car's pale blue exterior.

"I guess." She bit her lip.

"Want to go to the cemetery?" He grinned.

"Sure." She shifted her eyes and slowly stepped into the car.

They sped off and up into the hills while she replayed a speech in her head. She was going to break it to Sam slowly, ask for his support, and then what? What if he dumped her? She tightened her grip on the door handle.

They rolled to a stop at the parking lot. When they got out, there was a slight breeze, and she was glad she'd worn her sweater.

They started the hike to the cemetery, making small talk, when Annalisa suddenly felt like throwing up.

"Excuse me." She vomited over the trunk of an oak tree.

"Are you OK?" Sam asked. "Something is wrong."

She wiped her mouth and turned away. It wasn't supposed to happen this way.

"All right, so I'm pregnant." She looked down.

"What?" Sam's blue eyes couldn't have appeared wider.

She sighed. "I said I'm pregnant."

"How do you know?" he frowned.

"Mrs. Thompson thinks so."

Sam shook his head with a laugh. "The school nurse? What does she know?"

Annalisa glared at Sam. Why was he making this so hard?

"I've been sick for the past week, and I missed my monthly cycle. I think she's right."

Sam stopped walking. "I think we better go back to school."

"Fine." She turned and picked up speed.

Sam didn't say anything on the walk back, in the car, or when they parked at school. He simply nodded, and she left and ran to history class.

Later that day, he avoided her during their entire work shift.

She was furious. She needed support now more than ever. So, she decided to tell her mother.

But it wasn't that easy. She couldn't seem to find the right way to broach the topic.

Finally, she decided after a week that she'd waited long enough. She would tell her at dinner. It happened to be a night when her mother had fixed her favorite *cavatelli alla marinara*. She took a few bites of the chewy semolina noodles and paused.

"Mamma, I have to talk to you about something."

"What?" Her mother was still wearing her cleaning lady uniform under her red-checked apron. "You don't like *cavatelli*? Do you know how hard it is to get flour these days?"

"It's not that, Mamma." Annalisa tugged at the horn amulet. "It's just... Well, you see... I found out... I'm pregnant."

Her mother slammed her fork onto the table. Her heart-shaped face seemed sharper in the dim kitchen light as she glared across at Annalisa, a muscle twitching near her temple. She clutched the fork like a weapon with her other hand pressed down, stretching the edge of the sauce-stained tablecloth.

She frowned and shook her head, dropping the fork on the table and rising from her chair. Its legs scraped against the worn kitchen tiles, a grating sound, like a blade sharpening on a stone. Her knuckles were white as she grasped the wooden seat back.

"I must have misheard my daughter, because she told me she is having a baby." She slowly enunciated each word as her nearly black eyes seemed to bore holes through Annalisa's face. "My seventeen-year-old daughter."

She yanked off the apron as if it was suffocating her and twisted it with both hands as though she wanted to wring it dry. "Get out," she whispered.

"What, Mamma?"

"I want you to leave," she said louder. "Now!"

"But, Mamma..."

Annalisa felt a chill in the coldness of her mother's gaze.

"No." The woman shook her head. "You are not my daughter. My daughter doesn't fornicate. That's not how I raised my children. After everything I've sacrificed, you go and stain the family name."

She dropped the apron to the floor with a gasp. "How could you?"

Annalisa stared back at her mother, tears stinging her eyes. What had she expected would happen? Her mother had always been full of criticism and judgement, so tied to her Old-World ways. Still, this was different. Never—even in her harshest moments—had she seen such fury and bitter disappointment.

It made Annalisa think back to the *Jack Benny Program* she'd heard before the Pearl Harbor announcement, the one that featured his spoof on Dr. Jekyll and Mr. Hyde. A switch had flipped. One moment she was sweet and doting, serving Annalisa her favorite pasta, but the next, she was nearly unrecognizable, her voice like a razor, sharp and cutting.

Her mother stomped on the apron. "I want you to leave."

Annalisa got up and pushed her chair back into the table with shaking hands. Tears streamed down her cheeks. She ran to their room and began frantically tossing clothing into her backpack along with all her savings. Where could she go? She didn't have any real friends except for Sam. And now Sam didn't want to have anything to do with her.

She grabbed her hat and mittens, zipped up her coat, left

the apartment, and started walking—she wasn't sure where. Then she thought about the vacant apartment back in Pittsburg. She headed to the Greyhound bus station.

After checking the bus schedule, she saw one was headed out in just a couple of hours. So, she fished out her copy of *Pride and Prejudice* and returned to the world of Elizabeth Bennet, who seemed to be preoccupied with marriage. And she wondered if she could ever find a husband who would accept her after she'd been pregnant out of wedlock. She was halfway through the book when the bus rolled in.

It was quiet on the street when she got off in Pittsburg at around 9 p.m. She wasn't sure how far the bus was from the apartment where she'd gone with Sam, and it occurred to her she wasn't completely certain of the address. She panicked. Then it dawned on her. She definitely knew one address of a vacated apartment: the one she'd shared with her family.

So, she headed that way. It was chilly outside, and she could see her breath. She passed a street sign and looked up. It wasn't far now.

She walked for a good hour. It hadn't seemed to take that long when she'd left with her mother. Perhaps it was because they'd been talking. And now she didn't know when her mother would again speak to her.

It was dark when she finally arrived at her old apartment, and she knew the door would be locked. She searched the front yard for something, anything, to break the door window and found nothing. Then she thought about her hardback book. She took the book in her hand and slammed it into the glass pane as hard as she could. It cracked, and she slammed the book again, this time breaking through the glass but also cutting her wrist. Blood dripped as she reached through and turned the doorknob.

She opened the door, applying pressure to her cut as she walked into the living room. Suddenly, the light turned on.

"Who are you? What are you doing here?" a man wearing pajamas shouted at her.

"Oh!" She turned and ran out the door.

Annalisa ran all the way down the street to the harbor where she saw a bench and sat down. Panting now, she examined her hurt wrist. It was still bleeding. Blood had soaked through her sleeve and had dripped on her skirt.

Tears streamed down her cheeks. There was nowhere else to go, and it was getting late. She reached up and tugged at her necklace. And then she remembered her father's boat.

Half expecting it to be gone, she walked down the pier, but there it was. The little wooden boat swayed in the water as she climbed in. There, she opened up the fish hold. Even after a year, it still smelled of fish. She would try to ignore it, she thought, as she lay down a few sweaters and fashioned a little nest. It was surprisingly warm. She snuggled up and stared up at the sky. She saw a shooting star and made a wish. *Bring Papà home.* And then it occurred to her. She didn't have his address. How was she going to continue to write to him? She'd have to go back to the apartment to get it. And maybe when she returned, her mother would take her back. It was her last thought as she drifted off to sleep.

She shivered when she awoke in the pale light of dawn. After sitting up, she readjusted her sweater nest, so it covered her better. But it was no use. It was too cold, and besides, she was already awake. She scooped up her sweaters and loaded them back into her backpack. Then she set out for the Greyhound station.

But when she arrived at her apartment at 8 a.m. her mother made it clear that she had not changed her mind.

"I told you to leave." Her mother stood with crossed arms. "Go live with the man who did this to you."

"But I can't, Mamma."

"Go live with that friend, Mary, of yours you're always

studying with." She waved her hand. "Go anywhere. Just leave!"

Annalisa grabbed and pocketed her father's last letter. Then she ran out the door. She was going to catch a train. And then? She wasn't sure.

"Hey!"

Sam stood in front of his house, but she ignored him and continued walking.

"Wait," he called out. "Where are you going?"

"To the train station." She turned to him and met his eyes as she twisted her charm.

He pointed to her wrist. "You're hurt."

"Yeah? So what?"

She stomped off.

She was two blocks down when she heard a familiar sound: Sam's Model A.

Sam leaned forward and cranked down the window. "Hop in," he muttered, his voice tight caught between frustration and concern.

"No." She continued walking.

"Annalisa, I'm sorry," he called after her, and she stopped. "I got scared. Is that why you're running away?"

"No," she said. "My Mamma kicked me out."

He raised his eyebrows. "Kicked you out? Because you're pregnant?"

She released a hollow laugh and nodded. "Can you believe it?" With trembling hands, she wiped her eyes. "I don't know what I'm going to do."

"Let me drive you somewhere."

She met his blue eyes. "You'd take me? Where?"

He laughed. "Where were you headed?"

"Anywhere but here."

"Say." He lit a cigarette. "How about we go on that Route 66 trip I've been itching to take? We don't even have to go all the way to Chicago—just stick to the south where it's warmer and take it as far as this car will drive. You and me with no one stopping us!"

She nodded slowly. "You'd do that? But what about that new gas ration? I mean, there's only so many miles you're allowed to go."

Sam frowned for a moment. "Got any cash?"

"Sure do. Why would I leave home without it?"

"I know someone who sells extra ration cards. He's gotta have one of those X stickers... you know, the kind that traveling salesmen have? It gives you unlimited gas miles—unlike the measly four gallons a week with this one." He pointed to his car's A sticker.

"But that's buying from the black market... Won't we get caught?" She shook her head. It was outrageous. "Besides, who's going to believe we're traveling salespeople?"

"Rules are meant to be broken." Sam winked. "And for all they know, I might have a couple dozen encyclopedias in the trunk."

She paused, hand still on the door, and looked at him. Maybe he was right. After all, the ration was so new there were bound to be gas stations eager enough to take their cash that they wouldn't care how they'd gotten their sticker.

"Will you get in already?" Sam sighed. "It's getting cold."

Annalisa smiled and slid into the seat. As long as they were hitting the road, she didn't care what Sam did to get them there.

Annalisa leaned into the window as they headed south, passing through vast tracts of farmland. She saw almond trees, citrus groves, rows upon rows of grapevines, and stinky garlic fields between wide open spaces grazed by cattle.

It was taking a lot longer than they'd anticipated because they had to keep stopping for her to vomit or use the bathroom.

Sam rolled into a gas station where he was greeted by a blue-uniformed attendant and pointed to the new X sticker on the window. Annalisa felt her heart pound as the man stepped up for closer inspection.

"Ain't seen one of those yet." The attendant furrowed his ash-colored eyebrows.

"My wife and I sell Bibles, sir," Sam said with a mock drawl. "Tell me: Have you accepted Jesus as your Lord and savior?"

The attendant adjusted his cap. "Yes, sir. But I don't need no Bible. It's all up here." He pointed to his forehead.

Sam turned and winked at Annalisa as the man refueled the Model A.

"Will that be all?" the man asked after Sam had paid him.

"Actually, I'd like to buy a map if you've got one." Sam leaned out the window.

"Where you headed?" The attendant wiped his hands on his stiff pants.

"All the way to good ol' Tennessee." Sam rested his arm on the open window. It was almost casual except his fingers drummed lightly against the door.

The attendant nodded and adjusted his greasy cap. "I'm sure you'll find a lot of folks there whose souls need saving. I've got a map of all the major roads running across the country. You wait right here."

He slipped back into the store. The scent of gasoline and tobacco clung to the cool air. Annalisa gasped, releasing the breath she'd held, and turned to Sam with a smile. "Selling Bibles with my wife?" She raised her brows. "Seems he bought it."

Sam grinned but kept his eyes glued to the store door. "Sure did. Now, shush. Here he comes."

The attendant strolled to the car with something folded in his hand, a map, which he displayed at the window. Sam reached out to take it while slipping him another bill.

"Praise Jesus!" Sam called out as the man turned away.

The attendant tipped his cap. "Yes, sir," he called over his shoulder. "Praise the Lord!" Annalisa shook her head, willing herself not to laugh as Sam put the car in gear.

After a few moments on the road again, she burst into giggles, an explosion of nerves and relief. Sam shook his head and, with a smirk, pulled over. It was ridiculous: the notion of selling Bibles, pretending to be married, and driving off wherever the road would lead. She didn't want to think about it too hard, wanted to avoid fear of the unknown, and it was easier to laugh anyway.

Sam unfolded the colorful map, smoothing it out against the steering wheel.

"See this here?" He traced a line with his finger.

"That's where we're headed," he said. "The next biggest city is Bakersfield. We could stop there if you'd like."

She dropped her hand, which had been gripping her horn amulet, and relaxed into the leather seat. "Sounds swell."

Sam pressed his lips together for a moment and then met her eyes. "Listen. When we get there, we're going to need a place to stay. It's best if we continue to pretend we're married, OK?"

She nodded, again grasping the amulet between her thumb and finger. Twisting it made its edges warm from her touch. "Just call me Mrs. Wells." The words felt strange on her tongue, but in a way, oddly right. As Sam started up the car, her mind began to race. What if— What if it wasn't all pretend? Could she really be Mrs. Wells? The thought was thrilling but also a bit unsettling.

The sun was just about to disappear when they rolled through downtown Bakersfield and stopped at the first motel Sam spotted.

Annalisa stayed out in the car as Sam went in, and then they went upstairs to the room together. It had yellowed walls and reeked of cigarettes, but they didn't mind. Both were exhausted from their trip and quickly slipped into the bed with a sagging mattress.

It was warm in the bed and the pillows had a slightly musty smell. But she was happy to be lying there next to Sam.

"Sam?" she whispered into the darkness.

"What?"

"Thank you."

He rolled on top of her and planted a kiss. "Don't mention it."

TWENTY-SIX
DECEMBER 1942

Camp Forrest, Tullahoma, Tennessee

Hon. Edward Ennis
Alien Control Unit
Department of Justice
Washington, D.C.

Dear Sir: I am writing to you once again on the anniversary of my confinement to ask once more for my release or a rehearing. It is unfortunate that my involvement in a veterans' group would be seen as dangerous to the United States. I have committed no crimes and still wish to one day be a citizen of this country. I hope you will take my matter to heart and let me return to my family and work.

Respectfully yours,
Vincenzo Aiello

"Would you look at that?" Fino pointed at little flakes of snow gathering on the windowsill where he and Vincenzo stood.

"I haven't seen any snow since Missoula." Vincenzo's breath fogged the glass. "And that's now a whole year ago."

"We sure didn't see too much of that back home, hey?" Ernesto lifted a scraggly brow.

"Only in the mountains." Vincenzo nodded. But instead of Sicily, he was thinking about Pittsburg and the snow that sometimes fell atop Mount Diablo just to the south. He'd borrowed Giovanni Scotto's car and drove up there one year with the children. Mario and Annalisa built their first snowman. Annalisa was only four, but Mario was ten and eager for more snow play that season. It never panned out. There was always something else to do over the winter weekends. But the look on both kids' faces—particularly Mario's—when they saw the white powder was truly priceless. Vincenzo wondered if Alberto and Cristina had ever seen snow. No doubt Alberto would have had a similar expression to Mario's. What different lives the two boys had led.

"Another year in captivity," Fino sighed. "Is that what we have in store for us?"

The door slammed, and the men turned around. Karsten and Alrich had returned from an excursion in the forest with armfuls of pine boughs, which added a bright fragrance to the otherwise musty interior of the hut.

"What are you doing with all of those branches?" Vincenzo asked.

"We are going to build a Christmas tree." Karsten set down his load. "You can help if you'd like."

"Build a Christmas tree?" Vincenzo chuckled.

"*Ja*. We will tie the branches together with string from the canteen." Alrich demonstrated.

The two Germans began to pile the tied branches in a corner. When they were done with their waist-high pile, it did almost look like a little tree.

The idea of putting a tree in your living room seemed so

strange to Vincenzo. He had seen trees on display in stores, but had never put one up in his apartment as it wasn't part of Sicilian custom. Instead, Maria would set up a large porcelain *presepio*, the nativity scene he'd given her for their first Christmas in the U.S. She'd place it on a shelf positioned next to their radio. Throughout December, he could look forward to gazing at the brightly colored Mary and Joseph and sets of donkeys, oxen, cows, and sheep while sitting back to listen to American carols. They'd wait until December 24 to place Baby Jesus between his parents, and then, on January 6, the Epiphany, they'd place the Three Wise Men.

He thought back to his home in Isola delle Femmine and the intricate, hand-painted *presepi* displayed in store windows. He remembered the time he and Costanza had tried their hand at making one out of papier mâché. The siblings had taken some of their mother's flour and mixed it with water before dipping shredded newspaper into the homemade glue. He'd never forget the detailed way Costanza mixed blue with just a touch of white to capture the perfect cerulean shade for Mary's cloak. For his part, he fetched dried grasses from their yard and laid them down on a little cardboard box where they set their version of the Christ Child on Christmas Eve. The baby's head was slightly misshapen and a tad too large for his stick-figure-like little body. But once framed by the cadre of animals, his parents, and the three nearly identical-shaped wise men, he was the perfect focal point for the celebration of his birth. Or so said Vincenzo's mother.

"Now what?" Fino asked.

"We decorate it." Karsten clapped his hands. "It will be just like back home."

He took a piece of blue letter paper and folded it into a series of tight triangular folds. Then, he carefully ripped a diagonal line from the bottom left corner to the middle of the right edge before unfolding it to reveal a five-pointed star.

"Where did you learn to do that?" Vincenzo marveled at the simplicity and ingenuity.

"At my last camp I bunked with a Japanese man," Karsten placed the star on top of the makeshift tree. "He used to make all sorts of shapes by folding paper. He didn't even need scissors. He called it origami."

"What sort of shapes?" Ernesto asked.

"Here, let me show you." Karsten took another piece of paper. "This one is supposed to look like a bird."

He folded the paper in half diagonally to form a triangle, which he then unfolded. Next, he folded it diagonally in the opposite direction and again unfolded before turning the sheet over. Folding the paper in half horizontally, he pressed down the crease before unfolding once more. Then he folded the paper in half vertically, pushed in the crease, and unfolded yet again.

"See where the creases intersect at the center?" he asked, and the other men nodded. "You just bring the top corner of the paper down to that point, so it forms a smaller square like so."

He held it up for the men to examine. Then he folded the left and right corners of the top layer of the folded paper diagonally to the center crease so that he created a shape like a kite.

He showed the men the top point. "Now I just fold this down to form a smaller triangle. See that?"

Then he folded the little triangle in half upwards, making sure to reinforce the crease.

"And now I open these flaps just a bit and fold them along the creases. See? Now they are wings."

Vincenzo nodded as he watched the bird materialize before him as Karsten folded the bottom point upwards, tucking it into a pocket the flaps had created.

"And you just pull the wings apart like this." Karsten gave it a little tug. "*Hier ist es!*"

The men collectively oohed and aahed before trying their

hand at their own birds, using letter paper. When Vincenzo was finished, he realized he must have missed a step, because his little bird didn't quite look like it could take flight. Still, he followed the other men by tying it with string and affixing it to a branch.

"What now?" Fino asked when they'd decorated the tree with the star and birds.

"Now we sing." Karsten grinned at Alrich. The two launched into a rendition of "O Tannenbaum" for their Italian audience.

"We have our own song," Vincenzo said after the Germans had finished. He began singing "Tu scendi dalle stelle," and the other Italians soon joined him.

"What does it mean?" Karsten asked.

"It is about Jesus coming down from the stars," Vincenzo explained. "But yours is more fitting for our lovely little tree."

The men spent the rest of the afternoon teaching each other their respective songs and sharing stories of Christmases past when they were not confined behind barbed wire.

Under the sterile, flickering lights, Vincenzo sat hunched at a long mess hall table, facing another mediocre meal. He poked his tin fork at a rubbery chicken cutlet beside overcooked vegetables. It was certainly not like the meals Aldo had cooked for the internees back in Missoula. His upbeat friend managed to find his place in the face of indefinite imprisonment so far from home and the people he loved while maintaining his focus on Bella Vista, the beauty beyond the barbed wire. For the past year, Vincenzo had tried to emulate that, throwing himself into activities, befriending strangers, and sharing tradition.

He picked up his knife and began to saw into the hunk of meat, beige like the walls. Lifting a forkful to his lips, he considered how and why he still had to find Bella Vista at each stop.

Was it sheer willpower? A sense of desperation? Or was it like during the last war, a promise that he'd meet loved ones on the other side?

Some days, it was harder than others; some weeks, it was nearly impossible. There were moments when he questioned whether Bella Vista was a mere illusion, a trick to play to survive.

He clenched the fork at the plate's side as he mechanically chewed the flavorless chicken. It was sustenance, and he was grateful the government still cared to feed, clothe, and shelter him. He'd endured no torture, just the agony of limbo at every turn.

The mess hall buzzed with muted conversations, devoid of the joy he'd seen among the performers at his first camp. He glanced at Fino and Ernesto, who sat beside him. They had traveled with him from Dodd Field, where he was certain his brain had cooked in the heat.

Somehow, Fino had maintained a similar optimism to Aldo's, considering this experience a chance to see the rest of the United States, the rest of the country they'd left Italy for, a place where they were now only welcome in captivity.

Vincenzo reflected again on that radio program the family had heard the year prior, the morning they heard the initial news about Pearl Harbor. It was a silly show sponsored by Jell-O, but it was also his second encounter with the tale of Dr. Jekyll and Mr. Hyde.

He'd seen the film starring Spencer Tracy with Annalisa at the California Theatre back in Pittsburg, and he knew there was much more to the story. It made him think about how people could have two drastically different sides that shared one body. And, he realized, countries could, too.

The United States had an outward image of being warm and welcoming; in his case, the same nation had rounded up people who traded their sweat to provide food for American families. With every censored or confiscated letter and forced relocation, it could also be cold and punitive.

He wondered just how many Americans even knew the network of internment camps existed. And if they did, why didn't they care enough to stop it? This state of imprisonment was surely unjust and not reflective of the freedom he had been promised. While there were no chains and as of yet no violence, the limbo itself could be similarly torturous, making time seem endless as he lost his faith in justice.

"Vincenzo Aiello?" a guard called to him from the other side of the table. He was a young boy, about Mario's age—or at least the age he would have been.

Vincenzo wondered, if his son had chosen the Army, would he have ended up working in one of these camps? Surely, Mario would have empathized with the men more than this boy, who seemed bothered by the simple task of interacting with an internee. His side part and darting eyes mirrored his disciplined, hurried energy.

Vincenzo nodded, and the guard handed him a piece of mail. It was slim, rectangular, and bore a government return address.

Fino leaned over from his philosophical conversation with Ernesto. "It's not from your wife and daughter?"

"No." Vincenzo's voice rose with a touch of excitement. Could this be his moment? Had the government read his latest letter? Were they finally going to send him home? The thin envelope felt impossibly heavy. He had held out this long.

He tore it open and frowned. "It says I am moving again."

"Where now?" Ernesto asked.

"Oklahoma," Vincenzo said.

"And so," Karsten tapped the table, "your journey continues."

Indeed, it would. Another pin on a map. Another long, tedious trip. Would this so-called journey ever end?

TWENTY-SEVEN
DECEMBER 2, 1942

Palermo, Sicily

When Alberto arrived at the shipyard, Francesco informed him that they'd be broadcasting a speech from Mussolini at noon.

It had been eighteen months since Italy entered the war and almost a year since the nation declared war on the United States. Alberto wondered what il Duce would say this time.

As noon approached, he gathered with the other men around the loudspeaker. He could see in their faces a mix of anxiety and skepticism. He could not blame his fellow laborers for the latter, knowing that their workplace had been a war zone more than once. The promise of another speech did little to reassure them it would not happen again.

The speaker began to crackle, and they leaned in as Mussolini started to speak, first addressing his reluctance even to do so.

"It is my conviction that in time of war, when the cannon speaks with its powerful voice, the less we speak, the better."

He emphasized his belief that actions speak louder than words during war, and there was no need for excessive propaganda. Instead, he wished to provide a political and military report on Italy's involvement in the war for the past eighteen months.

While acknowledging the strength of Russia's military, he asserted that he had confidence in the Axis's ability to achieve victory and reshape Europe. He spoke of America's president, someone he felt had a "diabolical desire for war." And he posited that Japan could not wait for the U.S. to be the first to shoot and instead inflicted upon Americans a tremendous defeat.

He talked about the Anglo-American landing in North Africa, stating it was predictable due to the visible cooperation between American and French officers. And he made it clear that he'd advised Germany to occupy all of France and Corsica to prevent the French fleet from joining the British. He criticized Anglo-Saxon propaganda, which he felt exaggerated the heroism of the French response. He then spoke about British bombings of Italian cities, emphasizing that civilians had been targeted.

It was important, he said, to counter exaggerated reports by providing more accurate accounts of the number of buildings destroyed as well as the total number of killed and wounded. And Alberto listened as il Duce listed the stark statistics of death and destruction, something with which Palermo had become all too familiar through the earlier part of the year. Mussolini shared that more than 1,800 civilians had been killed and more than 3,000 injured since the start of the war. On top of that, casualties included more than 40,000 in the Army, over 33,000 in the Navy, and more than 20,000 in the Air Force. He addressed the number of Italians taken as prisoners of war—more than 232,000 Italians captured—and the 37,000 plus who had gone missing. Then he spoke to the number of homes hit by bombs, singling out damage and destruction in Milan, Turin, Savona, and Genoa, where a combined total of nearly 13,000 residences were hit, and about 400 were destroyed.

But what really got Alberto's attention was when il Duce said, "We must get the population out of the cities, above all the women and children. And we must organize a total evacuation or almost total. It is the duty of all those who can find a place to live far from the urban and industrial centers to do so."

Alberto inhaled sharply as his mind went to the Ferrantes. He didn't want anything to happen to Vittoria, Lorenzo, or their mother. He thought about Isola delle Femmine and how his own family had been spared from the past year's bombings.

Mussolini's booming voice continued with what he defined as a purpose of his address: to weigh in on criticisms from one of Winston Churchill's recent speeches directed at Italy's defense and leadership. He contrasted Italy's commitment to the war effort with Britain's hypocrisy, suggesting that the latter nation's true aim was "to reduce the globe to the state in which India is today" with a "world of slaves in order to guarantee for the British people their five daily digestions."

Then he concluded by urging Italians to fight, not only for the living and the future but also for the dead, so their sacrifice would not have been in vain.

"They, the dead, imperiously command us to fight through till victory," he said. "We obey."

Alberto heard cheers from the other end of the loudspeaker, followed by static. But the shipyard workers seemed more sedate, returning to their workstations in near silence.

He shuffled back to the ship panels he was painting, his thoughts far from British hypocrisy and Anglo-Saxon propaganda. Instead, his mind raced with images of destruction, and he considered the gravity of Mussolini's evacuation recommendation. Each stroke of red paint was another sign of urgency, a reminder of the city's bloodshed.

He looked down at his crimson-covered coveralls and

thought about the lasting stains. They were inherent in his work. So were the nightmares of post-raid cleanup. Not something he would have seen in a job description. For the first time he wondered what it was all worth and if he could ever just walk away.

He could have chosen another path. But then again, it might have landed him in Africa like Franco, separated from the people he loved, or a prisoner of war to suffer untold privations. Worse: He might have served as a grim statistic in il Duce's report, a life cut short, barely worth a footnote in the history of this ghastly war.

He reflected on his carefree childhood summers filled with soccer games and festivals. No matter how often he heard reports of il Duce's conquests and engagements abroad, he could always look forward to another match, another parade, another supper with family. He yearned for that sense of safety and normalcy—if not for himself, for Vittoria. He knew he had to talk to the Ferrantes about leaving. He knew he had to do something before it was too late.

The whistle blew, and he clocked out, strolling through Palermo's streets as if equipped with a new set of eyes. The city bore scars the British Royal Air Force had inflicted in the form of crumbling buildings and still-shattered windows. Then there were the dozens of casualties and thousands more shell-shocked, living in constant fear of future attacks. He thought about how he and the Ferrantes closed the curtains and ate by candlelight each night, the fear of punishment for not observing blackout orders hanging over them just as much as the awareness that one lamp's glow might mean their death in an enemy air raid.

"But where would we go, Alberto?" Vittoria said after he'd broached the topic of evacuation at the dinner table.

"You could go to Isola delle Femmine." Alberto leaned forward. "Think about it. This whole time, my family has been safe from the bombings."

Signora Ferrante shook her head. "Il Duce is asking a lot of his people if we're all just supposed to pack up and head to the countryside."

"Maybe he knows something?" Alberto shrugged. "Maybe there will be more bombings. Just think about it."

"But I have my students to think about." Vittoria crossed her arms. "I can't just leave my job. Besides, what about you, Alberto? With your job at the shipyards, you're in a worse place than we are."

And Alberto knew she was right, but he needed his job. His family, his livelihood, depended on it.

<h1 style="text-align:center">TWENTY-EIGHT</h1>
DECEMBER 1942

Route 66–Highway 64

"Just another hour, and we'll hit Oklahoma City," Sam said as he and Annalisa got out at a gas station.

They'd been following Route 66 for about a week now, sharing the road with logging trucks and sleeping through cold nights huddled in the back of the Model A. There was a patch of heavy snow near Flagstaff before crossing through milder albeit chilly weather in Santa Fe and Amarillo. There wasn't much time for sightseeing beyond what was directly on the route although they did stop at Santa Fe's Plaza to procure two woolen blankets.

Annalisa looked at the map once more. "And Tennessee's not all that far away."

She'd been thinking a lot about her father in the passing days, wondering what it must be like to miss the holiday season without his family. True, her mother would also be alone, but she'd made that choice—not her father. He didn't deserve to be locked away without any end in sight.

"Let me see that." Sam tugged at the map. He ran his finger

over the lines and nodded. "Yeah. That's what we'll do. We'll head to Arkansas today."

Annalisa wrinkled her brow. "Arkansas? But that's off Route 66."

Sam smiled. "And it happens to be on the way to Tennessee."

He put his hand on her shoulder. "Look, I know how much you've been wanting to see your Pops. We'll call it the Tullahoma detour."

She twisted her horn charm. "Are you sure you want to drive all that way for a short visit? What if they don't let us in?"

Sam nodded. "It's part of the adventure. Besides, we're too close not to. We'll just pick up Highway 64 and take that as far into Arkansas as possible tonight. Then we'll head to Memphis, and after that, we'll be in Tullahoma in no time."

Annalisa leaned back in the seat and let herself relax, knowing that Sam was going to take care of her after all. Did this mean he really loved her?

They rode another three hours into Arkansas, arriving somewhere outside the town of Russellville after dark, and Sam pulled into the parking lot of a diner.

"What will you have?" asked a gum-chomping waitress in a pink uniform.

"A plate of biscuits and gravy," said Sam.

"And for you, Miss?"

"We're sharing." Annalisa stared down at her silverware.

They'd taken to eating one meal a day and supplementing it with bread and peanuts they'd bought along the way. Annalisa knew she probably needed more in her condition, but she was also cognizant that funds were limited.

The waitress left the table, and Sam leaned back into the cushioned booth. "You've been quiet. Are you OK?"

Annalisa shrugged as she traced a finger along the rim of her mug. "Just thinking."

"You worry too much. We'll get there just fine." He gave her a half smile as he glanced out the window to the crowded parking lot.

She tugged at her hair. "Ugh. I'm not talking about the trip. I'm... What are we going to do when this is all over?"

Sam frowned. "What do you mean?"

She gasped, then leaned across the table, locking her eyes with his, willing for him to see her need for clarity. "I mean... I'm having your baby."

Sam clenched his jaw as he quickly leaned forward with a sharp inhale. "What more do you want from me? I've taken you halfway across the country." He shook his head. She'd never realized his blue eyes could be so icy. "You always expect more."

Annalisa's chest tightened. His words hurt as if they were piercing through her skin, and she aimed for a steady tone.

"I want more?" She pointed to her belly with a shaky finger. "I didn't ask for this pregnancy. This is your fault, too."

His gaze shifted, and she could tell she had hit him. Was that guilt? There was just a flicker of expression before he seemed to shrink back, crossing his arms across his chest. "I don't need to listen to this."

Then, to her surprise, he rose from the booth, his lips fixed in a hard line. "Why don't you find your own way to Tullahoma?"

"Fine, maybe I will." Annalisa grabbed her coat, slinging it over her shoulder. She stormed out of the diner, her loafers pounding the pavement. Each heavy step seemed to echo her hurt, rage, and the fear she couldn't outrun.

It was cold outside—so cold she could see her breath. She pulled her hood over her head, slid her hands up into her sleeves, and started walking—where to? Away.

Tears ran down her cheeks as she passed the remnants of a cornfield and headed back toward Highway 64.

When she arrived at the intersection, traffic was whizzing past, and she held out her thumb. Car after car and truck after truck passed. No one was stopping. She pulled her horn amulet up to her lips and kissed it.

Suddenly, she heard a beep. She turned to see Sam's Model A.

"Get in," he shouted.

"No." She shook her head. "I don't want anything to do with you."

"I said get in. You're going to get yourself killed standing there with all that traffic."

She looked at the highway and then looked back at the car.

"Fine." She got in and slammed the door.

They were silent for some time while he got back onto the highway.

"Where are we going?" she finally asked. "I thought we were stopping."

"I'm going to keep driving until I get tired. You're welcome to sleep."

She fished out a slice of bread. She was famished. "Want any?"

"I'm good. You need the food more than I do."

She nibbled at her slice of bread, watching the lights of cars headed in the opposite direction.

"I'm sorry," she said quietly.

He nodded. "Yeah, me too."

At some point, she fell asleep. A loud pop and a jolt of the car woke her. She looked at Sam, who was furiously spinning the steering wheel as the car spun around. She screamed, and then the car stopped. But it was facing oncoming traffic. Several horns blasted as traffic halted in front of them.

A man got out of his car and rapped at the window.

"Are you OK?" he asked as other people beeped their car horns.

Sam rolled down his window. "I think I popped the tire."

"We need to get you to the side of the road," The man glanced at the traffic as horns continued to beep.

He waved his arms in the air, and another man emerged from his car.

"We're going to push you," the first man explained. He and the other man went to the back of the car while Sam turned the wheel. People were still blasting their horns, but others got out to help.

With the combined effort of four people and Sam turning the wheel, they were able to get the car to the side of the road.

"Yeah, you definitely blew out that tire." The first man released a whistle. He was an older gentleman with kind eyes. "Got a spare?"

"Yeah." Sam went to the back to retrieve it. Annalisa exited and watched as cars sped past along the highway.

The man cranked the jack to lift the car. "Where are you headed?"

"Tennessee." Sam grasped the spare tire under his arm.

The man paused. "I mean tonight."

"Not sure." Sam shook his head. "Just driving as far as we can."

The man gestured for the spare and Sam handed it over. "Well, I'll tell you what." He switched the blown tire with the new one. "I live in Plumerville. Why don't you kids come and stay the night? It's getting late, and you just had that scare."

"Are you sure?" Sam carried the spent tire back to the trunk.

The man began screwing the bolts in place. "I insist." He

looked at Annalisa. "Besides, it looks like you could use a home-cooked meal. My wife won't mind."

The man, who said his name was Mr. Johnson, gave Sam his address.

When they arrived, Mrs. Johnson went to work, fixing up two extra dinner plates.

Annalisa thanked her.

"It's nothing—just leftovers." Mrs. Johnson pushed aside a loose lock of light brown hair.

Meanwhile, Mr. Johnson made up a bed in one of their bedrooms and fixed up another spot on their couch.

"Our son Riley's just a little older than you two." Mrs. Johnson gazed at them from across the table as they ate their chicken and rice.

"Is he in the military?" Annalisa looked up from her plate.

"Off in the Pacific," said Mr. Johnson.

"My brother was in the Navy." Annalisa twisted her horn charm.

"Is that so?" Mr. Johnson asked. "Which fleet?"

"He... Well, he was at Pearl Harbor."

Mr. and Mrs. Johnson exchanged a concerned glance when they saw Annalisa's eyes well with tears.

"Sounds like you've been through quite a bit, my dear." Mrs. Johnson leaned across and reached for her hand. And Annalisa let her take it.

When they'd finished dinner, Mrs. Johnson passed out towels, and Annalisa and Sam took turns taking much-needed showers.

"You can stay as long as you like," Mrs. Johnson said before the two headed for bed, Annalisa in the bedroom and Sam on the couch.

"Thank you, but we're anxious to get to Tennessee." Sam looked at Annalisa, who nodded.

"Well, sleep on it." Mrs. Johnson smiled. "The offer stands."

The next morning Annalisa awoke to the smell of bacon and eggs. She stretched out in the comfortable bed she'd slept in and sat up. It felt good to be in a home, a place with two loving parents. Did Riley realize how lucky he was?

She dressed and joined Sam and Mrs. Johnson in the sunny kitchen. Mr. Johnson was out back repairing a fence, as chickens pecked at the ground in front of a fallow field.

Mrs. Johnson followed her eyes. "Ben bought this farm thirty years ago. We've got a few hands to help us, but he still does most of the work himself."

"What kind of farm?" Sam asked.

"Mostly soybeans." Mrs. Johnson stood from her chair. "A few peach trees, too."

She started clearing their plates. "So, did you decide what you're going to do?"

Sam looked at Annalisa. "We're going to try to get to Tennessee today," she said.

"I thought you'd say that." Mrs. Johnson opened her pantry. "Well, I've got plenty of food to send along with you."

"Thank you." Sam smiled.

Mrs. Johnson helped the teens load up the car with food. "You kids are welcome to come back on your return trip."

"That would be nice." Annalisa gave her hostess a hug.

"Just in case you don't stop back, can I get your address?" Mrs. Johnson asked. "I'd love to send you some of my peach preserves."

Annalisa jotted it down, and as she did so, she wondered if it was still her home. Each stroke of the pen drew her back to those awful moments—the screech of her mother's chair, the sharpness of her voice, and the pain of her words. It had left Annalisa raw and hurting. She had no choice but to leave, and yet the gravity of it lingered, pulling her back into its orbit. Would she ever go back? Could her mother ever forgive her? Annalisa's hand trembled slightly, and she considered the deeper question: Would her mother even let her back in? She felt an ache in her chest, a jab of guilt that dug into her ribs. It reminded her she was fragile, and so much was still uncertain. How could she possibly belong when everything had fallen apart? She placed a fingertip on her still-small pregnant belly, reflecting on a future she'd never expected.

Meanwhile, Mrs. Johnson kept talking, her voice bright like sunshine on what appeared to be a gray day. She pocketed the piece of paper with the address. "You're getting a belated Christmas card, too!" *Christmas.* They had lost track of the days since they'd been on the road. Soon it would be time to ring in 1943. Annalisa realized she had no present for her father. Perhaps her presence would be enough of a gift. She hoped he wouldn't be too disappointed, that he'd not disown her like her mother. At any rate, she couldn't wait to see him again.

The Johnsons stood in their driveway, waving as Sam started the engine, and he and Annalisa rolled out and headed back to the highway.

They made good timing, stopping only a few times for bathroom breaks and eating lunch on the road. Then Annalisa curled up by the window and fell asleep.

When she awoke, they'd crossed the state line. Sam glanced over to her in the passenger seat. "Welcome to Tennessee!"

They passed through Memphis, continuing to follow Highway 64 all the way to Fayetteville, where they caught State Route 55 and hit Tullahoma by dinnertime.

"It's probably too late for visitors," Sam said. "How about we spend the night here and get up early to see your Pops?"

Annalisa nodded, mildly disappointed. "Sounds good."

. . .

After a night spent sleeping in the chilly backseat, she awoke early and watched the sunrise. It was a brand-new day and one of hope.

Once Sam and she had each scarfed down one of Mrs. Johnson's blueberry muffins, they checked the map against the address on Papà's last letter. Annalisa was even more eager as she saw how close they were.

Her excitement fizzled as soon as they arrived and saw a sign that read STOP beneath the letters for Camp Forrest.

A guard trudged through the ankle-deep snow to the side of the car. "Can I help you?"

"We're here to see one of the internees," Annalisa explained, looking at the bare trees.

The man showed them where to park and brought them to a concrete building where a man behind a desk flipped through pages of internee names.

"I'm sorry." The man frowned. "It looks like Vincenzo Aiello has been transferred."

"Transferred? When?" Annalisa gasped.

The man ran his finger over her father's record. "Earlier this week."

"Where?" Annalisa asked.

"Fort McAlester in Oklahoma. I'm awfully sorry."

Annalisa felt as if the room was spinning beyond her control. Had she ever had a grip? Or was it all a handful of sand? So many nauseating hours of driving, cold nights spent on the road, and meager meals of gas station snacks across endless highways that ultimately led to nothing. The weight of the trip and the miles behind her sagged on her shoulders, and with it, the crushing heft of disappointment.

She hadn't realized just how tightly she had clung to the idea of seeing her father again, of this journey bringing some kind of closure. They should have left sooner. They shouldn't have stopped at the Johnsons' place. If they'd only made different choices—before and during this trip.

Tears blurred her vision, and soon they began to cascade in torrents. It was all too much—this trip, this pregnancy, and the endless quest for something she felt she could never reach. She had lost her brother, her father, her mother—everyone and everything that had once grounded her. Now it seemed like nothing was beneath her; the emptiness would drag her down. What now?

"We drove all the way out here for nothing!" she sobbed.

Sam put his arm around her. "Shh."

"So sorry." The man closed the binder.

Sam pulled Annalisa along with him back to the car.

He opened his map as she continued to sob on the seat beside him.

"What are you doing?" She sniffled.

"We're going to Fort McAlester."

TWENTY-NINE
DECEMBER 1942

Fort McAlester, McAlester, Oklahoma

It had been some time—not since Fort Missoula—that Vincenzo had slept in a real building and one that was not vulnerable to the elements. In this building, a military barracks, he shared a room with twenty-four other men, several of whom snored throughout the night. But he was warm and dry, and it didn't smell like mold. It was the little things that mattered.

He lay there thinking of all the places he'd been, places he'd never dreamed of traveling. In just two days, he'd see the start of a new year, another spent in captivity. Again, he wondered how he got here, shuffled around like a pawn on a board, a number on a ledger, scrawled with an indifferent hand. He was done being bothered by it all. Instead, he felt numb.

There was the sound of the now-familiar reveille, the bugle call that meant it was time to rise. It broke through the sounds of men still snoring, perhaps dreaming of freedom beyond these blank walls and past the barbed wire. The Bella Vista Vincenzo once sought was now so far away.

The men began rising, grumbling as they dressed to shuffle off to the next stage: a new circle of hell.

He slid off his bottom bunk and dressed. Together the men filed out for breakfast. At least he could look forward to another meal.

He dug into his plate of pale-yellow eggs and wondered what this particular camp had in store for him. Scanning the room, he saw what he assumed were mostly Italian faces.

The air was crisp outside after breakfast, but he passed a group of three men, who had already gathered for a game of bocce ball.

"I need a teammate," a man called to him. "Come, join us."

"Cristiano." The man introduced himself. He had a large nose and bushy eyebrows and looked to be in his late forties to early fifties. "And this is Marcellino and Tonio."

"Vincenzo."

"We'll be red," Cristiano said as the other men moved four blue balls to their side.

"Vincenzo, why don't you toss the *pallina?*" asked Tonio, who was tall and slim, with a stoop to his posture. His teammate was shorter, with a slight paunch.

Vincenzo threw the smaller target ball to the end of the makeshift court. Then he rolled the first red ball. It landed about a hand's distance from the *pallina.*

"Good job." Cristiano smiled as he took his turn.

Vincenzo watched the other men roll their balls. Marcellino's knocked into the *pallina.*

"Two points right there," he said.

They played the whole morning. Vincenzo's team lost each round until it was time to head to lunch.

"So, where has the Grand Tour brought you?" Cristiano

asked as they sat across from one another in the mess hall with trays of chicken cutlets and green beans.

"Montana, Texas, and Tennessee before here. How about you?"

"Ellis Island, Fort George Meade in Maryland, and then here." Cristiano sawed his cutlet. "I came from Brooklyn."

Vincenzo took a sip of water. "I'm from near San Francisco."

Cristiano nodded as he chewed. "And before that?"

Vincenzo jabbed a piece of chicken. "Sicily."

Cristiano's amber eyes seemed to sparkle. "Ah, the stone that my Calabria is kicking."

Vincenzo smiled. "Or the stone that stubs your toe."

Cristiano playfully kicked him under the table. "You're a funny man, Vincenzo."

He sighed. "At least I've got that going for me. There's not much else these days. One has to rely on some sense of humor."

They finished their meal and were just walking back to the barracks when Vincenzo heard his name being called over the loudspeaker.

"Perhaps today is your lucky day." Cristiano patted him on the back. "You better go see what that's all about."

Vincenzo walked to the green central building where he'd been summoned and stepped up to a window at the reception.

"They called for me," he said, and the man behind the window looked down at a piece of paper.

"Oh yes, Vincenzo Aiello. You have a visitor."

Vincenzo blinked and tilted his head. Who would come to visit him all the way out in Oklahoma?

"A visitor? Are you sure you have the right guy?"

The man looked back down at the paper. "You are Vincenzo Aiello?"

He hesitated for a moment. What if it were someone from

the government? Would they bring him to the courthouse for more questioning? Perhaps there was news of his release and therefore a good thing.

He nodded. "That's me."

"There are two people waiting in the recreation room. You'll have twenty-five minutes to meet with them."

Vincenzo's heart pounded as he followed the guard, his heavy boots echoing through the dimly lit hallway and into the bright room. The sun poured through the windows and hit his eyes as he entered the place where men borrowed books and played games at scratched-up card tables. It wasn't much to look at, but at one of those tables between a red-haired young man and stiff-backed guard, he spotted Annalisa.

His mouth dropped open as his breath caught. His little girl. But how?

"What are you doing here?" He ran to the table, and she stood, somehow taller than he remembered.

"Papà!" He gathered her in his arms and felt her shoulders shake. Pulling back, he saw tears in her light brown eyes. She looked different—paler with exhaustion lining her face. But it was his precious Annalisa, and she'd come so far to see him.

"Ahem." The guard tapped his watch. "You have twenty-four more minutes."

Vincenzo turned, scowling, suddenly remembering they weren't alone. "I haven't seen my little girl in a year. Can I have some privacy?"

The man didn't flinch. "I'm afraid not." He pressed his lips into a frown on his pasty, rodent-like face.

Vincenzo inhaled sharply but decided to let it go. It wasn't worth a scene. Besides, his little girl was here. Nothing else could matter.

"Papà, I want you to meet someone..." Her eyes shifted as if in hesitation. "Sam, this is my father."

Vincenzo turned to the young man, a boy really. His clothes were rumpled, his red hair was disheveled, and Vincenzo saw dirty nails when he extended a hand. "Sam?" A simple enough name, but from the nervous looks of his daughter, why he was here seemed complicated.

Nodding, Vincenzo took the boy's hand but only briefly before he settled into a chair across from them. Both kids looked tired. Had they really driven halfway across the country on their own? His eyes swept across Annalisa, whose fingers were twisted in her lap. Her shoulders tensed as she took a deep, measured breath. Something was wrong.

"Papà, we don't have much time... I might as well just say it... Mamma kicked me out... I... I'm pregnant."

He must have heard incorrectly. A few men had entered and set up a game to their right. Surely their chatter had gotten in the way. But she tapped on her belly as if in emphasis. His little girl was pregnant?

Vincenzo nearly fell out of his seat. "You're what? But you are just..." He gripped the edge of the table to steady himself, and the men to the right looked his way. Meanwhile the rodent seated to his left stared at his watch.

"Seventeen years old, Papà. I know." Her eyes fell to the tabletop as she spoke. "You're probably disappointed in me."

Vincenzo's chest tightened as he sharply released a breath. His head spun as he tried to piece it all together.

He turned to the boy—Sam. So, this was the one. The one who had taken his daughter's virginity, stole her innocence while Vincenzo was locked away.

One of the card players took a sip of water, and he suddenly felt parched. From where he sat, the sun was directly in his eyes. He squinted to get a better look and assess the mixed-up situation.

Maria knew before him, and he wasn't there to protect Annalisa from her wrath. He could almost picture his wife's reddened face and hear her shout before turning her back on their only daughter.

He'd been absent from it all. Instead of supporting his family, he'd been locked behind barbed wire, biding his time with games of bocce, crafting origami birds, and fantasizing about a Bella Vista that no longer existed.

Had Maria cried afterward? He wasn't there to hold and comfort his wife, soften her anger, and help her understand. Did she have regrets? Did Annalisa?

The government had taken him away, leaving his wife and daughter to navigate a war-torn world alone. This wouldn't have happened had he been home. Instead, here she was, filled with tears, pregnant, and abandoned.

He'd longed to see his family for a year, but not like this. All that time behind fences, and his daughter couldn't be protected.

She was staring at him now, her light eyes imploring him. He had to respond and make this visit worthwhile. If only he could step back into the past, beyond the barbed wire, to fix it all. If only that darn sun wasn't in his eyes so he could really see the person who mattered.

He cleared his throat. "Annalisa, your mother..." How could he justify his wife's actions? "She's proud and stubborn. It must have been... a shock."

His daughter took the boy's hand, but his expression was unreadable. He sure had a lot of freckles.

Again, Vincenzo cleared his throat. He really could have used some of that water. "Your mother loves you like I do."

Annalisa wiped her sleeve across her eyes and pressed her palm into the table's surface. "But she kicked me out, and now I have nowhere to go..."

Vincenzo took her hand and closed his eyes for a long moment of silence. He held onto Annalisa as if it would change what he heard.

"Papà? Say something, Papà."

"What are you planning to do?" he finally asked, opening his eyes to look at her. Her hair was messy, and she had dark circles under her deep-set eyes.

Beside her Sam sat far too quiet and composed for Vincenzo's tastes. This boy should be the one losing sleep; this was just as much his doing. He needed to take better care of her. He was going to have to fix things because Vincenzo certainly couldn't.

"I'm not sure, Papà." Annalisa glanced at Sam. "I thought you could tell Mamma, make her understand."

Vincenzo ran his hand through his hair. That wasn't the solution. It was now up to the boy. Things like this happened sometimes back in Sicily. Like when his cousin got his girlfriend pregnant. He did the respectable thing and accepted responsibility. They raised two beautiful daughters. Things turned out well for them.

He turned to Sam with a frown. "And you? What are you planning to do?"

Sam looked back with wide eyes. "I brought her here. I guess I'll take her back. Maybe my Ma will let me take her in…"

"No." Vincenzo pressed his hands into the table. "You got my daughter pregnant. Now tell me: Are you going to marry her?"

"Marry?" Sam's voice cracked. For a moment his lips twitched into something almost resembling a smile. Was this amusing? Or was the boy simply in disbelief? Vincenzo was uncertain, but it left him incensed.

"Yes. Marry. You did this to my daughter. Now you're going to make it right."

"You have ten more minutes," the guard said.

"Will you shut your mouth!" Vincenzo snapped. He hadn't meant to; it wasn't the rodent's fault that this boy seemed incapable of rising to the challenge. He softened his tone. "Can't you see I am having an important conversation with my daughter and this young man?"

The guard looked down at the floor.

"Yes," Sam mumbled.

Annalisa turned to the boy with a surprised look on her face.

"You will marry my daughter?"

"Yes," Sam answered louder this time with a glare.

"Good boy." Vincenzo nodded with a frown. "It's for the best. I don't want my daughter carrying around a bastard."

Annalisa flinched as if stung. He hadn't meant to further upset her.

She took Sam's hand. "You'll write to Mamma?"

"I'll write to her, but I don't know when she'll get my letter," Vincenzo said. "I want you two to get married. Maybe then she'll feel better about the situation. I know I will."

"Time's up." The guard pointed to his watch.

"Thank you, Papà." Annalisa stood. Vincenzo went to her side.

"I said time is up," said the guard.

"I have to go." Vincenzo hugged his daughter goodbye.

"You be good to my daughter." Vincenzo looked at Sam. "Promise me."

He saw the boy nod before exiting the room. This was a distressing turn of events. Surely his absence was partially to blame. And it wasn't just this past year.

He thought back to all those years he'd taken for granted that family life could continue—even while he spent all that time away, fishing and providing for them in the only way he knew how. His father had done the same; his father had, too. But unlike Annalisa, as the boy, he had the chance to participate. It must have been hard for Costanza. No wonder his sister had married so early.

The light from the window was blinding, but he could clearly see that Annalisa needed him more than he knew. Especially after losing Mario. Even more so with a coming baby. A grandchild.

Maria would surely soften when the little one arrived; wouldn't she? His wife needed him, too.

He had to get back to California and make things right. His family's future depended on it.

THIRTY

JANUARY 1943

Palermo, Sicily

Just after midnight, when New Year's Eve switched to New Year's Day, Alberto heard it: the *pop-pop-pop* of what sounded like fireworks. But then the room shook with the sound of a boom. And he knew it wasn't just revelers ringing in 1943.

His first thought was of Vittoria. He'd wanted to celebrate with his fiancée, but she'd been home sick that day. Besides, with New Year's Eve falling on a Thursday, he'd have to be up early on Friday for work. But at that moment, he worried about her safety.

Another boom came. This time it was louder. He ran into the bathroom and slipped into the bathtub, kneeling with his hands over his head as the apartment shook.

He was shaking, too, and his heart was beating wildly as the bombing continued. Just how much were they unloading?

It had been quite a while—since March, to be exact. He'd thought the worst of the war had passed. And now here it was, and he didn't have a chance to escape to the air raid shelter down the street.

Again, and again and again, the building continued to shake, and the booms did not cease. He reached into his pocket, finding comfort in the touch of the wooden net shuttle he still kept there, even after all these years. He shifted his thoughts to the mundane chore of net weaving. There was a rhythm to it; he was certain. It was meditative, yet productive. He thought about the threads this shuttle must have carried, the ties that bound him to the past, and he somehow felt more secure.

He wasn't sure how long he was crouched in his position; his knees and back had begun to hurt. But he endured the pain, staying still even after the bombing ceased. When he finally moved, he had trouble standing, his muscles stiff and his body aching.

He surveyed the apartment. His window had shattered, and a fine layer of dust lay on the floor.

Then, without thinking, he ran across the street to Vittoria's apartment and pounded on the door. He was relieved when she answered, her body shaking as she collapsed into his arms.

"Come inside," she said between tears. "Mamma won't mind."

Like his apartment, her home was also covered in dust, with glass from windows littering the floor.

Signora Ferrante greeted him. "Come, sit down. Have some water."

Alberto slid into a chair across from Lorenzo, who held a blanket tightly around his body.

"We're all right, aren't we, Lorenzo?" Vittoria placed a hand on her brother's shoulder before sitting down to his left.

"Yes, we are all right." Signora Ferrante's hands trembled as she poured water for Vittoria and Alberto.

Alberto took a sip. "I don't know if I can sleep after that."

"You're welcome to stay here," Signora Ferrante said. "In fact, I insist."

. . .

After a few quiet days, Palermo fell back into its rhythms. People were again on the street, and on Sunday, the soccer team was back on their little field with Alberto blowing the whistle and cheering his players on.

Later that week, on the evening of January 5, he joined the Ferrantes to celebrate Epiphany Eve. After *antipasti* of *caponata*, stewed eggplant salad, and *panelle*, chickpea-flour cutlets with wedges of lemon, Signora Ferrante served *coniglio alla stimpirata*, rabbit cooked in a sweet and sour sauce with olives, capers, and pine nuts. They sang songs and played a card game until it was time for Lorenzo to go to bed.

Then the boy left out a glass of wine for La Befana, the kindly old witch who would visit to bring candy to good children and coal to those who had been naughty. Once he was fast asleep, the ladies and Alberto set to work filling his stocking with dried figs, dates, and *torrone* purchased with saved-up ration coupons.

It seemed like all was well with the world again, and so two days later, he thought nothing of a distant, low-frequency hum. It was a cloudy day, but there was a patch of blue sky in which he could see a cluster of about ten silver planes where the Axis scouts normally flew. He turned back to the panel he was coating, dipping his brush into red paint. He'd seen those scouts every day for the past year.

Just as he was about to apply the color to the surface, he heard a growing roar. The drone of the planes' engines had become more pronounced. The paint began to vibrate in the can, and soon, the ground seemed to shiver beneath the weight of the sound waves. He looked up again, and it was clear these were not the usual scouts.

Within that same moment of realization, he heard a series of high-pitched screeches. He dropped the brush into the can, causing the red paint to splash like blood as he raised his hands to his ears, blocking out the deafening whine that added a sharp contrast to what sounded like a swarm of angry bees. All around him, men were running and diving to the ground. And he watched, frozen in horror, as the planes began to unload bombs on the other side of the port.

Boom! Boom! Boom!

He felt each explosion in rapid succession.

Boom! Boom! Boom!

His heart felt as if it were in his throat.

He was on the ground, digging his fingers into the asphalt as the surface shook as if rocked by a quake. He shut his eyes and prayed the Lord's Prayer aloud, hoping to be delivered from this evil as the bombs continued to explode.

Then, gradually, the roar of the bombers diminished to a distant hum, and an eerie silence settled around him, broken only by the crackling and popping sounds of burning ships and boats. He was suddenly aware of the pungent smell of burning wood, metal, and fuel as acrid smoke billowed into the already overcast afternoon sky.

THIRTY-ONE

JANUARY 1943

Route 66–Route 93

After stopping in Oklahoma City to replenish their food supply, Annalisa and Sam returned to Route 66. They hadn't spoken much since they'd seen her father, and the heavy silence carried the weight of Sam's promise to marry the internee's daughter.

Finally, Sam spoke. "You know I just said yes to keep the peace, right?" He took a drag of his cigarette.

She stared at him a moment as he exhaled. "What do you mean?"

"I mean," he took another drag, "I'm not going to have someone tell me what to do."

Annalisa was stunned. "You mean... you don't want to marry me?"

He stubbed his cigarette on the steering wheel and opened the window to toss it out. "I didn't say that. It's just that I don't want to be pushed around. That's all. I had enough of that with my old man."

She sat there for a moment, staring out the window at the blur of bare trees. "You never talk about your father."

"What's there to say?" Sam fished in his pocket for another cigarette, which he lit. "My Pops just up and left one day. I don't know what happened. He just never came back."

"And he left your mother to raise you by herself?"

"Yeah." Sam inhaled. "Pretty much."

He blew out a puff of smoke. "I'll tell you what, though. She stays out of my hair. She doesn't expect too much from me with no father in the picture."

He took another drag. "Besides," he exhaled. "She's too tired after waiting tables to do much parenting."

Again, Annalisa looked out the window. "So, what now?"

"We figure things out ourselves." Sam tapped his cigarette ash out the window. "Isn't that what this whole trip is about?"

She wondered where he got his courage, the drive to move forward into the unknown. Perhaps it was born from necessity, all those years navigating life as a boy without his father. He was doing the best he could to take care of himself. And on the course of this trip, he'd been there for her, too.

But how far did that go? He seemed hesitant to commit; couldn't marriage, too, be an exciting journey? It seemed to be a logical step forward. And after all they'd endured, she couldn't understand why he'd say no.

"But my father's been through so much. It isn't much to ask... right?"

Sam took another drag. "It's not that easy." He exhaled. "If we're going to get married, it should be when we're good and ready, not because your Pops says we have to. Besides, marriage is about love."

Her throat tensed. What was he saying? Did all of this really mean so little? She was ready to move ahead. Was that naive considering the circumstances?

"But you love me, don't you?"

He took another drag and turned to her. "You know I do."

. . .

They rolled into Amarillo at around sunset, but Sam kept driving.

"I thought we were stopping." Annalisa frowned. She was tired but more concerned he'd fall asleep at the wheel.

"We can make it across the border tonight."

About two hours later, he slowed and turned into what the sign said was Blue Swallow Court in Tucumcari, New Mexico.

"How about we splurge a little and spend the night at this motel?"

And she nodded, silently counting in her head what funds she had left. She handed Sam some cash and waited in the car while he went in.

"You know what day it is?" Annalisa asked as they walked to their room.

"Jeepers, I've lost track!"

"I've definitely lost track on this trip. But I'm pretty sure it's already January."

He squeezed her. "Well, Happy New Year."

"Happy New Year," she said into his chest, grateful for the warmth and wanting the sentiment to be true. The next few months promised to be challenging, something wholly different from what she'd imagined last year at this time. Then, she'd simply wished for her father's return. Sam didn't yet exist in her mind or heart. Now it was up to the two of them to face this bridge. Was it strong enough for their crossing?

Annalisa awoke to find Sam seated at the bed's edge, already dressed and poring over the map.

"You're sure up early." She stretched and crawled up next to him.

He turned and gave her a kiss. "Good morning, sunshine."

She glanced at the outstretched map in his hands. They'd somehow made their way along so many of the little lines and through the funny shapes that marked borders. It made her think back to Mario's globe and how he'd dreamed of venturing off to South America. Back then she'd never even left California. Now, looking at this spread of colors and boxes, she could clearly see how much ground they'd still not covered. The United States was massive on its own; there was a lot more to learn and explore in her own country.

After visiting her father in his place of imprisonment, she realized there were some things that just didn't fit on a map—barbed wire fencing, silent suffering, and how this same country could so easily uproot a family's life without the majority of people knowing. Navigation was that much harder in a country that didn't want your kind. The lines on Sam's map were clean and fluid; nothing like her jagged and messy reality.

"So how far is it to Arizona?" she asked.

"About four hundred and fifty miles. We'll make it to Winslow by nightfall."

They slid into the car and were soon off again on Route 66, watching interesting rock formations rise like towers on the roadside and a rainbow of cars along the way. They ate en route, sharing a loaf of bread and a bottle of Coca-Cola.

Sure enough, as the sun set, they'd crossed into Arizona. Annalisa watched the diminishing light play upon the red rocks, the vastness of the desert stretching out before them mirroring the uncertainty she felt. And it wasn't long before they saw the sign for Winslow, where they got off on a country road and pulled into a ditch to car camp the night.

She shivered under the blanket as she looked up through the window at the wide array of stars in what seemed like bigger skies than she'd ever seen. There was an order to the constellations, something she yearned for in her own life. She thought about what her father had said and how she had undoubtedly disappointed him. For a moment, she wished things were different—simpler, for nothing in the past year had been easy, not even her relationship with Sam.

As she traced the invisible lines between the stars, she realized that her struggles had helped her grow. They had shaped her in ways she was only beginning to understand. She felt stronger and realized she could handle this baby. She wasn't a little girl anymore. Maybe she would be able to set things right with her mother. This wasn't just an aimless road trip; she'd found herself along the way.

She awoke in the cold of dawn with a crick in her neck. Sam was already in the front seat, munching on a hunk of bread. She rubbed her neck and noticed it was bare.

"Oh my God!" She sat up and desperately pawed through the pile of dirty clothes in the backseat.

"What are you doing back there? What's wrong?"

"My necklace!" she shouted. "Help me find it."

Together they searched the car from the back seats to the front. They even checked the trunk.

"Are you sure you brought it?" Sam asked as they searched the passenger seat once more.

"Of course I brought it," she snapped. "I wear it all the time."

Sam sighed. "It's just a necklace."

"Just a necklace?" She slammed her fist into the seat. "It was a gift from my brother! The brother who's dead, remember?"

"OK, OK." Sam held up his hands. "Where do you think you last had it?"

"I don't know. Blue Swallow Court?" She bit her lip.

"Jeepers! We're not going all the way back to New Mexico."

"Sam, please." She took his hand. "We have to. That was my brother's necklace. He gave it to me for good luck, and I promised to always wear it."

"Some luck that's brought you!" He huffed.

"Come on, Sam. Please?" She stared into his pale blue eyes.

He blinked. "OK, fine. You win."

She squeezed his hand. "We're going back?"

"We're going back, but we're not staying at the motel. Can't afford it."

It was late at night when they arrived back in Tucumcari, New Mexico, and pulled up at the familiar motel. They stepped out of the car together and walked up to the front desk.

"There's no vacancy," a gray-haired man said, and Annalisa wondered if he might be the owner.

"Please, sir." Sam leaned forward with his hands on the desk. "We stayed in room 10. We just need to check for something we lost."

The man eyed Sam. "How old are you, son?"

"Seventeen, sir."

"What are you doing taking a girl to a hotel at your age? Do your parents know?"

"Actually." Annalisa glanced at Sam. "We're married. We married young."

The man stepped back and looked the two of them up and down. "You don't say. Well, I'm afraid I still can't let you check the room. It's occupied."

"When do they check out?" Sam looked at Annalisa.

"They said they need two nights." The man rested his hand on the desk. "But like I said, there's no vacancy. You'll have to stay elsewhere."

"That's fine with us," Sam waved his hand.

"Wait," Annalisa held up her finger. "Maybe someone found it and brought it to you? It's a gold necklace with a gold horn charm."

The man shook his head. "I'm sorry, dear. Nothing like that

has turned up. Now, if you'll excuse me, I was closing the door for the night. You know, what with no vacancy and all."

"Of course," Sam said. "We'll be back. The day after tomorrow, right?"

"That's right, son." The man tapped the desk. "Best of luck to you."

"Thank you, sir." Sam took Annalisa's hand as they headed out the door.

They slept in the car on the side of the road for two nights before they pulled back into the Blue Swallow Court parking lot. A family of four was loading bags into their trunk, while a couple left their car, suitcases in hand.

Annalisa checked her bedhead in the dirty window of a parked red Chevrolet. She smoothed down her hair before making eye contact with a man she hadn't noticed in the driver's seat.

She quickly turned back toward the motel, catching up with Sam, who'd walked ahead.

The same man stood behind the front desk, where a pretty brunette woman in a sunny yellow dress was asking for directions. As the man explained with hand gestures, he paused and nodded to Annalisa.

"I'll be right with you."

"Oh, I'm sorry." The woman turned to Annalisa and Sam. "You go ahead. I'm in no rush."

The man smiled at Annalisa. "You're here to see room 10?"

"Yes." Annalisa nodded. "Is it vacant?"

"They just checked out," the man said. "But I can't promise you'll find what you're looking for. I'm sorry to say that we sometimes get unsavory characters here. Like those I-talians and Mexicans."

Annalisa caught herself reaching for her necklace. Instead, she forced a smile.

"Don't get me wrong. I love their food. Especially those I-talians. But you just can't know their intentions. You know what I'm saying?"

Again, Annalisa smiled, and Sam cleared his throat. "So, about that room?"

"Oh, yes, son." The man turned to retrieve the key. "Here you go. Just make it quick. We have plenty of customers coming in."

Annalisa breathed a sigh of relief after the door swung behind them.

"Are you OK?" Sam took her hand.

"I'm fine." She nodded. "Let's find my necklace."

They searched the room from the wooden desk and floor to the shower and closet before stripping down the bed and Sam crawling beneath it. They even checked the windowsill and under the tabletop lamp.

"It's not here," Sam said as Annalisa peeked behind the toilet.

"What am I supposed to do?" She sank to the floor.

Sam sat down next to her. "We have no choice but to move on. Your brother would understand. Trust me."

He stood up and held out his hand. She took it and stood, feeling a rush to her head. He grabbed her before she fell.

He gave her a squeeze. "We need to get you and that baby something to eat fast!"

Annalisa stabbed at a piece of scrambled eggs. "Thanks for this —for everything."

"Don't mention it." He took a sip of coffee. "Too bad we couldn't find the necklace."

She nodded, looking out the diner window at the bare, twisted trees. It was peaceful, if not depressing. Then she saw a flash of black and white as a magpie landed on one of the branches. She watched the large bird hop its way up the bough. It had an ebony-colored head and a white chest with iridescent blue feathers on its wings and long tail. It lifted those beautiful wings and took flight.

"I've been thinking." Sam twirled his fork between his hands. "What if we were to take a little detour to Las Vegas?"

"Las Vegas?" she asked. "Isn't that out of the way?"

"Not really," he said. "Once we get into Arizona, around Kingman, we can take Route 93 north."

"But why Las Vegas?" she asked, taking another bite of her eggs.

He slid out of the booth and kneeled in front of her on the floor.

Suddenly, it was as if time stopped, freezing everything and everyone in place. The red vinyl booth seemed to gleam more vibrantly in the bright light. The air was heavy with the rich aromas of coffee, bacon, and maple syrup. The waitress stopped at the center of the room, a plate of silver-dollar pancakes in hand, as patrons paused mid-conversation. Gone was the clatter of silverware; the only sound was the gentle hum of an overhead fan.

"What are you doing?" Annalisa asked, dropping her fork.

"Annalisa Aiello, will you marry me?" Sam grinned up at her.

Her body froze as people stared in their direction. She peered into his pale blue eyes and felt as if she were drowning in the depths of an ocean. Was this really happening? It was the same Sam who hadn't seemed committed, the source of her fear for what was to come.

"But I thought you said…"

"I told you when we're good and ready." His voice was steady and so was his stance. "I'm ready now." He cleared his throat as he took her hand. "It scared me. Still does. But I keep thinking about my mother and how she had to raise me alone. I don't want to be like my father. And with you, I won't be." He squeezed her fingers. "This baby's mine, too. And I want to be here. We can do this together."

She sat there for a moment more, absorbing the meaning of his words.

He met her silence with a small, almost nervous laugh. "Besides, it could be fun, right? Another adventure." He dropped his hand to his side as he repositioned on the food-stained rug. "So, what do you say? Are you going to make me stay kneeling on the floor?"

To that, she smiled. "Till death do us part and come what may?" she teased.

His eyes widened. "Is that a yes?"

"Yes," she replied to the sound of cheers and applause from their fellow diners.

Sam looked happier than she'd ever seen. For that she was glad. She needed him to be ready and willing to take this next step. He was the only good thing she had left in life. There was so much more to face, and she didn't want to tackle it alone. And it could be fun, too—at some point.

Sam and Annalisa crossed a desert highway soon populated with fancy cars and signs advertising saloons and showgirls. They passed something called El Rancho Vegas, with a sunburst shape on top of a tower boasting that it had an opera house, a casino, and a restaurant.

The two kept their eyes peeled until Annalisa spotted a sign for the Gretna Green Wedding Chapel. Then they pulled into an empty lot adjacent to a white picket fence in front of a little white house beneath a stone clock tower topped with a pointed steeple.

"So, this is it," Annalisa said. "We're really doing this."

"We are." Sam paused for a moment with his hands pressed onto the steering wheel. He stared out the window, and for a moment, she wondered if he regretted his decision.

She nervously licked at her hand and ran her fingers through her bedhead. If nothing else, she wanted to look somewhat presentable.

Sam opened the door and slid out of his seat, and she followed him along the stone path to the chapel entrance.

An older woman with shoulder-length white hair answered the door with a smile. She welcomed them and began a tour.

The chapel itself was rather small, just a few rows of empty pews in front of a wooden altar that stood before an arched window with a white candelabra and leafy plant on either side.

"We do our own flower arrangements." She gestured to a vase of white roses on the altar. "Would you like a bouquet?"

"No, thank you." Annalisa shook her head. "We just want something simple."

"Simple, we've got." The woman smiled. "Now, we just have some paperwork for you to sign. You are both at least eighteen years of age, correct?"

"We are." Sam squeezed Annalisa's hand.

"Wonderful. I'll call for the minister when you're ready."

Sam filled out a form with both of their names and wrote out their dates of birth so they'd both appear to be eighteen. He listed his address as their residence.

Then they sat in the pew and waited.

A few minutes later, a man with thinning gray hair and hollowed-out cheeks appeared.

"Do you have any special requests?"

"Not really." Annalisa looked at Sam, who shook his head.

"All right, then." The man clapped his hands. "Shall we proceed?"

Annalisa paused but saw Sam nod. It made her feel better about what they were doing. If he was certain, she could be, too.

The minister cleared his throat and began.

"Dearly beloved, we are gathered here today to witness the blessed union of..." He looked down at his piece of paper. "... Annalisa and Sam in matrimony."

He turned to Sam. "Do you, Sam, take Annalisa to be your lawfully wedded wife, to have and to hold from this day forth, for better or for worse, for richer or for poorer, in sickness and in health, to love and to cherish until death do you part?"

Sam looked blankly at the minister.

"You may say 'I do,' if you agree to those terms." The man rolled his eyes.

"Oh, yes." Sam released a nervous chuckle.

The minister turned to Annalisa and repeated the same words.

"I do." Annalisa nodded.

"Please present the rings," the minister said.

"Oh." Annalisa blushed. "We don't have anything."

The minister looked back at the older woman who had shown them in. "Do we have anything they can use?"

"I'm afraid not." The woman smiled softly. It reminded Annalisa of the fleeting moments of sweetness she craved from her mother. She wondered what she might think of what they'd done and if Annalisa could ever again be a part of her life.

"Not to worry," said the minister. "You can do a handshake instead. Sam, repeat after me. 'With this handshake, I thee wed.'"

And Sam repeated and took her hand.

"Now, Annalisa, please say, 'With this handshake, I thee wed.'"

The words were so simple but weighed so much. She had

never imagined she might be standing in a seedy chapel, getting married without rings or a dress. None of it was expected, but standing beside Sam she felt stronger, safer, and suddenly more certain that they could actually move forward hand-in-hand as they were now. She repeated after the minister.

"Sam and Annalisa." The minister looked at each one as he said their names. "By the power vested in me in the state of Nevada, I now pronounce you husband and wife for life. You may now kiss the bride."

Sam took Annalisa in his arms and gave her a peck on the lips. It was brief but sealing. They were now linked, and it was time to move forward. It didn't matter where, just so long as they were together.

"I love you," he whispered.

Annalisa began to cry, releasing all the pent-up emotion as she thought of everything she'd been through and lost—her brother, her father, and her life back home—and what she'd gained—a partnership and soon a new family. It was all so much. But she knew one thing for sure as a smile stretched across her face. And she said it with four simple words: "I love you, too."

After a romantic night and leisurely morning at the Wittwer Motel, a mile and a half up Main Street, the newlyweds were back on the road, this time to Concord.

"We really should get some rings." Annalisa tugged at her finger.

"I've got one for you." Sam turned onto the highway. "My Ma has been saving my grandmother's ring for me."

"Are you sure your mother will be OK with me staying with you at the house?"

Sam squeezed the steering wheel. "What can she say? We're legally married."

"You're lucky, you know." Annalisa stared at the desert roadside.

"Why's that?"

She turned to him. "It seems you never have to worry about getting in trouble."

"It's not always been that way," Sam said quietly. "My Pops was pretty hard on me—both of us, really."

They drove through the long, wide basin of the Mojave Desert past twisty, spiky Joshua trees, heading toward snow-capped mountains in the distance. Crosswinds rocked the car, and Sam held tight to the steering wheel.

About an hour in, they reached Barstow and got out to stretch their legs before hitting Route 66 again. Sam cranked up the radio and put his arm around Annalisa as he sang along with Judy Garland and Gene Kelly to "For Me and My Gal."

She joined him in singing about how they would build a little home for two or three or more, and she stopped.

"We'll see how things go with this baby."

Sam smiled. "You don't think you'd want more someday?"

"Maybe when we're a little older." She tapped at the window. "One's going to be plenty to tend to."

By the time they'd hit San Bernardino, they were both beat. Since funds were short, they again slept on the side of the road.

But the next morning, despite his efforts, Sam couldn't get the car to start. The air was crisp, and Annalisa stayed inside as he leaned over the open hood, trying to determine what was wrong.

He slammed the hood and came back into the car and put his head down on the steering wheel.

"Just another eight hours and now what?" He slammed the horn. "We're stuck here."

"Don't say that," Annalisa said. "There's plenty of traffic." She slid out the door.

"What are you doing?" asked Sam.

She began waving her arms for someone to stop. It didn't take long before a burly man in a pickup truck pulled over.

He stepped out onto the pavement in denim pants and a button-down shirt, his wide shoulders tense and his focus narrow as he glanced at Sam's driver-side window. His eyes shifted to Annalisa, and his jaw clenched.

"Do you need help?" His voice was low and urgent.

It took her a moment to realize it was a look of concern. She stifled a nervous laugh and ran a hand through her tangled hair. "It's the car… won't start."

The man's eyes softened as he nodded, gazing at her a moment longer before he stepped toward the front of the car and motioned for Sam to open the hood.

She watched her now-husband get out to explain what had happened. Meanwhile, the man crouched to inspect the engine. "Looks like a faulty spark plug." He grunted. "Lucky you; I happen to have a spare."

He went back to his truck, and Annalisa's eyes met Sam's, which seemed just as uncertain. They were still a long way from Concord. Was it really so simple? And she wondered if they could trust this strange man.

But soon there he was, with a spark plug in one hand and a wrench in the other. There was a sureness in his step as he approached the car again. He leaned in and moved his hands with familiarity. There could be a fix. Perhaps it wasn't so difficult—any of it.

"How much do I owe you?" Sam asked when the man had finished.

The man's eyes swept across their tired faces for a long moment. It was as if he suddenly somehow recognized them or something within. Annalisa wondered what.

But when he finally shook his head, she realized he'd seen their desperation. Perhaps he also understood they had many more miles to reach where they actually needed to go.

"It was nothing. You kids be careful, OK?"

It was a smooth drive north with them entering Contra Costa County late that evening.

They sat in the car for a few moments after rolling to a stop outside Sam's house.

"It feels funny not even checking on my mother." Annalisa said it but had no desire to deal with it. She wasn't sure which side of her mother she'd face when she walked up the stairs to that door.

"You can try talking to her tomorrow." Sam opened his door. "Come on; let's go to my place and get some rest."

The house was quiet when they entered. Smoke clung to the air in the small, sparsely decorated living room, where a gray couch was pushed against the wall behind a paper-cluttered coffee table. A brown wood tabletop Zenith radio served as the focal point from its perch on a dusty bookcase. Beside it sat a half-empty cup of what looked like cold coffee. Sam opened a small closet where he deposited his coat and held out his hand for Annalisa's. "Ma's probably not back yet from the restaurant. Still, I don't want her finding us and freaking out. I'll sleep on the sofa, and you can have my bed."

"You sure?" Annalisa glanced at the tiny couch.

Sam nodded. "Yeah, I'll talk to my Ma when she gets home. Everything's going to be fine."

Annalisa awoke to the sound and smell of sizzling eggs. She was famished, so she threw on her clothes and tiptoed down the hall.

Sam sat in the kitchen, looking deep in thought as a tall red-haired woman spooned breakfast on his plate. She looked up at Annalisa and nodded.

"Good morning." There was a hint of tension in Mrs. Wells'

voice. "Sam was just doing some explaining. He gave me quite a scare when I came home last night. But I'm just glad you kids are all right. You are all right, aren't you?"

Annalisa tipped her chin and looked at Sam.

"Ma, Annalisa and I have something to tell you..."

His mother looked at the two of them with wide blue eyes. "Oh no." She sat down. "You got her pregnant."

Annalisa blushed as she settled into an empty chair.

"He did, didn't he?" Mrs. Wells raised her hand to her mouth.

"Ma, will you listen to me?" Sam's voice cracked. "Yes, Annalisa's pregnant, but like I was telling you, we got married."

"Do your folks know?" Mrs. Wells turned to Annalisa.

Annalisa shook her head. "Not yet," she said quietly. "But my father suggested it."

"He didn't want a bastard grandchild." Mrs. Wells raised a brow.

Annalisa's face grew hotter. Maybe it would have been better to just go back to her mother after all.

Sam slammed his palm onto the table. "Ma! It's not like that. We love each other."

"So that's it?" His mother stood. "You're just going to walk back into this house and tell me you married a girl who's having your baby? I suppose you haven't even thought about how much school or work you missed. What are you going to do with yourselves? Or have you even planned that far ahead?"

Sam raised himself from his own chair. "I'll go talk to Mr. Reede and see if he'll take us back."

Mrs. Wells let out a long sigh. "Well, you're practically an adult and married, so I don't suppose I have much to say. I just hope you'll be happy."

And Annalisa hoped it would be true.

· · ·

Annalisa took a deep breath and knocked on the door to her apartment. She didn't want to just barge in and scare her mother.

Mamma answered, dressed in her cleaning lady uniform.

"Oh." She held the door open, her eyes falling on Annalisa's belly. "I was about to head out."

Annalisa clasped her hands. "I know, Mamma, but can we talk?"

"Walk with me. I don't have time."

But, Annalisa noted, her mother wasn't slamming the door in her face: a good sign.

"Where have you been?" Mamma grabbed her purse and keys.

"I saw Papà. They moved him to Oklahoma."

Her mother raised her eyebrows. "Oklahoma? You went all the way to Oklahoma? How did you get there?"

"Sam drove me."

Mamma walked down the stairs to the apartment entrance. "Is he the one who got you pregnant?"

Annalisa sighed. "Yes, Mamma. But he drove me all the way there."

"How is your father?" She stopped on the porch. "Are they feeding him enough?"

"Papà looked good. A little thinner, but it was nice to finally see him."

Her mother nodded and resumed walking. "Did you tell him about your condition?"

Annalisa trailed behind her. "I did."

Mamma turned. "And what did your father have to say about that?"

"He wanted me to marry Sam."

"Get married?" Her mother stopped. "We don't even know this boy. Is he Italian? What kind of name is Sam?"

Annalisa inhaled sharply. Why was this all so hard? She needed support, not needling.

"Mamma, we got married."

Her mother waved her hand and began walking faster. "I can't deal with this right now. I have to get to work. My daughter is telling me she eloped."

Annalisa quickened her pace to keep up. "But Papà asked us to get married. He said it would be better. I thought you'd understand."

"What's there to understand?" Her mother walked even faster toward the corner.

"Mamma, I'm not asking to come back... It's just... Sam is going to try to get a job so we can get our own place."

Her mother stopped to turn to her again. "What do you want from me?"

Annalisa wiped away a tear. "Sorry, Mamma. That's all. I'm sorry I disappointed you."

Her mother's eyes shifted. "I really have to go."

Annalisa was crying now. "So, you're still not going to talk to me?"

"We're talking, aren't we?" She threw up her hands.

"But you don't forgive me?"

Her mother shook her head, and Annalisa saw deep disappointment in her black eyes. "It's not how I raised you. Now, I really have to leave."

"Goodbye, Mamma."

"Goodbye." Her mother crossed to the bus stop.

Annalisa watched her and then turned back toward Sam's house. She'd thought seeing her father would fix things, but her mother clearly hadn't yet received any letter. She imagined getting married would help smooth things over. But neither Sam's mother nor her own were any happier to hear the news.

THIRTY-TWO
JANUARY–FEBRUARY 1943

Palermo, Sicily

It started with a faint hum. As the sound grew, Alberto immediately realized it was the stuff of his nightmares again come true. He looked up from the panel he was painting and saw the approach of ten planes he could only assume were American bombers—American because here they were, striking in daylight and without warning. At least with the British Royal Air Force, you could count on the sirens to sound into the night.

He heard what sounded like hundreds if not thousands of bees swarming, and then he dropped what he was doing and followed the other men in fleeing, for they knew exactly where these bombers were headed: the port.

He ran as fast as he could, sweat forming on his brow despite the crisp winter air, as he heard a loud whining sound. Men were passing him from both directions as he pumped his arms and sprinted to the closest bomb shelter.

There he met a mass of people trying to squeeze through the entrance all at once. He stepped behind them and pushed along with the rest until he, too, reached the door and could descend into the dark, damp concrete underground room.

About a hundred people huddled on the cold floor. He found a spot against a wall beside a mother with three small children and a baby. The baby was screaming and two of the children, little girls, were sobbing and clinging to their mother. The little boy, who appeared to be the oldest, sat upright, staring blankly at Alberto, and he wondered just what these poor children had witnessed previously.

Suddenly, he heard a loud whistling sound followed by an earth-rattling boom. Again, the baby screamed, joined by all three children, as they jumped into their mother's lap.

More whistling and another boom. And again, and again and again. Alberto realized he was holding the woman's hand, but he didn't let go until it seemed the last bomb had been dropped.

The baby whimpered, and the other children wiped their tears on their mother's faded blue skirt.

He looked around at the other people, searching for the Ferrantes, but he did not see their faces among those who'd managed to find shelter there.

Everyone waited for at least another half hour before a few younger men rose and slowly walked up the stairs. Alberto nodded at the woman and her children and then got up as well. He found himself dazed as he reached the top and slowly, as if sleepwalking, made his way back to his apartment.

When it came time to fish his key from his pocket, his hand hit a familiar piece of wood. There was the net shuttle, and he wondered if its presence had protected him yet again. He thought of his uncle, who had left him the tool, and wondered what the man must think about this war from his American vantage point now that the U.S. was attacking a place not far from his old home. Surely, he must feel remorse—perhaps even regret. And Alberto thought of his own similar feelings as he stood there instead of beside his family.

He glanced at his watch. It was midafternoon, but he had no desire to return to his work site. Instead, he turned and walked across the street to the Ferrante apartment.

Signora Ferrante opened the door and enveloped Alberto in a hug. "We hid in the bathtub—all of us."

Then he saw Vittoria, who ran to him and buried her sobbing face in his chest.

"You made it," Vittoria said.

He nodded and stroked her hair.

Signora Ferrante went to the kitchen. "Can I get you something to eat or drink?"

"Water would be wonderful." Alberto sat down in the living room on their green couch beside Vittoria. Lorenzo sat on an adjacent chair with his arms wrapped tightly around his knees.

Signora Ferrante brought out three glasses of water and placed them on the marble coffee table before turning to fiddle with their boxy brown radio.

It crackled a bit before they heard a news broadcaster at the tail end of an announcement about the bombing.

"...hit the port, and it is too early to determine the extent of the damage or if there were any casualties. In other news, the British Eighth Army has entered the Libyan city of Tripoli, which the Axis forces have largely withdrawn, having relocated to Tunisia."

"Did you hear that?" Vittoria asked.

"Yes, the port, I saw..."

"No, I mean Tripoli." Vittoria placed her hand on his knee. "That was our major supply base, and it sounds like the British Army just marched in and took it without a fight."

"My brother-in-law, Franco, was there," Alberto said.

His thoughts immediately went to Cristina and her little family. How long would they have to wait to be reunited? What if Franco was hurt or imprisoned? Then what? No. He couldn't let himself think that way.

He placed his hand on Vittoria's. "I just hope they can hold on to Tunisia."

She turned to him. "But what if they can't? Don't you see? It's over in North Africa."

She was right. The Allies already controlled the Mediterranean, and he'd heard that Italian men were dying of diseases from mosquitoes.

"And you think Italy's next?" He knew it was true in his bones.

She nodded, and he hugged her.

"Maybe Alberto's right: It's time to leave." Signora Ferrante stood beside the radio as if frozen by the bad news. "Who knows when the next bombs will fall? Or when the Allies will invade Sicily."

"You'd consider it?" Alberto looked at Vittoria. "I know you don't want to leave your students, but..."

"Yes, I've considered it." Vittoria spoke slowly. "But I need to give my headmistress some notice. I can't just not show up at school. At least a month would give them some time to find someone new."

"A month?" Alberto's voice rose. "But who knows how many more bombs will fall before the end of this month?"

"Don't worry." Signora Ferrante turned off the radio. "It won't be too much longer. Besides, we have to find a new place, and that also takes time."

Alberto nodded. It made sense, but it still left him feeling uneasy. "I'll let my parents know so they can keep a lookout for apartments near them."

"Would you still be able to coach me in soccer?" Lorenzo raised his head from his knees.

"Yes, Alberto, what are your plans?" Vittoria asked, and everyone looked in his direction.

He clasped his hands. "As long as you are all safe... that's what matters."

"But you wouldn't join us?" Vittoria frowned. "Not even after today? You had to leave your work site to escape an air raid!"

"I need this job," he said firmly. "My family is depending on me."

"Just think about it." Vittoria took his hand in hers.

He thought of it often as he and his coworkers cleaned up what was left of sunken ships and associated debris. And he found himself counting down the hours to when he could return to Vittoria's side. For despite the fact his work site had been hit, he was still more worried about what might happen to his fiancée and her family.

A week and a half later, he found himself again running from work to the neighborhood air raid shelter as what appeared to be dozens of bombers swept in toward the harbor. When he finally made it down the concrete stairs, he spotted the Ferrantes, who motioned for him to join them on the floor.

Lorenzo wore his Balilla uniform, his kerchief secured with a silver pin that read, "*Credere, obbedire, combattere.*" Alberto remembered his father helping him put on his similar uniform long ago, back when he'd promised that he would indeed believe, obey, and fight for Mussolini and Mother Italy.

A tear trickled down his cheek as he looked down at the boy and thought about how different life had turned out. The fervor that once drove him seemed like a faded memory, obscured by the clouds of war and related privations. He looked at this boy, who similarly dreamed of becoming a soccer player, and thought of how he, too, might have to leave it all behind for obligations to family and country. This boy had already seen and endured far too much in his thirteen years. Now here he sat, desperate for survival from the war his beloved Duce had entered and continued to ask Italy to fight.

The air raid shelter shook, rocked by a nearby explosion. Alberto draped a protective arm around Lorenzo, wishing to shield the boy from danger outside and disillusionment within.

Vittoria leaned her head against Alberto's as Signora Ferrante pressed herself against the other side of her daughter. And for just a moment, Alberto was happy that they were together. But the moment passed as the shocks from another explosion rippled across the floor.

They huddled for about an hour before slowly rising and climbing the stairs together, where they ascended into the evening's fading light. Then they walked back to the Ferrante home, where, after a quiet supper, Signora Ferrante insisted Alberto stay the night.

The next morning, he returned to his work site to see the remnants of burning ships. Rather than go to the paint locker as usual, he fell into his typical post-bombing routine of picking up a broom and joining the other men as they swept up the debris.

The air still reeked of burning fuel, and he heard chatter about the nearly one hundred people—all civilians—who had perished between the waterfront and the old city. He wondered just how many might have worked with him or manned the ships that docked nearby. The Ferrantes and he had been lucky.

That evening, as the men packed up to leave, Alberto felt a tap on his shoulder.

"Listen," Ascanio whispered. "A number of the guys are planning to do something big."

"You mean like a strike?" Alberto's eyes widened.

"Not like a strike, an actual strike." Ascanio raised a fist. "We're tired of having to clean up every time the port gets bombed, and after yesterday, with it happening while we were on our shift, conditions are just too dangerous. We deserve better wages and protection, don't you think?"

Alberto nodded slowly. "Count me in."

THIRTY-THREE
JANUARY–FEBRUARY 1943

Concord, California

Mr. Reede wouldn't budge. "You kids left me without cashiers for nearly two weeks. I had to bring in the family to cover for you."

"But I need the work, Mr. Reede," Sam said. "It's just… Well, Annalisa's pregnant and we'll soon have an extra mouth to feed."

"That's no longer my concern, is it?" The store owner looked away. "Besides, I've already hired a replacement."

Annalisa took a deep breath. "Please, Mr. Reede. It was my fault, not Sam's. We can work morning shifts… weekends… anything."

Tears ran down her cheeks.

Mr. Reede's eyes swept over her face, and he swallowed. "I'll tell you what. I have a cousin who works at the steel mill over in Pittsburg. He might be able to put a good word in for you."

"You'd talk to him?" Sam raised his brows. "Golly, Mr. Reede. That would sure be swell."

Mr. Reede pulled out a notepad. "Here's his name and number. Tell him who sent you, and don't go and screw it up. Now, if you excuse me, I have customers to serve." He gestured to the line that had formed behind them.

They left the store and walked in silence until they reached Pacheco Square. Then Sam sat down on a bench and lit a cigarette. He offered one to Annalisa.

She held up her hand. "No thanks, I'm still feeling a little nauseous."

Sam took a drag. "I suppose we could try our luck in Pittsburg."

Annalisa tugged at her hair. "I could get a job, too. At least until the baby comes."

Sam looked at her and took another drag. "What would you do?"

She slid a lock behind her ear. "They hire lots of ladies at the cannery. My Papà used to bring his fish there."

He flicked his cigarette. "But what do you know about canning?"

"I used to help my Mamma clean the salmon when he'd bring some home. It's no fun, but for the money, I could do that."

Sam tossed his cigarette on the ground and stubbed it out.

"There's no need for you to work." He took Annalisa's hand. "The pay should be good enough. We'll go back to Pittsburg and start a whole new life. How about that?"

Annalisa nodded. She wasn't so sure she was ready to take on the role of housewife just yet. Besides, a little extra money couldn't hurt, right?

Sam called Mr. Reede's cousin, who was eager for the young man to get started sight unseen. Within a week, Sam was driving from his mother's house for eight-hour shifts, six days a week, sweeping floors and shoveling coal. It was good money, but Annalisa was restless.

So, she took the Greyhound bus to Pittsburg and visited Booth Cannery where she was ushered into the office of the foreman, Mr. Hansen.

"Any experience?" he asked as he ran his hand through his light brown hair.

She told him how she'd cleaned her father's fish and offered Mr. Reede as a reference for her work ethic. She prayed that he would say something nice and not harp on the fact that she'd left for two weeks without notice.

But it didn't seem the man needed a reference. "Can you start tomorrow?"

She nodded. "Sure thing!"

Things were looking up for once.

She returned to Concord late that afternoon. While walking back to Sam's house, she ran into her mother, who was heading up the stairs to her apartment.

"Mamma, I got a job," Annalisa called to her.

"The boy is making you work?" Mamma paused with her hand on the door handle. "Doesn't he realize you're pregnant?"

Annalisa sighed. "Mamma, I want a job. He didn't tell me I had to. Besides, it will help to put some money aside for when the baby comes."

Her mother looked at her and gave a sad smile. It was as though she were peering into the past at someone or something long gone. "You always were a smart girl."

"But you're still mad at me?"

The smile vanished. "I can't take you back, I'm sorry." She shook her head. "Not after what you did to this family."

Annalisa watched her mother step through the wrought-iron door. It creaked closed behind her and her feet hit the stairs, and Annalisa stood there watching, listening, and resolving to never shut the door on her own child.

FEBRUARY 1943

Pittsburg, California

When Annalisa arrived at Booth Cannery, she was handed a white uniform dress with a white apron, a white cap that slightly resembled that of a nurse, and matching white cotton gloves.

Mr. Hansen led her to the floor, where she saw several rows of twelve women standing before a long wooden table.

"There's a machine that rapidly cleans the fish, but we still need ladies' fingers to thoroughly clean out the blood and skin that gets left behind," he explained.

He showed her to her place on the assembly line, between two women holding salmon under running water from an overhead faucet.

"See how they use their knives to just flick off any bits of what the machine doesn't catch?"

She watched as the ladies deposited their cleaned fish onto a conveyor belt in the center of the table that carted the salmon away for further canning processes.

"Now's your turn." Mr. Hansen pointed to the open space between the women—two brunettes, an older one with redder hair and doe eyes and the other who looked like she was not much older than Annalisa—who glanced at her curiously.

"And who might you be?" The older one grabbed another fish and scraped out the inside under the water.

"My name's Annalisa." She picked up her own fish and followed suit.

"Peggy." The older one tossed her fish onto the belt. "And that's Emily."

Annalisa held her fish under the water as she turned to Emily.

"You have to go faster than that, sweetie," Peggy said. "We can't have you holding up the line."

"Oh, sorry." Annalisa released her own cleaned fish.

"Don't mind her," Emily whispered. "She's just a big pussycat under that lioness act."

Annalisa smiled and tried to ignore the nauseating stench as she picked up another fish and started the process again. Still, her stomach churned, and when she felt she couldn't hold back any longer, she excused herself for the lavatory.

Sam shuffled into the bedroom after a long day of work at the steel mill.

"Something smells funny." He sniffed the air.

Annalisa lay in the little twin bed they shared with two fluffy pillows propped behind her head and a newspaper in her hands. Her eyes left the last headline she'd scanned after two stories that held her attention.

The Japanese troops had evacuated Guadalcanal, ending the Battle of the Solomon Islands. It was a victory for the U.S., but so distant from her own battles.

It reminded her of how much had happened over the past month, not to mention the entire year. She reflected on how Mario might have ended up entrenched in such a battle. If so, maybe he would have celebrated, although she couldn't imagine someone like Mario ever really fighting a war.

The news followed a story about a German Army surrender following the Battle of Stalingrad. The writer marked it as a turning point, but all of it was so far from her physically and mentally.

Still, she wondered if this really could be the beginning of the end to this war and the suffering. Perhaps the time would finally come for them to send her father home.

She lowered the paper and smiled.

"I got a job."

Sam sniffed at the uniform she'd tossed on his desk chair. "Smells like you brought the whole cannery back with you... I thought we talked about this."

Annalisa set the newspaper on the nightstand and met his glare. "I know you want to be the breadwinner, but I can't just sit around and wait for the baby to come. I want this. Don't you want me to be happy?"

Sam sighed and took her hand as he slid onto the bed beside her. "I do want you to be happy. But don't you think being pregnant might be a problem?"

Annalisa shifted her eyes. It wasn't as easy as she'd thought; she needed to get past the nauseating smell. But she wasn't about to give up just yet.

"The foreman doesn't have to know. Besides, it doesn't have to be more than a few months. I figure it might help us with a down payment on an apartment of our own."

Sam pulled her in closer. "OK."

Annalisa smiled. "You mean it? You're not mad?"

Sam shook his head. "We'll start looking for a place of our own this weekend. We'll definitely need a bigger bed."

By that Sunday, Annalisa and Sam had pored over newspaper listings and found a few prospective apartments in Pittsburg. Her old home, a place full of memories good and bad.

As they rode into town, they passed by the old playground where she and Mario used to play and her high school where her brother got her to ditch her first classes. But it was also where, because of her mother, they'd been driven out of their home. There, the FBI had taken not only her brother's treasured camera, but her father. It was also where they'd received Mario's fateful news.

She sat in silent reflection as they rolled to a stop in front of a red-roofed two-story white stucco home with two addresses to the right of the wrought-iron front door. It was nearly a miniature of her apartment in Concord, and for a moment, she thought about her mother. In another world she might celebrate with her the prospect of a new home.

"Why don't you go on in while I wait in the car?" Sam broke her spell.

So, Annalisa slid out of the car, checked her reflection in the window to smooth out her hair, and made her way to the front door. She rang the doorbell and waited. A plump blonde woman answered.

The woman frowned as she tapped her manicured fingers on the open door. "Yes?"

"I'd called you about an apartment," Annalisa said.

The woman eyed her closely, her other hand tightly gripped on the door frame. "What are you, some kind of wop?"

"No, my husband and I are Americans." Annalisa felt her face grow warm as the woman continued to stare.

"Cuz I don't rent to no dagos or krauts." She shook her head. "Is that going to be a problem?"

"No, ma'am." Annalisa felt her chest tighten.

The woman relaxed her grip and laughed. "Good. Those Italians, especially. I can't stand them. They cook with all that garlic. It stinks up the place. Plus, they're all Fascists, genuflecting to Mussolini and whatnot."

"Yeah, we're Americans." Annalisa offered a smile.

The woman nodded with another laugh and then tilted her head. "What'd you say your name was again?"

"Annie," she said quickly. "Annie Wells."

THIRTY-FOUR
FEBRUARY 1943

Alberto and Vittoria weaved through the crowd to board their train. It was a Sunday, a beautiful day to join the Cardinales for supper. They would also visit a little apartment that would be available later that month so Vittoria could report back to her mother and Lorenzo.

Despite the joy Alberto felt for Vittoria's coming move, he couldn't shake the anxiety that had plagued him since he'd agreed to join the shipyard workers in their strike.

The plan was simple: He'd show up at work the next day as usual, except when the morning whistle blew, he and the other 1,300 or so men would sit down.

And yet so much was unknown, namely how Francesco and the foremen would respond and whether he might lose this job in which he'd worked so hard to advance.

He took a deep breath and squeezed the wooden shuttle in his pocket. He was going to enjoy this day and not overthink it.

Several people brought not only suitcases but trunks aboard the train. It was a sign of the times, especially after the last bombing. And his mind shifted to how it would not be long before the Ferrantes followed these people in their flight to the countryside.

His father and sister greeted the couple with warm hugs when they arrived in Isola delle Femmine. The women chatted about the apartment that Cristina had found through one of her friends.

"Perhaps Lorenzo can babysit the children," Cristina said. "I've got some old curtains you can use. Isn't it all so exciting?"

Vittoria smiled and nodded, and Alberto knew she was not that excited. But especially after the last bombing eleven days prior, it made sense. They'd discussed how, after the war, she would rejoin Alberto, they'd marry in Isola delle Femmine, and he would return on Sundays to visit. And she hoped she could find another job at a school in the little village.

When they arrived at the Cardinale home, Mamma was ready to serve supper, which included a main course of tripe with a potato and green bean salad. After leading the table in grace, Papà poured each adult a glass of wine.

"A toast to new beginnings for Vittoria and her family." He held up his long-stemmed glass. "We look forward to having you as neighbors."

Everyone responded with a "*Salute!*" as they clinked their glasses together.

"How is Franco?" Alberto asked his sister.

Cristina sighed. "Letters are fewer and further between. But at least I know he made it to Tunisia in one piece."

She scooped Remo onto her lap. "You know this little one said his first word?"

"Oh?" Vittoria touched the baby's cheek. "He's getting to be such a big boy!"

"He said 'Ba.' I think he was trying to say 'Papà.'" Her eyes moistened.

"Franco will be home soon enough." It hurt Alberto to see his sister cry.

"But what if the Allies take control of Tunisia, too?" Cristina squeezed Remo. "Then what?"

Alberto shook his head and took a deep breath. "We can't assume the worst. Franco is strong and resourceful. He'll make it back to us."

"Don't worry." Vittoria patted her future sister-in-law on the back. "We're all here for you."

The table was quiet for a few moments as everyone dug into their tripe.

"So, Vittoria, you are going to see the apartment after this?" Mamma asked, and Alberto was glad for a change in subject.

"I'm so grateful that Cristina found the place." Vittoria held her fork. "So many people are moving back to the countryside and eating up all the available property."

"We're looking forward to having you here and seeing our son more often." Papà's hazel eyes met Alberto's.

"Next thing we have to plan is that wedding of yours." Mamma's light brown eyes twinkled. And for a moment, Alberto wondered why his own irises ended up so dark.

"Do you know what you're going to wear?" Cristina asked.

"My Mamma's dress." Vittoria smiled. "Would you believe it fits me perfectly? No need for alterations."

"That's a blessing." His mother sipped her wine. "Now we just have to make the arrangements with Maria Santissima delle Grazie."

"We were thinking of doing it in the spring, right, Alberto?" Vittoria turned in his direction.

Alberto's mind had wandered. He was thinking about how they could be planning a wedding in the midst of a war.

"What's that?"

"Spring," Vittoria repeated. "We want to get married in the spring."

Alberto nodded. "Perhaps spring will be a good time. You'll have had a chance to get situated here."

The apartment was near the waterfront, and the current owner boasted about sea breezes and the proximity to the church and market. Best of all, in Alberto's eyes, it was a short walk from his parents' place and not too far from Cristina's, either.

After touring the apartment, Alberto and Vittoria took a stroll to the west, dropping by the soccer field at Piano Ponente. Two teams faced off, with several young men trying desperately to ward off a forward's progress toward their goal.

"Soon, Lorenzo will be playing here," Alberto said.

Vittoria tented her eyes as she gazed at the players. "They seem like such big boys. I hope he fits in."

"He'll be fine. Maybe I can drop in with them one of these Sundays."

"He'd like that." She smiled and nodded. "He's going to miss you coaching him just as much as he'll miss his team."

Alberto grinned. "I know his big sister will take care of him and keep him out of trouble."

They turned and walked along the village's western shore, watching crooked-necked cormorants compete with gulls for fish as the white swells fizzled upon contact with the rocks and sand lining their grassy path.

It was early evening by the time they arrived at the train station, feeling like they'd accomplished something on their long day in the village.

They held hands as they sat in contentment, watching as the countryside slowly gave way to a more densely populated urban setting of blue, pink, and white houses. And Alberto thought about all the people who, like Vittoria, were heeding Mussolini's call to leave the city.

They walked swiftly past the remnants of buildings ruined by recent bombing, and he held her hand tighter, happy that she'd made her decision to leave.

She embraced him when they arrived in the street between their two apartments. "Just think: It won't be much longer before I'm not right across the street."

He squeezed her. "It seems strange to say it, but I can't wait for that to be the case. I'll feel so much better once you're finally there. Plus, it will be good for our families."

He gave her a kiss and watched as she turned her key in her door. Then he turned and entered his own building and readied for bed, mentally preparing himself for the events to come.

Alberto rose earlier than usual after a night of tossing and turning in his sleep.

When he arrived at his work site, he nodded at several of his coworkers before going to the paint locker and fetching paints he knew he was not going to use. Then he waited.

He looked around and saw similar nervous glances back at him. Then the bell rang.

Panic jolted through his body. Was he doing the right thing? He saw all the men at his station plop down and joined them.

They sat there in silence for several minutes, which stretched into at least a half hour, before Francesco reached their station, shaking his head.

"Get up." He spoke firmly. The men, including Alberto, sat still, staring into the space immediately before them.

"I said, 'Get up!'" Francesco barked loudly.

"Not until you meet our demands," a man named Pasquale replied in a loud, low voice.

"You want better wages?" Francesco whistled. "I can't change the work conditions, but you'll have no work if you stay seated."

Alberto didn't dare turn his head, but he could see the men in front of him remaining in their places.

"If you don't get up, I will have to notify the authorities," Francesco carefully enunciated each word.

The men stayed in their positions, and Francesco turned and quickly walked away.

"What now?" Alberto asked a man to his right, named Arturo.

"Shh," Arturo whispered. "We stay until they move us."

"But we don't resist arrest?" Alberto replied.

"No! Now be quiet and sit still," Arturo hissed.

And so, Alberto did for about an hour, with the cold concrete under his backside and the bottoms of his legs.

Finally, he heard voices approaching, and then, to his horror, five men in tight black shirts entered the area where he sat.

"Get up, now!" shouted one of the Blackshirts.

No one changed their position, but Alberto felt himself start to shake.

"If you will not move, we will move you." Another Blackshirt drew a nightstick.

Still, no one moved, so the men began methodically pulling the shipyard workers up. And as they did, Alberto heard someone shout, "Resist!"

Soon, that man was joined in a chorus of others chanting in resistance. The Blackshirts swung their nightsticks. There was suddenly a mess of blood and cries of pain as the Blackshirts carted men away.

Alberto stayed silent, frozen in fear in his seated position. But when one of the Blackshirts approached from behind, he swung his elbows back and jabbed the man.

The Blackshirt howled and launched his nightstick hard into Alberto's right knee. He buckled over in pain, and the man followed with a blow to Alberto's back.

"That will teach you all a lesson." The Blackshirt smirked.

Alberto lay crumpled on the ground and sobbed as waves of pain shot through his lower back and up his leg from his knee.

The Blackshirts continued to cart his coworkers away in groups of five at a time. But no one came for him. He stayed there long after everyone had left until Francesco appeared.

"Serves you right." Francesco shook his head. "After all I've done for you over the years, and you go and join this strike?"

Alberto lay in the fetal position as Francesco stepped over and assessed him.

"Looks like you need some medical attention." He turned to walk away.

"By the way," he called over his shoulder. "You're fired."

Alberto tried to get up and felt the pain shoot through him again, and he collapsed. He lay back down and writhed in agony.

He heard footsteps and turned his head to see two men dressed in white pushing a cart and Francesco at their side, pointing at Alberto.

Alberto cried out as the men lifted him onto the cart and then wheeled him to a waiting ambulance.

The cart shifted and bounced slightly as the ambulance rolled across the cobblestone roads, and Alberto found himself again sobbing. Finally, they reached the hospital, where the men wheeled him in.

"You're so lucky." Vittoria looked out the window of Alberto's hospital room. "You could have been paralyzed."

Instead, his back was covered in bruises and he'd sustained

another knee injury. After a few days of bed rest, the doctor said he could get around with crutches.

"Why would you have gotten yourself mixed up in something like that?" Vittoria turned to face him. "With all that talk about how you need this job; how you can't move with us to Isola delle Femmine because of work? And then you go and get yourself fired?"

"That job put lives in danger." Alberto looked down at his bandaged leg that was elevated on several pillows.

She shook her head. "And striking didn't put your life in danger? Look at you."

"I panicked."

Vittoria sighed. "Well, at least you can heal at home, away from that awful place, for a little while. Mamma thinks you should stay with us. She can bring you food and help you get to the bathroom—at least until you can manage on your own with the crutches."

"Thank you," Alberto said.

The sun glowed like a halo around Vittoria's head. Here was his guiding light, the one who had shown him how to love, who helped him see a world beyond war and fascism. He knew her anger was rooted in fear and frustration with his inertia. More than anything, she worried about his safety. She was ready to move ahead, while he remained anchored to uncertainty. It was standing in the way of their shared future. Now there was no choice. He had to reconsider what that meant.

A day later he was lying on the couch in the Ferrantes' apartment with a bell at his side. Signora Ferrante was quick to respond to his call. It felt funny having to depend on someone else when he'd always been so independent. But when he tried to stand and pain shot through his leg, he realized he needed time to heal. So, he was grateful.

A week passed, and he was back on one foot, hobbling around on crutches and trying to keep the other foot off the ground as instructed. Still, he stayed with the Ferrantes. Signora Ferrante continued to wait on him and bring him chicken soup and *caffè d'orzo* throughout the day before Vittoria took over at night, tucking him in with a kiss.

"What day is it today?" Alberto asked Vittoria one evening as she sat at his feet grading papers.

"Sunday the fourteenth." Vittoria made a strike with her red pen.

"Saint Valentine's Day." Alberto smiled. "And I got to spend it with you."

She stopped what she was doing and slid into a little space in front of him, taking care not to brush against his knee.

"I look forward to many more Saint Valentine's Days spent with you by my side," she said softly, drawing his arms around her.

He held her like that for a long time, falling asleep with her in his arms. He awoke when she rose in the pale dawn light and kissed him lightly on the lips.

"I have to go—can't be late for school. See you later?"

"I'll see you later." Alberto kissed her deeper before she drew away and joined her mother in the kitchen for breakfast. He drifted back to sleep with happy dreams of their wedding.

And then he awoke to a loud humming. Signora Ferrante shook him.

"Alberto, get up! We need to get to the bathtub. There's no time to get to the shelter."

He reached over and grabbed his crutches. "I can do it. Just go. I'll join you in just a moment."

He raised himself up and hobbled across the room that had begun shaking. Just as he crossed the threshold of the bathroom, a tremendous boom caused him to fall to the floor.

Alberto crawled, dragging his bad leg farther into the bathroom, and slid to the tub. Signora Ferrante pulled him from each arm and dragged him in. Then they put their hands over their heads in response to another boom.

The windows in the bathroom rattled, and he heard something break. He held Signora Ferrante's small bony hands and stared at the bottom of the tub between them.

They stayed in that position for more than an hour, his back bruises throbbing, his buttocks falling asleep beneath him, and a dull ache pulsing in his thigh where the net shuttle was pressed against his leg. Still, he held on to Signora Ferrante as tears streamed down her cheeks, and he felt his own eyes grow wet. But through it all, they stayed put.

Finally, the tremors in the building stopped, and he heard nothing—only Signora Ferrante's heavy breathing. He looked up at her and pulled her in for a hug.

"What about Vittoria and Lorenzo?" she asked.

And suddenly, Alberto panicked, trying to stand unassisted. A shot of pain ran through his leg, and he collapsed onto the floor. Signora Ferrante was immediately at his side, helping him back to the couch.

They sat together in the living room in silence for a few moments.

"Vittoria probably went to the air raid shelter with the children, and Lorenzo must have gone there with his teacher," Signora Ferrante said. "Don't you think? Yes... that's probably what happened. I should start dinner. We all could use a hearty supper after that."

She left the room, and Alberto sat there, staring at the radio. He stayed in that position as he heard pots and pans banging and water flowing and smelled onions and garlic cooking in the kitchen.

He kept checking his watch. Finally, he heard someone at the door, and he lifted himself on his crutches and made his way to the entryway. There, he saw Lorenzo, who had clearly been crying.

"Are you all right?" he asked, and the boy ran to him and hugged him.

"You're safe," Lorenzo whispered. "Mamma, too?"

"Yes, we're safe, but did you see Vittoria?"

Lorenzo's eyes widened. "She's not here?"

Alberto shook his head. "I thought you might run into her on the way home."

"She's probably with her students." Lorenzo's eyes shifted.

"Yes, probably." Alberto's heart beat faster. Where was she?

Signora Ferrante emerged from the kitchen and took her boy in her arms.

"Where is your sister?"

"I don't know." Lorenzo's voice cracked. "Maybe we should turn on the radio?"

And he turned the knob to bring the brown box to life.

There was an ongoing news bulletin.

"We are hearing about extensive damage to the shipyard and harbor as well as many parts of the city, where rescuers are at this moment pulling bodies from the rubble. There are reports of damage to the Church of San Giorgio dei Genovesi, the Church of Santa Zita in Via Squarcialupo, the Oratory of the Compagnia del Rosario di Santa Cita in Via Valverde, the Church of Santa Maria in Valverde in Piazza Valverde, Bonservizi School, and..."

But Alberto couldn't hear anything else, for Vittoria's school, Bonservizi, had been damaged.

Lorenzo dropped to his knees on the floor, crying and leaning toward the radio. "Did you hear what he said?"

Alberto nodded, too stunned to make sense of it.

Signora Ferrante appeared in the living room, wringing her apron. "What can we do?"

"We wait." Alberto's fear coursed through his veins. "Maybe she made it to the shelter."

They waited the whole night, but Vittoria never came home.

Morning came, and Alberto remained glued to the radio. The news had only gotten worse with reports of more than one hundred assumed dead.

He and Signora Ferrante sipped *caffè d'orzo* in silence, and then he heard a knock.

Signora Ferrante opened the door to a slim woman in a dark suit, who explained she was Signora Solafi, the headmistress at Vittoria's school.

"I'm afraid she didn't make it." Signora Solafi clutched her hands tightly. "I'm so sorry."

Alberto swallowed and stared at the worn wooden table where he'd sat with Vittoria just two days prior. Valentine's Day. He thought of how he'd held her, all the precious moments they'd shared, and their dreams for the future. She was his light through the darkness of war, and now that was gone.

"What happened?" He raised his tearing eyes to the woman's narrow face.

"Most of us had escaped to the shelter, but Vittoria went back when she realized some children were missing." Signora Solafi paused. "And that's about when the bomb hit."

"You... saw her?" Alberto asked as a tear streamed down his cheek.

"No," Signora Solafi said. "But I saw the damage. There was no way she could have survived that. I'm so sorry."

"But there's a chance she might be under the rubble." Alberto's voice rose. "There has to be."

"I'm sorry." Signora Solafi shook her head.

Signora Ferrante and Alberto sat in silence for a long time after the headmistress left.

"Why didn't she just move when she had a chance?" Alberto pounded the table.

"Her job was important to her," Signora Ferrante sighed. "It sounds like she was dedicated until the end."

"But she had so much more to live for... We were going to marry this spring. She wanted children!"

"You were so good to my daughter," Signora Ferrante sobbed.

A cold weight dropped in Alberto's gut. He lowered his coffee cup, no longer able to drink.

"We have to leave," he said in a measured tone. "We'll take the train tomorrow and get away from this place."

Signora Ferrante nodded. "Even if they can't find the body, I'd still like to have a funeral."

He traced his finger around the cup's rim. "Of course. And we can do that in Isola delle Femmine. It just doesn't make sense to stay here any longer than we have to."

That evening, Alberto broke the news to Lorenzo. As he held the weeping boy, he saw Vittoria in his face. This young man had been taught to believe, obey, and fight, striving for those ideals just as he once had. Now Alberto saw it clearly as a simple slogan, because what more was there to believe in? Why should one obey a government that could not protect them? It was not worth the effort to fight. As he squeezed Lorenzo, he wondered how they could each move on. How could life ever be so carefree?

THIRTY-FIVE

FEBRUARY 1943

The lunch bell rang, and Annalisa followed the other women, removing her gloves and waiting in line to wash up in the bathroom. The fishy smell clung to her skin no matter how much she scrubbed, but the warm water felt good after a full morning of handling fish under the cold faucet.

"So, any plans this weekend?" Emily asked as they settled into seats across from one another in the breakroom.

"Not really." Annalisa shook her head. "Just catching up on my rest."

"This job can certainly drain you," Emily sighed. "I was going to ask if you'd like to join me at a dance Saturday night at the community center."

"A dance? Well, I'm married, so I don't think I'll be doing any dancing unless it's with my husband. And after a week of working at the steel mill, he's definitely not going to be up for doing much."

The past couple of weeks had been difficult. Sam would come home with his clothes and face blackened by the coal he'd been shoveling all day, and after hopping in the shower, he'd soon be off to bed, falling asleep nearly as soon as his head hit the pillow. So, she was surprised that night when she returned home to find him cleaned up and hovering over a pan in the kitchen.

"I thought I'd make a little something for dinner." He held up a spatula. "Just some chicken and vegetables."

"I didn't know you cooked." Annalisa set her handbag down on a chair.

"There's still a lot you don't know about me." He gave her a kiss. "So, how was your day?"

"Same as usual. How about you?"

"Just looking forward to Sunday. I thought we could take a drive up into the preserve for old time's sake—maybe even visit our favorite graveyard."

Annalisa smiled. "Sounds good to me."

"Say, before I forget, there's some mail that came for you from Oklahoma."

Her eyebrows shot up. "My father?"

She opened the letter he handed to her.

Dear Annalisa,

Thank you for your letter. I am so proud of you for finding your own home, and I hope you are enjoying married life. I have written to the Alien Enemy Control Unit multiple times now and finally heard that it would help my case if I could provide some letters attesting to my character. Would you be able to help reach out to people I knew who could provide a reference? Thank you, my dear, for anything you can do to help your father at this time.

With Love,
Your Papà

"So, what does he say?" Sam plated the food.

"He says he needs help. He needs letters vouching for his character. It sounds like there's a chance for a rehearing."

"Well, that should be easy, right?" Sam slid into his chair. "Just find some of the men he fished with."

"Yeah." Annalisa lifted a forkful of chicken. "I suppose that would work. And maybe our old landlord. My Papà always paid him on time."

"Who else? Maybe his barber?"

"Barber?" She laughed.

"Just thinking of people who might have talked with him a lot. I chat with my barber."

She chewed for a moment. "I just don't know when I'll have time to reach out to all of these people."

"I'll tell you what." Sam put down his fork. "Instead of going up to the graveyard on Sunday, let's plan to make a few visits around town. It will be like a scavenger hunt; we'll make it fun."

She loved this about him, his laid-back approach to what was seemingly insurmountable. It wasn't just easy confidence; he believed in her and respected what mattered to her. With him on her side, she sometimes felt like she could do just about anything. It was a nice thought to keep her moving forward in this frustrating struggle called life.

Sunday delivered a bright and clear morning, a rare respite from the winter rain. It seemed like all of Pittsburg was out on the streets, flaunting their finery. Ladies in church-appropriate dresses topped with fur collars and fascinator hats strolled beside men in single-breasted suits with narrow lapels as bobby-socked girls and boys in cardigans scampered ahead. Annalisa took in the view as they rode to their first stop to visit her father's old friend, Mr. Scotto.

She'd heard that the man had been evacuated like her mother and that he'd found a place in the town of Oakley while his American-born wife and children had stayed behind. But the government had since rescinded evacuation orders, so she figured he'd be back at his apartment.

"Ready for your mission?" Sam asked.

"Ready, sir." She saluted as she left the car with the Alien Enemy Control Unit's address in hand.

A blue scrub jay screeched overhead in a sycamore tree in front of the white picket fenced yard. Mr. Scotto was watering pink geraniums out front. She waved to get his attention.

"Annalisa!" The man lowered his tin watering can. "Is that you?"

"It is." She smiled at the gate. "Do you have a moment?"

"Of course." He approached. "Just tending to my garden. It's the least I can do now that we Italians can't fish. You know they requisitioned my *Giuseppina*?"

Annalisa had heard about how her father's former colleagues, who were not citizens, had been banned from fishing. Many had had to give up their boats as well as their livelihoods.

She glanced at the charming two-story building with a light gray exterior and white trim. She wondered how he could afford the apartment now and how much longer he could hold on to it without work.

"How is your father?" Mr. Scotto asked. "Any news?"

"That's what I came to talk to you about." She explained the situation.

"Of course, I'd be happy to tell them about what a good man your father is," Mr. Scotto said. "And I'm sure I can convince a few of the other fishermen to do the same."

"Thank you." She hugged the man before handing him the address.

"Give my regards to your Mamma," Mr. Scotto said, and

she promised to do so, although she wasn't sure when she'd again see her mother.

"One down," Sam tapped the steering wheel as she returned to the car.

"Actually, he offered to get more men to send letters."

"That's terrific." Sam turned his head as he backed out the car. "Now we just need to ask the landlord."

"And the barber, right?" She smiled.

"Yes, the barber. Definitely the barber!"

Annalisa gazed out the window as they drove on to their next stop, her family's former apartment to see their old landlord, Mr. DeRosa. Memories of her childhood washed over her, of when they raced up and down the street with her brother and gathering around the table for supper. That apartment had been her parents' first home, their beachhead upon arrival in the U.S. With so much that had happened, she wondered if they'd been better off staying in Sicily. Still, the sunny streets of Pittsburg seemed brighter today, ripe with possibility. She glanced at Sam, glad she was no longer facing uncertainty alone and resolved to finally make things right for her father.

Fort McAlester, McAlester, Oklahoma

Vincenzo walked back from lunch with a sense of hope. He'd received two letters: One from his daughter detailing her progress in rounding up character witnesses and a second that announced he would be moved back to Fort Missoula, his favorite camp thus far and, if he was lucky, his final destination.

"Hey, Vincenzo!" called Cristiano as he walked past. "Care for a little bocce?"

Vincenzo stepped up and accepted the *pallina* his friend handed him.

"I'm leaving Friday." He launched the little ball across the gravel to a spot about ten feet away from them.

"Who will I have to beat in bocce with you gone?" Cristiano asked as Vincenzo tossed the ball in the direction of the target. "Look at you. Nearly three months, and you're still throwing too short."

Vincenzo waited until Cristiano had released his ball before scooping his own up and throwing it so that it rolled right next to the *pallina*. "Looks like you spoke too soon."

"You can't always win." Cristiano tossed his second ball.

"Indeed." Vincenzo rolled another ball. "But it's time for my luck to change, don't you think?"

"I hope so." Cristiano launched his third ball. "For me, too. It's been a long road, this Grand Tour."

"And what do we have to show for it? More gray hair and weight loss. Our families aren't going to recognize us when this is done."

After the men had each tossed out four balls, they walked to the *pallina* and measured the distance between the balls using their feet.

Cristiana shook his head at Vincenzo. "Looks like you're the winner—at least for today."

Friday came sooner than Vincenzo had anticipated. He said his goodbyes and climbed onto the back of a truck with twenty other men en route to the train that would take them north to Montana.

He slept most of the journey, feeling less anxious, knowing he was returning somewhere familiar. Had any of the musicians from his previous stay remained? He decided it didn't matter. He was determined to get his rehearing and disembark from what Cristiano called the Grand Tour once and for all. So much depended on his release. The future of his family was at stake.

MARCH 1943

Fort Missoula, Missoula, Montana

Vincenzo stepped out of the train into the cold, dry air. Snow covered the blue mountains, and small flakes cascaded from the afternoon sky. Bella Vista, indeed.

Two of his bocce rivals, Tonio and Marcellino, were among

those who joined him in the back of the truck that bumped along the road to Fort Missoula.

"Look who decided to join us." Tonio nudged Vincenzo.

"I guess I just couldn't stay away from you guys." Vincenzo shook his head.

"I hear they have real bocce courts where we're going," Marcellino said.

"They do." Vincenzo nodded. "Soccer fields, too."

"The better to beat you on!" Tonio grinned.

"I wouldn't get too cocky if I were you," Vincenzo winked. "I've been here before, you know."

They slowed to a stop, and the men filed out, making their way toward the white stucco barrack building. When he entered, the air was musty and smelled of cigarette smoke.

He scanned the room and saw some vaguely familiar faces. He nodded and made his way to an empty bunk, closely followed by Tonio.

"I'll take the bottom bunk!" Tonio called over his stooped shoulders as they approached the beds.

"Fine by me." Vincenzo climbed up to rest after his long journey.

He closed his eyes, and it wasn't long before he was dreaming. He was back home, but this time, home was Isola delle Femmine. His sister, Costanza, was there, but she was a teenager and he realized so, too, was he.

It was springtime. The sky was powder blue and a light, cool breeze carried with it the briny scent of the sea. Somehow, he'd missed the tuna *mattanza*.

He raced to the shore and watched the men haul in the net. They sang with each tug, and then he saw them lean over to stab at the giant fish. The water was a brilliant azure shade, and the sun sparkled across the waves as sea birds circled overhead.

All the colors seemed to merge, contrasting with his muted feelings of loss and longing. He heard Costanza laughing behind him, and then her laughter turned into that of a man's.

He awoke and remembered where he was and that Tonio was below him.

"What's so funny?"

"You were snoring. That must have been a deep sleep."

"I was dreaming." He closed his eyes again.

"Hold on to those dreams," Tonio said softly. "It's all we have these days."

A bell rang, the sound bouncing off the bare walls.

"Dinnertime." Vincenzo climbed down from his bunk, still groggy from his interrupted nap.

"I'm starving." Tonio rubbed his belly as the two followed the other men out the door into the cold evening.

"This place had the best dinners." Vincenzo waved his hand. "Some world-class chefs were interned here."

When they reached the mess hall, they were pleased to receive pasta in red sauce alongside Italian sausage and green beans on their metal trays.

The two surveyed the rows of wooden picnic-style tables, and Vincenzo spotted a familiar face he raced to greet.

"Aldo!" He nearly dropped his food tray as he went in for a hug.

"*Paesano!*" Aldo smiled. "You came back?"

"Yes, we just got here from Fort McAlester, in Oklahoma. This is Tonio. Tonio, Aldo. Aldo, Tonio."

The two men shook hands.

"Come, sit with us." Aldo motioned to open seats, and they slid in among men Vincenzo remembered from his previous stay.

"So, you're still here?" Vincenzo shook his head. "They didn't move you?"

"No, I think as long as Italy is at war with America, we will be here serving our own tour of duty," Aldo said. "Isn't that right, Niccolò?"

A shorter man with a pudgy, olive-toned face nodded his head.

"So, what shows have you all been putting on since I've left?" Vincenzo asked.

"We're doing *Pagliacci* now. If you can believe it, the men have gotten better."

"I used to work at the ticket booth." Vincenzo turned to Tonio, who nodded. "And the public's still coming for the shows?"

"It's definitely earned us some good public relations, especially after there was a story in the newspapers about how we eat better than local Missoulians." Aldo pierced a piece of sausage. "I said maybe we should cook for them, too. So, how's life? I take it you haven't had a rehearing."

"Funny you should mention it." Vincenzo tapped his fork. "I'm working on that very thing."

Aldo arched a brow. "Well, my friend, perhaps our Bella Vista will be yours."

Vincenzo pressed his lips together and nodded. For the first time, it felt like he was close to what he'd been chasing for so long.

THIRTY-SEVEN
MARCH 1943

Alberto watched the sapphire waves crash into the rocky shore, and he thought of the violence and heartache that had brought him back to Isola delle Femmine. A month had passed, and while he was walking again, he carried with him the pain of having lost Vittoria. The memories had begun to haunt him, mingling with a growing sense of responsibility for his family.

He thought of Vittoria's soft smile and gentle touch, recalling her strong sense of justice and unwavering convictions. She would have been intrigued by the news of yet another strike, this time involving tens of thousands at Fiat's Mirafiori plant in Turin, where workers dropped their tools and walked off the job. The men demanded a 192-hour bonus, but it was more than that: Their home had been rocked by Allied bombs and they faced food scarcity. Perhaps his own strike had meant something after all, inspiring other men to act on behalf of their workforce, families, and nation as a whole. The people had spoken. It was time for change, but would the government listen? He longed to contemplate with Vittoria the answers to his many questions, to again hear her sweet voice, and walk by her side with deliberate steps forward despite the uncertain future. He closed his eyes. Nearly feeling her presence there alongside him made the void even more unbearable.

He'd brought the Ferrantes back with him. The apartment Vittoria had secured was out of the question without a job. Instead, they were sharing space with his parents in their home. Signora Ferrante was sleeping in Cristina's old room and splitting meal preparation duties with his mother, and he was bunking with Lorenzo in his former bedroom.

He sat down on a jagged rock, staring out at the deep blue horizon. As his mind turned over his next steps, he saw something: a small weather-worn but seaworthy *gozzo* boat, bobbing in the azure waters. Memories of childhood suddenly swept over him like the sea-foam accumulating on the shore. He thought of the net shuttle his father had gifted him, a present passed down from his uncle. It had once symbolized hard work, age-old tradition, and, for a time, prosperity.

He still had that shuttle, even after all these years, a charm that he thought had served him no good luck as of late. But now he realized it held the key to a better future. It had no place in the big city, but here, in the slower-paced countryside, one could take the time to sit down and repair a net and possibly even salvage the web of life he once knew. He thought of the afternoons he'd played soccer while his father and other fishermen worked diligently, mending nets on drying racks nearby. How their fingers and wrists rhythmically flexed as they slid their shuttles through gaps, repairing the damage wrought by massive fish and harsh elements.

He stood up, feeling the weight of his body on his still-weak leg, and took a deep breath of the salty yet healing air, determined to change course.

. . .

"Papà, I've decided to start fishing," Alberto announced over a dinner of rice and vegetables.

Supplies were running short and the black market was cost-prohibitive without his paycheck. The family had taken to eating a meal a day, and it was showing in his parents' thinner faces as they exchanged a puzzled look across the table.

His father tilted his head. "But you never wanted to fish before. Why now?"

"Why not?" Alberto shrugged. "I need to pull my own weight around here. You said so yourself: It's in my blood. It's time."

"It won't be easy." Papà shook his head. "If you're planning to fish tuna, you'll need at least thirty men, strong ones. All the young men have left for the war. The rest of us are no longer fit for the sea."

"I'll bring strong, hard workers who can help us rebuild the fleet, maybe in time for another spring *mattanza*," Alberto said.

"I'll help!" Lorenzo raised his hand.

"Yes, strong fishermen like Lorenzo." Alberto smiled. Now he just needed another twenty-eight men, and he knew exactly where to find them. He just hoped they'd have the strength and willingness to heed his desperate call.

Alberto emerged from the train alone onto a platform in Palermo Centrale, full of determination tempered with dread. The city had suffered two enormous blows in the past week, and all around him were reminders of that fateful February day when he'd lost Vittoria.

Hundreds of bombs had once again rained down on the city, damaging even the once-grand Cathedral. Nothing was sacred anymore. The Americans and British had made that abundantly clear with their relentless air raids that ran from day to night.

He walked for an hour past gutted buildings and piles of rubble. Men shoveled through the remnants of the city that had delivered and destroyed his dreams. And he wondered how many more hearts had been broken.

When Alberto reached the port, he saw still-burning ships, a demolished dry dock, and men picking up the pieces. He stood there for some time, inhaling the stench of burning fuel, metal, wood, and God only knew what else. Amid the popping and fizzing sounds, he considered all the hard work wasted, the hope shattered, and the expectations that shipyard workers keep toiling on. And then he took a step forward.

"Excuse me," he called to a man with whom he'd crossed paths over the years.

The laborer was sweeping up debris, and few other men were in sight.

"Alberto Cardinale?" the man replied, and Alberto remembered his name: Leonardo Giordano. "Where have you been?"

"I returned home to Isola delle Femmine after the strike. How are things?"

"Not good." Leonardo ran a sooty hand through his curly brown hair.

Alberto adjusted his shoulder bag. "Like I said, I came from the village. I'm looking to recruit some men for fishing. The money wouldn't be the same as here, but it'd be far safer."

"You came here to recruit men?" Leonardo whispered, looking around to see if anyone had heard them.

"Yes." Alberto fished out a piece of paper on which he'd scribbled an address. "We'll meet here. Please spread the word. I know there must be men looking to leave the city."

"I know a few men who would jump at the chance." Leonardo nodded as he pocketed the paper.

"Excellent," Alberto said. "Even if you don't decide to join me, I wish you the best of luck."

"Thank you." Leonardo tipped his chin. "Good luck is hard to come by these days."

As Alberto walked away, again passing through the shell of this once great city, he looked ahead with optimism. Although he knew the days ahead would present numerous challenges, he found solace in a renewed sense of purpose. This crew of fishermen would reel in not only sustaining food but also hope for a better future.

If only Vittoria could be there by his side to see it through.

THIRTY-EIGHT
MARCH 1943

Fort Missoula, Missoula, Montana

Vincenzo picked up a large basket and carried the men's dirty laundry out the door to the camp tailor and laundry shop. Entrance was limited to men tasked with mending items such as socks and pants and those who were put on laundry duty.

Still, the shop was bustling with activity as the actors from the *Pagliacci* production had lined up in front of this week's tailor for alterations to their respective costumes.

"Hey, Vincenzo!" Aldo's friend Niccolò called to him, and Vincenzo nodded. "What, they've got you on laundry?"

"I guess it's my lucky week." Vincenzo began transferring the stinky clothes from the basket into a free washer. Then he moved to another machine, unloading clothes into the wringer to remove the excess water. Finally, he opened a dryer, unloaded clean clothes into his empty basket, and carried them back to the barracks.

Everyone had written their names inside the waistband or collar, which made it relatively easy for Vincenzo to deposit all the clothing in the men's assigned lockers. What was tricky was when multiple men had the same last name. He'd wisely written a V before Aiello, knowing that back home in Pittsburg, five directory pages were allotted to his surname.

But when he approached the barracks, he heard men shouting. As he stepped through the door, he encountered what appeared to be a riot, something he'd never seen at Fort Missoula. More than a dozen men were grappling on the floor like wrestlers surrounded by a large ring of onlookers.

"What's happening?" he asked Marcellino, who was among those gawking.

"Someone wrote an anti-Fascist letter, singling out the camp Fascists, and Dr. Grimley posted it on the wall of the infirmary and well... I guess one of the accused Fascists saw it."

Vincenzo raised his eyebrows. "And he started a fight?"

"He told the other accused Fascists, and the three of them sneaked up on the guy who wrote it, and well, then it turned into a much bigger fight with other guys jumping in on the anti-Fascist side."

Vincenzo stared at the men with wide eyes. "This is ridiculous. They're going to get hurt—all because the doctor decided to post a letter on his wall?"

Just then, five guards entered and began spraying a canister of gas at the men in the center of the ring.

"All of you, enough of that!" shouted one of the guards, and the men in the middle of the ring stopped fighting and began choking.

The guards rounded up the men and took them to the infirmary.

"And they're going to see the letter, and then we're back where we started." Vincenzo traced a circle in the air. "Unbelievable!"

"I'll tell you something." Marcellino raised a plump finger. "I highly doubt half those guys were really Fascists. It's just a lot of pent-up frustration. There's not enough to do around here."

"Just wait till it's their turn for laundry or kitchen duty." Vincenzo chuckled.

Marcellino shook his head. "Even that's not enough. It's still too cold to go outside, and who can blame a guy for getting stir-crazy?"

Vincenzo picked his basket back up. "I have to put these clothes away. Want to help me?"

"Sure thing, my friend," Marcellino nodded, and the two split up the job of loading clothes into lockers.

When they were finished, it seemed everyone had calmed down. The day's excitement had ceased, and now several men were lying down to take a nap or read from one of the camp's communal newspapers.

"Any news?" Tonio asked from the lower bunk after Vincenzo climbed atop his.

"News? You mean about the riot?"

Tonio chuckled. "No, silly. Your daughter's campaign to get you out of here."

Vincenzo leaned over the edge. "She asked a few men to write letters. I don't know if they did or didn't. Mail takes so long to reach us anyway these days with the extra layer of censors they've added in the past few months. Everything goes to New York now, before coming our way."

"It's stricter, too." Tonio lay on his back with his arms behind his head. "My wife sent me some photographs, and they confiscated them. All I had was a letter with the words, 'Here are the latest family pictures.' And no pictures inside. I can't see how much my three-year-old has grown up without me there."

"I didn't even think about that. You know my daughter's pregnant? Pretty soon, she's going to have a baby, and I don't suppose I'll see him or her anytime soon."

"A baby?" Tonio sat up. "You're going to be a grandfather?

Congratulations, my friend. That's good news, which means luck could be on your side after all."

"I hope so," Vincenzo said. "For you, too."

"Let's toast to it, eh?"

"With what? Water?"

"No, silly." He dropped his voice to a whisper. "The guys in the kitchen have been saving up the dried fruit they serve to keep us regular. No one's supposed to know, but there's a small supply of what they're calling prison wine."

"Well, I'll be... It's been an awful long time since I've had a fermented beverage. We'll definitely have to have a drink of that."

"They're serving it up at dinnertime. You just have to know the code word."

Vincenzo smiled. "And what might that be?"

"Mussolini."

Vincenzo chuckled nervously and shook his head. "Are you serious? 'Mussolini'? Not a name I'd ever expected to toast to—especially after all of this."

Tonio shrugged. "Hey, I'll say whatever they want if it gets me a drink."

Vincenzo considered his friend's words and carefree spirit. Maybe it didn't really matter. After all, it was just good fun. At least they could still find something worth toasting.

The dinner bell rang, and Vincenzo was feeling jovial. He was going to enjoy a glass of so-called prison wine and what promised to be a splendid meal: veal parmigiana and a side of *penne alla marinara.*

He stepped up to the counter and requested his food. His eyes met those of the server, who seemed to share a knowing smile. Still, he hesitated, reconsidering his use of the name steeped in such infamy here in the U.S.

Mussolini had misguidedly led his nation to war with the very same people Italy had been aligned with during Vincenzo's service. He'd led disastrous campaigns in Greece and Africa in a desperate effort to reclaim the empire, misguided crusades that ultimately led to suffering. And for what? His people were dying, industries were crumbling, and Italy's reputation was shattered. It was because of Mussolini Vincenzo ended up in this mess. Yet, here in this camp, the man's name was reduced to a joke. Perhaps that was fitting. A mock toast with wine made from rotten fruit was one way to strip the vainglorious man of his power. Maybe that, in itself, was a victory.

It made him smile. "Oh yeah, and Mussolini, too!"

Two men approached him from behind and pinned him against the counter.

"What did you say?" one of them hissed into his ear.

"What do you mean?" Vincenzo tried to push them away. "I just asked for my food."

"No, you're a Mussolini-lover, aren't you?" A third man joined from the side, effectively boxing Vincenzo in.

"But I'm Sicilian; what good has Mussolini done for me?" Vincenzo gasped. "Besides, I left before the March on Rome."

None of it seemed to matter as a group surrounded them and began chanting. "Fascist! Fascist! Fascist!"

And soon, the first three men had Vincenzo pinned to the floor. He struggled to block their punches but to no avail. They pummeled him while a crowd gathered to watch.

"Leave him alone!" Aldo shouted, having rushed from the kitchen into the ring.

"He must be a Fascist, too!" shouted a broad-chested man, and three men joined him in tackling Aldo to the floor.

"Fascists! Fascists! Fascists!" chanted a growing crowd.

"Stop it, now!" shouted a guard, who held a can of gas. "I'm warning you."

The anti-Fascists stopped beating Vincenzo and Aldo, and the crowd quickly dispersed.

"Are you OK?" the guard asked as he bent down to help the men up.

Vincenzo's nose was bleeding and his head ached, but he nodded.

"You don't look so good," the guard said. "I'm taking you to the infirmary."

Vincenzo never got to eat his eagerly anticipated supper nor had a chance to sip the prison wine. But on his way to the infirmary, he was handed a letter. He was being granted a rehearing.

THIRTY-NINE
MARCH 1943

Pittsburg, California

Dear Annalisa,

I have good news! A rehearing has been scheduled for April. Now I just hope those men have come through and written the letters you asked for. I appreciate your help. You must be so busy with the new job, and I hope you are feeling well. I wish there were space to write more, but I can tell you that the snow is finally melting, and the hills are covered in the prettiest shade of green. Perhaps that means new beginnings are in store for us all. Please take care of yourself, my precious girl.

Love,
Papà

Annalisa's eyes were moist as she folded the letter and placed it on her nightstand on top of the pile she'd saved from her father.

"What's the matter?" Sam asked as he entered the room.

She clenched the side of the bed where she sat. "My Papà has a rehearing scheduled."

"Well, that's good news, isn't it?" He slid next to her. "Why are you so upset?"

She turned and faced him. "Because he thinks all those men wrote letters, and I just don't know."

"Why wouldn't they have written letters?" He brushed a stray hair out of her eyes. "Don't worry, it will all be resolved soon, and your Pops will be back before the baby comes."

But Annalisa wasn't sure. And it kept her up most of the night.

"Are you OK?" Emily asked her the next day while they were cleaning their fish. It was shad day, and the smell of the fish was particularly pungent.

"I need to run to the ladies' room. Cover for me?"

"Sure thing, sweetie."

In the bathroom, Annalisa splashed her face. The smell still made her nauseous, but she was also exhausted. She looked at herself in the mirror. Her face had gotten fuller, and she had a cluster of pimples on her forehead.

She sighed. Not much she could do about it. And then she thought about her father. There had to be something more she could do for him.

She returned to the assembly line, and Peggy shot her an annoyed look. The other ladies were starting to notice how often she had to leave. She just hoped no one suspected she was pregnant—especially not Mr. Hansen. Their foreman would certainly fire her on the spot.

She stole a look at her burgeoning belly. Perhaps they would think she'd put on some weight. She'd casually mentioned having to go on a diet to Emily, hoping that it would help bide her time. And now she was one month into her second trimester. There was only so much more time that she could hold on to this job.

"So, what's with you lately?" Emily asked as they munched on their respective sandwiches in the breakroom.

Annalisa shifted her eyes. "The smell just got to me, that's all."

Emily took a bite, and lowered her baloney sandwich. "But you seem so tired, too. Are you sleeping OK?"

"Not really." Annalisa tore at her bread's crust. "I've got a lot on my mind."

"Spill it." Emily smiled. "You know I won't tell anyone."

"Well, it's just that..." Annalisa looked down at the greasy table. "Well, my father's been away for a while."

"What? Your daddy's in prison?" Emily whispered.

Annalisa took a sip of her water. "Something like that. He's Italian, and they sent him off to one of those camps you hear about."

Emily raised her brows. "Like Camp Stoneman?"

"Yeah, like that, except he's not a POW." She waved her hand. "Anyway, it's complicated." She bit into her cheese sandwich as her friend nodded.

"Sounds like it." Emily chewed thoughtfully. "So, what's wrong?"

Annalisa lowered her sandwich. "He's up for a rehearing and needs someone to vouch for his character. I tried to find people, but I don't know if they've actually written letters on his behalf."

"Wait a minute." Emily raised a finger. "What about your brother?"

Annalisa stared at her a moment. "My brother? What do you mean? My brother's dead."

"I know." Emily leaned forward. "You told me, remember? Doesn't having a war hero as a son make you like a Gold Star Parent or something?"

Annalisa ate another two bites and considered her friend's words. If she wrote a letter revealing her father's status, it could change everything. It was highly likely that the government had no idea who they'd actually imprisoned. It was just what she needed to push her desperate effort over the edge. She suddenly felt like she could kiss the girl.

"Oh my God, Emily. You're brilliant. Why are you working at a cannery?"

Emily winked as she blotted her lips. "I know, right?"

Hon. Edward Ennis
Alien Control Unit
Department of Justice
Washington, D.C.

Dear Sir: I am writing to you on behalf of my father, Vincenzo Aiello, who has been interned since December 8, 1941. I understand my father has been granted a rehearing. Several individuals have offered to vouch for my father's character, which I hope you will consider as evidence of his good standing as a prospective citizen. Additionally, I wanted to let you know that my father also happens to be a Gold Star Parent. His son, Mario Aiello, was killed on December 7, 1941, aboard the USS Arizona during the attack on Pearl Harbor. My father and my family are very proud of my brother's legacy, and my father wants nothing more than to honor my brother by becoming a naturalized citizen if given the chance. I hope that you will consider releasing my father, so my family can finally mourn my brother's passing together.

Respectfully yours,
Annalisa Wells

Annalisa sealed the envelope and brought it, along with her

latest letter to her father, to the post office. She felt hopeful, and she was grateful for her friendship with Emily. The girl was definitely brilliant. Perhaps this idea was what they needed to push things over the finish line—letters or no letters.

The next Monday, they were still cleaning shad, and Annalisa was still feeling nauseous. After about two hours on the assembly line, she had to bolt to the bathroom.

When she returned, she froze. Mr. Hansen stood in her open spot, clipboard in hand.

"Annalisa, may I see you for a moment?" her foreman asked with a concerned look.

"Certainly, Mr. Hansen." Annalisa caught Peggy's eye as she followed him.

"Have a seat." Mr. Hansen closed the door to his wood-paneled office that reeked of cigarette smoke.

After they had both settled into chairs on the opposite side of his tidy desk, he leaned forward with his hands folded and cleared his throat.

"I'm getting reports you're leaving the assembly line quite a bit, shirking your responsibilities and whatnot," he said. "Is this true?"

Annalisa felt her face grow hot. "I wasn't feeling well. It was probably something I ate."

"I received reports on more than one occasion. You must be eating quite a lot of bad food. Aren't you Italians supposed to be good cooks?"

"It's passed." She waved her hand. "I promise it won't happen again."

"Can you make that promise?" He leaned back in his chair. "From the looks of you, it appears you may be in the family way."

"I beg your pardon?"

"Pregnant." Mr. Hansen's eyes settled on her belly. "You are pregnant, aren't you?"

Annalisa burst into tears. "I'm not that far along. I can still manage."

Mr. Hansen sighed. "I need ladies who can stick to the assembly line. We can't afford to have anyone leaving their spot. It's just not fair to the others. Besides, what am I paying you for? I'm sorry, Missy, but I'm going to need your uniform."

She gasped. "You're firing me?"

"Yes, I'm afraid so." He jotted something in a ledger on his desk. "We will pay you through today. Now, if you'll excuse me, there's plenty of work that still needs to be done. Just drop your uniform off when you can."

With that, Annalisa yanked the white cap from her head and flung it onto his desk. "This isn't fair—none of it."

Tears blurred her vision as she turned on her heel and stormed out. She wanted to get far away from that smelly place and for life to change once and for all.

FORTY

MARCH 1943

Isola delle Femmine, Sicily

Each morning, Alberto would rise, drink a few sips of *caffè d'orzo*, and head out to Piano Ponente, where he'd asked the men to meet. After a few hours, several boys would show up to play a pickup game of soccer, but no one from Palermo came.

Still, he kept going until one afternoon on Wednesday, the 24th of March, he heard someone call his name. He'd been watching the boys play soccer and was so engrossed that he hadn't noticed about a dozen men amble onto the field behind him.

"Alberto!" Leonardo called out again, and Alberto turned in surprise to see his former coworker and the men he'd brought, including his friends Ascanio and Fausto.

"You came!" he shouted.

"You should have seen it," Ascanio said sadly. "Twenty-four bombers. They sank six merchant marine ships along with several smaller boats. One of the ships was loaded with ammunition and just blew up, causing all kinds of damage."

"And the *Granatier*..." Fausto interjected.

"Yes." Ascanio shook his head. "They damaged the *Granatier*."

"No!" Alberto clenched his fists. "She was one of the first of the ships I'd worked on that was sent into service."

"I'm afraid she'll need some extensive repairs." Ascanio sighed. "That is if they can make her seaworthy again."

Alberto shook his head. "It happened while you were on the job?"

The men all nodded.

"We decided together that we were either going to strike again or leave." Leonardo's eyes shifted to the other men. "And well, some of us chose the latter."

"Well, I hope you'll find you made the right choice," Alberto said. "If nothing else, you'll be far safer here."

A few of the men nervously chuckled, and Alberto could see in their gaunt faces how much their experiences had drained them.

"So, when can we start fishing?" Fausto asked.

Now Alberto released his own nervous chuckle. "Well, my father and I will need to train you. It won't be easy. Tuna fishing can even be dangerous."

"You said they fish every May and June." Ascanio tilted his head. "We have a couple of months, no?"

"That's right." Alberto nodded. "Just a couple of months. If that still sounds good to you, you're welcome to join us. I can't fit you all in my parents' home, but I do know of an apartment that might still be available. If you don't mind sharing."

The men turned to one another.

"I'm in." Leonardo lifted his chin.

"Of course, I am." Ascanio grinned.

"Me too," Fausto echoed.

Several of the other men stepped forward and raised their hands. Only three men expressed their regrets that they could not stay.

"I'll spread the word, though," said a man named Flavio.

"Excellent." Alberto clapped. "Thank you all for coming here today. We have nine more sets of hands than we did. I assume we're bound to find some more."

He hugged the men who were leaving and then left the remaining nine to watch the soccer match while he fetched his father.

For the rest of the week, the men met in the same place. Between practicing technique with Papà, they worked on fixing up abandoned wood-hulled *gozzi* and mending portions of the linen net. Meanwhile, Alberto greeted what amounted to a dozen more men. All had come from the shipyard and felt compelled to do so because of the most recent air raid.

That Saturday, Alberto stood back and watched as men held a net at the edge of one of the boats, some laughing as they fell in and others helping them back up. He wondered how this ragtag crew of men without experience might fare when it was finally out at sea.

He was not alone in his doubts. As he settled into the pew on Sunday for Mass with the Ferrantes and his family, he heard whispers and saw questioning stares. But the priest Padre Isadoro's sermon gave him some hope.

"Dearly beloved, as we gather here today, we are this week reminded of chapter four of the Book of Matthew, verses eighteen through twenty-two: 'As Jesus was walking beside the Sea of Galilee, he saw two brothers, Simon called Peter and his brother Andrew. They were casting a net into the lake, for they were fishermen.' And Jesus said, 'Come, follow me, and I will send you out to fish for people.'"

Padre Isadoro paused, making eye contact with Alberto, and continued. "This village once boasted a thriving fishing industry, but most of our fishermen had to put down the net and take up arms. They had to learn a new trade just as our new guests from Palermo heeded the call to fish our waters. Remember: Jesus called upon ordinary men to join him as disciples. These men may not have had skills, but they had faith and determination. That's what I'd like to see from this community. With faith and determination, these novices will bring this village not only food but a future. And I ask you each to open your hearts and minds and accept them into the fold, to have your own faith and determination."

Alberto smiled at the priest and felt a wave of relief wash over him. He turned his head and saw several nods in response to the man's words, and he knew he would not be alone in his endeavor.

As he walked with his family and friends out of the church, his eyes met those of a beaming Padre Isadoro.

"Thank you." The priest took his hand. "You are bringing life back to this community when we need it most. And something tells me this feeds your soul as well."

"Yes, Padre." Alberto hugged the older man.

"I also wanted to say you can count me in." Padre Isadoro pointed to his chest. "I may not have sea legs or the blessing of youth, but the time has come for men to stand up and pitch in for everyone."

"Really?" Alberto was moved by his pastor's words. They had worked so hard and needed all the support they could get in their effort. "You would join us? Thank you, Padre. Now God will truly be on our side."

"The Lord is always beside you." Padre Isadoro again grasped Alberto's hand. "Remember that."

FORTY-ONE

MAY 1943

Fort Missoula, Missoula, Montana

Vincenzo took a bite from his *spiedini* skewer of rolled-up breaded sirloin steak and then washed it down with a glass of water.

"I can't believe it," Aldo said. "Think about it: By this time next week, you could be a free man going home to your family."

Vincenzo smiled. "I just need to get through the hearing."

"Don't take this the wrong way, but I hope I never see you again."

The time had come. In two days, Vincenzo was due in the same little courtroom where he'd initially been condemned to internment more than a year prior.

It seemed a lifetime ago. He'd taken so much for granted: his job, the regular letters and postcards from Mario, Maria's hearty and creative suppers, Annalisa excelling in school, clean sheets and comfy pillows, and the evening shot of grappa. Now all he could hope for were meals minus rationed foods, the linens, and maybe, if he were lucky, there'd be some grappa. He knew from their letters that his daughter and wife were barely speaking, but he hoped that his return could end that. They needed to properly mourn his son together. And maybe he could finally share their secret with Annalisa.

Dinner ended, and a band of seven violinists, an accordionist, a mandolin player, and a singer lined up along the wall opposite the serving counter. They began to play "Ciuri Ciuri," a traditional Sicilian folk song about the beauty of flowers and love.

His mind went to Maria's birthday, a year before they knew the war would separate them. He'd spotted some wild gladiolus on the roadside near Piano Ponente when walking from where he'd docked his boat to see her at her parents' home. The flowers were a vibrant purple, her favorite hue.

"No one has ever brought me flowers." She didn't care where they'd come from, only that he'd been thoughtful enough to gift them to her.

That was Maria, the same girl who said yes to marriage without a ring and didn't mind that he reeked of fish and had blood-stained clothes.

Why hadn't he given her more flowers? Surely, he could have at least picked some spring blooms from their front yard. So many missed chances to make his wife happy. As soon as he got back, he'd make up for lost time with a lovely spring bouquet —yes, soon. He had to think positively.

The musicians launched into a *tarantella*, and he was instantly transported again to Isola delle Femmine, this time to his cousin's banquet hall where they'd held their wedding reception.

There was an accordionist as there was now, and several tambourines had been handed out to the various couples on the dance floor. Then the music started with the men and women moving their feet in swift, small steps, the women's skirts unfurling like colorful blossoms, while the men hopped side to side. The music picked up pace, and the couples weaved in and out of each other's paths, eventually forming a circle that devolved into a line of dancers. As they clapped their hands and slapped the tambourines, he'd looked across at Maria twirling in her white lace dress, a hand-me-down from her mother. Her forehead was beaded with perspiration above a radiant smile. And he'd pulled her in for a kiss before the applauding crowd, dozens of people he now wasn't sure he'd ever see again.

After a few more songs, the musicians packed up their instruments, and Vincenzo walked with Aldo, Marcellino, and Tonio back to the barracks.

"You sure you won't miss nights like this when you're back on the other side?" Tonio asked from the lower bunk once they'd settled down.

"I'll tell you what I won't miss: your snoring!" Vincenzo said, and he felt his bunkmate playfully punch the bottom of his bed.

It was morning when they came for him, right after breakfast, so at least he'd gained some sustenance. Vincenzo turned as he walked and looked out at green pine trees lining the graceful mountain peaks, the Bella Vista. He silently asked God for strength, for his knees were shaking, and despite the cool spring weather, he was beginning to perspire.

They led him to the same building, T-1, inside the same wood-paneled courtroom where they'd declared him "potentially dangerous" and sentenced him to internment. And he settled into the same wobbly and uncomfortable wooden chair, feeling himself awash with hope, tinged with dread.

There they were again—the three men who had faced him last round—Scott Fitzgibbon, U.S. Attorney; William Pratt, Immigration and Naturalization Service; and Donald Martin, Federal Bureau of Investigation, along with a panel in the front composed of men from the Bay Area.

A man named Sutherland spoke. "We are gathered here today for the rehearing of internee number 14613212385, otherwise known as Vincenzo Aiello of Pittsburg, California. We have received four letters, providing testimonials to the character of said internee, and we have conducted follow-up interviews with each character witness."

Vincenzo exhaled in relief as the man spoke. He was already envisioning his homecoming, the loved ones gathered to greet him, the pasta he might have when he returned, holding Maria in his arms... Finally, it would come.

But then he heard Sutherland's tone change. "Mr. Aiello? What do you have to say?"

"Excuse me?" Vincenzo looked blankly at the three men with their penetrating stares.

"I asked what you had to say about the allegations that you had expressed pro-Fascist sentiments that resulted in a fight last month. Did you or did you not profess your allegiance to Mussolini, as has been reported?"

Vincenzo thought for a moment, then could not help himself but laugh.

"So, you think this is funny?" Sutherland tapped the desk. "This is a very serious allegation. Did you or did you not?"

"It was... about the wine," Vincenzo stammered. "Some internees made wine from dried fruits. There was a code word you had to say to be served a glass. For some reason, they chose 'Mussolini.'"

He shook his head. "It was silly, and I regret it now. The whole thing definitely wasn't worth it in the end."

Sutherland stared at him with a frown and looked at the other men, who shook their heads.

"We will have to investigate this story of prison wine further." Sutherland made a note with his pencil. "Until then, and in light of the fact that you were involved in a fight, we have decided to deny you parole."

"No!" Vincenzo groaned.

"You may leave now," Sutherland pointed to the door.

As he descended the dim staircase, Vincenzo felt lower with each step. He'd dug his grave with that ridiculous request for wine. Would this damnation be eternal?

He exited the building and stood in the cool spring breeze. There in the lush, green hills was Bella Vista, so much farther from his reach.

FORTY-TWO

MAY 1943

Pittsburg, California

Annalisa grabbed a couple of boxes of macaroni and cheese and dropped them into her grocery basket. She wondered what her mother would think of her feeding her husband something orange from a cardboard box. Then she considered what her mother might be doing and how she might be faring with the news of her father's parole being denied.

She couldn't believe the news herself, and it pained her to think that her father was so deprived that he might risk everything for a glass of prison wine. The details were murky as her father only had twenty-four lines to explain himself, but he'd mentioned he'd been in a fight, which worried Annalisa. She thought back to when Mario had been involved in the brawl with the neighborhood bullies and how Papà had invoked Jesus, suggesting that Mario turn the other cheek. What had internment done to her father? Would the same man return, and when might that be? It was all so frustrating. She'd tried her best and even that wasn't enough. Perhaps Edward Ennis hadn't yet gotten the letter. Wouldn't being a Gold Star Parent get her father out?

Passing a stack of canned fish, now rationed, she thought of the job she'd briefly held. She'd wanted to do her part, but now everything rested on Sam's often sore shoulders.

Upon approaching the counter, she unloaded her goods, handed over her ration coupons, and then paid the bill. It was a simple and routine exchange at a time that was anything but simple or routine.

She waddled down the sidewalk, weighed down by three bags. At six months pregnant, such tasks were growing harder. But who else was going to do it? Sam was all she had left in her life; he was the rock she could depend on for most everything else.

She spotted the legs of that rock sticking out from beneath his aging car when she arrived in front of their apartment. He slid out, covered in grease, when he heard her.

"Let me help you unload." He rubbed his stained hands on his trousers.

When they got inside, she collapsed on a kitchen chair in tears.

"Hey, are you OK?" Sam reached for her.

"You need to wash up." She wiped her eyes.

He turned to the sink and began scrubbing his hands. "So, what got you so upset?"

"All this with my Papà...We were so close to getting him out, and then he had to get into a fight." She sniffled. "And then my Mamma..."

"You miss her, don't you?" Sam turned off the faucet and dried his hands on a towel.

"I guess so." Her expression soured. "She disowned me when I needed her most."

Sam was cradling her now. "Well, I'm here, aren't I? Who needs her?"

"Don't talk about her like that. She's lost so much, and then I had to go complicate things."

Sam stroked her cheek. "Well, maybe when your Pops comes back, things will change."

She shook her head. "It won't be the same. Not without Mario. Nothing is ever going to be the same again."

"Sure, it will be different, but why does it have to be the same, anyway?"

Annalisa leaned into Sam's chest and said nothing for a moment.

She was thinking of her mother and how she had looked at her with such pride before she made her First Communion. Mamma had Annalisa stand on a chair as she pinned the hem of a white lace-trimmed dress.

"This was my dress, you know." Her mother paused with fabric between her fingers.

Annalisa remembered nodding.

"Stand up straight." Mamma tapped her leg. "This will be an important day for you. You know why?"

"It's my First Communion?"

Her mother sighed. "Yes, but do you know what that means?"

"I get to stand in line and eat bread?"

Her mother laughed. "You're joining the Church in accepting the bread that is Jesus's body."

Annalisa frowned. "But doesn't Jesus need his body?"

Her mother shook her head. "Silly girl. It's a symbol of the sacrifice that he made."

"What's a sacrifice?"

Mamma added another pin. "Don't they teach you anything in that school? It's when someone does something really hard, no matter how much it hurts them so they can make a better life. Like your Papà and I did when we left Sicily."

"What do you mean?"

Mamma dropped a pin on the floor, and as she picked it up, she muttered, "Someday you'll realize all the sacrifices that have been made for the life you have."

And now she was starting to understand her mother's harsh rhetoric, erratic temper, and even her moments of resentment. Her mother had endured a hard life, and Annalisa had only made it more difficult.

"I'm going to do it," she said suddenly, pulling away from Sam.

"What?"

"I'm going to write her a letter and see if she still won't be a part of my life. What do I have to lose anyway, right?"

Dear Mamma,

I hope you are well. It's a shame Papà was denied parole. I'm sorry it didn't work out the way we wanted.

I miss you. Even though we didn't always see eye to eye, it hurts to know I disappointed you. And I know I hurt you, and you didn't need that with everything else going on. The truth is I was scared, angry, lost, and made some mistakes. Sorry for that.

With Papà's situation, I've been thinking a lot about both of you. You only wanted the best for me, and you were always there for me in the past. Being without you these past few months has made me realize how much family means to me and how much I need you in my life.

I'd like to find a way for us to come together again. It won't be easy, and I know I can't go back and change what I've done to upset you. But I hope one day you'll forgive me.

In just a few short months, I'll have your first grandchild. I'm excited but sad to think our baby might not have a chance to meet his or her Nonna.

Hopefully, for your grandchild's sake at the very least, you'll consider reaching out to me. I'll be waiting for your reply.

Until then, you are in my thoughts. I love you, Mamma.

Your daughter,
Annalisa

FORTY-THREE

MAY 1943

Isola delle Femmine, Sicily

The moment had come. Forty men plus Alberto lined up on the pier off of Piano Ponente to pile onto the decks of the awaiting three large *gozzi* and a smaller rowboat as a crowd gathered, already cheering from the shore.

Padre Isadoro, whom Alberto had appointed in the role of *rais*, leader of the hunt, lifted a paddle in the air and called out, "Praise his name! Praise Jesus!"

And everyone shouted, "Amen!"

Alberto scanned the faces of the assembled men, the majority from Palermo, but also some of the village elders who had come out of fishing retirement to join the day's crusade.

It had been a challenging two months of grueling training for himself as well as the other novices. But the day had finally come. He was optimistic yet anxious.

He looked out at his father, who stood on the shore beside young Lorenzo. The fourteen-year-old had begged to join, but Alberto promised him his time would come, that he had enough grown men to help him this time.

The older men sang as they rowed, the lyrics to songs passed down from generations upon generations of seafarers before them, while the newcomers from Palermo hummed along. Their voices and humming grew louder with excitement and anticipation until they'd plied about three miles from the shore to an invisible line their forefathers had defined as the best location and distance to set up the *tonnara* and ensure a successful catch.

Then they waited, their eyes and ears peeled for any disturbance on the water's surface. After about five minutes, they heard the shrieks of approaching seagulls flying in by the dozens to a spot about a hundred feet away. The crew in the smaller rowboat paddled toward what was now a frenzy of splashing water and diving gulls to corral the tuna. The other men quickly gathered and dropped the net, positioning the *tonnara*, so it was ready to intercept the schools as they passed through. It didn't take long for the fish to be herded toward the central part of the net. Then, as he was trained, Padre Isadoro made the call, and the men began to pull in the net. The elders again sang with each heave as their weathered hands gripped the linen threads with calculated strength. It was important to close the *tonnara* around the tuna without causing damage to the fish or the net itself.

Alberto felt every fiber of his body engage with each tug and shift in position on the unstable deck. Then, he felt a pop, which caused him to drop his portion of the net. Pain shot through his leg, and he screamed as he lost balance. Two sets of hands caught him just as he plunged toward the tuna death chamber.

It was Ascanio and Fausto, his first friends from the shipyard. They pushed him backward onto the deck, where he collapsed safely but in excruciating pain. Tears welled in his closed eyes as he clutched his throbbing, re-injured knee.

"That was close!" Fausto shouted.

The men around them didn't seem to notice as they began tossing enormous bloody fish onto the deck, one writhing uncomfortably near his face.

"We have to get you out of the way," Ascanio said as he and Fausto carefully moved Alberto, who howled in pain.

They moved him to the bow of the *gozzo*, where he lay in a fetal position, watching as fish accumulated on deck. Ascanio and Fausto left his side to help shove the giant, flopping fish into the hold while he shut his eyes and waited in agony for it all to end.

An hour later, the *gozzi* were heavy with fish, and the Palermitani led the men in a raucous rendition of "C'è la luna mezzo mare," laughing their way through the bawdy mother-daughter coming-of-age lyrics. Everyone but Alberto, Fausto, and Ascanio. The three friends remained huddled at the boat's bow, while men behind them rowed between the chorus, "*O mammà, pisci fritti baccalà! O mammà, pisci fritti baccalà!*"

Alberto watched as they neared the shore, where he met his father's concerned eyes. When they arrived, Ascanio, Fausto, and two other men lifted him onto the landing.

"I'll get the doctor." Mamma raced off.

Papà approached "What happened?"

"My knee," Alberto grimaced. "I re-injured it. It was all a mistake. I shouldn't have gone out there in the first place."

"No mistake." His father pointed to the celebration unfolding around them. "Look at what you've done. This is all because of you. Your knee will heal. Look around you! You've made everyone so happy. More than that: You've delivered more food and created capable fishermen. That's more than most people can claim in a day's work."

The doctor arrived and examined Alberto's knee as the men continued to sing and now dance with friends and family members.

"Yes, it appears to be another medial collateral ligament

injury." The doctor ran his hand through his thinning gray hair. "I want you on bed rest for a couple of weeks. Then limit your weight-bearing movements for another month until you heal. No more fishing—at least for a while—for you."

One of the men let Alberto and his family use his donkey cart to bring him home. He winced as the cart jostled and bounced on each bump along the cobblestone road, backed by the soundtrack of what seemed to be the entire village singing as they marched in triumph for a brand-new day in Isola delle Femmine.

Back in his childhood bed with his leg propped up, he thought about Vittoria and how she and her mother had doted on him as he healed just two months prior. He smiled as he realized how happy she would have been despite his injury had she seen how the men had set down their shipyard tools to come together for a greater good, their eyes brighter with hope for a peaceful and prosperous future.

FORTY-FOUR
MAY 1943

Fort Missoula, Missoula, Montana

Vincenzo trudged back to the barracks from the court building along the gravel path. He inhaled the sweet scent of the fresh-cut grass—the smell of growth and newness. The birds chirped overhead in the leafy green trees, reminding him it was spring. But it meant nothing to him in his depressed state, and the big, blue sky only seemed to add to the weight.

He entered the barracks and looked down as he made his way to his bunk. It was lunchtime, but he didn't feel like eating, only sleeping. He hoped to find some comfort in the blanket of dreams.

He lay his head on his flimsy pillow and stared at the wood-beam ceiling. There had to be a way to reverse the decision so he could be granted parole. It couldn't end this way, and he couldn't see how he could continue to bounce around between barbed-wire-enclosed camps for the rest of his life. Why was he being punished, he who had been such a model prisoner?

And there it was. The answer seemed crystal clear. He'd

been a model prisoner, so much so that the guards had remembered him when he'd returned to Fort Missoula. His fellow internees hadn't forgotten him either. There was one fight, but he didn't fight back. It had been a huge misunderstanding and one he was sure he could prove.

He sat up in bed. He was going to do something. Today.

Men had returned from lunch, including Tonio, who greeted him as he plopped down on the bunk below him. "So?" he asked.

"So, I was denied parole," Vincenzo sighed.

"Denied? I thought the deal was sealed. You had testimonials. Why on earth would they deny you parole?"

"That fight."

"Did you tell them what really happened?"

"I tried. But listen," he whispered over the edge of the bunk. "I have an idea. What if I get a bunch of internees to write letters?"

"I'd write one for you if you write one for me." Tonio met his eyes.

Vincenzo tapped the metal frame. "Exactly. I'll write letters for everyone who can vouch for my character."

Vincenzo sat with his head propped up in his bed as he scribbled on camp-issued stationery. He had received promises from five other internees that they would draft letters to Edward Ennis, director of the Alien Control Unit. In return, he promised to write letters on their behalf. Still, he wondered if it would be enough. Besides, what kind of character witness was a prisoner?

He finished the letter and placed it on top of a stack to his left. Then he slid down from his bunk, carrying the letters, and proceeded to the administrative building from which letters were mailed.

It was a sunny day, and he passed a dozen men playing soccer on the field. He stopped for a moment to watch them, and he heard someone clear his throat behind him.

"So, Aiello, can we count on you for the ticket counter this Sunday?"

He turned and saw Thomas, the INS officer with whom he'd become friendly.

He nodded, and then a thought occurred to him.

"Say, Thomas. You've known me for a while now, since I started working with the productions... I am gathering character witnesses from the camp. Do you think you might be able to vouch for me?"

Thomas narrowed his blue eyes. "How so?"

He swallowed. "I need a letter to Edward Ennis."

Thomas looked at him with a frown. "You're looking to bust out of this place?"

"It's been a year and a half now." His voice cracked as he considered all he'd lost and left behind. "It doesn't need to be long, just something that speaks to my character."

Thomas stared at him a moment longer and then sighed.

"Sure. Why not? Although we'd miss you around here."

Two weeks passed, and camp life carried on. Vincenzo attended practice for a production of a play called *Pirati* and tried not to think about his fate with the review board. But it was difficult. Every day, he went to the administrative building in anticipation of something, anything, in response to his outreach.

Instead, there was news for Marcellino. Several letters, including Vincenzo's, provided the character references he needed for a rehearing. He would face the review board on Friday, and Vincenzo knew it wouldn't be long before his friend would be going home.

Marcellino's big day came with fanfare, for it seemed

everyone Vincenzo knew was abuzz with anticipation. He shook his friend's hand before his fateful walk to the courtroom and expressed his best wishes.

About an hour later, Marcellino returned to the barracks wearing a broad smile.

"They've issued parole!" He pumped his fist in the air. "I'm going back to San Francisco for processing and then home. Can you believe it?"

"That's wonderful." Vincenzo gave him a tight hug as if squeezing the man could strangle his jealous feelings away.

"I have you to thank for your report on my character at camp," Marcellino said. "Hopefully, your letters will help you, too."

The next day, Vincenzo threw himself into camp activities. He started the day with a game of bocce before he made his way to the theater building and helped Thomas prepare the ticket counter for the evening debut of *Pirati*. Meanwhile, the twenty-three actors dressed in pirate costumes ran through their rehearsal, and a chorus of thirteen warmed up their voices.

Before the show, he visited the administration building to see if he'd gotten any mail.

"Yes, sir." The clerk produced two envelopes.

One had a stamp bearing the insignia of the Department of Justice.

He tore it open right there in front of the clerk.

Dear Mr. Aiello,

We have reviewed your additional testimonials and considered your status as a Gold Star Parent. We wish to extend our condolences, as well as express our sincere appreciation for your exem-

*plary contributions and conduct during your internment. In
light of these considerations, we are pleased to inform you that
your application for parole has been approved. You are to
undergo further processing at Silver Avenue Detention Center
in San Francisco in preparation for your release. Congratulations.*

Sincerely,
Earl G. Harrison
Commissioner Immigration and Naturalization Service

He lowered the letter, a broad smile stretching across his
face. Then he read it again to ensure he hadn't missed something. But there it was in black and white.

He pressed his hands on the desk and jumped up, feeling
light on his feet. The heavy weight was gone.

"They did it! They approved my parole!"

He was really, finally going home.

The clerk gave a bored nod. For him it was just another day
overseeing a desk, while for Vincenzo, it was all his dreams
come true.

"What is a Gold Star Parent?" Vincenzo asked.

The clerk cleared his throat as if giving a recitation. "It's a
distinction given to a parent who's lost a loved one in the war.
Why?"

Vincenzo thought about Mario, how his son must be smiling
down at him, like in those moments after they'd packed their
boat hold to the brim with fish. Or when he stood on that
theater stage, yearning to sing like the big men. He thought
about the groundbreaking for the Golden Gate Bridge the
moment when those carrier pigeons took flight. Now he wanted
to spread the news to the world.

He felt and understood that childlike wonder he'd seen in

both of his children. And his mind shifted to Annalisa. This was likely her doing. Such a smart, courageous girl. He couldn't wait to see his daughter and help her welcome her child into the world.

FORTY-FIVE

JUNE 1943

California

Annalisa felt every bump as Sam drove along the winding road up to Black Diamond Mines Preserve, entering the familiar hills, this time dotted with vibrant wildflowers. There were patches of bright yellow (California buttercups, mustard, and sweet fennel), splashes of magenta (red maids, shooting stars, thistle, and clover), sprinklings of blue (blue-eyed grass, blue dicks, larkspur, and lupine), and pops of orange (poppies and fiddlenecks) poking through the tall blades of grass. The California buckeye was in full bloom, its pale pink spiky flowers standing above deep green leaves shaped like hands. And the evergreen oak leaves seemed to shimmer in the brilliant sun that hung high in the pale blue sky.

It was a beautiful Sunday afternoon, and after receiving her father's latest letter, they had something to celebrate. After nineteen months in captivity, he would finally be released. At last, he'd have the chance to properly grieve the death of his son. The government he once embraced had robbed him of his pursued freedom and opportunity. He was never going to get that time back. Homecoming would surely be bittersweet.

She'd missed her father. That and the pain of losing Mario would stay with her, like a scar. Together, they'd shaped the woman she'd become—or at least hoped she could one day be.

Her hand rested on her now-enormous belly. This was some big baby. Perhaps he'd be a soccer player; he was constantly kicking from all directions.

Her world had changed once and twice in the span of two fateful December days, both of which would live in infamy for her. Then it kept changing. She had helped her mother navigate an even more foreign country. The burden it placed on her young shoulders was enough to break someone. It did break her in some ways. But now, with one less worry, perhaps she could set aside time to rebuild. Her baby would need her.

"I can't believe releasing my father took them so long," Annalisa said as Sam rolled to a stop in the parking lot. "I just keep thinking of how he lost so much. And now so much time has passed."

Sam nodded while exiting the car. "Your letter really sealed the deal." He pulled out their picnic basket and handed her a rolled-up yellow blanket. "I'm proud of you."

Annalisa smiled as they made their way to a clearing, where they laid out the blanket and settled down for lunch. She'd had a big breakfast, but she still felt famished. She rubbed her large belly. This baby was really hungry.

"You haven't heard from your mother yet?" Sam took a bite of an egg salad sandwich.

Annalisa sighed as she reached for a purple grape and popped it into her mouth. "Not yet."

"Give it some time," Sam said. "Things will be different when your Pops comes home."

They munched on their meal in silence, backed by the buzz of bees and the occasional fly. Annalisa thought about how much had changed in her life since she'd first come to this park with her big brother. It had been a thrilling adventure, and she'd seen a different side of Mario. He was proud to show her this special place, a secret he'd kept from their parents. Then she thought about the first time she'd visited with Sam. It was a wholly different period in her life when she yearned for escape and freedom from the confines of reality and her mother. In some ways, she'd blamed her mother for what happened to her father. She hadn't learned English nor encouraged him to get citizenship. And there was a time when she thought both her parents had driven Mario away. Those resentments had faded, and now, more than anything, she wanted to be with her family again.

Annalisa saw an azure flash as a Western bluebird landed in a nearby Coulter pine.

"Kew, kew, kew," it sang down at them.

"Hey, little bird." Annalisa peered up at his deep-blue face and rusty breast. "Maybe it's a sign."

"What do you mean?" Sam asked.

"The bird." Annalisa readjusted herself on the blanket. "He's trying to tell us something."

"Maybe he's a symbol of spring—birth, renewal, and all that stuff."

"Isn't that the robin?" She smiled.

The bird continued to sing as the couple watched and listened.

"You know what that reminds me of," Sam said. "That song, 'When I walk down the street, coming on with my sweets...'"

"I hear bluebirds," she sang and squeezed his hand. "Maybe he is a sign of renewal, like you say."

"A fresh start." He leaned in for a kiss. "I know it's been a long road, but we got to where we are together, and things are shaping up. Just wait and see."

* * *

Vincenzo waited as the guard went through his belongings, taking care to check for contraband and weapons.

The indifferent expression on his ruddy face did little to calm Vincenzo's nerves as he held his breath, afraid that something could go wrong that would delay the day's release.

"All clear." The guard handed Vincenzo a small sack with his belongings.

"Clear?" asked Vincenzo.

The guard nodded. "Best of luck to you."

The sun shone brilliantly as Vincenzo exited the dim interior of the concrete building, greeted by dry, hot air and two familiar faces: Annalisa and Sam. But hers was much fuller; so was her belly. It was almost as if she were a balloon, ready to pop. For a moment he wondered if it was just one baby; he'd seen a twin pregnancy before.

"Papà!" Annalisa shouted, and she waddled into his outstretched arms.

He felt the bulge of what was going to be his grandchild and her tears on his chest, and he began to cry, for it was all suddenly real. He was free, going home, and his little girl was again in his arms.

"*Mia cara*," he breathed. "I've missed you."

He wiped his eyes and turned to Sam. "I knew you'd do the right thing."

As he looked at the red-haired, blue-eyed boy, he experienced a wave of mixed emotions. While he appreciated that he'd driven all the way out to San Francisco to pick him up, he couldn't completely erase the resentment he felt toward him. Yes, Sam had married his daughter, but did he truly understand the gravity of the situation? Was he even ready for the responsibility of being a father? He was just a kid. They both were. Not tested like him on the battlefront. But then again, they had endured their own war.

It remained to be seen just how they would adapt to their changing circumstances. He'd been blessed to have his sister take on part of the load the first time around. When it came time for Annalisa, he and Maria had finally found their footing. He had been earning a decent living, and Mario had been already nearly six years old.

Annalisa stayed by his side as Sam stiffly shook his hand.

"Let's get you home." Annalisa led them to his car.

Vincenzo grimaced when he saw the state of the Model A. "You drove all the way to Tennessee and Oklahoma in that thing?"

"She's been through a lot." Sam patted the car's dusty roof. "But hasn't everyone?"

"My being away was hard on you," Vincenzo said quietly to Annalisa, who nodded.

She took his hand. "But I can't imagine what it's been like for you."

"Would you like to sit up front, Mr. Aiello?" Sam asked.

Vincenzo nodded and slowly opened the door, determined to set aside his feelings about Sam and savor each moment of his new freedom. He kept his eyes peeled as they rolled through residential neighborhoods along the western edge of the San Francisco Bay. His thoughts shifted to the Bay Area men he'd encountered as he wondered just how many had made it back home. The car was silent save for jazz music on the radio, so different from the opera and folk songs he'd heard back at Fort Missoula, so much noisier and chaotic than the songs of his own youth.

Sam drove across the wide Bay Bridge, and Vincenzo took in the panorama of distant hills beyond the brilliant blue, the water he'd missed, having been so landlocked and barbed-wire bound for such a long time. He rolled down the window, despite the heat, determined to catch a breath. He inhaled the fishy scent, closed his eyes, and sighed. It was starting to feel like home.

They crossed the bridge to the industrial port of Oakland, where he saw cargo ships, ferries, and fishing boats, another reminder of home. They drove through the city with Annalisa describing her short stint at the cannery, and soon the Model A was climbing hills and passing redwoods. Again, he rolled down the window, breathing it all in.

They descended the hills into another residential area, flanked by tall trees and homes featuring flower boxes. And Vincenzo thought about the tulips Maria had planted in their front yard at a home he'd not be returning to, their lives forever transformed by the follies of middle age. He'd joined the wrong organization. Neither sought to secure citizenship—until it was too late.

They passed through several towns until they reached a stretch of road from which he could see a mountain in the distance. It was Mount Diablo, the same mountain where he'd taken the children to see snow, just one time.

Now they were in Concord, passing a small, abandoned crop-duster airport and hangar next to acres of strawberry fields.

"The Japanese folks used to work these fields." Annalisa pointed out the window. "Until they got sent away."

And his mind went to Satow and all the Japanese men he'd encountered at the various camps. He thought about all the families—so many more than the Italians—who had been uprooted, their homes and businesses lost, too.

They entered an area with more traffic, and Annalisa pointed out various sights: the bank, the variety store where she and Sam had worked, and a large square with a lovely wisteria-draped pergola. Suddenly, the car slowed as they turned onto a quiet street and parked in front of a white stucco building at the corner.

He sat in the car for a moment as Sam and Annalisa exited and waited outside. He looked up at the apartment building's arched doorways and windows, rounded turret, and red-tiled roof. It was so different from what he'd imagined. He had thought of the move to Concord as a punishment. What he hadn't expected was something so graceful yet quaint.

He slowly got out of the car and gazed at the wrought-iron door.

"Welcome home, Papà." Annalisa patted him on the shoulder.

They walked up the sidewalk to a set of clay-colored steps, each adorned with two colorful Spanish tiles, and Annalisa led the way inside.

They walked past a table with a wooden duck and up the stairs to a sturdy door.

Annalisa knocked and then turned back toward the stairs.

"What? You're not going to stay?"

"Mamma won't want to see me," she said quietly, shadows accentuating her high cheekbones beneath her downcast eyes.

"You're our daughter." Vincenzo drew her gently but firmly to his side on the landing in front of the door. "I've seen enough fighting. Let's have some peace."

And just a beat later, the door opened.

FORTY-SIX
JUNE 1943

Isola delle Femmine, Sicily

The aroma of grilled fish wafted through the hot air, intermingling with the scent of the salty breeze that lifted the yellowed lace curtains that hung on the window of Alberto and Lorenzo's bedroom.

There Alberto lay, his right leg elevated on a couple of pillows, as he listened to the festivities going on in the street below. Musicians were there, playing a *tarantella*. He heard the distinct sounds of the small, high-pitched *friscalettu*, the so-called shepherds' flute, and the twangy *marranzano*, the mouth harp, along with the slapping of tambourines and the reedy, expressive brightness of an accordion.

"La la la, la la la, lala lala lala la…" voices sang.

He thought back to times when he, himself, had danced to the tune as a wedding guest. The lively, fast-paced music brought people together to celebrate a romantic bond, the beginning of an important journey for a special couple.

No doubt they would have played it at his wedding to Vittoria.

While his knee had begun to heal in the past few weeks, his heart continued to ache, a pain he did not want to go away. The more he sat with it, the more he hurt as he reflected on all the what-ifs and could-bes.

He heard a knock at the door, and he turned.

"Can I get you some food from downstairs?" Lorenzo asked.

More than a bedside nurse, the boy had served as a faithful companion during Albert's period of convalescence, never complaining and always offering a shy smile. And he hoped that their brotherly bond served as a styptic stick to the wound left with his sister's death.

"Maybe I can join you." Alberto shifted his position and leaned over to take hold of one of his crutches as he lowered himself from the bed.

"Are you sure you can make it? The doctor said..."

"The doctor said to limit my weight-bearing activities." Alberto lifted a crutch. "I'm just going out to eat, not dance."

Lorenzo nodded with a frown.

"Don't worry, I won't be out there too long." Alberto smiled.

Lorenzo slowly led the way down the stairs and out to the buzzing street.

There Alberto saw the fishermen gathered, sweating as they danced, hand in hand with village women and elders. He watched as they spun in a circle, the women's brightly colored skirts twirling and everyone's feet moving rapidly to steps passed down over the ages.

One of the women shook a tambourine in the air at the end of the tune and the dancing ceased, with people queuing up before a man stationed at a charcoal brazier, who'd been grilling some of the day's catch.

"Alberto!" Ascanio called out to him, breaking away from the girl who'd been on his arm. "How are you?"

"The knee is healing." Alberto patted his leg. "How was the *mattanza*?"

"Better than we'd expected." Ascanio raised his shoulders. "Of course, it's not the same without you."

"Thank you for saying that, but I'm sure you didn't miss having to save me from falling into the chamber of death." Alberto chuckled.

"I was glad to have been there that day," Ascanio said softly. "You know I'd do anything for you after you delivered us all from that evil."

"Anything?" Alberto asked, his eyebrows raised.

"Well, within reason." Ascanio winked. "I wouldn't go back to Palermo even if you paid me."

They moved forward in line amid the bustling scene, and Alberto's eyes landed on Lorenzo, who chatted with a group of other young soccer players. Alberto thought of his own days as a youth, participating in the post-*mattanza* festivities. Just like Lorenzo, he'd seen it as an opportunity to further solidify bonds. But unlike the boy, he had no dreams of taking part in the big event they celebrated. Now he saw things differently. The war had changed him, harkening him back to his fisherman roots. He adjusted his crutch and reached in his pocket, where he still kept his uncle's wooden shuttle. Running his finger across its smooth surface, he had an idea.

"Lorenzo!" he called, and the boy was quickly by his side, with a look of concern.

"Do you need something, Alberto?"

"I need to talk to you," Alberto shifted his weight. "You know Ascanio, right?"

Lorenzo nodded shyly, looking at the older man.

"Well, I want you to work with Ascanio." Alberto looked at his friend. "He's going to take you fishing."

Ascanio's eyes widened at first but softened in understanding.

"And maybe, when you're ready, we can take you out for the *mattanza*." Ascanio patted Lorenzo's back.

"How would you like that?" Alberto asked the boy, whose mouth hung agape.

"You really mean it?" he whispered.

Ascanio and Alberto nodded.

"But first, I want you to have something." Alberto adjusted his crutch so he could pull the shuttle from his pocket. "It's an heirloom I inherited, but I know you can put it to better use."

He handed it to Lorenzo, who fingered it gently as if it were something more fragile.

"Thank you," the boy breathed. "I'll guard it with my life."

"And it will guard yours," Alberto said. "I've carried that shuttle in my pocket throughout this war."

Lorenzo reached in for a hug and thanked him again.

They reached the brazier, and each got a plate full of tender, browned grilled tuna. The flesh was rich and buttery, with a hint of sweetness.

When they finished their meal, Alberto decided he was up for a longer walk, and he, Ascanio, and Lorenzo made their way toward the rocky beach overlooking the Spanish-era tower on the islet. The sun was setting, casting a deep orange glow onto the surface of the cobalt water, as seagulls swooped in to snatch their evening meal and a gray heron waded through the gentle waves that lapped at the rocks. He watched Ascanio chatting with Lorenzo, who was once again fingering the shuttle in the palm of his hand. He thought about his family's legacy and how Lorenzo now held a key, something to hold on to in these days of uncertainty.

FORTY-SEVEN
JUNE 1943

Concord, California

Maria stood at the door, her eyes wide and nearly instantly filled with tears.

Vincenzo, too, felt himself awash with a wave of emotion as he looked at his wife, who looked gaunt and tired, her tightly bound hair appearing thinner and newly streaked with silver.

It had been too long.

"Maria." He reached for her almost timidly and slipped his now-shaking arms around her shoulders.

She sobbed into his chest, soaking the fabric of his cotton T-shirt, and he closed his eyes as he inhaled her familiar scent—a mix of soap and baby powder.

They stood there, locked in an embrace, and his mind was flooded with memories of his return from war all those years ago when they'd shared similar tears that washed away his insecurities and doubts that she'd want to marry a shell of the carefree dreamer he'd once been. The war had hardened him in many ways, making him more serious, but it also made him appreciate the smaller things, life's details that framed what truly mattered.

As he looked down into her deep, dark eyes, he saw himself changed even more, his experience having stripped away any remaining idealism, leaving behind a core sense of resilience.

He thought about all the nights he'd spent, many shivering without adequate linens, and the days where he was a mere number in a ledger, devoid of dignity behind the barbed wire. Then there were all the birthdays, holidays, and boring Sunday afternoons he'd missed. It all added up to a gap he could not fill, a void that would forever be felt, and a life forever changed by decisions and circumstances. But now, he thought, as he squeezed her tightly, he was finally home.

She raised her head, and he felt her shoulders tense. He turned and remembered Annalisa's and Sam's quiet presence.

He stepped back and placed his arm around his daughter. "She brought me back, you know. And it was her letter to Edward Ennis that finally got me out."

He saw Maria's eyes cloud with more tears.

"Thank you," she whispered, turning toward Annalisa. "I'm just... so sorry. Can you ever forgive me?"

He looked at his daughter, who was now overcome with her own tears.

"Oh, Mamma." Annalisa stepped forward and embraced her.

Vincenzo watched his daughter and wife and thought about the family's missing piece. Mario would have done everything to travel back for this reunion.

Tears slid down his cheeks, and he suddenly caught sight of Sam, who stood awkwardly behind them, leaning against the white stucco wall with his hands in his blue jean pockets.

"And I have Sam to thank for driving me." He pulled the boy forward. "We're all here now, Maria. Isn't it wonderful?"

She nodded, still holding Annalisa. "What are we doing standing around? Come in and sit down, so we can celebrate."

They stepped over the threshold and into the living room,

where Vincenzo saw a small framed photograph of the family posed with Mario in uniform over a cheap-looking pink couch beside a matching chair. It certainly wasn't like the nice blue tufted set he'd purchased when they'd first moved into their Pittsburg home, but he knew they'd had to leave it all behind.

He lifted the picture from the wall and sat on the couch as Annalisa settled to his left and Sam to her left, leaving the chair open for Maria. But she didn't sit down.

"Let me get you something to drink." She disappeared into the kitchen.

Vincenzo stared down at the photograph. It was taken on the day of Mario's departure to Hawaii. He'd asked one of his fellow sailors to snap it with his box camera, and afterward, he'd handed the camera to Annalisa for safekeeping.

"Do you still have that camera?" Vincenzo asked.

"What camera?" Annalisa frowned.

"Mario's."

Annalisa shook her head. "They took it when they searched the apartment."

"So much this country has taken from us." Vincenzo clutched the wooden frame in frustration.

"Relax, Papà." Annalisa placed her hand on his shoulder. "What matters is we're back together."

"You're right." Vincenzo stared at a patch of afternoon light that fell on the hardwood floor as Maria returned with four glasses of lemonade. He took a sip. It was tart, and he thought about how much more sour lemons were in the U.S., nothing like the sweetness he'd experienced in Sicily. And with that, his thoughts turned to his left-behind family—especially Alberto. He knew Maria hadn't heard from them with war-time communications restricted.

"Maybe when this war is all over, we can go back to Sicily."

Maria nodded. "I'd like that. It's been too long to not hear anything. Oh... that reminds me. Something came in the mail for Annalisa!"

She raced down the hall, and Vincenzo took a sip of his lemonade. It really was tart. Then he remembered hearing about the sugar ration. He wondered what other privations his family had suffered.

Maria returned with a small box, which she handed to Annalisa. "This came in the mail some time ago. We weren't speaking, and well... I decided to wait to give it to you."

Annalisa fingered the brown paper packaging and carefully tore at a corner. She shook it, and he saw a glint of gold. Then he saw his daughter was crying.

"What's wrong?" He draped his left arm over her shoulder to hug her. Then he saw what it was.

On her lap was a gold necklace—the gold *cornicello* necklace he'd given to Mario now so many years ago. It couldn't be. Had they found Mario's necklace with his body? But why was it addressed to Annalisa?

"The Johnsons." She turned to Sam as she wiped her eyes. "They found the necklace in the bed I slept in."

"Who are the Johnsons, and why did they have Mario's necklace?" Vincenzo asked. He was so confused.

"We stayed with them in Arkansas." Annalisa stretched the necklace between her fingers. "And Mario gave this to me as a gift before he left for Hawaii. I know it means something special to you, too, Papà. You gave it to him."

She handed him the necklace, and he felt the weight of history wash over him as he saw Mario's wide eyes when he'd first opened his present. He'd kissed it every morning before they dropped their net. It had been his good luck charm. The boy had never taken it off—even in the shower and when he slept. And yet, he'd given it to his little sister.

"You know." Vincenzo ran his thumb and finger along the

twisted horn. "When a woman wears it, it's a symbol of fertility."

Annalisa blushed.

"I mean, it's a sign you'll have a healthy child," he said quickly.

"Here." He opened the clasp and draped it around Annalisa's neck. "He wanted you to have it, and so it shall be."

"Thank you, Papà." She kissed his forehead as he leaned in to secure the necklace in place.

Vincenzo caught Sam's eye as he settled back on the couch. Again, he wondered whether this boy would be able to rise to the occasion. He reflected on how he, at just a year older than Sam, had gone to fight a war. Just what stuff was this Sam made of? Just who had his daughter married? He knew nothing of his family or his heritage. Still, he could tell his daughter loved this boy. And that meant something.

He turned again to his daughter. "Annalisa, now that we're all together again, don't you think it might be a good idea for us to have a church wedding for you?"

"But Papà... we're already married." She let out a tense laugh.

"Yeah, why do we need a church wedding?" Sam frowned.

"Because, young man," Vincenzo smiled tightly, "shouldn't I be able to walk my daughter down the aisle now that I'm a free man?"

He saw Sam raise his eyebrows as he looked at Annalisa with a hard stare. Apparently, he didn't think Vincenzo should have such a right. What kind of person had his daughter brought into their family?

"It's fine, Papà," she said quietly. "I'll do it if it's important to you."

Her words thawed the heat of his anger. She sounded so young at that moment, like she had as a sweet, inquisitive little girl. It took him back to their father-daughter *contradanza*, the dance they'd spontaneously shared in front of all those people in San Francisco. He could still remember her wide smile as they hopped and swayed, snapping their fingers as they stepped in time, honoring their Sicilian tradition in a place once far beyond his dreams.

She was a woman now, and he was finally free to walk her down the aisle. His precious girl, who soon might have a daughter of her own. He glanced at her belly. Maybe two.

FORTY-EIGHT
JULY 1943

Isola delle Femmine, Sicily

The fishing season had passed, and plenty of tuna and swordfish had been canned and stored to last the village for at least two seasons. Hotter days had arrived—even hotter when it was announced on July 10 that the Allied troops had stormed Sicily's southern shores before dawn. Twelve days had since passed. He knew, for he'd been counting, wondering just how long before they'd reach Palermo.

Alberto stood on the beach overlooking the islet of Isola delle Femmine, staring beyond the white-capped azure waves at the Spanish-era stone tower that once safeguarded the coast. He pondered the island's complex history—the Phoenicians and Greeks who colonized it, the Romans who rolled it into their empire, the Arabs, Berbers, and Saracens who conquered and cultivated its lands, the Norman invaders, and its Spanish rulers. Now he anxiously awaited as the Americans and British made their way north.

He thought about his family in California. Surely the Americans weren't all bad. Perhaps there was some truth in their claims of "liberation." Could this invasion bring some good?

The radio announcer said the Allied troops numbered more than 100,000 men with thousands of tanks and other vehicles. Many Sicilian soldiers had surrendered, others had been taken prisoner. Alberto knew liberation would not come without a fight, and he sadly knew Sicily was no match. Just how much could this already beleaguered island take? Just how many more lives would be lost? And he wondered just when this war might ever end.

He picked up a smooth, flat stone and, after twisting backward, launched it into the sea. It skipped three times. And he thought of the Father, Son, and Holy Ghost. Three in one was the trinity, a concept that had once given him comfort, but one shrouded in mystery. Understanding it required blind faith, like stepping off a ledge with the certainty that someone would catch you when you fell. That person had once been Mussolini; now he had faith in the strength of his community. As the ripples from that stone's triple skip faded from the crystalline water's surface, he found himself praying for similar certitude to guide him along the murkier days ahead.

He slowly limped his way back along the dusty, narrow streets. And he thought of how they had hosted so much new life, thanks in a large part to the past months' fishing expeditions. The men from Palermo brought a glimmer of hope as well as sustenance. What would this American invasion mean for a village so close to resurrection?

He stopped as he reached Piano Ponente, and he saw Lorenzo head a ball that came across the little soccer field in his direction. Alberto clapped and shouted for his young friend, now with a lower voice, a taller, surer stance, and a set of sea legs to boot. As the boys ran, dribbled, and stole the ball from one another, he reflected on the energy of youth and how, despite the lines drawn on the field, their enthusiasm knew no bounds. Here was a stark contrast to the pervasive torpor of the older townspeople, who he feared had resigned themselves to their looming fate, their homeland under a slow-burning siege.

The game ended, and Lorenzo ran to Alberto's side.

"Did you see that?" He panted. "I blocked the goal with my head."

Alberto nodded. "Just don't tell your Mamma. She'll worry about your brain cells."

"Is it true?" Lorenzo asked, as they began their walk back to the family apartment. "What they say about the Americani?"

Again, Alberto nodded. "But don't you worry. No one's coming to Isola delle Femmine. Not as long as we have men like you to defend it."

The radio buzzed with a broadcast as they entered the apartment through the living room, and Lorenzo ran to their bedroom to change clothes. And then Alberto heard it.

"We are reporting from Palermo where the Americani have entered the city and planted their flag," the announcer said. "The enemy was met with little resistance and not a shot was fired."

It didn't surprise him that Palermitani hadn't resisted. The city had been battered beyond recognition and lost its will to survive. The Allies had weakened Italy's once-firm grip on the Mediterranean and gained a foothold in Southern Europe. Alberto thought about what that would mean: supply lines disrupted, strategic positions lost, and, for the Axis powers, an embarrassing forced retreat. Just how much more could Italy hold on? Was this the beginning of the end?

"But we're safe here, aren't we?" Signora Ferrante asked from her seat on a worn mauve chair. Beside her on the matching couch sat Alberto's mother with her head in her hands.

"For now." Alberto nodded. "But things are going to change around here—for all of Italy."

Alberto stood in his closet, pulling out shirts and slacks that needed mending. He placed them in a tidy pile before scooping them up and carrying them down the hall to his parents' bedroom, where his mother sat behind her sewing machine. It was a simple task and one he readily accepted.

"How could you let yourself wear these things?" His mother shook her head.

These clothes and he had seen better days. It was a matter of delaying the inevitable. Eventually, he'd have to discard these pieces. At some point, he'd have to face reality. The Americans were here in Isola delle Femmine.

They'd arrived early in the morning, their tanks rumbling down the sleepy streets, taking down a few trees and cacti in their path and bringing sleepy residents to their balconies.

Alberto looked out the open window behind his mother.

"They're still down there." He pointed to a gaggle of children surrounding one of the tanks on the street below. The military men were smiling and passing something out to the youngsters. And then he spotted Lorenzo among them.

"Lorenzo!" he shouted out the window, and his mother sprang to his side.

"What's he doing?" she asked. "Doesn't he know they're dangerous?"

"I'll get him." Alberto turned and raced down the hall.

When he arrived on the street, he made eye contact with one of the soldiers, a boy with sandy brown hair. He stood among several men who seemed just as young. And had they not been wearing their green uniforms along with a curious white armband, he might have assumed they and the children were a homogenous group.

"Lorenzo!" he called again to his friend, and Lorenzo left the men and trotted over.

"Alberto, they gave us candy!" He held up an American chocolate bar.

"Don't eat that; it's probably poisoned."

Lorenzo chuckled. "But, Alberto, they're nice. Besides, I saw other boys eating the candy, and they didn't seem sick."

Alberto looked back at the military men and again caught the eye of the sandy-haired boy, who began waving for him to approach.

"You stay here," he told Lorenzo, and he steeled himself as he walked toward the side of the tank where the boy stood.

The boy held out his hand, and Alberto stared at him. But then the soldier held up a finger and turned toward the tank.

He's getting a weapon! Alberto thought, and he felt himself freeze in place. But then the boy produced two cans. One was a can of mixed vegetables and the other was something called SPAM that looked like meat, according to its label. The soldier held the cans in front of Alberto, gesturing for him to take them. They were sealed, so perhaps not poisoned? Alberto thought of how much his mother would appreciate the extra food. Their dinners, as of late, consisted of bits of canned fish mixed with rice. If nothing else, this provided some variety. He reached forward and took the cans, bowing his head in thanks.

The boy reached into his pocket and pulled out a small rectangular package that read WRIGLEY's on the wrapper, and he placed it on top of the cans.

Alberto again bowed in thanks, and he carried the goods to Lorenzo.

"You're right." He smiled. "Seems safe enough. I just wonder why they're being so nice to us."

"Maybe they don't want this war either." Lorenzo shrugged.

Alberto left Lorenzo and took the goods upstairs. He set the cans down on the white-tiled kitchen counter and opened the rectangular package. There were five flat rectangles wrapped in silver paper inside. He took one, unwrapped it, and saw something beige that appeared to be food. Was it candy? He placed it on his tongue and began chewing it. It was sweet and minty flavored but didn't break up like regular candy. Instead, the more he chewed it, the more it formed into a glob. He spat it out, wondering if he had indeed ingested poison with this strange substance.

Lorenzo was behind him now. "Don't eat that." Alberto pointed to the silver-wrapped rectangles.

"Oh, that?" Lorenzo laughed. "They showed us how you eat it. You don't swallow it; you just chew it. Like this."

He slid one of the beige rectangles in his mouth and began chewing as Alberto watched on in horror.

"But what if it's poisonous?"

Lorenzo shook his head. "No, it's refreshing. Nice and minty."

Alberto clicked his tongue. "Leave it to the Americani to make food you can't eat."

That evening, the Ferrantes and the Cardinales gathered at the supper table and bowed their heads as Papà said grace.

"And we also thank the Lord for the food the Americani have brought us," he prayed with his eyes closed. "May they leave us in peace."

As he joined everyone in saying "Amen," Alberto couldn't help but wonder how it had come to this that they were now showing gratitude to the people who had so ruthlessly massacred fellow Sicilians, including Vittoria. He wondered if the boys in the street had any connection to the bombs that fell. Even if they didn't, they still wore the U.S. uniform and fought on the Allied side. Then he thought about his own country, whose uniform he once wore with pride. How far the nation had since fallen. Vittoria was right. Il Duce had led the nation into a war for which they weren't prepared. It wasn't until long after air raids had killed hundreds of Palermitani that he'd even suggested evacuation. He didn't have a plan to do so.

As Alberto lifted his forkful of SPAM, he heard a loud boom and dropped the meat back on his plate.

"What was that?" Papà stood, and the rest of the table joined him in rushing to the window. The tank had cleared from the now-empty street. They heard another boom, followed by three more in rapid succession.

"It sounded like fireworks," Lorenzo said. "Maybe the Americani are shooting off fireworks?"

The families laughed, releasing their nervous tension.

"You're right, Lorenzo." Alberto patted his back. "It's probably fireworks."

Alberto walked with Lorenzo to the soccer field the next morning. His knee had healed, and he thought he might even play with the boys—at least as the goalie.

But when they reached Piano Ponente, they met an agitated crowd of men and women. Ascanio was among them, and he waved to Alberto.

"What's up, *amico*?" Alberto asked.

Ascanio took a deep breath. "The Americani... A bunch of them got drunk and took their tank to the shore. You should see what they did to the tower on the islet."

"What do you mean?" Alberto frowned. "Graffiti?"

"Worse." Ascanio shook his head. "They nearly blew it up."

"That must have been what we heard last night," Lorenzo turned to Alberto. "We thought it was fireworks."

"Must have been the Americani version of fireworks."

Ascanio shook his head as he clicked his tongue. "A blatant disregard for history. Come with me. I'll show you."

The three wended their way through the streets to the shore, and even before they arrived, Alberto could see the damage in the distance.

"Oh my God." His chest sank. "You're right. They have no respect."

They stepped onto the rocks and looked across at the three-hundred-year-old tower, once a sturdy Spanish-era fortress, now partially reduced to rubble. It was as if the building had belched out rocks.

"They were using it as target practice," Ascanio said.

Alberto thought back to the soldiers he'd seen—really just boys. This was a game for them. The Sicilians had hardly shown resistance. The children had flocked to them. They were the so-called liberators, so they could do what they wanted.

It was unsettling to see just how much the line between saviors and oppressors had blurred in this war. He then thought back to the soccer players he'd seen on the field and their youthful exuberance. These young military men had the same potential, but battlefield experiences had jaded them. Now they'd left a scar on Isola delle Femmine soil, another reminder of war's desecration.

"Where are they now?"

"Gone since this morning." Ascanio waved his hand. "And good riddance, too."

Alberto sighed and picked up a rock. He swung it into the air and watched it skip twice. Lorenzo and Ascanio silently followed suit, each watching their efforts sink another rock to the bottom of the sea, a rock that could take decades to make its way back to the shore.

He thought about how this, too, was an act of vandalism—less violent but disruptive all the same. The ripples faded from the cerulean surface, and he considered how the harsh effects of their current reality were often masked from daily life. They may not have been as visible as a ruined fortress, but they were no less significant.

A cool breeze ruffled his hair, and Alberto turned to his friends with a renewed sense of purpose. He was ready to return to the sea, to resume fishing, and to support his fellow villagers. Many challenges lay ahead—the recovery of his injured knee, ensuring his family had food, and enduring the pain of Vittoria's loss—but he was determined to face them with resilience. Someday soon they would leave these days of war and hardships behind. It was only a matter of time.

FORTY-NINE
JULY 1943

Concord, California

"We interrupt this broadcast for an important news bulletin," said the announcer. "Italy's King Victor Emmanuel has accepted Prime Minister Benito Mussolini's resignation and has appointed Pietro Badoglio as Head of the Government."

Vincenzo sat back on the stiff couch, stunned as the program, a radio play involving a detective, resumed. He wondered what lay between the lines of that brief announcement. With the recent invasion of Sicily, he had known the writing was on the wall for Mussolini. But he was especially surprised to hear just who would replace him.

Badoglio had been a senior officer, holding the rank of Lieutenant General and involved in numerous operations on the Isonzo Front during the Great War. But his leadership of the XXVII Corps during the Battle of Caporetto gained him notoriety and scorn. His sector collapsed under the Austro-German assault and contributed to the overall Italian retreat. He failed to adequately prepare his sector's defenses and didn't effectively counter enemy infiltration tactics. Yet somehow, in the aftermath, he was appointed Vice Chief of Staff. The man was a career opportunist, remarkably unscathed by his blunders. And now he was to lead as Prime Minister. Vincenzo wondered how the king could have chosen such a man to helm the government of a nation so crippled by Mussolini's mismanagement.

He thought about his sister, Costanza, and her family. It had been so long since he'd heard from them. He wondered how they'd endured without his regular checks in the mail. He didn't even know how Alberto had fared in Palermo amid all the bombings. There were many unknowns.

Mussolini's fall marked the end of an era, one that he'd missed entirely with his emigration overseas. Now, even with a new regime, the future remained uncertain. He hoped that his reservations about Badoglio were wrong. Perhaps new leadership would provide the people with much-needed hope, a glimmer of light to carry them through the chaos, and maybe even an end to their involvement in the war.

In the meantime, he had something to look forward to. Annalisa's wedding was set for Saturday.

* * *

Annalisa stood on tiptoe in the tiny church bathroom, trying to get a better look at herself in the heavily smudged mirror. Her mother had added an extra panel of rayon to the waist of her own white wedding gown, and in the right light, the seams were nearly invisible. Still, she was hot, and the thin fabric had already begun to stick on her back and her broad belly.

"It's just about time." Mamma entered, her face red with beads of sweat on her brow. "What's wrong?"

"Mamma, I look like a whale." Annalisa brushed away a tear.

Her mother stepped behind her and adjusted her long lace

veil. "No, you're beautiful. Who's going to judge you? The priest?"

Annalisa laughed. She knew how important this church wedding was to her parents. "Thank you, Mamma. I'm ready now."

She walked with her mother out of the bathroom, carrying a single large calla lily, down the hall, and through a wooden door to the back of the church. Through the window, she saw a row of her father's friends, Sam's mother, and a few strangers from his side. She looked beyond them to the altar. The priest was there, but where was Sam?

Annalisa turned to see her father, his eyes full of tears.

"*Mia cara.*" He smiled. "You don't know how much it means to me to be here and see you—all of it."

She reached forward and hugged him, momentarily forgetting about her delicate dress and veil. "I'm so happy, too. But where's Sam?"

* * *

Vincenzo was furious as he stormed into the men's room, finding not a trace of the groom. So, *this* was who his daughter had married. He couldn't even be bothered to show up—to his own wedding!

He clenched his fists as he made his way down the hall and to the back of the church. There, he saw his beautiful daughter crying. Maria was comforting her. For that, he was grateful; he needed some air.

He slipped out the church entrance, and it was there in front of the church that he saw Sam. The boy was sitting on the front steps with a cigarette in one hand and his head in the other.

Vincenzo walked over and sat down beside him.

He said nothing momentarily, just staring at a crack in the

step where a dandelion grew. He looked at the puffy cloud of seeds that stood up, ready to be captured by the wind.

"You see that." He nudged Sam. "That little plant pushed its roots through the concrete. It fought against the odds and broke through a hard surface just to survive."

Sam looked up with red eyes and flicked the ash from his cigarette. "What do you mean?"

"Responsibility is what I mean." Vincenzo tapped on his leg. "It doesn't wait for perfect conditions. It helps us grow no matter what stands in the way."

He watched his son-in-law take a drag from his cigarette.

"You listen to me." Vincenzo raised his index finger. "There's a crying young woman standing at the back of that church because of you. She needs you to show up and push through, no matter how hard it is. That's what it means to be responsible. That's part of being a husband and a father."

Sam nodded as he slowly exhaled and stood up. Without a word, he tossed his cigarette down, stubbed it out, and walked back to the church.

Vincenzo stayed on the step for a moment longer, still staring at the dandelion. He reached forward, picked it, and blew the seeds from the top. As they took flight, he wondered how far his words would travel with Sam. Then he, too, stood and entered the church.

* * *

Annalisa dropped her calla lily to the floor and pressed her crying face into Sam's chest. She knew seeing the bride before the wedding was bad luck, but she didn't care. He was there, after all.

She straightened his white bowtie, something he'd found in his father's old drawer, and looked up into his red eyes.

"What happened?" she whispered.

"I'm so sorry." He draped his arms around her shoulders. "I just got scared, and... I don't want to be like my Pops. He ran away when things got tough. But I won't; I promise."

Annalisa smoothed a red lock from his forehead. "You aren't your father. You're still the man I married in Las Vegas, and you're here now. That's what matters."

She heard a throat clear, and she looked to see her father standing behind them. He reached out his hand to Sam, and she watched her husband take it.

Sam turned to her. "I'll see you inside?"

She nodded and watched him walk through the door into the church.

Papà bent down, picked up her calla lily, and handed it to her. He straightened her veil and adjusted her necklace.

Annalisa heard the rich resonance of the church organ as the player launched into "Ave Maria."

"Are you ready?" Her father gazed into her eyes.

"Ready, Papà." She kissed him on the cheek.

He stepped to her side, slid his left arm through her right, and pushed open the door. Then they began their march up the aisle.

Light poured in through the rose-shaped stained glass window that hung above the crucifix-adorned altar piece, illuminating her path as she stepped forward, supported by her father. And all was as it should be.

She made eye contact with Sam and saw what looked like tears. She thought about how much their lives had changed in what was really a short amount of time and considered how fate had led them there. There was that first meeting at Reede's Variety Store and the coincidence that they were neighbors. Then, there was the fact that he chose to bring her to Black Diamond Mines Preserve, a place where she'd shared a final moment with Mario. She reflected on how he rose to the challenge of driving her halfway across the country; how, thanks to him, she'd been able to see and help her father. Through so much uncertainty and upheaval, he'd stepped up to stand by her side. Now she realized he, too, needed some reassurance.

As she approached the altar, past the smiling faces of Mr. Scotto and the other fishermen and their wives, she turned toward her mother and saw the face of the woman she'd disappointed. Annalisa didn't blame her for that. Instead, she thought of the pain and shame she'd caused during a period where her mother needed her most. She remembered the day her mother had disowned her and that terrible night when she felt the most alone. It was a bitter memory, but now she saw strength and humility to forgive and move on. It hadn't been easy, and the path forward was far from smooth. But now there was a smile on her mother's face, directed at her.

Annalisa's eyes drifted to the empty space at the end of her parents' pew, and she thought about Mario, remembering the promises they'd made, the dreams they'd shared, and his treasured necklace she now wore. His gentle spirit had stayed with her and brought her comfort in the past year and a half. He would remain a part of who she was.

She felt her father tighten his grip as they reached their destination. This was a culmination for him after such a long period of limbo. He had endured so much just to end up here again by her side. She was grateful for this opportunity to honor his simple wish. He leaned in and kissed her on the cheek before slipping into the pew alongside her mother. Then she turned to Sam.

Tears of joy filled Sam's eyes. She'd never seen him look so happy, not even on the day of their Las Vegas wedding. That was different. Here they were stronger following a long journey to find themselves through each other.

As they stood there through the readings and into the start of the Gospel, she felt a slight cramp.

"I need to sit down," she whispered to the priest, and he nodded.

Her parents scooted over to let her have a seat, and Sam stepped to her side.

"Are you OK?" her mother asked.

"Just a cramp." She rubbed her belly.

Sam held her hand as she got back up. Then he turned to the priest. "Can we skip ahead to the vows?"

The priest nodded.

He turned to her. "Annalisa, repeat after me, 'I, Annalisa, take you, Sam, to be my husband. I promise to be true to you in good times and in bad, in sickness and in health. I will love you and honor you all the days of my life.'"

She repeated the vow and smiled as Sam repeated his.

"Now it is time to exchange the rings," the priest said, and Mamma stepped forward and dropped two rings into his hand.

"Sam, repeat after me, 'With this ring, I thee wed.'"

Sam slid his grandmother's diamond-encrusted ring on Annalisa's finger. "With this ring, I thee wed."

The priest handed Annalisa a ring, and it was her turn. It was a simple gold band that had been her grandfather's, something her father had inherited and brought back from Sicily. She thought of the ties that bound her just like the necklace she again wore on her neck. The ring symbolized heritage and continuity, and now she was extending that to Sam. It marked a union that represented a more certain future.

"With this ring, I thee wed." She slipped the ring on his finger.

"Now, let us pray." The priest closed his eyes. "Heavenly Father, you have given us the joy of witnessing the union of Annalisa Aiello and Samuel Wells in marriage. Bless them as they begin a new life together. May their love grow stronger and deeper each day, and may their union be a reflection of your love. Through Jesus Christ, our Lord, Amen."

He opened his eyes and turned to Sam. "Now you may kiss the bride."

Sam took her in his arms and kissed her.

Suddenly, she felt another more intense cramp followed by a sudden rush of warmth as a distinct wetness spread through her panties and trickled down her legs onto the gray carpet of the altar. She looked down in horror.

"It's happening," she shouted. "The baby is coming!"

* * *

The waiting room buzzed with the chatter and coughs of the sick and injured, who sat beneath the harsh yellow light. A distinct ammonia scent permeated the stifling air as Vincenzo paced. It had been three hours and still no word about Annalisa.

He peered out the window at the emergency vehicles and parked cars. In the dark of the lot, he spotted the faint but steady glow of a burning cigarette. So that's where Sam had wandered off, he thought.

He glanced over at Maria, whose eyes were closed as she ran rosary beads through her fingers. Perhaps she was thinking of her own childbirths, the first so much more complicated than that of Annalisa. The blessing and the sacrifice. The life they left behind.

He slipped out the door, focused on a small ember that seemed to pulse with an orange, steady hue, and made his way to his son-in-law's side.

"Any word?" Sam took a drag.

Vincenzo shook his head. "How are you holding up?"

"Better than expected." Sam exhaled.

Vincenzo nodded. "Can I ask you something?"

"Sure." Sam flicked his cigarette.

"What happened back there... before the wedding?"

Sam paused, took a drag, and let the smoke out slowly. "I got scared."

"But why? You were already married."

"It's just that it's now so real... with this baby coming and... Well, what if I end up like my father? He left my Ma and me, you know."

Vincenzo stared at the glowing tip of his son-in-law's cigarette as it shook in his hand.

"I understand that you're worried," he said. "Fatherhood is a tremendous responsibility. There are decisions you make... sacrifices... but what you've done for my daughter, how you brought her all that way to see me... You're here when my daughter needs you most."

"But what if I screw it all up?" Sam's voice cracked, and Vincenzo remembered just how young he was.

He placed his right hand on Sam's shaking shoulder and looked him in the eye. "Everyone makes mistakes. That's part of being human. We all have our regrets about things we did or didn't do. Decisions we made. But if I learned anything from being interned, it was this: despite everything, you just need to move forward—no matter how tough things get."

He squeezed Sam's shoulder. "No one's asking you to be perfect. Just focus on being present, and the rest should follow."

Sam dropped his cigarette and stubbed it out. "Thank you, I needed that."

"Sure, any time. And I'm here for you, too... if you need anything more."

Then he pulled Sam into a tight hug. "Let's go back inside."

They walked together back into the waiting room, sharing stories about the past year and a half to pass the time. Vincenzo was starting to understand why Annalisa was so drawn to Sam —a young man who needed her just as much as she needed him.

As they chatted, a man's sharp voice cut through the murmur of the waiting room. "Mr. Wells?"

They looked up to see a tired-looking doctor in a rumpled white coat. Vincenzo gently squeezed Sam's hand, and they both stood, moving toward the doctor as Maria crossed the room to their side.

"Is she all right?" Sam's eyes were wide, his voice trembling.

The doctor gave a reassuring smile. "She's doing fine and so are the babies. Two boys."

"Twins?" Sam blinked.

Vincenzo looked at Maria and nodded. They did say twins ran in families.

"Yes, healthy twins. Congratulations, Mr. Wells. You can see them now, if you'd like."

Vincenzo and Maria hugged Sam, feeling the weight of their earlier fears lifted as they together faced new beginnings.

FIFTY

MAY 1945

Concord, California

Annalisa lowered little Max onto the sidewalk next to his brother, Robert, and looked up at her mother, waving from the wrought-iron balcony.

"I'll be right down to help you," Mamma called.

Annalisa watched the two boys waddle aimlessly through the grass before they both plopped down near a patch of dandelions. She smiled as she lowered her hands and helped them back up.

"They're quite the handful." Maria chuckled from behind her before approaching to scoop Max up. "I certainly couldn't have managed it."

Annalisa lifted Robert, and together they made their way up the tiled stairs to her parents' second-floor apartment.

"What have you been up to, Mamma?" Annalisa asked as she settled onto the couch, her eyes on the boys as they crawled about a wooden playpen her mother had set in the living room.

"Just tidying up around here," Mamma said as she set a

coaster on the table in front of Annalisa. "Let me get you some lemonade. You must be thirsty."

Robert let out a giggle, and she rose to the playpen's side to see Max break into a smile. The two were identical with light brown eyes and wavy auburn hair. She lowered herself to the floor so she was at their level, peering through the wooden framework across the room to where the radio sat. Her eyes settled on a large green book, propped against its side. It was thick and worn at the binding, and she wasn't sure if she'd seen it before.

She scooted across the floor and picked it up. It was heavier than it looked. She carried it over to the couch and began to page through.

It was a collection of photographs of people gathered in a garden, standing in front of a church, and a man holding a large fish on a beach in front of the water. The sea. It was Sicily. These were her relatives back in Isola delle Femmine, no doubt.

She continued to turn the pages until she saw something that stopped her cold. Mario. He was dressed in some kind of military uniform, but it didn't look familiar. And why was he standing with her aunt and uncle? Why was Mario in Sicily? When was this photograph even taken? She'd never seen it. Come to think of it, she'd only ever once seen a picture of her aunt and uncle on her father's dresser. He hadn't shared this album, these photographs. She'd never asked.

She slowly flipped the page and saw more photographs of Mario. But it couldn't be. What was going on?

"Mamma!" she called out, and her mother entered the room with a frosty pitcher and glass, which she set down on the table before reaching to close the album.

They made eye contact and Annalisa saw the older woman's panic. "Mamma, what is this? When was Mario in Sicily?"

Her mother sank into the sofa to her left and buried her face in her hands. She was quiet for a moment before releasing a heavy sigh and turning to Annalisa.

"It's not Mario."

Annalisa stared into her mother's dark eyes, so much more full of mystery than she'd ever imagined. "What do you mean? That's Mario's face in those photographs."

Mamma nodded. "They're identical. Just like Robert and Max."

Annalisa frowned and shifted her gaze to her sons. Max was playing with Robert's hair. His twin.

"Twins?" Annalisa said slowly, looking back at Mamma.

Her mother nodded.

Annalisa swallowed. "But how? Who is he? I don't understand."

Her mother reached for the pitcher and slowly poured a glass of lemonade, which she pushed in front of Annalisa. "His name is Alberto. Your aunt and uncle raised him. One baby was enough for us at the time. And a few years later you were born, and well, we managed all right."

Annalisa stared at the golden liquid in her glass before raising it to her lips to take a sip. It was bitter and sweet at the same time. Just like the revelation.

"But you never told us," she whispered. "I had another brother... have another brother."

She slammed down her glass. "How could you keep that from us?"

Mamma clutched the edge of the couch, her nails digging deep into the cushion as if she was holding on for her life. "I wanted to tell you. But the timing was never right."

She inhaled sharply, her voice cracking, "You don't know how I suffered, always wondering if I did the right thing."

Mamma paused to wipe away a tear. "Leaving him behind, losing Mario, and knowing they never had a chance to meet. Then wondering what had happened to him during the war."

She let out a sob. "No one could possibly know what that was like."

And suddenly it all made sense. All that talk about sacrifices. Her mother's misplaced anger. The way her father always wanted them to think of the future and not the past.

"I have a brother," she said quietly, opening the album again to look more closely at his face. He had a birthmark like Mario's, but it was on his right cheek. And his hair was parted down the center rather than to the side as Mario had always worn it.

Mamma twisted her ring. "Now that the war is over, maybe we can go and see him."

Annalisa nodded.

"Yes, that is what we'll do." Her mother traced his face with her fingertip. "We'll go and see what's become of our beautiful boy."

They spent the rest of the afternoon paging through the old album with Mamma reminiscing about Sicily and Annalisa asking questions like she never had. And Annalisa could see it made her mother happy.

By the time her father stepped through the door, sooty from his day at the steel mill, a job Sam had helped him get, the two women had shed a number of happy tears and drafted a letter—together—to Alberto.

"You're not angry?" Papà asked Annalisa as they embraced.

"A little bit," she admitted as she twirled her horn charm beneath her chin. "But I understand you did what you thought was best. Like you always did for Mario and me."

He nodded. "There's no room in this life for regrets." He raised his lemonade glass. "Instead, we have much to celebrate."

"*Salute!*" Annalisa lifted her glass toward his, her thoughts on how far they'd come, facing a lighter, brighter future together.

FIFTY-ONE
JULY 1947

A band of woodwind and brass players played a rendition of "Il canto degli Italiani" as they marched to the beats of drums. Behind them, more than a dozen men in white pushed a silver cart, atop which wobbled the statue of Santa Maria delle Grazie with the Christ Child on her right hip. Crowned with a halo of golden stars and draped in a gold-embellished blue cloak, the simulacrum was surrounded by silver branches adorned with yellow-and-white lilies, a vibrant celebration of faith and renewal.

Alberto stood in Piazza Umberto I, watching with a sense of nostalgia mixed with pride. Isola delle Femmine had come together to celebrate their patron saint, giving thanks for the sea's bountiful harvest, a symbol of hope and recovery following the years of trials they'd collectively endured. The narrow streets were lined with villagers of all ages, some holding colorful banners that flapped in the sea breeze, singing the words of a new national anthem. Many faces were awash in tears, which he knew came from a place of gratitude and remembrance.

He turned to his right, where his American family stood. His biological parents, Vincenzo and Maria, had sailed across the sea to join them in celebration and reconnect with their roots.

It had been a shock when his parents told him and shared with him a heartfelt letter from Maria and Annalisa. But he'd long wondered why neither of his parents had such dark eyes and where his pointed chin had come from. Somehow connecting the dots made it all more special. His parents' choice to bring him up was a gift as well as a sacrifice. They had always loved him. He would always be their only son.

Vincenzo and Maria brought along Annalisa, a young woman he hoped to know as a second sister. Her husband, Sam, stood to her right beside their four-year-old twins, Max and Robert, who marveled and pointed at the marchers. He reflected on the joy in their faces, these people who had also lost so much. The waves of war had shaped them all, but the ripples were now dissolving into prosperity. This momentous celebration served as a testament to their resilience and optimism.

Feeling a tug at his pant leg, he looked down to see his seven-year-old nephew Remo and lifted the boy up for a better view. He smiled at the boy's nine-year-old brother, Teodoro, who stood on tiptoes at his left side, flanked by Cristina and Franco. Reflecting on his brother-in-law's sacrifices in Africa, he considered Franco among the lucky ones to return from the unforgiving battlefront. His presence, too, was emblematic of the resilience of the Italian people. The little family was a symbol of its enduring spirit.

Behind them stood Giuseppe and Costanza, whom he still regarded as his parents. He thought of their attempts to preserve normalcy—especially throughout the war, how they had supported him when he needed to quite literally get back on his feet, how they'd welcomed Signora Ferrante and Lorenzo as family.

Now he looked ahead to where those friends stood, closer to the procession alongside his former coworkers Ascanio and Fausto. They had settled into their own place, adopting Isola delle Femmine as their home. This parade was somewhat of a farewell to Lorenzo as he prepared to sail to Taranto for naval training. Alberto hoped peace would persist for his sake and that the boy who had become his brother would soon return to participate in the *mattanza* once again.

Cymbals clashed as the band launched into a new tune, and the crowd erupted in cheers, seemingly oblivious to the hot afternoon sun. Everyone was finally safe, in the right place, on the other side of trials and war. At last, the ripples of the past had cleared, revealing depths of joy and renewal, delivering a hopeful end to their collective journey.

A LETTER FROM THE AUTHOR

Dear Reader,

Thank you for reading *Beneath the Sicilian Stars* and for following Vincenzo, Annalisa, and Alberto's journeys. If you want to join other readers in hearing all about my new releases with Storm Publishing, you can sign up for my newsletter!

www.stormpublishing.co/lindsay-morris

If you enjoyed this book, I would be grateful if you could leave a review. Your feedback is invaluable, and even a short review can make all the difference in helping other readers discover my book. Thank you so much for your time and support!

Over the course of writing this novel, I had the privilege of meeting several Italian Americans living in California's Contra Costa County. Their shared experience of having relatives who endured injustices enacted by the federal government when President Franklin Roosevelt signed Executive Order 9066, authorizing the military to exclude and relocate persons from designated areas, provided a unique and personal perspective.

At least 10,000 Italian Americans were evacuated from their homes in California, and about a third of Pittsburg, California's entire population was forced to leave with their photographs displayed like criminal mugshots across the front page of Pittsburg's *Post Dispatch*.

Lesser known were the stories of hundreds of Italians interned in a network of camps across the United States. The Federal Bureau of Investigation began arresting Italians believed to be "potentially dangerous" the night after Pearl Harbor—four days before the U.S. and Italy were at war. Title 50 of the U.S. Code, based on the 1798 Alien & Sedition Acts, gave the government the power to detain "enemy aliens" in emergencies.

The government effectively declared war on much of its immigrant population, imposing restrictions on about 600,000 Italian residents without U.S. citizenship who, on Dec. 8, had been designated enemy aliens by presidential proclamation. These "enemy aliens" were required to re-register as such; FBI agents raided homes and confiscated weapons, radios, cameras, and even flashlights. Non-citizens on the West Coast were placed under a strict curfew, required to carry "alien enemy" ID booklets, and told they would need a permit to travel more than five miles. Those who did not comply were subject to arrest and detention.

For some reason, these events and restrictions were, as author Lawrence DiStasi wrote, *Una Storia Segreta*, a secret story and hidden history. In writing this novel, I have sought to shed light on this experience and to bring it to life.

Equally, I wished to share the plight of Sicilians subjected to some of the worst bombing campaigns of World War II. My cousins in Palermo live in a city rebuilt, a portrait of resilience amid the ghosts of the past.

Through my storytelling, I aim to provide a portal and encourage readers to further explore often-overlooked histories. And I am grateful you have joined me on my journey. I hope you'll stay in touch—I have many more stories and ideas to share!

KEEP IN TOUCH WITH THE AUTHOR

lindsaymariemorris.com

x.com/lindsaymmorris
instagram.com/lindsaymariemorris
linkedin.com/in/lindsaymmorris
threads.net/@lindsaymariemorris

ACKNOWLEDGMENTS

This book began with a fall down a rabbit hole. While researching Italian prisoners of war for my first novel, *The Last Letter from Sicily*, I read about Italians held in United States internment camps. I live in Los Angeles, home to the Japanese American National Museum, where visitors encounter the story of Japanese internment. But I had no idea that Italians and Germans were also interned—albeit on a far smaller scale.

My research led me to *Una Storia Segreta*, edited by historian and author Lawrence DiStasi. The book followed the success of a traveling exhibition of the same name, which is Italian for secret story and hidden history.

DiStasi remains one of the few who have shed light on this dark chapter. His efforts and compiled testimonies persuaded President Bill Clinton to pass the "Wartime Violations of Italian American Civil Liberties Act" signed into Public Law 106-451 in November 2000. While no reparations were distributed, the act acknowledged the injustices suffered by Italian U.S. residents during the war.

Through DiStasi's books, which also include *Branded: How Italian Immigrants Became 'Enemies' During World War II*, I learned that my state, California, was among the most restricted, particularly the Bay Area. I found one chapter of *Una Storia Segreta*, entitled "Pittsburg Stories," particularly illuminating. Nearly 2,000 noncitizen residents were ordered to evacuate from their homes. Most of these people were of Sicilian descent with ties to Isola delle Femmine.

I was drawn to that story and wrote a few introductory chapters about a Sicilian fisherman and his Pittsburg-based family before setting it aside. I am grateful to Storm Publishing Commissioning Editor Kate Gilby-Smith, who read those pages and believed there was potential for another novel.

Kate's developmental edits on my first draft provided me with clear direction and enough inspiration to add more than 25,000 extra words. She also suggested I consider weaving in a secret, which I figured out after brainstorming with my incredibly supportive husband, Matthew Sirolly.

In addition to Kate, Editorial Operations Director Alexandra Begley, and the rest of the Storm team, I am indebted to my beta readers, Santa Maria Morris, Maria Kuehn, JoAnna Agnello, Salvatore Agnello, Catherine Maita, Annika Hagros, and Margaret Sirolly. My aforementioned husband, Matt, not only read a draft and provided constructive feedback but also took time out to take me on a two-week research road trip.

On that trip, I had the chance to visit the Historical Museum at Fort Missoula with an informative tour from Education Director Kristjana Eyjólfsson. I stood in an internee barrack, stepped into the loyalty hearing courtroom, and saw the so-called Bella Vista beyond what was once surrounded by barbed wire. HMFM Education Assistant Austin O. Haney provided me with a treasure trove of photographs and even camp menus from Fort Missoula.

Separately, I visited California's Contra Costa County, where I stayed in Pittsburg and spent half a day camped at the Pittsburg Historical Museum in the company of Vince Ferrante, the museum's Vice President & Historian. I am grateful to the kind people at the Concord Visitor Center, who provided me with a historic walking tour map of the city where many "enemy aliens" found homes after they were evacuated during World War II. And I spent several hours on the road tracing and chasing history with the fabulous Carol A. Jensen, an East Contra Costa County historian and author, who connected me with additional sources.

Martinez, California, residents Mary Goodman and Mary Hatch drove out to meet with me in Pittsburg to chat about the ways the war impacted the area's Italian residents. Pittsburg, Martinez, and Monterey are today Isola delle Femmine sister cities, thanks largely to the efforts of Friends of Isola delle Femmine President and Co-founder Frank Bruno. Frank shared what brought so many Isolans to Pittsburg and provided important insights that helped me further shape this family's world.

During the course of writing this novel, I had Friends of Isola delle Femmine's Liaison to Isola delle Femmine Salvatore N. Coniglio on speed dial. Salvatore was born in Isola delle Femmine and played on Italy's 1964 Olympic Soccer Team before joining his father and family members in Pittsburg. In addition to sharing stories of his Isola delle Femmine youth, he and Frank Bruno provided fact-checking. Salvatore also introduced me to his Isolan cousin Giuseppe Lucido, who shared more about the town's customs and history.

Along with those valuable personal interactions, I was able to interview and correspond with so many others touched by the events of World War II, including Velio Alberto Bronzini (whose father lost his store because it was in an enemy-restricted part of Oakland), Bob Scudero (whose mother, Rose, was evacuated from her Pittsburg home to Concord), Steve Lucido (whose family tree includes internee Francesco Lucido), Frances Gianno Hammond (whose father and grandparents were evacuated from Martinez to Concord), and Paula Wherity (whose grandparents were evacuated from Pittsburg to Concord).

Fact-finding is integral to writing historical fiction; even the most minor details matter. The first paragraph of this novel was informed by antique radio experts, including Petaluma, California, pre-transistor era electronics repairer Tom Harris; Simon's Vintage Electronics Repair's "Inveterate Tinkerer" Simon Favre of Milpitas, California; Antique Wireless Association Museum Curator Lynn J. Bisha; Arizona Antique Radio Club Past-President Larry Stencel; and California Historical Radio Society Secretary Jaime Arbona. Vintage Dancer CEO and Owner Debbie Sessions guided me on historic fashion. And in the following pages, you'll find my bibliography, which I have provided for your own further exploration. Any errors are my own.

There are so many people to thank. I am grateful to everyone who encouraged and advised me along the way. And thank you, dear reader, for your interest in this story!

BIBLIOGRAPHY

- DiStasi, L. (Ed.). (2001). *Una storia segreta: The secret history of Italian American evacuation and internment during World War II*. Heyday Books.
- DiStasi, L. (2016). *Branded: How Italian immigrants became "enemies" during World War II*. Heyday Books.
- Department of Justice. (2001, November). *Report to the Congress of the United States: A review of the restrictions on persons of Italian ancestry during World War II*. U.S. Department of Justice.
- Baliva, Z. (Director). (2021). *Potentially dangerous: A documentary on the Italian American experience during World War II* [Film].
- Fox, S. (1990). *The unknown internment: An oral history of the relocation of Italian Americans during World War II*. Twayne Publishers.
- Van Valkenburg, C. B. (1995). *An alien place: The Fort Missoula, Montana, detention camp 1941–1944*. Pictorial Histories Publishing Company.
- Chopas, M. E. B. (2011). *Law, security, and ethnic profiling: Italians in the United States during World War II* (Doctoral dissertation). University of North Carolina at Chapel Hill.
- Chopas, M. E. B. (2017). *Searching for subversives: The story of Italian internment in wartime America*. University of North Carolina Press.
- Soga, Y. (2008). *Life behind barbed wire: The World War II internment memoirs of a Hawaiʻi Issei* (K. Hirai, Trans.). University of Hawaiʻi Press.
- Cione, J. (2003). *Sicily on my mind: Echoes of fascism and World War II*. AuthorHouse.
- Musumeci, N. (2023). *La Sicilia bombardata: La popolazione dell'isola nella Seconda guerra mondiale (1940–1943)*. Rubbettino Editore.
- Gioannini, M., & Massobrio, G. (2007). *Bombardate l'Italia: Storia della guerra di distruzione aerea 1940–1945*. Rizzoli.

- Bellomo, A. (2016). *Bombe su Palermo: Cronaca degli attacchi aerei 1940–1943*. Soldiershop.